WORLD TRIBUNAL
FORCE OF THREE

Hugo Wolfgang Holzmann

Order this book online at www.trafford.com
or email orders@trafford.com

Most Trafford titles are also available at major online book retailers.

Printed in the United States of America.

ISBN: 978-1-4907-3097-4 (sc)
ISBN: 978-1-4907-3096-7 (hc)
ISBN: 978-1-4907-3095-0 (e)

Library of Congress Control Number: 2014905159

Trafford rev. 04/26/2014

 www.trafford.com

North America & international
toll-free: 1 888 232 4444 (USA & Canada)
fax: 812 355 4082

WORLD TRIBUNAL

Force of Three

A historical fiction novel by Hugo
Wolfgang Holzmann

The third novel of a trilogy: *Terror, The Great Hoax,*
World Tribunal

This book is dedicated to all victims
of crime and terror.

"Law without Force is Impotent."

"Force without Law is Terror."

-Pascal

CONTENTS

INTRODUCTION

A wise man said, "You are as important as the rest of the world!" meaning, the world exists because you are alive; you die, and there is no longer any world, relative speaking. This is how precious your life—anyone's life—is!

Long ago (two generations removed) there was a terrible war; history calls it the Second World War, when an untold number of people were killed needlessly.

Well, not needlessly as the world was forced to combat Nazi Germany, led by the egregious mass murderer Adolf Hitler. Perhaps as many as forty million or more men, women, and children were killed or murdered. Half of them were soldiers killed in battle; the other half were men, women, and children who were murdered.

The Soviets lost over ten million soldiers killed in battle; the Germans almost as many.

Yes, there is a vast difference in human terms between killing and murdering. Killing can be intentional as in battle or unintentional as in air raids where the targets are cities and their inhabitants but not specifically any particular person. So, for example, a hundred thousand Germans—most of them the elderly, women, and children—were killed by Allied bombing attacks in retaliation to German terror attacks, and half as many of British subjects died in German air attacks. Countless civilians were killed during actual military operations throughout Europe.

Murder—the intentional killing of men, women and children. For example, during the winter of 1941-42, two million Soviet prisoners of war died in camps due to lack of shelter, starvation, and inadequate medical care. As one of the German military commanders (General Walther von Reichenau) declared, "We need not concern ourselves with the care and feeding of Soviet prisoners." That was murder.

And then there was the genocide of Jews, Slavs, gypsies; the murder of hostages taken in all conquered countries; punishment mended out to communities all over Europe by the German military and SS; villages and towns wiped out.

In the case of murdering Jews, orders were given to do so in an aura of terror, of brutality, and the German agencies committing these atrocities did so.

Why is mankind so atrocious, even bestial? I have no answer; neither do really those who study man or write the sorry history of mankind. Why this lack of mercy, compassion, empathy for others? We can read about the Roman circuses of blood and gory: spectator sports, public executions of quartering, burning at the stake, or other grizzly killings attended to by multitude, which delighted in them. The impalement of men, women, and children in the Balkans viewed by many—what a horrible way to die. The terrible tortures of the Inquisition in the name of God.

Did mankind become civilized since? The genocide by the Turks against the Armenians, the brutalities inflicted on the Chinese by the Japanese, and the Holocaust of the twentieth century show *it* has not!

Six million innocents murdered. Alone over a million children were put to death, each child's life so precious. Humiliated and terrorized before being shot, beaten to death, gassed, burned alive. Who were their cruel murderers? Men and women of our present civilization: Germans, Lithuanians, Latvians, Ukrainians, and the collaborators of the enlightened nations of the West like the Vichy government of France.

Has the world improved since? Genocide in Africa, the Balkans, the murders by the Mexican drug cartels, of Somali pirates, and the religious atrocities committed by Islamic fundamentalists tells us it has not.

Rarely have such vicious killers brought to justice. Bin Laden has, a few other criminals. We wished we could rid the world of all or most of these murderers.

In this story we can and do so. Three dedicated men, one a scientist who invented a death ray, band together to eliminate those murderers they can reach and bring to justice.

It won't be vigilantly elimination as the three will hold a trial to justify their actions.

And they will give warning against those tried and found guilty to desist from their murderous actions or their hate mongering before they are eliminated.

And *you* may be part of the Force of Three by adding to and justifying your wish for the dismissal from the world of those who need to be removed.

PROLOGUE

THE THREE ENFORCERS
PROFESSOR MAX KLAUSNER
POLICE INSPECTOR ANTON HOFER
TAXI DRIVER SEPP KAINZ

Police inspector Anton Hofer was born in Munich in 1965, the son of Otto and Rosemarie Nagil. Otto Nagil was during the Second World War an SS officer and attained the rank of *Standartenfuehrer* (colonel). He was in charge of Fort IX, in Kovno, Lithuania, and with the Einsatzkommando 3. Under his command sixty thousand Jews were shot and several thousand Soviet prisoners. At the end of the war, he fled with his wife, Rosemarie, to Cairo and lived a comfortable life with SS funds secreted out by the Odessa organization. He was declared a war criminal but was protected by the Egyptians, as were many others of the SS and Gestapo.

Otto Nagil was a strict disciplinarian and brutalized his wife, Rosemarie. This was the reason she went to Munich to give a healthy birth to their son Anton. Anton was raised in Cairo and learned Arabic, later in school, also English and Russian.

When Anton was thirteen, he witnessed a severe beating his father gave to Rosemarie; and when she called for help, "TONY, HELP ME. HE IS KILLING ME!" Anton, to save his mother, shot his father. That her son would never feel guilty of committing patricide, she let him read his father's war diary; and Anton realized that he killed a monster, a child murderer who may have been his father but was no longer thought of such.

Later in life he (Anton is Catholic) married the Jewish girl Hanna with whom he grew up in Cairo.

When the parents of Hanna moved to Jerusalem and Rosemarie back to her ancestral house in Munich, Anton and Hanna joined Rosemarie. Anton took a job with the Munich police and became a successful police officer, and since he spoke Russian and Arabic (also English and Hebrew), he worked with the antiterror squad and the criminal investigation division.

In the year 2010, when his mother, Rosemarie, died, he moved to his family in Jerusalem as Hanna's mother, Amal, lived there. By then Anton and Hanna had adopted three children: Daniel, Esther, and David. (Hanna was barren.)

With the death of Rosemarie, in December of 2011, Anton changed his family's name from Nagil to the maternal name of his mother, Hofer. Nothing should remember him of SS Colonel Otto Nagil.

In Jerusalem he joined the police and was accepted as a senior police inspector.

Josef (or Sepp) Kainz was a taxi driver and longtime friend of Anton. Not only was Sepp the personal chauffeur for Anton and his family when they lived in Munich, but he also assisted Anton in various matters such as when Anton rescued his kidnapped mother or pursued criminals and terrorists, often in a manner Sepp would call "illegal in a legal sense." Sepp was always available to Inspector Nagil for "just causes."

In fact, at the police department Sepp Kainz was known as Inspector Nagil's private detective.

Sepp Kainz was sixty-five, married to Inge and living in Planegg where Anton had his ancestral house. With Anton now living in Jerusalem, Sepp was the caretaker of the house.

Sepp had no formal education besides grammar school but was a man of great experience and wisdom.

Professor Max Klausner was the energy expert of the Max Planck Institute in Munich. He was a theoretician, experimentalist and teacher, a brilliant scientist.

He lived alone in the north of Munich in a nice villa. Dedicated to his work, he had never married but had a girlfriend, Ingrid, with whom he had a daughter, Erica, five years old.

In January of 2005, two American nuclear scientists, graduates of MIT, came to the Max Planck Institute in Munich to learn about neutron emission in conjunction with reactors for slow and chain reaction fission. Dr. Wahaj and Dr. Jaafari met with Professor Klausner and were advised by him to study more extensively scientific German before taking the course; they had taken German at MIT. This they did for three months, and since Klausner lived alone in his villa, they rented the second floor. With them lived their two Iranian chauffeurs, really bodyguards. The four had parties with high school girls. They also brought a beautiful young woman, Monica, who seduced Klausner. He was in her power and participated in their parties; pictures were taken, and the good professor was compromised. When the four returned for the fall semester, he checked their passports and saw an entry to Pakistan and then to Iran where they stayed for several months. This was when Klausner realized that they could not have been refugees but supposedly Sunnis who went to America to escape the Iranian totalitarian regime.

When he refused to admit them to the institute, they blackmailed him by warning him that they would release the pictures of sex escapades with school girls to the newspaper.

Professor Klausner admitted the two.

In November 2005, Inspector Nagil was warned by the head of the Egyptian military intelligence, Brigadier Amer (Anton worked for Brigadier Amer while serving in the Egyptian army), about the two American scientists who were supposedly Iranian refugees but in reality were Shiites and members of the Revolutionary Guard—in fact, atom spies. Inspector Nagil informed the FBI through his acquaintance, agent Johnson, who, after doing research, found that the two had come to the United States in 1997, seeking asylum as they were Sunnis, and had not only lied about their religious status but also claimed that they had fled with their families who, however, were still in Iran. The FBI will go to court to nullify their citizenship and deport them back to Iran.

Inspector Nagil requested agent Johnson to hold the matter in obedience for a couple weeks as he will be working on a plan to avoid the two scientists from taking their learned knowledge to Iran.

Inspector Nagil, with the help of taxi driver Sepp Kainz staged a robbery; forced them to turn over their wallets and the chauffeurs their pistols; and, by giving the scientists injection of cyanide, eliminated Wahaj and Jaafari.

He called agent Johnson with the news that both scientists had died of heart attacks.

Agent Johnson understood and offered Inspector Nagil a job with the CIA where his expertise and language skills could be very useful—he declined.

Afterward, Anton visited Professor Klausner, and after revealing what he knew and showing the professor a compromising picture of him with a nude girl (which Nagil had found in the wallet of one of the chauffeurs), Klausner made a complete confession.

It was then that Inspector Nagil identified himself as a police inspector but assured the professor that he worked private on the matter and that he didn't have to resign from the institute or experience any harm if he gives up his passion for young girls and will never again teach nuclear science to unauthorized people.

Professor Klausner assured Inspector Nagil, "Never again."

In fact, Inspector Nagil and Professor Klausner became friends, called each other by first names, and when Max asked Anton to please visit him again, Anton said he would as soon as Ingrid and Erica were with him.

After the begin of 2006, Max Klausner married Ingrid, and Anton became a frequent visitor as both were interested in astronomy and astrophysics and would discuss these subjects extensively.

While the author realizes that not every reader is interested in astrophysics, he wishes to record some of their conversations as they lead ultimately to the invention of death rays.

CHAPTER I

Inspector Anton Nagil and Professor Max Klausner

(At this point in time, Anton was still Inspector Nagil. It was only in the year 2011—after his mother, Rosemarie, died—that he changed his family's name to Hofer.)

I t was at the beginning of 2006 after Max Klausner had married Ingrid that Anton visited Max and they became close friends. Both were interested in astronomy, and they discussed the subject extensively and also delved into astrophysics.

Anton, who was a chemical engineer, had studied nuclear science for his master's at the University of San Diego, and his hobby was astronomy.

Once again, after a good dinner Ingrid had cooked, the two sat together in front of the hearth, with a glass of hot-spiced wine. Outside it was still winter, and it snowed heavily. Ingrid and Erica went to the movies, and the two sat alone.

Max smiled at Anton, "The last time you mentioned that you don't believe in the

Ur-Knall, the big bang. Why not, Anton?"

"For many reasons of which one is Einstein's grand formula 'energy equals mass times the speed of light squared'—that is, energy equals one gram of mass multiplied by 186,000, squared. And the result would be in ergs, a tiny energy measurement, similar to an electron volt. With the mass of our sun, the energy would be tremendous. But go further, there are supposed to be hundred billion galaxies with each in the average composed of hundred billions stars, all this mass contained in a single point of energy, the point called singularity, smaller than a subatomic particle. It is just common sense that such a point of energy could not exist or the energy be contained for any period, a scientific fairytale. There is also the question of where did this singularity come from?"

"Maybe God put it there?"

Anton laughed. "I thought we are talking about science and not religion."

"You are right, Anton. Science it shall be. I have no rational answer to the question how all this energy could be contained in a miniscule point. There are speculations of how the singularity came into being, the brane theory, the rapid expansion of space, repeating the big crunch of the universe, with the subsequent expansion of the big bang. Of course, I admit that there must have been a first time."

"And we are right back at our present big bang."

"So, Anton, you must have thought about it. Give me your theory of how our universe came into being."

"Yes, I have thought about it, with more common sense than the big bang theory. And by the way, Einstein never believed in the big bang. His theory of the singularity was just a thought experiment, a star crushing itself into a tiny point."

"Like a black hole?"

"Einstein also denied the existence of a black hole. That was first thought of by the German scientist Schwarzschield, based upon Einstein's thought experiment. I have to use philosopher Occam's theory: 'Use the simplest explanation if all else fails.' Let's think of nature and exclude at this point the mystery of life. The universe consists of matter and energy. On earth, the planets and the sun, all matter is composed of only ninety-two elements. Whatever we find in the universe, spectrographs tell us that matter is composed of the same elements."

"Plutonium?"

"Manmade. This does not mean that there are not undiscovered elements somewhere in the universe. Perhaps eons ago there was just hydrogen. And if you asked me wherefrom the hydrogen came, I cannot tell you. The same with energy; energy is movement. How did energy begin? I don't know. Energy is also the attraction and repulsion of matter, of charged particles. We made a name for it, positive and negative charges, which all particles have."

"Neutrons?"

"The combination of a proton and electron, and we must not forget the neutrino. Just because the neutrinos complement the charges, that does not mean that these particle are not energized."

"And how big would your universe be?"

"Astronomers tell us that wherever we look, we can see or measure objects up to 13.7 billion light-years away. That would be the radius with us nicely placed in the middle.

That makes a universe 27.4 billion light-years in diameter. You and I, our world, our solar system—in fact, our galaxy—or rather the particles thereof were in existence shortly after the big bang and were part of the explosion or expansion. It just is not possible that we are now right in the middle. This is another fallacy of the big bang theory.

"An explosion like the big bang, expands in a shell-like formation. We should be within this shell. Only if we are at a point somewhere in this shell and can see in every direction to a distance of 13.7 billion light-years is our present theory of the universe possible. Then we would have to extent the shell in a sphere-like configuration, which would make the universe many times larger.

"How big is my universe? I have no idea. I only believe in common sense that tells me that as far as space goes, the universe is infinite in size. I know it is difficult to visualize infinite. However, matter is finite. All matter kept in check by the gravitational force of the whole. This also means that nothing that is matter is ever at rest but driven apart or attracted by gravitational forces and the inherent energy of matter."

"Well, Anton, you gave a simplistic but rational theory, perhaps even more realistic than the big bang. As far as energy goes, there are other forces. You did mention gravity. How about charges?"

"You know, Max, it is amazing that science understands what gravity does but not the *why* of it."

"Mass attracts!"

"But why does mass attract? Perhaps the neutrinos are gravitons?"

"Because mass of matter causes this attraction."

Anton laughed. "That is not a scientific explanation of the why."

"Well, if you don't let me bring in religion, perhaps we can explain these phenomena philosophically?"

"Not permitted. Let's us stay with pure science. Interestingly, Einstein never gave an explanation what pure energy means. He stated that matter can be transformed into energy, but what type of energy? You know, Max, I firmly believe that energy cannot exist independently of matter. Energy is a manifestation of matter, velocity, vibration, oscillation, etc. Even the charges you mentioned conform to the same type of energy."

"Well, it is true that Einstein never explained what matter transforms into when it becomes energy; maybe he means photons. But it is the foundation of his special relativity. You believe in his theory, don't you, Anton?"

"I am sorry, Max, but I believe very little about his special relativity."

"That you have to explain. Time dilation, foreshortening, mass increase—it all has been proven. His famous equation?"

"Pure clever speculation. He was very smart. He took this equation from the Lorentz-

Fitzgerald contraction equations. Einstein was asked if he found the theory by experimentation. He answered he didn't come near a laboratory for years. Nothing has been empirically proven. Take time dilation. Time is manmade; nature does not need time."

"But they proved time dilation. Scientists on planes carrying atomic clocks showed a slowing of time when compared to similar clocks on the ground."

"This was not a scientific endeavor. These were not scientists but students and people interested in proving time dilation. I mean, how can you compare a plan flying at 600 miles per hour, or 0.17 miles per second with the speed of light at 186,000 miles per second? First of all, even Einstein stated that these phenomena only occur at 90 percent of the speed of light.

"Besides, if I remember correctly, the clocks showed both a slowing and speeding up of time in nanoseconds. Now NASA, with satellites, moving at a much greater speed, could perhaps prove this slowing of time—that is, if there is any."

"Haven't they done so?"

"I don't know. I wrote once to them and asked if clocks in the satellites showed the time dilation. They were nice enough to write back. Wrote briefly 'We in NASA are not in the business to prove or disprove Einstein's theory.' I read another article about such an orbital test. In 1977, a cesium atomic clock was placed into orbit. At that time no adjustments were made to account for Einstein's special and general theory of relativity.

However, a frequency synthesizer was added that could be switched on to make the adjustment. After twenty days in orbit, it was necessary to make these adjustments to account for Einstein's postulates. It is a complicated affair as a number of phenomena must be taken into account. The clock would move slower due to the velocity of the satellite; the nearer to the earth, the greater the velocity. However, the clock would move faster because of lesser gravity depending on the distance to the earth. These plus and minus time factors would cancel each other. Then, satellites are not in a perfectly circular orbit. Also, satellite signal receivers are moving on a rotating earth.

"Adjustments are made; else, the global positioning systems would be off by several miles a day. There is also the question how possibly can a cesium atom be affected by the velocity of its carrier and the warping of space, especially since NASA attaches more importance to Newtonian gravity than to Einsteinian warping.

"I believe that any adjustments made are only due to the time frame of how long it takes for the signals from the moving satellite to the receiver on earth.

"And again, Einstein's theories subscribe these effects of slowing of time to happen only at tremendous velocities. Even satellites travel only at less than twenty miles per second.

Take the increase of mass at velocities near the speed of light. Einstein said that at 90 percent the speed of light an object would double its mass—that is, a spaceship traveling that fast would become twice as massive; consequently the people inside would also double their mass, become twice as big and heavy. Now, we don't have to worry about a spaceship moving at that velocity; but we propel particles that fast and, in fact, a lot faster. We have accelerators that propel particles, protons, at over 99.999999 percent the speed of light. While Einstein did not give us graph showing what happens to matter at these velocities, the increase of mass at that speed would be great and the proton becoming like a cannonball or even bigger and get stuck in the tube of the accelerator.

Also, the particle would become as thin as a sheet of paper, and time dilation would become so effective that the particle would never arrive at its destination."

"I have to think about what you said, Anton. Let's go for walk. I love to walk in a snowstorm," suggested Max.

They dressed warm, went outside, and had a brisk walk. By the time they returned, they looked like snowmen. Ingrid and Erika had come back, and they sat together by the warm fire, Erika telling importantly about the Disney film *Bambi* they had seen.

Anton showed the Klausners pictures of his family who lived in Jerusalem and of his beautiful wife, Hanna. Hanna was a pediatric nurse and worked as a volunteer at the Hadassah Hospital. He also showed pictures of her mother, Amal, and their three children, all adopted. The first one they adopted was Daniel, now two years old (his mother had died in childbirth); David, seven; and Esther, four years old.

Anton had told Max and Ingrid the tragic story of David and Esther. The Cohen family had immigrated to Israel from South Africa and joined the kibbuz Kfar Etzion in the West Bank. One night, Palestinian terrorists cut through the fence of the kibbuz, entered the house of the Cohens, shot the parents of the two children, and kidnapped David and Esther to be used as a trade-off for a thousand terrorists in Israeli prisons.

Anton, who had been visiting his family in Jerusalem, was asked by the police deputy commissioner Avi Barlev to go to the Hebron to seek information about the children.

He could do so as he held Egyptian citizenship with the name of Achmed Nabil. He was told by Barlev that a Nazi fugitive known as Hassan Abu-Sharif, formerly the SS officer Hans Stettner, was involved in the murder of the parents and the kidnapping of the children. He visited Stettner; Stettner and Anton's father, Otto Nagil, were colleagues in the SS. Through a collaborator of Israeli's Shin Bet (secret service), he discovered where the children were held captive. He was also informed that the children were terribly mistreated, three-year-old Esther repeatedly hurt by the Mukthar Abu al-Adhami from the village of Bani Na'im. For Anton it became no longer a mission of getting information but to rescue the children. This he did and brought them safely to Jerusalem and the Hadassah Hospital. In the hospital, David and Esther were visited by Hanna; and when she mentioned that she was the wife of the man who rescued them, they wished to be visited by the "man."

After the children had been healed and returned to Kfar Etzion, they were despondent and only wished to live with Hanna and the man. Anton and Hanna were then able to adopt David and Esther.

This is how the Nagil family suddenly became a family of six. Amal, of course, was happy to be a grandmother to three children.

While Anton lived with his mother, Rosemarie, in Munich, he visited his family in Jerusalem every month for a long weekend and also on holidays besides his month vacation. It was only a four-hour flight from Munich to Tel Aviv.

Of course, five-year-old Erica wished very much to meet the children of Uncle Anton and did so when the Klausners visited Jerusalem or the Nagil family came to Munich.

There were many visits by the Klausners to the Nagils and vis-à-vis. And over the years Anton and Max held many sessions discussing astronomy and physics.

Here is one important discussion as it gave Max the idea for a death ray.

The subject was the atom, and Anton suggested that scientists really don't understand what an atom is composed of.

"Well, Anton, with the exception of hydrogen, all atoms are composed of the nuclei of protons and neutrons, orbited by the electrons, simple enough."

"While this is true, it is the construction of the atom that is the puzzle. The nucleus, while only a tiny part of the atom, contains most of its mass, right?"

Max nodded.

"In fact, the nucleus, which resides in the center of the atom, is so small that the sphere of the atom is a hundred thousand times bigger."

"That is true, with the electrons circling or let's say orbiting the nucleus in a quantum unknown orbit. The electrons are so small that their mass cannot be given and their energy described in electron volts."

"Am I correct to visualize the atom like an astrodome-type structure but fully rounded, with the nucleus presented by a—well, let's say—by a peanut?"

"Hugely enlarged—I guess that would be a proper description."

"Now tell me, Max, when we look at a bar of iron or similar substance or any solid element, what are we seeing?"

Max laughed. "Of course a bar of iron."

"Wait a minute. With all the empty space an atom is composed of—and we certainly can never see the speeding electrons—are we then looking at a multitude of nuclei?"

"It is the reflection of a multitude of iron atoms we see, held together in a crystalline configuration."

"Tell me, Max, are the atoms little spheres or what?"

"Yes and no. Single atoms we must visualize as tiny spheres; when bound together with other like atoms, like in your bar of iron, they may change appearance especially when in this crystalline form and exchanging electrons."

"But even then, if no longer a true sphere, would it be correct to say that each iron atom still has this massive nucleus with this huge empty space around it?"

"Yes, that would be correct."

"The space around each nucleus a hundred thousand times bigger. Yes? Then, even if you have billions of atoms, like in an iron bar, with all the empty space within each atom, we should be able to stick a finger right through this iron bar, and I still ask, what are we really seeing? Is it a reflection of the nuclei?"

"Ah, Anton, you are asking difficult questions, and I should know the answers, but I don't have one except to say that with billions of atoms in togetherness we can see the solid."

"I look at this problem and compare it with our solar system. The sun the nucleus, with the planets orbiting like the electrons. Our nearest star is Alpha Centauri, with lots of space between our sun and Centauri, other nearby stars in every direction. There was a debate a long time ago with some astronomers saying that with stars in every point of view, the sky should be luminous, night as bright as daytime. But it is the distance between stars that prevents that. The same with atoms, it is the distance of empty space between one nucleus and the next one. We should not see anything, yet we do. I saw once pictures of atoms. In 1998, Don Eiger controlled thirty-five xenon atoms and arranged them to spell IBM, then took a picture of it with an electron microscope. Each atom was shown as a nebulous outline of a pearl. How is that possible? Unless each atom is visible because . . ."

"Because of what, Anton?"

"Because there is more to an atom than a teeny nucleus and then this huge empty space with electrons orbiting, electrons 1,800 times smaller than a proton."

"And what might that be?"

"Photons. Millions or billions of photons ready to be expelled at this fantastic speed of light. Expelled in a continuous beam of electromagnetic radiation when the atom is energized. Free to zoom out into space or confined to a wire, or in a wire, when a charge is applied to the atom. And each atom needs a certain compliment of photons to be satisfied, photons which are freely available. I mean, electromagnetic radiation is all over space and even surges into and through solids like our bodies. Take radio waves. We can get the signals even in a basement. It surges right through walls of wood and brick. Electricity is nothing but a flow of photons guided along or within a wire."

"This is new to me that electricity is a flow of photons. Present science pictures electricity as energized electrons."

"And electrons are not supposed to surge through the wire, right?"

"Right. When a charge—voltage we call it—is applied to a wire, it energizes the electrons in the wire and does so almost instantaneously."

"Well, I believe that electrons become energized when voltage is applied but kick out photons, which then flow as current. And as we know, electromagnetic radiation can either surge unhindered through space or guided along a wire. In fact, this current of photons could be concentrated that we can send it as electricity from producer to receiver without wires."

"How?"

"By taking away the positive charge of each photon, this would make the beams of radiation no longer spread out, as it is done in laser beams."

"That would be a great scientific achievement. Let me think about it, Anton. But one more question about your theory. What do you think makes the atom visible, like these xenon atoms looking like pearls? I mean, if an atom is filled with photons, they are not standing still but move around in the shell of the atom."

"Yes, near the nucleus they would be orbiting at great velocity; but close to the outside of the atom, they would slow down and even stop moving, form a sort of shell, a crust around the atom. Scientists can slow speeding photons to crawl speed. What scientists can do nature can do usually better."

"I think about it and maybe do some experimentation."

CHAPTER II

The Invention of the Death Ray

Professor Max Klausner did some experimenting and found that certain atoms such as cooper and silver were suitable for sending energy in the form of photons from a sending apparatus to a receiver. Max told Anton at his next visit and demonstrated the sending of electromagnetic energy as photons through air in a narrow beam. They discussed the implications of transmitting energy without wire, which would revolutionize energy transmission.

Anton asked, "By which frequency?"

"With experimentations I found that energy can be best transmitted through air in long-wave frequency. Longer even than radio waves."

"But could you transmit in shorter waves too?"

"Like what Anton?"

"Let's say in the range of light or even infrared?" answered Anton.

"Yes, it would be possible; but in both frequencies the beams would spread out, become less concentrated, and therefore less energetic."

"Is there any way, a method by which the beams remain narrow and concentrated, Max?"

Max laughed. "You think of one, and I try."

"I have thought about such rays," said Anton. "To come back to the photon, I believe it has both charges, positive and negative. The positive charge comes from the spinning or as science believes its vibration or oscillation. The negative charge is caused by velocity. In fact, all subatomic particles have both charges. With both charges cancelling each other, the photon appears neutral. Take away the vibration, and the photon is only negatively charged. Now, if it were possible to create a sort of tube to guide the negatively charges photons, you could keep them concentrated regardless of the frequency."

"Ah, Anton, you are dreaming. Where would we find such a tube?"

"Make one. Use the atoms of cooper or silver, you have an abundance of electrons, which are easily separated out. Electrons, because of their strong negative charge, may not oscillate. Shoot a beam of electrons, it could accommodate the photons, perhaps become even more negatively charged and thereby concentrated."

Max smiled. "I believe you are thinking of something else than transmission of energy, Anton."

"I am, Max. A death ray, a heat ray in the frequency of infrared."

Max lifted his brows. "I thought so. It would be nice if we could do away with the baddies in the world. But as you know, electromagnetic radiation travels in a straight line."

"Bounce the rays off satellites?"

"The rays would bounce off and scatter."

"Let me think about the problem, Max."

At Anton's next visit to Munich and Max, he had a proposal. "Let me first explain the visual beam in the frequency of light. When the combined beams of photons and electrons hit the satellite—and it must be an orbital one—the beam scatters somewhat. This is all right as it gives us a wider view of the regions below. By adding, or really concentrating the negativity of the beam, we can narrow it and thereby zero in on the target we wish to view. Perhaps right up to a person? In the same manner we can send the infrared rays guided by the visual beam. Then all we have to do is to adjust the strength or temperature and send a jolt of heat. Possible, Max?"

"If it is possible, Anton, it would take a lot of experimentation and the use of several powerful computers."

"Work on it, Max."

"But what do I tell my director? Director Glaser would like to know what for I need these computers and what I am doing."

"Tell him half the truth. Say that you are working on wireless energy transmission. A big plus for the Max Planck Institute if you succeed."

This is the story professor Max Klausner told Director Glaser. The directors let him buy the necessary equipment and gave him the small but solid-built former observatory for his experimental work. This had a dome that could be rotated and an opening from which the powerful sending and receiving antennas could operate.

Also Director Glaser had Professor Klausner sign an agreement that 50 percent of any financial benefit would go to the institute. The former observatory was now called the Energy House.

It was now June of 2012, and Anton, who had changed his family name from Nagil to Hofer, was hired by the institute as a consultant to Professor Klausner. Anton had a degree as a chemical engineer with a minor in nuclear science.

Later, at the recommendation of the professor, Sepp Kainz was hired as a part-time computer expert to assist Professor Klausner.

However, it was Klausner who taught his new assistant how to work the computer.

A that time, Sepp, in his late sixties, had semi-retired as a taxi driver and welcomed the work he did for a beneficial, if modest, salary. He received a badge that allowed him as an employee of the Max Planck Institute to come and go as the professor needed him.

At the beginning of his employment, Sepp Kainz had no idea that the professor was working on a death ray. As he understood it, they were working on wireless energy transmission—a secret.

Anton Hofer came mainly on weekends, arrived Friday mornings after his early morning flight to Munich and left Saturday, and arrived in Tel Aviv at 4:00 a.m. Sunday morning where his faithful housekeeper Eliahu waited for him. He was home by six with a welcome with his family, and then he's off to work at the Jerusalem police department. At least he slept the four hours on the flight.

By the end of June Klausner had succeeded with an isotope separator to form the main electron beam, actually composed of four individual rays into which he imbedded the photon beam. But before he developed and used an infrared ray, he worked and succeeded on a visual ray and with trial and error was able to view almost any place on earth.

The exceptions were the areas directly opposite from Germany, from 140 degrees east to 145 degrees west longtitude, mainly the Pacific with parts of Australia and New Zealand.

The second powerful computer was managed by Anton as this computer adjusted the strength of the infrared ray and also had the ENTER key to send it. Again with trials they found that three thousand degrees and duration of a tenth second should kill a man. They tried it on trees and were able to set a tree aflame. To have abundant photons available Klausner built a black box with heat lamps. To be able to set a car or house on fire, they adjusted the infrared beam up to five thousand degrees, with a time frame of from one-tenth to one second.

At Anton's suggestion, Klausner used a third computer for audio sending and receiving. Of course, this would only work if an active audio apparatus was at the receiving end, such as an activated phone or radio or TV.

For their first killing they decided to kill a wildebeest. They found such animals in abundance in Kenya National Park. This killing would not go to waste as there were predators that would eat the carcass.

While Max used the view computer to zero in on Kenya, Anton was at the power computer to adjust the temperature of the infrared beam and push the key to send the charge.

For viewing a certain place on earth, Klausner used a computer that gave him Google Earth, and he found easily Lake Victoria and the grassland of Kenya National Park to the east. Then he adjusted his view computer to the same area. The many tiny black points were a herd of wildebeest. He zeroed in on one animal; it was grassing and standing still. He brought the view closer to the animal's head until about a foot away.

"Give him the charge, Anton!" Anton on his power computer had the same view. He had adjusted the heat ray to three thousand degrees. He pushed the ENTER key. They did not see the surge of the infrared beam but saw the animal fall at once dead. Fire enveloped the head, and white smoke or steam issued from the head of the animal. They did not know if any noise was associated with the killing, but nearby wildebeest were spooked and galloped off, and then the herd moved away. Raising the view they saw coyotes come and tear at the dead animal. "I guess they have cooked meat for dinner," said Klausner.

Their first attempt to kill had been a success. And they knew that a surge of three thousand degrees of infrared heat, which killed the animal, was enough to kill a man.

"What now, Anton?" asked Max. "We have the death ray developed and can kill any person on earth. Who are the baddies who deserve to be removed, either to punish for committed crimes or to protect mankind from criminal misfits?"

"Haven't you thought about it, Max?"

"Yes, I did. There are two groups of people I would kill." Anton interrupted, "Let's not use the word 'kill'; it is so drastic a word. They kill. We eliminate and only after a trial. We prosecute, defend or mitigate, then judge."

"All right, Anton, one group I wish to eliminate, as they are a danger to mankind, are the Somali pirates. I mean, in our modern-day-and-age piracy? They attack ships with machine guns, with rifle grenades. Capture crews and hold them for ransom, kidnapping on a big scale. They have murdered innocent seafarers. I read about such dastardly executions. I just don't understand that the great powers let it happen and seldom interfere."

"I agree with you, Max, that the pirates are a danger to mankind and should be eliminated. Why the big powers? Don't they do anything about it?"

"Well, they do but not enough. They really should send an expeditionary force on land to wipe out the pirates; they know where they are hiding and living. I guess it is political. The government of Somalia is caught in a civil war against the al-Shabab militia. Even in their capital Mogadishu, the militia is active against the government, and a weak government it is. Probably corrupt and getting a share of the ransom. So the government does not permit foreign forces to come in and wipe out the pirates. There are navy ships of many countries in the Gulf of Aden and the Indian Ocean to protect commerce, but we are talking about a huge body of water. Also, there are many fishing boats around, so who are the pirates? Another problem is that the crews are kept imprisoned on their ships, guarded by armed pirates. You attack them, and they would kill the hostages.

"I have to look around, especially in the Gulf of Aden and see if I can differentiate between legitimate fishing boats and pirates. They use speedboats and are armed. The other groups of people who deserve to be eliminated are the Mexican drug cartels. I read about horrific killings, torture, and dismemberment. And you, Anton, who are your baddies, though I can imagine who you would be after."

"Who?"

"The same people or groups who caused 9/11 in America, the Muslim jihadists."

"You are right, Max. By the way, does Sepp know anything about what we plan?"

"No. He believes we are working on wireless transmission of energy. The same as director Glaser thinks we are doing."

"Max, I think we should bring Sepp Kainz into our project. He is a simple and decent person. He would represent the common man, the public. He has been with me through many adventures like when the neo-Nazis kidnapped my mother. When I eliminated the Iranian atom spies. He has been only understanding of what I do, calls its illegal in a legal sense. He is faithful and loyal to me and would be to our world tribunal."

"Maybe you are right, Anton. He would represent the common man. Besides being a decent person, supported you loyally in your illegal-legal doings, he might put the brakes on when we become fanatical about our mission to eradicate the baddies in the world. He also has a lot of wisdom. I have talked to him about the scourge of the Mexican cartels. He puts a lot of blame on America, the insatiable lust for illegal drugs, and he is right of course. He thinks that the Americans should call it what we call it, *Rauschgift,* intoxicating poison. But he also says that the Mexicans should try to execute the most vicious members of the cartels. Why don't you talk to Sepp, feel him out what he thinks about a power that could eliminate the worst of the offenders?"

"All right, I do that. If we are a power of three, we can institute a real tribunal. We can have an accuser or prosecutor, a litigator or defender, a judge. The three of us together are the jury. We are the world tribunal."

CHAPTER III

The Force of Three

It was the same day—Saturday, the fourteenth of July 2012—that Anton invited his good friend Sepp Kainz to supper at the Heide Inn. He had called him from the institute but declined to invite Sepp's wife, Inge. He explained that he needed Sepp privately. This was nothing new for Sepp as Anton had the help of him for many special jobs he did when a police officer in Munich. In fact, Sepp Kainz was known as the private detective of Inspector Nagil during his years with the Munich police department.

While they had supper, they talked only about their families. After, when Anton lit his pipe (they sat in the smoking section of the inn), Sepp asked, "An all-night job, Anton? I told Inge I might not be back until tomorrow morning."

Anton laughed. "Nothing of the sort. A talk. Want to come over to my place or walk in the woods?"

"You have excellent whiskey and good cigars. Let's go to your place."

This they did. Anton's house was only a block from the inn. The sat in the comfortable and rustic living room. Anton served his Jim Beam bourbon and brought a box of habanas, Cuban cigars.

Sepp puffed. "So what is up in this secret meeting?"

Anton smiled. "Secret is right. Sepp, what I tell you and offer you, even if you decline, must be kept a secret. Promise?" Sepp nodded, which was like an oath he took.

"How do you like your job with Professor Klausner?"

"It is only part-time. But I appreciate the extra money I make being semi-retired and on pension. Oh, it is interesting as the professor taught me how to use the computer. Now it is even more interesting as he uses Google Earth to go to different places on earth and repeats the same thing with another computer but in real time. He taught me how to do it, and I can go and view just about any place, see what is going on right now. He also made an audio beam so we can talk. I operate that computer. It is his secret to do so, and he said that only he and you know about it. And only with you can I discuss it."

"There is more to it than just beam this visual ray to any place on earth, Sepp. We can also send a death ray along with the visual ray. Mankind has been and is always threatened by very evil people. Klausner and I wish to eliminate the worst of them. Think about this: eliminate evildoers who have committed crimes against mankind or are doing it now." Anton looked deeply into the eyes of his friend. Sepp's head was bobbing imperceptibly, thinking and agreeing. Then he said, "That would be a blessing for mankind." His eyes looked serious at Anton. "I wished it could be done. I would help. What could I do?"

Just as serious, Anton said, "It can be done. We shall do it. Professor Klausner, I, with you, would form a team to combat the worst of the criminals. Not the usual criminals who steal and rob, even murder, but more of the type of war criminals, the fanatics who kill for political, racist, or religious reasons. Like the Nazis did, the Serbs in Yugoslavia, the warlords in Laos and Cambodia, the slaughtering of the Tutsis in Rwanda."

Said Sepp, "Or the neo-Nazis now. They still believe in Hitler and what Hitler did, only that they are without power; else, they would continue slaughtering the Jews and other minder-blooded people. They still subscribe to being the *Herrenvolk* and that stupid blood cult. That is the reason they call their secret organization the Blut und Erde Bund. It used to be that most of their younger followers were skinheads, but now they attract also students and the sons of well-to-do folks. And with their slogans of '*Rauss mit die Auslaender* [out with the foreigners],' they find sympathy with others."

"Is Horst Bachleiter and his son Gustaf still the leader of the Bund?"

"Yes, according to Fred Schultheis. I am friendly with Fred, and we talk often about you. Fred still works for Inspector Wagner as a secret informer of the Bund. Fred took me along one time to one of their meetings. I was as an interested guest. Many in brown and black uniforms, Swastikas all over the place. And all the bull they talked about, blaming the Jews for Europe's recession. If I could, I would kill them all."

"That is what Klausner and I wish to do. Punish those who committed terrible crimes against mankind and those who are doing it now. Prevent them from continuing their misdeeds. Klausner and I wish for you to join us."

"Anton, I m just a simple man, not educated."

"That is one of the reasons we want you. You would represent the common man. But more than that, you are a good man; you have a lot of experience with the common folks, a lot of wisdom, a man of integrity. Also perhaps, a brake on Klausner and I when we become too radical. Before we kill—and we won't use the word 'kill' but instead 'eliminate'— before we eliminate a miscreant or condemn a group, we hold a trial. Whoever of us three brings such a criminal of mankind before our court, he will detail the crimes committed; one will be the defender, one the judge. And the three of us will be the jury."

"Sounds good and fair. We three will be like a Force of Three."

"A good name for us. We will call our group seeking justice the world tribunal and sign judgments with the Force of Three. You are with us then, Sepp?"

"Count me in, Anton. I will be proud to serve. Let justice be done."

"Sepp, then think about the evildoers you wish to bring before our court. The professor already stated his desire to accuse the Somali pirates of crimes against mankind and also the Mexican drug cartels; they have become mass murderers, torturing and dismembering their victims."

"When do we begin?"

"No hurry, Sepp. And importantly, the way Klausner has trained us, he will do the search and close in on the one to be eliminated. You take the computer for audio signals—that is, if we wish to talk to the criminal. I adjust the heat beam and push the trigger, a key on my computer. I am flying back to Israel tonight to be with my family for Sunday. I thought next Friday we all fly to my dacha near Moscow and hold our first trial. We come back on Sunday, all right?"

"Fine with me, Anton. I have to explain to Inge why she can't come along this time."

"Just tell her that the professor is coming too and we talk technical business."

Sepp then took Anton to the airport for his flight back to Tel Aviv.

CHAPTER IV

The Dacha Meeting

Anton had it all arranged and procured visas (courtesy of General Orlov). They met at noon at the Domodedovo Airport in Moscow.

The limousine was waiting to take them to the town of Alexandrov, twenty miles northeast from the city. At the housing office they received the guest passes for professor Max Klausner and Sepp Kainz to permit them entry to the restricted government housing area. Anton Hofer, of course, had his permanent pass. Driver Ivan awaited them in his troika, an open carriage drawn by three white horses; and with jingling bell, they rode through the meadows with cattle grazing fields of wheat and corn.

At the birch forest was the guardhouse where they had to show their permits. Then along the creek, over the stone bridge, there was Anton's dacha, a one-story large log house with a tower in front. Ivan cracked his whip and called his "hoi-hoi" and Sasha, the caretaker came running. Sasha addressed Anton as *Kommissar* Hofer and was introduced to Professor Klausner and Sepp Kainz. While Sasha brought their luggage in, Anton took his friends into the kitchen where they met Sasha's wife, Isabella.

Isabella had the table set with various cold cuts; cheeses; herring; caviar, of course; and black bread. There was also Crimean wine, a bottle of vodka, and Anton's favorite bourbon.

Sasha returned in his car to Alexandrov after Isabella had inquired what they would like to eat; for Sunday she had ordered a turkey, which Sasha was to pick up.

They ate a hearty meal and drank wine; also the obligatory tea was served.

Anton had just lit his pipe when Isabella asked him to come into the living room. There she told Anton her secret.

Apparently, this dacha known as *dacha odin* was used for favorite foreign visitors; and every room was bugged, the listening devises built into the walls and ceiling, the microphones voice activated. There was a security office of the FSB (formerly the KGB) in Alexandrov, and after every visit to the dacha, an FSB agent came to take the tapes. In Sasha and Isabella's nearby cottage was a small room where the tape recorders were located. Sasha knew of the tapes but was under strict orders not to reveal their existence.

Isabella did not think that General Orlov, friend and benefactor of Anton who had done great service to Russia and was given the dacha by the general with permission of President Putin, knew that the tapes were still recording. She thought that it was an overzealous local FSB agent who was responsible. Sasha was threatened with banishment to Siberia if he warned Kommissar Hofer or any of the visitors.

"And why are you telling me this, dear Isabella, though I am grateful that you did?"

She answered, and tears came to her eyes, "Because you are a good landlord and very kind to me and Sasha."

Anton padded her arm. "You are a good woman, Isabella, I thank you. Here, buy yourself something." And he gave her a thousand rubles (about 300 dollars worth).

This, of course, presented a problem. He had been given the dacha two years ago on a ninety-nine-year lease for giving the Russians information that permitted them to intercept terrorists who wanted to nuke Moscow. Since, he had visited the dacha a few times with his family. Also a few of his former colleagues from the Munich police departments had visited. He would have to warn them about the listening devices that no compromising discussions were held. He chuckled to himself when he remembered his lovemaking with Hanna in their bugged bedroom. Words of love and endearment, moans and groans.

He would have be more subdued, though he wished not to tell Hanna. She would resent to visit here in a house where everything was recorded.

But for now, nothing about what they wished to discuss can be spoken about in the dacha.

Anton returned to the kitchen where his friends sat, and Isabella served tea and cake.

"Isabella, what have you prepared for supper for us?"

"I made shishkebab. I have them ready on spits, and they are marinating."

Anton turned to his friends. "How would you like to have them for a picnic this evening? It is two o'clock now, a half-hour walk, and we can be at the lake. There is a firepit. We take a bag of charcoal along. Do some fishing at the lake, full of carp. Isabella, can you prepare everything for us? Put it in baskets some wine too."

"I make everything ready, Kommissar Hofer. It is a nice day, but they say that we have a thunderstorm tonight."

"We will be back by then," answered Anton.

Max, "Does Isabella speak German? No? I thought we discuss our subject this afternoon."

Anton put his finger to his lips. "Not a word, Max, except about fishing."

A half hour later they were walking along the path through the birch forest, carrying the baskets and fishing rods.

Anton, "Now I can tell you. Isabella told me that the dacha's every room is bugged with listening devices. The dacha was at one time used by foreign dignitaries; it was bugged so the secret service could listen in. It is still bugged. I can't believe that my friend General Orlov would do that to me. Isabella thinks that he knows nothing about the continued bugging, and it is just the local FSB that mandates the continued use of the microphones that are voice activated. We have some debugging devices in our police department, and I shall bring one along. Activate by talking and finding one that is within a wall. Then I drive a nail in as if to hang a picture. Holla, there is something open behind. I wonder what. That I tell General Orlov. Then I see how he reacts."

Sepp took a deep breath. "That is all we needed, reveal the Force of Three to the Russian secret service before we even got started."

Max, "Yes, that was close and so unexpected. How come that she told you, Anton? I mean, she must be sworn to secrecy by the FSB."

"She is very fond of me because I treat her and Sasha nicely. Sasha must not know that she told me. He was threatened with Siberia if he did not cooperate. Isabella thinks that the continued use of the microphones is just a local eager-beaver act," said Anton.

It was a hot summer day but cool in the forest. Close to the lake the birch changed into pine trees. They came to the lake, with a meadow separating the forest from the water.

Along the lake were the many raspberry bushes, and there were bears noshing.

At the edge of the forest, where the path led to the lake, was the picnic place and firepit. The sun had crossed the zenith, and they had shade. They left the food basket covered with a cloth. Sepp took from the other one a bottle of red wine and glasses and served them.

"Look who is coming!" said Max.

One of the bears, a large one, came trotting toward them. Then about ten meters away stood up and growled. Anton took a fishing rod and swished it from side to side and yelled at the bear. It growled angrily. Anton yelled louder. The bear then trotted back to the lake, and all the bears moved farther away.

"Just protecting their young," explained Anton. But they gathered some dead wood and built a fire in the pit. "Keeps the bears away."

They sipped their wine. "It almost tastes like Tokay," thought Max.

"It is sweet wine from the Crimea, heavy in body." Anton took his etui with cigars.

Max smoked cigarettes took one; so did Sepp who rarely smoked but liked a good cigar. Anton, the pipe smoker, also was fond of a good Habana.

Anton: The world tribunal is in session.

Max: If we begin to eliminate miscreants, should we warn them? Warn the world of who we are and what the purpose of the world tribunal is?

Sepp: Especially if we wish to eliminate groups. Give those a warning who are just like *Mitlauefer* run-alongs? Like with the pirates who were fishermen before and might still be?

Max: Then let them fish and not kidnap people, hold them for ransom, and often kill their captives.

Anton: Yes, I believe we should let the world know. A warning to all evildoers to desist. But also eliminate those who have committed crimes against mankind and who are beyond jurisdiction. Like former war criminals who might still be around and are in hiding or in countries where they are protected.

Sepp: And how can we let the world know? Write a letter? And to whom?

Anton: I thought about it. We explain the world tribunal and its purpose to a prominent newspaper, deal only with this paper. Write a manifesto stating our reason and purpose. Then, when we have held a trial, write up the judgment, send it, and proceed.

Max: Write a letter? The authorities will trace the letter, and even if we don't put a return address, EUROPOL, INTERPOL or the Bka (Bundeskriminalamt) will set all machinery in motion to find the source. If need be they would watch every mailbox in Munich, take a picture of everyone who deposits a letter.

Anton: We will use a forwarding post office. There is one in Rome that is used by the mafia. This private post office will not reveal the sender or from where the letter was sent. Also, we should send the letter to them from different cities, even from foreign countries.

Sepp: If I understand right, within this letter, is the letter addressed to this newspaper?

Anton: Yes, the letter to the paper within a larger envelope.

Max: The *Berner Nachrichten* is the most prominent newspaper in Switzerland and read all over Europe. I can get their address from internet.

Anton: All right, then we chose this newspaper.

Max: What if they don't print it? If they think it is a hoax?

Anton: With the first letter and manifesto we send an appeal to the chief editor to hold the letter until the world tribunal has proven its existence. Then publish.

Max: I also get the name of the editor.

Sepp: How much does it cost to have the office in Rome forward the letter?

Anton: A hundred dollars or its equivalent in euro.

Max: I pay.

Anton: You and I share. Sepp is on pension.

Sepp: All right, now who begins? I guess we all have our evil ones in mind.

Anton smiled genially at Max. "You begin, Max. To fight the pirates is a proper start. Also the Mexican drug cartels need to be stopped in their murderous gang wars."

"Another cigar Anton, please," asked Max. All three lit a new cigar, and Sepp refilled their glasses. Anton threw more wood on the fire and the bears left them alone.

Max: In our modern day and age, it is unbelievable that piracy exists and does on a continuous basis. The pirates are mostly fishermen from north Somalia. Most, if not all, are Muslims. However, religion has little to do with their piracy as they also hijacked a ship from Saudi Arabia. Yet we cannot over look their ethnicity; some are Arabs and Shi'tis. It seems the only ships that are safe from them are Iranian and Syrian vessels.

Also their leaders are associated with the terrorist group of al-Shabab, again Shi'tis.

The government of Somalia is weak, torn by internal strife; and even in their capital of Mogadishu, they battle al-Shabab. By stating that their government is weak, we must also include the fact that many officials are corrupt and paid off to do nothing. Therefore, the government does not permit outside forces to wipe out the pirates in their nests. An expeditionary foreign force could easily put an end to piracy if it landed near their bases which we know where they exist. At first the pirates restricted their capturing of ships to the Gulf of Aden, which lies north of Somalia. Once foreign naval forces entered the gulf, they extended piracy to the Indian Ocean, around the Horn of Africa. This, of course, diluted the presence of these naval forces to immense areas.

The pirates operate from mother ships, which are fishing cutters, and therefore difficult to distinguish from regular fishing boats. They search nearby areas with speedboats; and when they find a large vessel, they attack it, usually with two or more boats. They fire their Kalashnikovs and rifle grenades at the ship to force it to stop, then shoot ladders over the railings to board the ship. Most ships are unarmed, and once the pirates boarded the ship, the crews become helpless captives. They force the captain to steer the ship to their favored anchorages. Then they demand ransom. Depending on the size of the vessel and the number of the crew, the ransom demand is in the millions. They may hold the ship and crew for many months until the ransom is paid and the money delivered by plane, dropped by parachute, delivered in a small boat, or even by an emissary from land. Crew members have been killed—or I should say murdered—as a warning to expedite the delivery of money. Crews have been killed when boarding the ship, especially if there was resistance.

Sepp: Why don't the countries of the ships provide naval personnel? I mean, even if there are two or three boats involved, if there are several trained navy men onboard with machineguns and hand grenades, they could put up a good fight.

Max: I don't really know. Perhaps it has to do with insurance. Once navy people are aboard, it becomes a war vessel. Insurance companies don't cover such ships. The other reason could be that many ships are registered in foreign places for tax reason. A German ship might be flagged as a ship from Malta or some other tax heaven. Only Israeli ships, special targets for Muslims, carry armed guards or navy personnel. Then there are ships that have great speed, like passenger liners or cruise ships, which by zigzagging makes it difficult or impossible to board.

Anton: I think we agree that piracy and using deadly force is a crime against mankind. But to try them and convict, we need a specific case!

"All right," said Max, "I give you such a specific instance of wanton murder by pirates."

He took a clipping from his pocket. "This is dated 23 August 2011. Let me read it to you."

Norfolk, Virginia, USA—a pair of Somali pirates were sentenced to life in prison for their roles in the hijacking of a yacht that left all four Americans on board dead. One of the pirates argued he had unsuccessfully tried to persuade his fellow pirates that the two women on board should be released.

The owner of the *Quest*, Jean and Scott Adam of Marina del Ray, along with friends Bob Riggle and Phyllis Macay of *Seattle*, were shot to death in February several days after being taken hostage south of Oman. They were the first Americans to be killed in a wave of piracy that has plagued the Gulf of Aden and the Indian Ocean in recent years.

A band of pirates had hoped to take the Americans back to Somalia so they could be ransomed, but that plan fell apart when four U.S. Navy warships began shadowing them.

The navy offered to let the pirates take the yacht in exchange for the hostages, but the pirates said they wouldn't get the kind of money they wanted for it. Hostages are typically ransomed for millions of dollars. Yusuf and Mohamed are the first of eleven men who have pleaded guilty to piracy. Each of the men faces mandatory life sentences. Three men are charged with murder and other death-penalty-eligible charges. In all, nineteen pirates boarded the *Quest*.

"The Adams had spent much of their time delivering Bibles around the world.

End of this article."

Sepp: How stupid. I mean, here they hold four hostages but are followed by four American warships. Did they expect to get away with it? The Americans abandoning their countrymen?

Anton: There could be a religious bias involved. Christians who delivered the scriptures pertaining to Jesus?

Max: Religious fanatics like the suicide bombers.

Sepp: Elimination of pirates a must! I speak them guilty.

Anton: I agree. I vote guilty.

Max: Guilty. Elimination.

Sepp: We must be careful to differentiate between bona fide fishermen and pirates.

Anton: Best if we can catch them attacking a ship.

Max: I have been viewing their anchorage of ships and the place nearby that seems to be their hideout. It is near Karin, on the north coast of Somalia, and not far from the town of Berbera where many pirates, leaders probably, have nice villas.

The road from Berbera to Karin is guarded by armed men, pirates. If we can't find their ships, we can start eliminating their guards, if only as a warning.

Anton stood up and stretched himself. "We have convicted the Somali pirates as a first act by the tribunal. Tomorrow we listen to the accusations against the Mexican drug cartels. Let's cook our shishkebab."

Anton threw charcoal on the wood fire; Sepp opened a second bottle of wine. Soon the charcoal turned white; and Anton, the cook, placed the spits with pork, lamb, and veggies over the stones and turned them often. Soon the vagrant smell of roasted meat was in the air. Sepp cut the loaf of bread; Max brought paper plates from the basket. They sat down and enjoyed a fine meal.

A wind came from the lake, and dark clouds rushed overhead; in the distance they could hear thunder.

Anton: We better pack up, or we get wet.

They left, walking fast, soon trotting as big drops came with the storm; and then they ran but got soaked by the time they got to the dacha. It also had gotten cold, and they were wet and shivering. They went to the sauna, which Sasha wisely had already fired.

Anton shrugged his shoulders and put his finger to his lips. "I don't know but it seems likely." They understood and spoke only about the beauty of the lake, the forest, the bears they had encountered and their fine meal.

Later they had tea with cake, then watched Russian TV in the living room, though only Anton could speak Russian. But there was a beautiful presentation of ballet from the Bolshoi Theater.

Unknown to the three friends, there was a call from the local FSB office to Sasha in the evening inquiring why there was no conversation recorded all afternoon. Sasha explained that his guest had picnicked all afternoon at the lake and had said they would again go there the next day. To the office it was important to listen in on the conversations of a police kommissar, a scientist, and a third person, all Germans. They told Sasha to call them if his guests once again go to the lake for a picnic.

For their Saturday picnic Isabella had prepared an assortment of sausages, which they could roast over a grill. In a jar was potato salad and loaf of bread, and they definitely needed a bag of charcoal as everything would be wet. Also, there were bottles of Crimean wine they liked.

Anton had refilled his etui with Habanas. This time Max took his photo along to take pictures. Before they left with their baskets, Isabella slipped Anton a note. "A secret note," she said sadly. He read it; it said, "Beware. Sasha had to tell THEM where you are picnicking." He asked Sasha for his battery-operated radio.

On the way through the forest, Anton explained to his friends that they might be spied upon, "Maybe they use a listening device. That is why I brought the radio."

"Maybe they play a good concert," laughed Max.

At their picnic place they saw the bears in the nearby bushes eating the raspberries. The big one stood up again and looked at them but didn't growl.

Anton turned the radio loud; yes, there was a Tchaikovsky concert. He faced the loudspeaker toward the forest.

Softly he said, "Let me see if we have unwanted guests."

Max: Be careful, Anton!

Sepp: Yell if you need help.

"I want to take pictures of the bears," Anton said loud. He took the camera and walked toward the bushes. When the big bear stood up and growled, Anton took his picture, then disappeared into the bushes but to the left of the bears. The big bear still stood and sniffed the air. Anton walked quickly farther to the left away from the bears, about a hundred meters to where the bushes extended close to the forest. He walked into the forest and circled around the picnic ground. Slowly he worked his way from tree to tree toward the music. Soon he saw two men. He had expected one or two in the uniform of the security personnel; he was glad to see them dressed as peasants. He could pretend he didn't know they were security but rather strangers who spied on them. He was close enough to hear them talk; of course, they spoke in Russian. The one in the brown tunic just said, "If they don't turn that damned music down, all we record is the concert."

The green-shirted man answered, "I wonder why they turned the radio toward the forest."

Brown tunic: They probably don't want to disturb the bears. I can't see the one who took pictures of the bears.

Green shirt: The big bear is still standing up and sniffing. If he get's too close, the bear will attack him.

Brown tunic: Would serve him right. Russians bears always love to eat a German.

Anton was now only a few trees away, maybe five or six meters. He took a picture of the two, sorry that they showed him their backs. He needed their faces. He stepped out from the tree. "Strastvutje druzya [Hello, friends]."

The two turnedl Anton snapped their picture. He knew it wouldn't be a good picture; their faces showed surprise—or was it shock? He walked to them. Then he saw the setup.

On one tripod was a camera, on the other a receiving antenna like a concave dish. A cable ran down to a car battery, another cable to a tape recorder. He was disappointed; you would have thought that by now the FSB had more modern equipment. He smiled. "What are you doing? Spying on us? What? You think we are three lovers and give you a titillating performance?" He took their camera, opened it and tore the film out, and put it in his pocket. Then he took the pole with the receiver from the tripod and threw it away. He tore the cable from the battery, and just as quickly he took the recorder and smashed it against a tree. It was all done and completed in less than a minute.

Green shirt rushed at him with clenched fists. Anton received him with a karate jab against the throat, and he fell. Brown tunic came next; he had a knife in his hand. Anton intercepted the stab and twisted his forearm. He let out a scream, and his wrist was broken, letting the knife drop. Anton picked up the knife to add to his collection.

Brown tunic said, "We are security agents, wanting to see who you are and what you are doing here. This is a restricted area."

Anton laughed. "I don't believe you. You are either Peeping Toms or bandits. Help your cohort to the car. You came in a car? Of course! And get the hell out of here."

Anton watched brown tunic help green shirt get up who was in distress breathing, and both disappeared into the forest. Anton returned to the picnic ground.

"Well," asked Sepp, "how did it go, you the karate expert?"

Anton smiled. "When I left them, both were in bad shape. They should make it back to their car all right. Their equipment they left behind the trees. Amazing the old junk they use to spy on people. Let me roast our sausages. I am really hungry." This he did while Sepp poured the wine. Apparently the smell attracted the bears as several came toward the forest. Max turned the radio toward them and increased the volume. No, they didn't appreciate the concert and returned to the bushes.

After they had eaten their feast, Anton passed his cigars.

"Next chapter," began Max, "the horrific doings of the Mexican drug cartels. Mass murder, torture, beheadings, and dismemberment, extortion, kidnapping for ransom, blackmail, threats—that is how they corrupt the police."

"Specifics dear, Max, specifics," asked Anton.

Max: Before I give you the specifics you asked for, let me tell you about this reign of terror in Mexico, who they are, the cartels and their leaders, where they are located.

As to why they are so vicious and brutal and kill so many innocents, I have no clear answer.

Sepp: Perhaps to intimidate the public and foremost the local police?

Max: That must be part of it. However, they corrupt the police, even prosecutors and judges, by threatening them and their families. Especially journalists, they have killed many who wrote about them.

Anton: And pay-off. Mexico is famous for pay-off corruption both to officials of the judiciary and the police.

Max took pages from his pocket. "This is from Internet."

There are several large and most brutal drug cartels and then smaller gangs. They all control certain territories and fight each other when one intrudes on the other. The more powerful also extend their control over areas of weaker gangs. It would be nice if they would fight only each other but most of the killed are innocents, bystanders, mistaken rivals, or migrants. Sometimes they conduct a mass-murder spree, like when they killed a bunch of teenagers at a party, which is believed they did to warn the public not to cooperate with the federal police and the army. President Calderon who had declared war on the cartels is soon out, and the new president Pena Nieto will continue trying to eradicate them. However, Calderon's fighting the cartels increased their violence, and we can expect the same under Nieto's regime. He will be sworn in in December.

The main problem, is of course, the insatiable demand for illegal drugs in America. "I wished the Americans would call illegal drugs what we call them Rauschgift, intoxicating poison; it may shy away young people from even trying them. The latest information about illicit drug use in America speaks of over twenty-one million people using them. That is 8 percent of the public. Worldwide the use of these drugs is 5.7 percent, mainly marijuana. In some states in America the use of marijuana is legal on prescription, but the federal government prohibits its use. While marijuana is perhaps benign, it leads to the use of more potent drug like cocaine and heroin. Then its users become addicts, it destroys family life and leads to crime. Besides the obvious danger of a driver using any of these drugs, he is intoxicated like with alcohol.

The largest and most violent cartel is the Zetas. Interesting, the Zetas were founded by rogue Mexican special forces to provide protection for the gulf cartel. Now a cartel in its own right, the Zetas have used extreme violence to extend their reach and claim key smuggling routes. Their present leaders are Heriberto Lazcano and Miguel Trevino Morales. Their main bases are in Monterrey and Nuevo Laredo, that city lies near the U.S. border.

The gulf cartel was once the most powerful trafficking cartel but lost its prominence with the arrest of its leader Osiel Cardenas Guillen in 2003 and the more recent departure of its enforcement wing, the Zetas. The gulf and Zetas cartels are now at each other's throats. Its sole leader is Jorge Costilla Sanchez, known as El Coss. Its coleader Antonio Ezekiel Cardenas Guillen, Toni Tormenta, was killed by security forces.

It main base is Mexico's gulf coast.

The Sinaloa Federation is a loose federation and has proved resilient to Mexico's offensive against organized crime. Its long-time leader is Joaquin Guzman Loera, known as El Chapo. He was captured but broke out of prison in 2001. Certainly bribery or threats, probably both. Guzman Loera is even on Forbes list of richest people and on the authorities' list of most wanted men. The base of the cartel is the Sinaloa province of western Mexico and Chihuahua province in the north with the city of Ciudad Juarez, which they share with the Juarez cartel.

Juarez Cartel also known as the Fuentes Organization has lost ground to the Sinaloa cartel. Its leader is Vicente Carrillo Fuentes. Its main base is the city of Ciudad Juarez, which lies across from the U.S. city of El Paso.

"By the way,"—Max looked up from his notes—"the city of Ciudad Juarez is considered the deadliest city in Mexico."

"Why is that?" asked Sepp.

Max explained, "Besides the usual killings of turf war, of innocents and migrants, more women are murdered than anywhere else in Mexico. Their remains found all over the city or in mass graves."

"How come?" asked Anton.

Max: With so many traffickers of cartels in operation—and these people are very primitive—I guess it is the macho image. Women and girls are to be used and then thrown away. Second-class citizens.

Anton: Very similar to fanatical Muslims, women are to be used and abused.

Max: Another minor cartel that was once powerful is the Beltran Leyva Organization.

It was founded by four brothers and was part of the Sinaloa cartel but broke away when they accused the Sinaloas of snitching on Alfredo Beltran Leyva who was arrested in 2008. Then another brother, Arturo Beltran Leyva, was killed in 2009. Now they have broken into two factions: the South Pacific Cartel and the Independent Cartel of Acapulco. That cartel is lead by Hector Beltran Leyva. Bases are the provinces of Morelos, which include Mexico City, Guerrero with Acapulco, and scattered territories.

The Arellano Felix Organization, once known as the Tijuana group and a ruthless cartel, fell apart when the brothers Benjamin, Eduardo, Javier, and Ramon were captured or killed. The present leader is a nephew, Fernando Sanchez Arellano, known as El Ingeniero. Main base is Baja California with the city of Tijuana. However, the Sinaloa cartel controls these routes into the U.S., and the Arellano gang has to pay them for access. So much for the drug cartels, who they are, and were their bases and strongholds are located.

Now for specifics and these are recent reports: April 12, tortured bodies of seven men dumped in Lazaro Cardenas; April 17, Mutilated bodies of fourteen men left in minivan in Nuevo Laredo; May 5, Bodies of twenty-three people found hanging from bridge or decapitated in Nuevo Laredo; May 9, eighteen bodies left near Guadalajara; 13 May, forty-nine bodies are found alongside highway near Monterrey. This act of wanton murder is the specific one I wish to accuse them with. Let me read from Internet:

> Forty-nine bodies with their heads, hands, and feet hacked off were found dumped on a northern Mexico highway leading from Monterrey to the Texas border. A message left near the scene suggests that the Zetas cartel was responsible. Nuevo Leon state security spokesman Jorge Domene said that the forty-three men

and six women would be hard to identify. It is believed they were migrants.

Sepp: Why would they kill these people and in such a gruesome fashion? I mean, they had nothing to do with the drug trafficking, just innocent people who wanted to get into America to find work.

Anton: It could be that these migrants didn't have enough money to pay, or more likely, the Zetas took their money then killed them to safe a long trip through the desert and across the border. It is in the nature of these gangsters to break any promise they make.

Cutting off their heads and hands was to prevent their identification as migrants. Taking migrants across the border is probably a lucrative sideline of their illegal drug business. In this case they saved themselves a lot of work.

Sepp: How merciless and cruel.

Max: Do we find the drug cartels guilty of crimes against mankind that warrants their elimination?

Sepp: Guilty, eliminate.

Anton: Horrendous! Guilty, eliminate.

Max: A thousand times guilty. Eliminate. Though we can never eradicate the trafficking, not as long as America imports the Rauschgift.

Anton: But we can reduce the trafficking once the members realize that there is a world tribunal and the Force of Three can eliminate them, even if it is only one by one.

I work on the manifesto, the first one against the pirates?

Max: Yes. I have spent a lot of time searching for their anchorage and found the one off Karin. Maybe next weekend we can go after them?

Anton: Make it in two weeks; that gives time to send the letter and have it forwarded to Bern. That would be Friday, the third of August. Tomorrow morning, before we leave at noon, we compose the manifesto and letter. Then on Monday or Tuesday, you, Sepp, take a train to Vienna, buy Austrian stamps at a post office, and mail the letter.

Max: Why not send it from Moscow?

Anton: Someday, the authorities in Europe and America will try to find the source of the letters they receive. We cannot be certain that the Rome forwarding agency will not divulge wherefrom the letters came. Officially they won't, as we are told they even resist a court order. Privately, someone with a deep pocket might give the information. If the authorities then go back and get the list of passenger that came and left Moscow on the twenty-second of July, our names would be known. Fine, but if our names appear again as suspicious characters . . . know what I mean?

Max: You are smart, Anton.

Anton smiled. "As a police inspector I have to think of all probabilities."

Since it looked like another storm was brewing, wind and dark clouds came from the lake; they soon packed up and walked back to the dacha.

It was early evening that Anton called the dacha of Alex, his friend General Alexander Orlov. Since he was there with his mistress Natasha, Anton asked for a short audience, which Alex granted him. He had Sasha drive him over. After a hearty welcome, embraces, and kisses by both Alex and his quasi-sister Natasha, Anton sat alone with Alex.

Anton told him of the incident of the two men spying on their party on Saturday when they were picnicking by the lake., that they had a camera and a listening device, that he believed they were Peeping Toms. He gave Alex the film with the picture he took of the two men. Alex had him describe what the men looked like, how they were dressed. He told Anton that they have security people in the area, but they were dressed in uniform.

Then Alex said, "Let me check on it, Anton. I have to make a call."

Ten minutes later Alex came back; he looked at Anton. Then he laughed uproarly,

"Peeping Toms? These were my agents." Then he looked serious. "They had no business spying on you." He turned to Sasha. "The recording devices were left on all the time?"

Sasha: Yes, general, I was told by Captain Rokosovski to keep them on and turn the tapes in after each visit. He, the captain, threatened me with Siberia if I told anyone. Isabella and I would be transferred to Siberia.

General Orlov: It is Captain Rokosovski who will be transferred to Siberia. Disconnect all recorders and return them to the FSB office in Alexandrov. He turned to Anton. "I am so sorry, Anton. I apologize. Yes, dacha odin was bugged, to use the slang term. But when it became your dacha, the order was to disconnect all. Captain Rokosovski took it upon himself to keep the listening devices on. All tapes will be destroyed.

You heard me tell Sasha to return the recorders. We cannot remove the microphones, which are in walls and ceilings. I assure you, Anton, as a friend to a friend and all you have done for Russia, the spying business is over, all finished. By the way, the Peeping Toms are in the hospital.

One needed surgery to repair his windpipe; the other has a cast on his arm. The two friends send their greetings." He laughed. Then he looked serious again. "Tell me, Anton, you knew, of course, they were my agents."

Anton: I knew they were your agents, but I also knew that in this case, they were not working for you.

Alex: Right again, Anton. Let us have a drink to our eternal friendship.

What Anton was afraid of, Alex brought a bottle of vodka, and they had a number of drinks, which included Sasha who had only done what he was told and was mighty glad that the spying business was over.

It was late when Anton returned and told Max and Sepp what had occurred. When the two wondered if the general would keep his promise, Anton assured them.

The same night Sasha disconnected the two recorders and tore out the cables.

Sunday morning.

They had a sumptuous breakfast then sat together in the living room where there was a small desk with a computer and printer. The children used the computer for games, Anton and even Sasha sometimes to play chess. Sasha had called Anton outside where his car stood. He showed him the two tape recorders and said he would take them to Alexandrov.

Then he looked at Anton sadly. "I am so sorry, Kommissar Hofer, that I deceived you."

Anton: I understand why you did it. You are forgiven but not more surprises, please.

"Never again," said a happier Sasha.

Together they composed the manifesto and the judgment, both in bold print, and Anton wrote the letter to the editor (on German computer paper). These, they put into an envelope and addressed it to the chief editor of the Suisse newspaper in Bern.

Sepp wondered, "What happens if authorities should get hold of the envelope and find that it was made in Russia?"

Anton chuckled. "It will really confuse them." He then gave Sepp a hundred-dollar bill to include with the larger envelope. Sepp was to take a train from Munich to Vienna, go into town and buy a larger envelope at a stationary store. Address the envelope to the forwarding agency in Rome, include the letter and money, for return address to print FIRENZE (Firenze was the code name Anton obtained from the agency), and mail it from a post office.

Before noon the limousine came that took them to the airport where the three friends parted. Max Klausner and Sepp Kainz returned to Munich, Anton Hofer to Israel.

Anton was home in Jerusalem before it got dark.

Hanna had often wondered what her Toni was doing on his many visits to Munich.

She knew he visited his colleagues in the police department, maybe even had police business with them, saw that his house was in order, paid his bills, and drove around with Sepp Kainz. But for the past few months he had been gone almost every weekend.

So when the children were in bed, Amal in her room in the basement, and they were alone she asked, "Toni, the truth. It isn't that you have a mistress in Munich?"

If any wife can read the face of her husband, it is Hanna, and she saw that he was truly shocked. He took her in his arms. "Hanna, how could you even think such an idea?

But it is true; there is another business I attend to. I never told you as I wanted it to be a surprise. I told you that I had business with Professor Klausner; most of the time in Munich I am with him at the institute. Max and I are working on a great invention. It is to send energy, electricity without a wire, wireless transmission of electricity. If we succeed, we will become famous and rich. I never told you I have become a part-time employee of the Max Planck Institute, though without pay. Let me show you my employee card. It is still secret work Max and I are doing. We have an agreement that if we succeed, while the institute will get the patent, we get 50 percent of any proceeds."

"Oh, Toni!" Hanna held her husband tight. She cried, "I am just a woman, darling. When a woman loves as I do. Forgive me, just this stupid thought came. I had to ask."

She looked up, tears still running down her cheeks. "Now I am your happy Hannerle again. Can you forgive me, Toni?"

He kissed her tears away. "Nothing to forgive. You are just a loving wife. Let's go to bed."

When they undressed, Hanna said, "By the way, they offered me a salaried position at the hospital."

Anton asked, "Why don't you take it?"

"Then I would be committed to six days a week and night shift."

He smiled. "No. Better not, I need you at night." They laughed, embraced, and kissed in love as they had been since high school.

On Monday, twenty-third of July, Sepp took the morning train to Vienna. He bought a pack of large envelopes, addressed one to Rome in block letters, wrote Firenze for return address, and mailed it at a nearby post office. By early evening he was back in Munich.

The letter was received in Rome on Wednesday and the next day mailed to Bern, Switzerland, where it arrived on Saturday, 28 July.

Frau Matilde Gruber, the secretary of chief editor of Konrad, opened all mail addressed to him. When she opened the letter postmarked from Rome and read the three pages, she hesitated but then called Herr Konrad.

"Herr Konrad, you received a letter from Rome; and I don't know if it is a prank, a hoax, or real. But it can't be real as it is too farfetched. Want me to read it to you?"

"How long is it, Matilde?"

"Three pages, and it is in English."

"Then it can wait till Monday. Have a nice weekend, Matilde."

"Thank you. You too, Herr Konrad. Goodbye."

When chief editor Sebastian Konrad came to work Monday morning the letter from Rome laid on his desk over the other mail. There were three pages. He read:

CHAPTER V

The First Manifesto

MANIFESTO I OF THE WORLD TRIBUNAL

L et it be known that as of July 2012, the world tribunal has come into existence.

The purpose of the world tribunal is to accuse and judge those who commit crimes—*hostis humani generis*—enemies of all mankind, who are beyond national/international jurisdiction, and when found guilty to be eliminated.

The active arm of the world tribunal is the Force of Three, signed STE:

S—international scientists who developed the death ray
T—tribunal, composed of men of jurisdiction
E—eliminators who will activate the death ray

JUDGMENT
AGAINST THE SOMALI PIRATES

The Somali pirates were accused of forcefully boarding peaceful ships in the Gulf of Aden and the Indian Ocean, capturing the crews and holding them for ransom.

The Somali pirates were found guilty of piracy, kidnapping, extortion, and murder.

Specifically, they boarded the yacht *Quest* of the American couple Scott Adam; his wife, Jean; and their friends Bob Riggle and Phyllis Macay. The pirates killed the four innocent seafarers. The pirates were also found guilty of murdering others, guilty of kidnapping and extortion for ransom.

JUDGMENT: The elimination of all pirates, Somali and other nationalities, by death ray—*erga omnes.*

To the chief editor of the *Berner Nachrichten*, Sebastian Konrad,
In regard to enclosed manifesto.

July 2012

Herr Konrad:

Please do not destroy this manifesto. This is not a prank letter but a message of reality.

A group of international eminent scientists has developed a death ray, which can be used against any person at any place on earth.

We all know that there are people in this world who are evildoers, and it would benefit mankind if these miscreants were brought to justice and, if found guilty of crimes against mankind, eliminated.

However, most of these evil persons are beyond anyone's jurisdiction, often part of or protected by totalitarian governments.

Therefore, the world tribunal was established to bring these criminals to justice.

There will be a trial. The crimes of the accused will be enumerated by the prosecution; there will be a defense demanding proof of crimes committed. Mitigating circumstances will be voiced. A tribunal of judges will then pronounce guilt or innocence.

If found guilty: in some cases a warning will be given to desist from further criminal acts. If found guilty of murder: the sentence of elimination by death ray will be carried out.

Please again, Herr Konrad, let the tribunal reiterate: do not destroy the manifesto and judgment. Keep it secure until you have verified the existence of the world tribunal and its power to eliminate. Your prominent newspaper will be the *only* media agency contacted, and hopefully you will then publish for worldwide dissemination.

Signed: The Force of Three

After chief editor Konrad read the contents of the letter, he called his secretary on intercom to contact editor Schramm and have him come to his office.

"By the way, Matilde, I hope you have not told anyone about this letter. No? Good, let's keep it for now—confidential."

When political editor Schramm came into his office, Konrad had him read.

"What do you suggest, Schramm? Is it a prank, a hoax?"

Editor Schramm shrugged his shoulders. "I wished I knew. It would be nice if such a force existed. There is, of course, the danger that such a force has an agenda, political maybe? Stopping the Somalis from piracy would be great, but after?"

"I know what you mean. For now I hold the letter. If we hear of such a death ray used, we publish, and I shall contact the federal police."

"Where did the letter come from?"

"Rome."

Saturday, fourth of August.

Anton came at noon to the institute; he had taken the morning flight from Tel Aviv. He rang the bell at the energy house, twice long and once short, his signal.

Sepp opened and told Anton that they were trailing speedboats in the Gulf of Aden.

After greeting Max, he sat before his computer, which showed the same view Max had.

Max explained, "We have been trailing the speedboats for an hour. When I raise the view, we can see a large freighter accompanied by another boat. I guess they called for help as the freighter is zigzagging and moving at a good clip."

"Who is calling for help?" asked Anton.

Sepp answered, "We think the one speedboat called for help. It just can't get the freighter to stop."

Max: We also saw the mother ship; it is about seventy kilometers northwest from the freighter. The one boat tries to herd the freighter to the south, toward Somalia, but it keeps heading in the general direction of east. Let me close in again. Now you can see the two boats speeding toward the freighter.

Anton: How far apart are they?

Max: Maybe ten, fifteen kilometers.

Anton: What is the time difference between us and them?

Max: Three hours ahead. It is noon here, so it would be three in the afternoon there. Lots of time before it gets dark.

Anton: Any navy ships around?

Sepp: Nothing. We looked around.

Max: The closest is a British frigate, at least a hundred kilometers to the east.

Anton: I wonder, why don't they call for help?

Max: They probably warned them that they will fire on the ship if they radio for help. The captain probably thinks he can hold them off until it gets dark. He doesn't know there are two more boats coming.

Anton: Can you see the nationality of the ship?

Max: From our above view, I cannot read the name of the ship. It flies the Panamanian flag.

Anton: Which doesn't tell us anything. A lot of ships register in Panama.

Max: It is a fast freighter, going about thirteen knots, slows to ten when curving.

Anton: I get the infrared ray going. If they attack, like climbing over the railing, we eliminate.

They watched fascinated. Sepp sat with Max as there was little chance to use and need the audio beam.

Another half hour and the three boats were alongside the freighter. Max had moved closer, and they could see the big freighter and two boats along one side the other boat opposite.

Six men were in each boat, and while one was steering, the others held their Kalashnikov rifles and rifle grenades. They were pirates all right. One pirate with a turban took a bullhorn and shouted something up to the ship. There were sailors squatting behind the railings and sometimes one looked for a moment down. The ship again curved away and almost hit the single boat, which also had to turn away. The turbaned pirate now took a rifle grenade and fired up at the ship. It went over the ship. But the next one hit the deckhouse; in fact, it went through the window and exploded inside. All the windows in the deckhouse shattered, and smoke came pouring from it. A man came out; he wore a blue jacket with insignia, probably the captain (it was Captain Jack Harris of the *Houston*). His jacket was torn, and he was bleeding in the face. He stood at the platform outside the deckhouse and raised one arm. The ship slowed and then came to a stop.

The sailors also stood up and raised their hands. The turbaned pirate now fired a rope ladder over the railing; with his rifle slung over his shoulder, he climbed up, followed by four more pirates with rifles.

Anton: Max, when the five pirates are on deck, zero in on turban. I want to give him a good charge so all can see, then three more. One I want to escape and report back.

All five stood now in a group on deck holding their rifles directed at the sailors. The turbaned pirate held his up toward the captain who came down the stairs to the deck.

Anton saw the turban appear on the screen, maybe a foot away. He had adjusted the temperature to five thousand degrees; the timing of the jolt would be one-fifth of a second. He hit the ENTER key. They saw the head explode in fire and the body burst into flame. The other pirates stood like transfixed, and one after the other was immolated though Anton had readjusted to three thousand degrees. At last, one pirate turned and jumped over the railing into the sea. He was soon picked up by one of the boats. The boats were seen speeding away.

The captain—wounded with a bloody face, and one arm seemed hurt—talked to his men who brought hoses and sprayed them at the burning deckhouse. The captain then disappeared into the ship. While Max followed the speedboats, they could see the freighter make way to the east.

A few hours later they saw the mother ship, it was stationary. It looked like a regular fishing cutter, but it had several more speedboats on the afterdeck and a large forklift to lower the boats and pick them up. The two boats made fast and the pirates climbed on deck. One of them, probably the diver, was surrounded as he gave witness to what he had seen.

Max: I wonder if we can sink the cutter.

Anton: In the close-up I saw of the boats, they had a big canister in the back by the outboard motor; it must be an auxiliary gas tank. Let me fire it with a good jolt.

This he did; the tank exploded and caused the back of the cutter to burn.

Sepp: I think we taught the pirates a good lesson. Now together with the manifesto, which I hope they learn of, perhaps they give up their piracy business?

Max: I think we should at least free one ship off Karin from pirates.

Anton: We still have a couple of hours before it gets dark. Let's see what they do.

They watched as the crew put out the fire in the back, but apparently the machinery or something was out of order as they took ropes and tied the cutter to the two remaining boats, which dragged the cutter to the southwest in the direction of Karin.

Max gave a view of Karin. There was the small town, a poor-looking place as many of the houses were mere mud huts. In the bay were about a dozen ships anchored. They chose a big tanker. The sun was just setting in the west; it would be soon twilight and dark. On the afterdeck they saw the crew eating guarded by a half-dozen pirates. *One in white, surely the cook, was ladling soup or stew into bowls.* Most of the pirates they had seen were dark skinned; a few were whites, probably Arabs. Among the guards was such an Arab.

Anton: Take the turbaned one first.

Max zeroed in on his turban, three thousand degrees infrared and one-fifth of a second. He fell, his head flaming and greasy smoke rising. Again the others were too stunned to run, which would have saved them, and one after another they were eliminated. The sailors were also at first immobile, watching in surprise and probably shock. Then they ran to the bodies and took their weapons, rushed up to the deckhouse. Two dead pirates were thrown down on deck. One pirate who had come from the inside saw the sailors with weapons, saw the smoldering remains of his cohorts, and jumped overboard.

Before it was dark, the tanker got underway.

"Mission accomplished. I sincerely hope the pirates get the message and return to fishing," said Max.

It was on Wednesday, the eighth of August, that Anton received a brief email from Max Klausner. It read, "K. free of birds." "Birds" was their codename for ships; the message meant "Karin free of ships." The pirates let the ships and crews go; they had gotten the message of the death rays. There were still other anchorages, but in due time the pirates must also get the message and hopefully return to fishing.

The same day editor Schramm rushed into the chief editor's office, "Guess what, Chief, I got a call from a Reuters agent in Mogadishu if we are interested to buy his report of death rays used in Somalia against pirates. Are we interested?" He smiled.

Chief: Get it. But I also want you to fly to Mogadishu and get more news, if possible a firsthand report. Come back at once. I hold the manifesto until then.

Saturday morning, 11 August, editor Schramm came to the office of the chief who expected him.

Schramm told, "Yesterday morning I visited the captain of the *Houston* in the hospital in Mogadishu; he was injured in the pirate attack. He was hit by shrapnel of an exploding grenade that was shot into the deckhouse; two of his crew were killed. He brought his ship in the day before for repairs; his deckhouse was demolished. Captain Jack Harris told me that about a hundred kilometers north of the Somali coast, he was shadowed by pirates in a speedboat. With deft maneuvering he prevented it from boarding the ship.

Then two more boats showed up, took his ship in between. He still managed to escape them. Then a pirate addressed him with a bullhorn and told him to stop the ship, or he will shoot at it."

The chief interrupted, "In what language did the pirate address Captain Harris?"

Schramm: In English. The *Houston* is an American ship. The captain didn't stop but kept on twisting and turning. Then the pirate fired a grenade up. The first missed; but the second hit the bridge, injured the captain, and killed the navigator and steersman. The bridge burned, and the captain knew he lost. He came out, stood on the stairs, and raised his arm to give up. So did his sailors. The pirates then shot a rope ladder over the railing, and five climbed up. Then the pirate who had addressed him and shot the grenade—he wore a turban, an Arab as he was a white and bearded—suddenly was engulfed in fire, fell dead, burning and smoking on deck. And within a minute three other pirates were killed by fire and smoke. Just suddenly burst into torches and fell dead. The fifth escaped by jumping over board. Captain Harris then told his crew to put out the fire in the deckhouse; his mate took the bridge, and they went underway to Mogadishu. He went into the dispensary and had their medic dress his wounds, shrapnel in the face and a big piece sliced into his left arm.

I gave the captain a thousand euros as I had promised him, and I was the first to interview him. Outside his room, the American ambassador and an FBI agent were waiting to see him, also government officials and a bunch of reporters.

I saw my friend the Reuter reporter, and he told me that he was in touch with a Somali government official who has connection to the al-Shabab militia. I gave him 500 euros as he had to pay the official too. Someone from the militia told the government man that on the same day a mother ship of the pirates was attacked with heat rays; gas tanks in the speedboats on deck exploded, which caused the cutter to burn. They put out the fire, but the cutter couldn't move and is being towed to land to one of their hideouts. That is it, chief.

Chief Konrad: Fine work, Schramm. Let's get the manifesto and judgment into print for the Sunday edition and your story as a byline with your name, your visit to Mogadishu.

The Sunday *Berner Nachrichten* broke the story with the headline in big print:

MANIFESTO DES WELT TRIBUNALS

By Tuesday, the fourteenth, most major newspapers carried the story.

Friday, seventeenth of August, 9:00 a.m., FBI Headquarters in Quantico, Virginia

The FBI had called for the emergency meeting. Present were the director of the FBI, his deputy James Adams (as recorder), the deputy directors of the CIA, NSA, the defense secretary, Professor Golomb of MIT, expert on laser technique, and FBI agent Smith who had flown in from Mogadishu. They sat around a large table; each one had a folder with a copy of the Suisse newspaper and national papers.

Director of FBI: We all have seen the newspaper reports that originated with the *Berner Nachrichten*. Let me introduce agent Smith from the embassy in Mogadishu with a firsthand report.

Agent Smith gave the report of his interview with Captain Harris of the *Houston*, which was similar to the newspaper accounts.

Director: Any questions for agent Smith?

Professor Golomb: Did the captain mention any light rays he might have seen when the pirates were killed? No? Were you able to interview any crew members?

Agent Smith: Yes, I was permitted on the freighter and spoke to crew members. One told that he saw one pirate jump overboard and that he was picked up by the two boats there. The boats immediately hightailed it out of there but nothing about seeing a light ray. Just that suddenly each pirate killed fell down and his head started to burn and smoke. Only the first one killed, the suggested Arab, turned at once into a flaming torch.

Defense Secretary: The form of killing, torching, does suggest a laser beam. How is that possible, Professor Golomb?

Professor: The torching of the Arab and the killing and subsequent burning heads suggest, of course, that it was done with a laser. Yet a light beam should have been visible, well, maybe not as it was in daytime. Of more interest would be wherefrom did the laser originate? Horizontal? Which suggests a nearby ship. From above? No one spoke about seeing or hearing a plane. Our present technology permits the sending of a powerful laser, but how was the beam directed? Since it hit people, in the case of the Arab, his head just about exploded. It seems that whoever sent the laser had also a visual view and that technology is not available.

CIA Deputy: How far can we shoot, if that is the correct terminology, a laser beam to kill, professor?

Professor: Laser pulse would be more correct. It is not the distance that is surprising but the accuracy of the beam. With a large-enough apparatus we can destroy a satellite hundreds of miles away, a combination of radar and laser, but not to aim at a person miles away. I suggest the laser came from a nearby ship.

NSA Deputy: I like to ask the defense secretary if we have such weapon capability.

Secretary: No.

CIA: If not American made, who else? It was an American ship they rescued.

Director: The ship flew the Panamanian flag.

CIA: But the freighter's name was *Houston*. Who else but American?

NSA: Of importance is, who is this world tribunal? Does it represent any danger to the United States?

Director: To combat the Somali pirates is of international interest. The manifesto speaks of "eminent international scientists."

CIA: Americans included, surely.

NSA: Maybe, I am not sure.

Director: We have to await further manifestos and judgments. Is there is anything else? As soon as we have more information, I call for another meeting. Defense Secretary, you keep President Obama informed?

Secretary: Of course. It was the president who wished for me to become part of this. Well, let's call it advisory group. I shall keep the cabinet informed.

Director: I think we shall keep this, so aptly named Advisory Group, for now confidential. No media involvement at this time please. Thank you for coming, Professor Golomb. Goodbye then, gentlemen. The meeting is adjourned.

The same day, Friday the seventeenth of August, there was also a meeting in the chief editor Konrad's office of the *Berner Nachrichten*. Present were editor Schramm and Superintendent Willi Biergli of the Suisse Federal Police. Chief Konrad had invited the super to visit in regard to the manifesto of the world tribunal. He had the super read the personal letter attached to the manifesto.

The chief explained, "When the letter arrived, I really did not know, prank or factual?

But then when the news came of possible use of death rays against the pirates, I called you. You read the manifesto and judgment in our paper, also the report of editor Schramm from Mogadishu. Since our Suisse newspaper is involved, I thought we should get together and discuss things."

Super: You did right, Herr Konrad. Since you also told me that the letter was sent from Rome, I queried a contact I have with the Italian Carabinieri. My contact at once thought that the letter came through the forwarding agency in Rome. For money, a bribe really, he received this information from the secretary of the agency that the letter originated in Vienna. This, of course, complicates matters. A manifesto of combating crimes comes to us in Switzerland from Rome and originates in Vienna. It is written in faultless, though common, English. The ship rescued from the pirates is American?

Chief: Yes, it is. Yet the manifesto and judgment speak of eminent international scientist, so?

Schramm: If the killing rays or death rays are fact, who else has the scientific know-how but America?

Super: We have to query the FBI. By the way, our forensic laboratory would like to inspect the letters and envelope.

Chief: I have them here. You can use them. I like to keep them in my archive.

Super: Good. I return them. I spoke with our government officials. While we believe that there is no present danger to Switzerland, we have to await further communication from the tribunal. As long as the tribunal confines its activities against criminal elements that are out of reach of normal national authorities, all is fine. But if they become political, know what I mean, Herr Konrad?

Chief: Yes, I understand. If I receive another communication, I call you at once.

That afternoon Superintendent Biergli called Herr Konrad and told him that the envelope originated in Russia. The paper was produced in Germany, mailed in Vienna, Austria.

On Saturday, eighteenth of August, Anton was home in Jerusalem. He was off and wanted to use the free day to compose the next manifesto. He made his notes in German, which neither his wife Hanna nor her mother, Amal, could read. He worked in his office, which was air-conditioned as the house was. The children—David, Esther, and little Daniel—were in the swimming pool supervised by Amal. Hanna was working at the Hadassah hospital.

The bell rang; it was his old friend Mordechai Nevot, the former Mossad deputy.

Anton welcomed him joyfully, "Old friend, come in."

Anton got a bottle of cool wine and poured the glasses.

"Nevot, it is good to see you." (Anton had always made it his practice to address him by his last name.)

Nevot smiled. "How nice to find you at home for a change. I have come by often on your day off, and Hanna always told me you are back in Munich."

"Business, Nevot, business."

"What possible business could you have in Munich, Anton? You are settled here, working for the police department, so?"

Anton looked serious. "Nevot, you are one of the few people I trust explicitly. Yet I cannot tell you. I can't event tell Hanna, and we have no secrets from each other."

Nevot smiled. "Unless you go on one of your secret 'seek-and-destroy missions.'"

Anton laughed but said nothing.

"I don't want to pry, Anton. Does it concern Israel?"

"Not at this point. But you deserve at least a hint. I work at the Max Planck Institute with Professor Klausner. Remember, he was the one who taught the Iranians. We work on wireless transmission of energy. I have become an employee of the institute, of course, only part-time and without salary, kind of consultant to the professor. If we succeed, we become famous and rich. And yes, Israel would benefit by our invention."

"Look, Anton, what you just told me, it will remain a secret in my mind. I know, in due time you will tell me. I have a good friend in America, a rich man and philanthropist. He is hundred percent trustworthy. He will help with anything that has to with the security of Israel, financial or otherwise. You ask, he will help. Just tell me what you need."

"Without revealing my secret, wor Nevot?"

"Without."

"I might need his generosity. Perhaps even a certain favor. Let me think about it and talk to the professor. We really work on wireless transmission."

"And more, Anton?"

Anton remained silent.

"Let us consider this talk and offer as a confidentially, Anton?" Anton nodded.

Else they talked about the family, police work, and politics.

Soon Nevot left, and Anton returned to his work. He finished the draft of the manifesto.

CHAPTER VI

The Second Manifesto

Friday, 24 August 2012.

A nton came during the morning to the institute and found Max and Sepp busy viewing Mexico, mainly the cities and towns in the north bordering on America.

Though central northern Mexico being seven to eight hours behind in time, that is ten o'clock in the morning in Munich, it was now 2:00 a.m. in Mexico and little could be seen even in the well lit city of Monterrey they were viewing.

Max: We are looking for members of the Zetas, the most violent of the cartels. The ones who killed the forty-nine people, including six women, chopped off their heads, hands, and feet—gruesome. And according to reports, they were just migrants, innocents.

Max shut off the computers and said that they would return to it at four in the afternoon when it would be morning in Mexico.

Anton showed his friends the draft of the manifesto and asked for any changes or additions. Max and Sepp thought it was proper as presented. Then together they worked on the judgment. Then typed it on the computer and printed both out.

Anton thought that he would take the letter to London and mail it from there.

Before noon he was on a flight to London and arrived at 3:00 p.m. He had used his Egyptian passport in the name of Achmed Nabil. For customs, he filled out the information for foreigners who were not part of

EU (European Union) and added the reason for his visit as correspondent for the *Al-Ahram* Cairo newspaper—post-Olympic business. At custom he produced his passport and identification as reporter for *Al-Ahram*. Looking tanned and having black hair, he was seen as an Egyptian and had no problems.

From Heathrow he took a double-decker bus to Victoria station. At a department store he bought a packet of large brown envelopes and a box of regular white ones. He had already a typed stick-on label with the name and address of the *Berner Nachrichten*.

He included the manifesto in the white envelope, closed it, put it and a hundred-dollar bill into the large envelope, sealed, and writing in block letters addressed it to the forwarding agency in Rome. Then he went to a nearby post office and paid in English money to have it airmailed to Rome. He would have liked to spend a day in London, but with the many tourists in London, he knew he would find it difficult to get a room. He returned to the airport and took a night flight to Frankfurt, spent most of the night there, and then flew in the morning to Munich. He took the S-train to Planegg and went home. He cleaned up and by early afternoon on Saturday was back at the institute.

Max and Sepp had much to tell. Yesterday afternoon at four, they scanned the highway leading from Monterrey to the town of Reynosa where the massacre of the forty-nine migrants took place. It was then 8:00 a.m. there. At a side road, a short distance off the highway, they saw a car standing. Max zeroed in on the car; it was an old Chevrolet, the window open and smoke curling out. Someone was in the car waiting and smoking.

He also waited. A short time later a new model van came, branched off the highway, and followed the dirt road to the old car. Two men came out of the van and a man in police uniform from the car. They spoke to each other. Then one of the two men gave a paper bundle to the policeman. They drove back to the highway and sped off. Max refocused on the policeman who still stood there by his car and counted what was obviously money, pesos. He then got a cell phone from his pocket and spoke to someone.

Max immediately had Sepp activate the audio signal on his computer. Max put on a headphone with attached microphone and listened in.

Apparently the man had received 5,000 pesos and had been expecting more. When Max heard him say adios, he at once signaled to Sepp for sending. He spoke in Spanish, "Como se llama [What is your name]?"

Max signaled receiving. The man replied "Carlos Villarreal."

The following conversation then ensued as told by Max:

Carlos: Who are you? Why do you cut into my phoning?

Max: You were talking about pesos, and then you finished and said adios.

You are finished with the other man, right? He signed off?

Carlos: Yes. And then you came on my line. Who are you?

"Listen, Carlos Villarreal, whatever you do and say to me or listen to me, DO NOT CUT ME OFF. Stay on the line; else, you get hurt, understand?"

"*Si*, senor, but who are you?"

"Tell me, Carlos, have you heard something about death rays used on pirates by the world tribunal?"

"Si, senor, I read something in the paper about death rays used against pirates."

"Good. Now first of all, understand that I can see you. You are standing before your old car and hold the bundle of pesos in your left hand. Now you are scratching your head with the right hand. So you know that I can see you, and more, you are in my power and I can hurt or even kill you. Let me prove it to you. Look at the fence post off to the side.

Can you see it?"

"Si, senor."

Max, while talking, adjusted the view to the post, close to the top of it, and moved over to the power computer. He used three thousand degrees and a half-second duration. He pushed the ENTER key, and the wooden post burst into flame. It burned like a big torch, smoke rising from it.

"Carlos, you see the post burn? Of course you do. Just remember that I can torch you, and I will burn you if you don't do as I command you, understand me? As to who I am,

I am with the world court who killed many pirates. Now the world court will combat the Mexican drug cartels. Will you do as I tell you?"

"Si, senor."

"Carlos Villarreal, you must tell me the truth or you burn. You are a policeman.

Which prefect do you belong to?"

"The Monterrey police."

"You also work for the Zetas cartel. Why do you work for them? For the money?"

"No. They threatened me and my family. That they torture my wife and children and then kill them."

"What do you do for them?"

"I tell them where the checkpoints are and if they are manned by policemen who work for them."

"Many Monterrey policemen work for the Zetas?"

"Si senor."

"For money like with you or that they threaten them and their families?"

"Nobody works for the money. The Zetas even cheat us. I was supposed to get 10,000 pesos. I got only 5,000."

"Tell me, Carlos, do you know Heriberto Lazcano or Miguel Morales?"

"I know Lazcano; he is their leader here in Monterrey. Morales is the leader in Nuevo Laredo."

"You know Lazcano, and you visited him. You know where he lives. Here is what I want you to do for the world tribunal. After you do that, you are free. Continue serving the Zetas as before. I let you even keep the money. I promise you nobody will ever know that you also worked for the tribunal. Drive into Monterrey. Drive by the house of Lazcano. When you are there, throw a burning cigarette out of the window."

"I will do it, senor. Can you follow me?"

"Of course, Carlos. Look, there are some cars coming your way; probably the smoke attracted them. Put out the fire, throw some dirt on it, and off you go."

Max: I watched him as he kicked dirt on the still smoldering stump. He waved the two cars off. Driving fast he returned to Monterrey. I had to raise my view to see his car. He drove through downtown, then into a southern suburb where there were nice villas, many with swimming pools. In front of such a villa he slowed down. There was a man at the entrance gate who waved to Carlos. Then the cigarette flew out the window.

I let him go then but took a picture of the screen showing the villa. Then a more distant overview to get the section of the city.

Well, Anton, we got the house of one of the leaders of the Zetas gang. Sepp and I thought we visit the house at noon, our time eight o'clock in the evening. See if we can catch and eliminate this Lazcano.

Anton: You two did a wonderful job. It is four o'clock now. Let's go out and eat and be back at seven, my treat.

They drove to the Grosse Wirt, a typical Munich inn that served fine Bavarian dishes.

While they ate, Anton told them about his brief London trip and then about his friend Nevot's offer to help financially.

"I don't think this is a good idea" said Max. "The fewer people who know about us, the more secure our operation will be."

Anton: Nevot doesn't know, though I suspect he imagines me associated with the tribunal. We could use financial help for our travels. Also, if his benefactor is trustworthy, we could send a letter by way of America.

Max: Get some more information about his benefactor.

Soon it was time to get back to the institute.

It was now eight in the evening and noon in Mexico. Max got Monterrey; then the section he took a screen picture of a sunny, cloudless day. And there stood the white villa with a flat tar roof, a wall around the roof. They saw two rifle men on the roof and two more in the garden who carried Kalashnikovs. One man stood outside the barred gate; he was not armed, at least not visibly.

In back the swimming pool, now empty, to the side of the house a small one, the garage.

In back of the garden a wooden shed close to the fence and back gate, there also stood a guard.

Sepp: I wonder what is in the shed. Drugs?

Max: Most likely. Unload from the back gate; else, they wouldn't need a guard there.

What do we do now? Just wait?

Anton: They might have lunch or take a siesta. We might have a long wait.

Max: Let's burn the house down.

Anton: Tar roof with lots of wood underneath. I give three short pulses of five thousand degrees; then I switch back to three thousand so I don't deplete the black box.

In three different places Max lowered the view to just above the roof, and each time Anton gave a pulse that caused at once a fire. Max raised the view, and they saw fires and lots of smoke. The two guards had disappeared down a stairway.

Max: Sorry, they were too fast for me.

Sepp: Please, Max, only armed people. They might have innocent visitors in the house.

Max: Innocent visitors in the house of a druglord? But you are right. We want to be careful whom we eliminate. Here, they come pouring out of the house.

They saw men, women, and a couple children run into the courtyard and gesticulating, pointing up at the roof. Some of the men and women were well dressed, but who was the leader Lazcano? Then a car came out of the garage and sped into the courtyard. A well-dressed man jumped in; so did a woman and the two children. The gate was open, and the car sped away.

Max: I hope that wasn't him. Now another car is coming.

This time Max was fast, and when another man opened the door, he zeroed in; and when close to his head, Anton gave a jolt, and the man fell, burning and smoking. Others who ran to the car changed direction and fled out of the gate. Just then a fire engine drove up, and men unrolled hoses. Two armed guards stood at the gate. Max and Anton eliminated them, their bodies lying by the gate burning. One fireman brought a small extinguisher and sprayed the bodies; soon they just smoked. There was now pandemonium, running in all directions and out the gate. Those armed had thrown their rifles away.

Max: Let's just burn the shed in the back.

That shed too had only a tar roof and soon burnt acrid smoke rising from it.

The place was now empty except for the firemen who sprayed the house but could not save it or the shed.

The Force of Three shut of their computers and went home. Satisfied that at least they had made a beginning combating the violent Zetas drug cartel, Anton flew back to Israel.

On Thursday, thirtieth of August, chief editor Sebastian Konrad received another letter from Rome. He decided to hold it for the Sunday, second of September edition, which was international and read in many countries.

MANIFESTO II OF THE WORLD TRIBUNAL

The world tribunal has accused members of the Mexican drug cartels, also members of FARC, the Columbian terror organization, and members of drug traffickers of South and Central America of mass murder.

The drug traffickers, especially those belonging to the Mexican Zetas and Sinaola organizations, have committed mass murder, often with torture and horrific dismemberment. Many of the victims were innocents, often youth and even children; many were migrants.

SPECIFICALLY, THEY COMMITTED THE ATROCITY OF MURDERING AND DECAPITATING FORTY-THREE MEN AND SIX WOMEN ON 13 MAY 2012 NEAR MONTERREY. ALL INNOCENT MIGRANTS.

JUDGMENT: The drug traffickers were found guilty of kidnapping and holding for ransom, torture, and murder.

SENTENCE BY THE WORLD TRIBUNAL: The elimination of all drug traffickers by death ray.

Signed: The Force of Three

The *Berner Nachrichten* printed the manifesto in their Sunday edition, second of September 2012.

With the manifesto was an editorial by chief editor Sebastian Konrad:

When the *Berner Nachrichten* received the first manifesto, judgment, and personal note to chief editor Konrad, in which the sender asked us not to consider it a prank but to hold for confirmation, we did so.

The confirmation we received was in the form of an interview editor Schramm had in Mogadishu, Somalia, with the captain of the American freighter *Houston*, who described the killing of pirates with death rays.

Only then did this newspaper decide to print the first manifesto and judgment, which held true in regard to the use of death rays or, as scientists described it, as laser beams.

This newspaper has now received a second communication from the world tribunal in regard to finding the Central and South American drug cartels guilty of having committed murder, torture, dismemberment, often against innocents.

Drug traffickers to be sentenced to elimination by death rays.

This newspaper does not condone vigilante-type killings. However, the world tribunal, while extraterritorial, claims jurisdiction by power and extranational jurisprudence.

By Wednesday, most major newspapers reprinted the manifesto and editorial.

On Monday, 3 September, Superintendant Biergli visited editor Konrad. He read the original letter and was given it and the envelope to be examined by his laboratory. The super also told Herr Konrad that this time the letter to Rome was sent from London!

A day later Superintendant Biergli returned both the letter and envelope. The envelope was of British manufacture; however, the paper the letter was written on came again from Germany.

It was time that Superintendent Willi Biergli of the Suisse Federal Police got in touch with the German Bka (Bundeskriminalamt).

Anton, when he returned home to Jerusalem after their attack against the Mexican traffickers, had a queasy feeling. Had they covered their tracks so far? Nothing must happen twice, therefore the changing of the posting of letters to Rome. He had his doubts that the agency in Rome was totally secure. All right, a letter from Vienna, then from London. He would try to have further letters mailed from America. He wanted to have the authorities, which he knew would be on their trail, think it was an American operation. It was logical anyhow; most good scientists were American, and so were the bigger research laboratories. The first envelope was from Russia, the second from England. What made him uneasy was that the sheets of paper were now twice from Germany. He must never again use German paper or envelopes. Best, to get a supply from the United States. For that he needed Nevot.

He called Mordechai Nevot and asked him to come by his office at Jerusalem police HQ.

Since both smoked, Anton lit his briar, Nevot a cigarette.

"How can I help you, Anton?" Nevot asked.

"Tell me about your American friend in New York," answered Anton.

"His name is John Resnik. He is into real estate and wealthy. So if it is money you need, name the amount and I have him send it. You want to remain incognito, he will send it to me."

"Yes, I need to remain incognito. No, it is no longer money I need but help with something else."

"OK, Anton, how can he help?"

"First of all I need a package of normal-size envelopes, self-sealing Manila envelopes. Then a small stack of regular computer paper, letter size."

"American computer paper is a little smaller, I believe 8 ½ x 11 inches."

"It will work in our printers. Next, and most important, every so often we wish to send a letter from New York."

"To Rome?" interrupted Nevot.

Anton frowned then smiled, "Perhaps. Nevot, you are not supposed to prey."

"I am sorry, Anton, but don't forget that I was a deputy in the Mossad. Mossad is monitoring what goes on, as is every other intelligence agency."

"Are you still working with them?"

"As advisor, yes, but not on this project. I listen but do not advise. Not until you wish to associate with them and seek their help. Now as

I understand, you wish for my friend in New York to send this letter to Rome. Tell me in detail how, when, etc."

"I would enclose in the letter certain details for the Suisse newspaper to publish. Seal it in the regular envelope and address it to the *Berner Nachrichten*. John Resnik would put the envelope in a larger one, plus a hundred-dollar bill. Address it to the forwarding agency in Rome. We were asked by them to write as return address FIRENCE, but I think we do this no longer. Just stick a note in with the bill that says FIRENCE. 'Firence' is our secret code with them. That is it."

"It might be a good idea to put a fake nonexistent return address on the larger envelope. Without a return address an envelope might look suspicious."

"Yes, Nevot, a good idea. Can John do all that. Do it right and secure."

"I tell you what, Anton, I fly to New York and talk to John, explain it all to him, step by step." Then Nevot shook his head. "No, we are doing it all wrong. Why involve John? How often do you send these letters, Anton?"

"Infrequently, maybe two more times, weeks apart, rarely after that."

"Give the letter to me. I fly to New York. Mail it according with your instructions."

"Yes, that would be better. I agree. But I still need the envelopes and paper."

"I fly right away to New York and get them. John likes for me to visit, and he pays first-class accommodation. You are sure you don't need any funds for your project?"

"No, Nevot, it was only meant for travel to different countries in Europe."

"Let me ask you one question, Anton, and I assure you that there is no contact between myself and the Mossad on this project. I think it is great that both the Somali pirates and the Mexican drug cartels are brought before the world tribunal. Both groups are vicious killers, especially the drug cartels. Will the world court also judge those who wish to harm Israel?"

"In due time, Nevot. The third manifesto will be judging war criminals, both old Nazis who were involved in the Holocaust and are still alive and those who still profess this racial philosophy, neo-Nazis, fascists, extreme right-wing groups. The fourth manifesto, and probably the last one, will prosecute jihadists and similar fanatical Muslim groups."

"All-inclusive?"

"Yes, Nevot."

CHAPTER VII

International Conferences

On Wednesday, the fifth of September, Superintendent Willi Biergli of the Suisse Federal Police had an appointment with Kriminalkommissar inspector Vogel at the headquarters of the German Federal Police also known as the Bka (Bundeskriminalamt) in Wiesbaden.

He had taken a flight from Bern to Frankfurt, and from there a taxi took him to the nearby Wiesbaden, the place called Geisberg where the big office building was located.

At the gate he had to state the purpose of his visit, his appointment with Inspector Vogel, and show his identification, his Suisse passport. A little card encased in plastic had been prepared, which had his title and name, signed by Inspector Vogel. With that, which he was to carry at all times, he was admitted. He was punctual for his visit at 2:00 p.m., and a guide was waiting who took him to the inspector's office.

Super Biergli had never met Inspector Vogel; he usually came to a conference with another inspector, but apparently Vogel was the one who dealt with the phenomenon known as the world tribunal. There was another man present who was introduced as Professor Kohl from the Psychiatric Forensic Institute of the Free University of Berlin.

The three officials sat together by a small round table, and coffee was served. Then they sat alone.

Vogel: The Suisse Federal Police designated you, Superintendent Biergli, as researcher in regard to the World Tribunal?

Super Biergli chuckled. "At this point the Suisse government is not doing any active research yet. I am an acquaintance of the chief editor of the *Berner Nachrichten*, who called me in when he received the first manifesto. I did some work researching the communication of both the first and second manifestos. That is the physical part, the material, the envelopes, and computer printout, the sheets of paper. And here I found some interesting and intertwining connections. That is why I asked for an appointment with the Bka."

Vogel: And what did you find?

Super: The first letter, which was mailed from Rome, was sent by a forwarding agency. However, it originated in Vienna. The Carabiniere who have an informer with the agency gave me this information. I had our laboratory inspect the envelope and sheets of paper. The envelope was Russian; the computer paper came from Germany. The letter with the second manifesto originated in London, the envelope was British, the paper was again German. This makes me believe that the operation of the world tribunal is located in Germany.

Vogel: That is interesting, and you may be right. But here at the Bka we strongly believe that the operation is from the United States. Who else has the scientists and laboratories to develop a death ray, which, by the way, we think is a laser beam?

Professor Kohl: I am not an expert on lasers, but how was the laser beam sent? From where? We must also think in terms of who benefited by combating both the pirates and drug cartels. The ship rescued from pirates, and where four of them were killed was American. Punishing the Mexican cartels benefits again America and Mexico.

Super: But why the German paper both times? Are they available in America? Does Germany export computer paper to America?

Prof.: The people of the world tribunal are international if we are to believe their writings. I think that they are desperate to hide their origins. Russian and British envelopes, German computer paper. Mailed from Vienna and then London.

Vogel: To research the posting in Vienna is fruitless. By train, bus, car, plane. It is impossible to find a clue there. However, we can ask Scotland Yard to check flight lists of persons who flew in an out of London on the twenty-fourth of August. Then distribute those names to all major police agencies here in Germany, see if anyone recognizes a familiar name. The other thing we can do, we can query the major research centers in Germany that conduct laser business if some do work on long-distance lasers.

Now to something else, I spoke to our forensic scientist professor Kohl to advise us who these people could be. Please, professor?

Prof.: It is feasible but unlikely that we succeed in profiling these people. First of all, I suspect that it is a very small group. The judgment is signed by the Force of Three. In their first communication they explain the force. *S* stands for international scientists, *T* for tribunal, *E*, the eliminators. It is my personal opinion that the designation of STE is only a cover for three people who developed the death ray and use it.

Now to the question who are they and what are their philosophies? Liberals, right-wing extremists, or left-wing? Do they have a political agenda? We cannot fathom their beliefs at this point. What they have been doing so far is combating criminal elements, the pirates, and even more so the violence of the drug cartels. It benefits all nations, especially those countries who send their ships through the Suez Canal and Gulf of Aden. To stop the drug traffic is almost impossible but a matter for America and Mexico.

Vogel: Illegal drugs rarely come from America to us, and if it happens it is usually a small amount found on a passenger. Not really trafficking that comes from the Balkans.

The question we have to answer is it really worthwhile for us to expend our resources in finding who the tribunal is? I mean, except for the sending of the manifestos from Europe, that a Russian envelope and German papers are used, Europe directly is not involved.

Super: We are committed with a minimal effort and only because a Suisse newspaper is involved.

Prof: I think we should try to find the source, the people, if only to stop them if they become political and harm us or any other nation of the European Union. Of course I didn't know that the material is European or that the mailing was done in Europe.

I like to hear about anything new, a third manifesto perhaps. It might give us an idea of the tribunal's origin. I suspect that the first two targets were chosen by the Force of Three to establish their credentials as bona fide international crime fighters. At this point we can only guess at the identity of the tribunal. The targets definitely benefit America. Everything else points to a European connection. So? If there is nothing else, I like to return to Berlin. Please keep me informed.

The two police inspectors then sat together and discussed other police matter of interest to Switzerland and Germany.

However, at the suggestion of Inspector Vogel, the Bka sent an official query to the major laboratories and research centers in Germany where laser technique is used and taught, asking for information on long-distance use of lasers and/or use of laser techniques to kill, requesting to treat the query and anything pertaining to it confidential.

Also, the Bka sent a request to Scotland Yard to supply a list of names of those who entered and left the two airports in London on Friday, the twenty-fourth of August.

Of interest, the query was also sent to the Max Planck Institute in Munich. Director Glaser gave it to Professor Klausner to reply to. When the professor objected because he was not working with lasers, the director told him, "That is the reason I give it to you. You are our foremost researcher on long-distance transmission of energy. Lasers are energy. It is because you are not working on lasers that I need your opinion and knowledge about our laser research, that is if there is a possibility that one or the other is involved in that business with the world tribunal. You heard about it?"

Klausner: Only what I read in the newspaper.

When the query came, Klausner answered with a brief reply that the use of lasers here at the institute is strictly for medical research and used in distances of centimeters.

When at their next get-together he mentioned that he was the one to write a comment on the use of death ray, supposedly lasers, he said, "That is like having the fox supervise the chickens."

(Inspector Vogel of the Bka was a brilliant investigator. His request to Scotland Yard in regard to a passenger list on 24 August was complied within a week. He sent copies of the list to all police departments in major cities of Germany. In Munich, the list came to police commissioner Max Kolb, who gave it to head inspector Stefan Wagner of the antiterror unit. When Wagner scanned the list, he came across the name of the Egyptian Achmed Nabil. He was quite familiar with this name, which was an alias of former police inspector Anton Nagil. However, Anton Nagil was a personal friend of his, and if he was involved in the world tribunal, he would keep his secret. In his estimation, so far, the tribunal was doing only good in combating the pirates and drug cartels.

Inspector Wagner attached a note to the list when he returned it, "List of names unknown," and signed it. By beginning of October Vogel had all replies; none of any helped. However, as persistent as Inspector Vogel was, he scanned the list of passengers again. Many of the passengers who had flown into London that day were foreigners. He sent letters to the German embassies of the countries these foreigners came from requesting personal information from that countries intelligence agencies. By the end of the year, he received most queries. None suspicious. No replies from Russia, Egypt, Saudi Arabia.)

Thursday, 6 September.
Conference at FBI Headquarters of the Advisory Group
The director introduced General Roberto Garcia of the Mexican Army.

Director: As we have read in various papers, there was another manifesto sent to the *Berner Nachrichten*. This time the tribunal accused the Mexican drug cartels of mass murder and other horrific crimes. The Mexican government informed our embassy that there was a possible attack against the Zetas cartel in Monterrey. We requested more information, and Mexico sent us General Garcia. General Garcia is in charge of federal troops combating the cartels. General, please.

General Garcia: There was a strange incident on Saturday, 25 August. It was first reported by a Monterrey newspaper as a fire that burned down a mansion. We requested further information from the Monterrey police department. Accordingly, on that Saturday, at noon, the mansion of a respectable businessman—his name is Nazario Moreno—burned down. Cause of fire is unknown. Senor Moreno was killed in the fire as were two other men. We know, of course, that Monterrey is a stronghold of the Zetas gang, as is Nuevo Laredo, both cities south of the border to the United States. We also know that many of the police in Monterrey are in pay of the cartel. And, gentlemen, let me explain that most police who work for the cartels, especially the violent ones as the Zetas and Sinaloas, do so not for greed but because they and their families are threatened if they don't cooperate. Just as these gangs have informers with the police, we have informers with the police who report to us—that is, to the federalis—double agents.

One agent told us that this Nazario Moreno was a sublieutenant of the Zetas cartel and that his house was one of the hideouts of the Zetas leader Heriberto Lazcano. While this agent was not there, he was told this a few days later by one of the guards.

Apparently the roof started to burn, and the fire quickly spread down into the second floor. People evacuated the house, and one of the first to flee was this Lazcano with his family. When Moreno tried to flee, as he entered a car, he suddenly burst into flames. So did two of the guards in the courtyard. This was not reported by the newspaper.

Does it match with the reported manifesto of the world tribunal?

Director: It does. It matches the information we received from Mogadishu about pirates suddenly bursting into flames. Killed by what we believe are laser beams.

CIA: If this happened on the twenty-fifth of August, it was before the Suisse newspaper received and published the second manifesto targeting the cartels. How in the world did the tribunal know about Lazcano hiding out in that mansion in Monterrey?

General: Yes, we in the military wonder too. We didn't know.

NSA: And why did the police in Monterrey not know?

General: We are sure that some in the police knew. Maybe even their chiefs. But again, there is this code of silence in our police. Afraid to do something and afraid to tell us in the military. Now, gentlemen, we certainly would like to know if the tribunal is American.

Director: Let me assure you, General Garcia, that our government is not involved. The operation is not American; at least we don't believe so. It is only one newspaper that receives the manifestos, a Suisse paper. It seems to be an European operation.

General: First going after the pirates in Somalia, now against our drug cartels. I wished it were American. We like to cooperate.

NSA: How can you or we? While the tribunal speaks of being international, we have no idea who they are. So how can we cooperate?

General: We thought of supplying names and locations of the cartels. Print in our newspapers or perhaps supply this information to you and your papers can print it?

CIA: We can do this regardless—help the tribunal. But it is amazing that they found the hideout of this leader Lazcano.

General: It is. This is why we thought the tribunal is American.

Director: It is a splendid idea to publish information about the cartels and their leaders. If your papers are afraid to publish, our major papers will gladly to it. And yes, it will help the tribunal who apparently can combat from a distances and do it safely.

General: Like invisible men?

Director: I don't believe anyone has the technique how to become invisible. But with lasers from a safe distance? Let us then cooperate, General Garcia. If there is nothing else, I have one of my men take you to your hotel, General; you are our guest while in Washington.

After the conference was adjourned, the director told deputy director James Adams to fly at once to Holland and attend a meeting of EUROPOL scheduled for Saturday, 8 September 2012. EUROPOL requested that an official of the FBI attend.

James Adams flew on Friday to Amsterdam, stayed overnight, and early Saturday morning took a train to Den Haag, where EUROPOL is located. A taxi took him there.

EUROPOL is the investigative arm of the European police while INTERPOL—which is located in Lyon, France—is the active agency combating crime for member nations.

EUROPOL is not investigating crime but the people who beget crime.

EUROPOL researches and analyses reports from national police departments, detective agencies, and courts. It keeps a vast amount of information on criminal elements: individuals, gangs, and terrorist groups.

EUROPOL devises strategies on how to combat serious crimes such as trafficking in rauschgift, kidnapping, extortion, sexual abuse of children, white slavery, murder for pay, illegal weapon sales, terrorism of individuals and groups; and it gives advice to local, state, and member nation police authorities how to find their perpetrators.

The twenty-seven-member nations of the European Union and associated nations like Norway and Turkey send special crime experts to EUROPOL where they work for several years and return home enriched by mutual experiences. There are about five hundred steady employees at EUROPOL of which 37 percent are females. With experts sent on a temporary basis, there are 650 people active.

The director of EUROPOL since 2009 is the Englishman Rob Wainwright.

While an international crime research organization, EUROPOL is not free of politics.

Especially "weaker" nations of the EU send as their delegation heads and politicians who are often more interested in furthering their national interests instead of EU cooperation.

For interpersonal relationship and common meetings/conferences, English was chosen to the detriment of France who wanted French spoken and Spain who stated that more people in the world speak Spanish than French or English and were probably correct.

But then English was the language taught in just about every school in Europe.

This particular conference on Saturday, the eighth of September, was called for by the chairman Michael Juergens of Germany. Chairmanship is rotated on a monthly basis.

The meeting was held in the minor conference room and attended to by the ranking member of each delegation of the twenty-seven-member nations and associated countries like Norway, Albania, Turkey. They sat around a large table; on one side stood a lectern. Each delegate had a small national flag on the table before him.

Chairman Juergens took the lectern. "This conference, as announced, pertains to the world court or the Force of Three, whichever is the correct way to call this group. While we had several meetings before on this subject, we have invited an American representative as many of us believe that it is an American operation. May I introduce the deputy director of the FBI, James Adams?"

Deputy Adams took the lectern. "I believe that we all understand the seriousness of this matter, that we have an organization or group of people who have tremendous power, in fact, as we understand it, over life and death of everyone on earth. The world tribunal—and we in the

United States prefer this designation—reserves the right to accuse, judge, and eliminate criminals who are beyond national and even international jurisdiction. We also know that their first target were the Somali pirates. They prevented the capture of a freighter in the Gulf of Aden, killed four pirates, then proceeded to the mother ship, which they set aflame. And further, in the anchorage of captured ships off Karin they freed a tanker, killed six more pirates. Our latest surveillance of Karin shows that all ships were freed and left.

The second incident of attacking criminals was on the twenty-fifth of August, at noon. A house, a mansion belonging to a subleader of the Zetas drug cartel, was burned. The leader, Senor Moreno, was killed as were two armed guards. The mansion was the hideout of the leader of the Zetas gang, a Heriberto Lazcano, who, however, escaped.

This happened in Monterrey, Mexico, which is controlled by the Zetas and gulf cartels.

I believe we are all familiar with both manifestos and judgments. By the way, the second manifesto pertaining to the Mexican drug cartels was received in Switzerland five days after the incident in Monterrey." Deputy Adams smiled. "Not that the Zetas would have paid any attention to the warning if they had received any warning to desist and disband before the incident. This much we know officially. I invite any question you may have."

Chairman Juergens: Wherefrom did you get this information about Monterrey?

Adams: We first found out through our embassy in Mexico City. Then we invited General Garcia to Washington. General Garcia is the military man in charge of combating the cartels. He gave us particulars about the incident in Monterrey.

Britain: Deputy Adams, do you know if this an American operation?

Adams: Not government sponsored. We don't know. However, we believe it is with a European connection.

France: Most of us believe it is American. The *Houston* freighter was an American ship. The fighting of the Mexican drug cartels benefits America and Mexico, of course.

But mainly, who has the know-how to construct a death ray? Who has as many laboratories and research centers to construct such a ray? Does America believe as we do that the death ray is a laser beam?

Adams: Yes, we do. However, we do not know or even understand its form of delivery.

Norway: By drones of course. Your military uses drones in Afghanistan, indiscriminately kills people, many innocent civilians.

Adams: We do not target innocents; we kill the enemy, terrorists, the Taliban who fight us. If we killed any civilian, it was accidental. Accidents happen in war. We are sorry.

Norway: Your sharpshooters even killed four innocent fishermen without trial.

Adams, with anger in his voice, "These were not fishermen. They were pirates holding hostages."

Norway: They did you no harm; they might have been fishermen, and what you thought were hostages might have been guests on board the fishing vessel.

Adams, showing true anger, "These, what you call fishermen, had Kalashnikov rifles and rifle grenades. It's that how you fish in Norway?"

Norway: And even if they were pirates, the killings violated fundamental human rights, including the right not to be deprived of life without due process of law.

Adams: You Norwegians have a strange way at looking at law. You even treat Anders Breivik more like a pocket thief and not the mass murderer he is. You call it Norwegian dignity. And your laws—he can get only a maximum of twenty-one years in prison for killing seventy-seven young peole. That is less than a year in jail for three people killed.

Chairman Juergens: Gentlemen, please, keep some decorum.

Adams: I apologize.

Chairman Juergens looked at the delegate from Norway, but there was no response.

Bulgaria: The comment from Norway was uncalled for. But nevertheless, his question about drones was realistic. We wonder, of course, how can a laser beam shoot, if this is the correct term, from a far distance? No other ship was seen; it must have come from above, from a drone?

Adams: A pulse of laser beam is more correct. It is, of course, a possibility. If high enough, the drone cannot be seen or heard. But who has drones in the Gulf of Aden?

The delegate from Bulgaria smiled. "You, of course. The same in Mexico, close to the border of America.

Adams: Possible. But let me again assure you that the United States is not involved in this . . . this . . . let's call it crime-busting project.

Holland: Then America is not opposed to the doings of the world tribunal?

Adams: We wished it did not exist. Yes, we are opposed to it.

While it does good work in the case of the Somali pirates and trying to eradicate the brutal and violent cartels per *erga omnes* (as an obligation to mankind), we cannot have such an extranational organization in existence.

We do not know what the future holds. Fighting crimes against mankind? What else does the tribunal consider crimes against mankind? We do not know, and we dread these implications of total power.

Hungary: I believe it is Israel that calls itself the world tribunal. The Jews are smart and clever people.

France: And why does my colleague from Hungary think so?

The Hungarian delegate took a newspaper clipping. "This is a statement made by Iran's vice president Mohammad Rahimi at a UNO-sponsored drug conference in Tehran. It was published by Iran's semiofficial FARS news agency. Let me read it. 'The prevalence of narcotics and drug addiction throughout the world finds its roots in the erroneous teachings of the Talmud, one of the Jewish Holy books. The book teaches them how to destroy non-Jews so as to protect an embryo in the womb of a Jewish mother. The Zionists' direct involvement in the illegal drug trafficking is such that you cannot find a single addict among the Zionists." He looked up. "The Zionists combat the Mexican cartels because of their competition in trafficking."

Bulgaria: This is nonsense. How would the Israelis get their drones on the Mexican-American border?

France: Catherine Ashton, the European Union's high representative for foreign affairs, said, "I am deeply disturbed by the racist and anti-Semitic statement made by Vice President Mohammad Reza Rahimi." And France seconds her statement. Anti-Semitic slander.

Hungary: If I have offended any Jewish person, I apologize.

Chairman Juergens: Your apology is accepted and recorded.

Ireland: We still don't know from where the world tribunal functions. Anyone has any idea? Any clues to the origin?

Chairman Juergens: I have had a report from Switzerland. Superintendent Biergli of the Suisse Federal Police sent me a letter with the following information. The letter is dated

5 September 2012.

To the chairman of EUROPOL:

I was requested by chief editor Sebastian Konrad, of the *Berner Nachtichten*, to research the origin of the manifestos and judgments his newspaper received on 29 July 2012 and the second on 30 August. Both letters came from Rome. Through contact we at the federal police have with the Italian Carabiniere, I found that the first letter was posted in Vienna, sent to Rome to a forwarding agency, and passed on to Bern. The second letter was mailed from London, again by way of Rome. I had our forensic laboratory examine the letters and envelopes. The first letter, the envelope is Russian, the writing paper is German. The second letter, the envelope is British, the paper again German.

Sincerely, etc.

Britain: Points to Germany as source?

Chairman Juergens: Mailed from London?

France: Obviously they are trying to confuse the issue. Austria, Italy, Russia, Germany, Britain, and Switzerland as recipient. We can be almost certain that none of these countries are involved.

Bulgaria: Leaves America?

Deputy Adams: Or Mexico?

France: No, not Mexico or Somalia. All involved indirectly.

Spain: The question is, shall we pursue the matter? So far, the tribunal has been doing only good work.

Bulgaria: Perhaps we can petition the world tribunal to go after Hezbollah. They committed that dastardly crime of bombing a tourist bus in Borgas; killed five people, including a Bulgarian subject; and wounded thirty.

Chairman Juergens smiled. "We better not become involved."

Deputy Adams: Let me reiterate no government agency of the United States is involved. My government will pursue the matter as we feel that it is dangerous to have such a powerful and unknown entity in the world.

Chairman Juergens: Let us put the issue to a vote. If your country wishes to pursue, please a show of hands. Spain, Portugal and Hungary, Lithuania, Latvia, no?

Spain: I say let's wait.

Portugal: Wait.

Hungary: First, let us ask Israel if they are involved.

Lithuania: I second Hungary's motion.

Latvia: I agree with Hungary.

France: Nonsense! A waste of time. Any country involved wouldn't admit to it.

Chairman Juergens: Nevertheless, to satisfy our colleagues from Hungary, Lithuania, and Latvia, I shall inquire at the Israeli embassy in Den Haag. This then concludes our conference; if I or anyone else has any important news, we shall meet again.

And I thank Deputy Adams for joining our conference.

On Tuesday, the eleventh of September, it was the eleventh anniversary of 9/11, and there were solemn rites in America. The Middle East exploded. In Benghazi, Libya, the American consulate was sacked and four Americans killed, including the ambassador to Libya. Anti-American riots in Cairo and Saana, Yemen. Demonstrations in other Muslim lands. Was it due to some American film defaming the prophet Muhammad? Or al-Qaeda at work remembering their dastardly work? Arab leaders and clergy mongering, of course Iran involved. Most likely all of it. It is so easy to get Muslims in a fury of hate and America their main target. Primitive people need to hate—their entertainment!

How proper and wonderful it had been if the world tribunal trio could have been at work, using the death ray at the worst rioters, those who threw Molotov cocktails, mongering the loudest and carrying signs "KILL THE AMERICANS! KILL THE CHRISTIANS! KILL THE JEWS!"

However, Inspector Anton Hofer was like all the police and army in Israel on standby and could not leave until Saturday. Max and Sepp without him did not dare.

CHAPTER VIII

The Force of Three
Continues Its Work

Nevot had been in the United States and brought back a box of self-sealed envelopes, a package of larger envelopes, a ream of computer paper, and a roll of stick-on labels.

Anton appeared in midmorning on Saturday, the fifteenth of September, at the institute and found Klausner and Sepp busy scanning the anchorage at Karin. There were only fishing boats to be seen.

Max: We viewed the road to Berbera. There is still a checkpoint of armed pirates. They haven't given up yet. I thought one more lesson and at least the piracy along the north coast of Somalia might be finished.

He moved the view from high up along the road from Karin and zeroed in on the checkpoint. The place, really just a mud hut, was at the entry to a small village. There were several people by the hut, in front and across the dirt road a wooden barrier. The men, while armed with rifles slung over heir shoulders, were all blacks.

"Let's just burn the barrier," suggested Sepp.

This they did, Anton giving one end of the wooden barrier a five-thousand-degree jolt, which made it burst into fire, and at once the four guards jumped into a car and raced off toward Karin.

Max: That should do it. Now back to Mexico. Sepp and I have been tracking a group of illegals walking toward the U.S. border of Texas. About fifty kilometers west of Ciudad Juarez, probably heading for El Paso. No roads, all barren hills and scrubland there. While we are not in the business of stopping Mexicans from crossing the border, we saw several men armed with rifles guide to take them across. Now, why would guides be armed? They are not fighting their way into America? This is Zetas territory. We suspect that they want to kill the migrants. It is almost noon here, and it would be four in the morning there. It should get light soon. They probably spent the night in one place where we saw them when it got dark, bad walking; and with rattlers around they wouldn't dare to walk at night. So let me see if I can find them again. But it was still dark.

Max had a pot of coffee ready, and they drank while they waited.

One hour later Max tried again, and there was dawn, all shadowy still; but they could see people moving around, packing up blankets.

Sepp counted the people. There were forty-two: eight were women, three children, and one woman carrying a bundle, which must be a baby. When the first rays of the sun appeared, they walked down the hill they were on, in front of the two armed guides. Another half hour and they were in the flatland. Max raised the view, and they saw it, a car coming from the east raising a cloud of dust. He moved in closer; it was a Land Rover. The car stopped by the people. Three men came out, holding rifles; the two guides joined them.

Five men holding their rifles pointed at the people and talked to them. The people then emptied their pockets, throwing money on the ground, some their watches. More talking and both men and women took rings off and threw them down.

Max shouted, "They are robbing them! Quick, Anton, get the ray ready. I zero in on the speaker; he seems to be the leader. Let's eliminate him before they shoot."

Anton, who wisely had his computer ready, adjusted to three thousand degrees. When Max brought the head of the spokesman into view, Anton pushed the key. The head burst into fire; the man fell down, and his clothing were aflame. Quickly Max zeroed in on another figure; the jolt of infrared went into his shoulder, and he fell, his clothing and body burning, smoke rising. He was still squirming, and Anton gave him another jolt, which killed him. By then the other three bandits had fled into the car and sped off.

Max: It would be difficult to follow the car; besides, let them bring the message of the use of death rays to the others.

He brought the view back to the people who stood stunned around the two burning corpses, then apparently talked to each other, and picked up their dropped money and rings.

Anton: They are lost here without guides in the middle of nowhere. We have to help them, but how?

Max: There is just nothing for many kilometers around. The closest place to civilization is north to the Texas border.

Sepp: Maybe we can find border guards. Let them know that there is a group of migrants south of the border.

Max: They dare not come across the border into Mexico.

Anton: But they can notify the Mexicans or get permission to fly across in a helicopter and at least bring them water.

Max: All right, let's try it.

He raised the view, and they moved to the north over more hills and desert until they saw the border fence. Farther north a broad highway with traffic went both ways.

Max: There was a dirt road along the fence. Let's follow it. Maybe we find border guards.

This they did, and soon they came to a cove of trees and a wagon standing in the shade.

Max: Sepp, see if you can pick up any voices.

They did not hear voices but music.

Max: They must have the radio on. Your turn, Anton.

Anton spoke in English into the microphone, "Attention please, we interrupt the program to bring you important news."

Voice: Must be something important Frank if they interrupt the program.

Anton: Frank, can you hear me?

Frank: Sam, did you hear that? They called me by name.

Sam: You must be kidding. That is in the studio. OK, one in the studio is Frank, and the other didn't know that the microphone is on, stupid.

Anton: Listen you two, Frank and Sam, this voice is not from a studio. I have an important message for you two. Are you listening?

Voice: Yes, we are listening, and who are you? How are you able to interrupt this program and talk to us?

Anton: Have you heard about the world tribunal?

Voice: Yes, I read something.

Anton: All right then, this is the voice of the world tribunal. Besides talking to you two, I can see you. You parked your wagon under a cove of trees, palm trees. We were just across the border in Mexico where we spotted forty-two migrants heading toward the border. Two armed guides were with them. We were suspicious as guides usually don't carry weapons; they had rifles. About an hour ago they broke camp and went down the hill into desert land. Then a Land Rover wagon came along with three more men. They were also armed; and the five now pointed their rifles at the group of men, women, and children and made them empty their pockets. Made them throw their money and even rings on the ground. We realized they were about to shoot the migrants and eliminated the leader of the bandits and one more man. The other three fled in their wagon.

The migrants are without a guide now and probably without water; they need help. One woman even had a baby in her arms.

Voice: How can we help? We are not permitted into Mexico. Besides, due south there are no roads but all desert and steep hills.

Anton: You can at least send a helicopter and bring them water. Notify the Mexicans in Ciudad Juarez to get them out, either with cars or helicopters.

Voice: Do you now their location?

Anton: Who am I speaking with?

Voice: I am Frank.

Anton: All right, Frank, looking at the map, I see the group about fifty kilometers west of Ciudad and about the same distance south of the border at a point due south-southwest of your town Canutillo.

Frank: Got it. We'll try to send a helicopter. Mainly we want to tell them to stay where they are. If they go back up into the hills, we have a hard time finding them. And we get word to the police in Juarez to pick them up. Thanks by the way.

Anton: Goodbye, Frank and Sam, and be sure to report it all to your authorities. Out.

Max returned the view to the migrants. They had dug two graves to bury the two bandits.

Max spotted a radio a boy had listening on the audio they heard music.

Max sat by the audio computer and spoke in Spanish, "Hola, tu hablas espanol?"

The boy looked around, then replied, "Si, senor." "Listen, boy," continued Max, "I know you can't see me, but I can see you and your people. Don't worry, everything will be all right. The Americans will send a helicopter with water for all of you, and the police from Ciudad Juarez will come to pick you up. Just stay where you are. Don't go back into the hills or continue in the desert; else, they won't find you. You understand?"

The boy looked around again and nodded. A woman nearby heard the voice. She was from Spain and heard Castilian Spanish spoken from the radio.

It took a few days for their report to trickle up to Homeland Security from where it was disseminated to the FBI. The director of the FBI requested the two border guards to come to Washington for a full report.

Of special interest was that the world tribunal had audio contact with the border guards in English and were able to use their SUV AM-band radio for communication.

The FBI sent a fax to the CIA, NSA, and the defense secretary with a full report of the incident near El Paso, including a report that Mexican authorities picked up the migrants and that the migrants buried the two bandits.

Deputy Adams, with permission of the director, sent a fax to Michael Juergens of EUROPOL, detailing the incident in the northern Chihuahua Province of Mexico, near the city of Ciudad Juarez, where forty-two migrants were saved by the world tribunal when they were about to be shot by bandits of the Zetas cartel. Two of the bandits were killed by laser. Of special interest, he noted, is that United States border guards were alerted by using their car radio in British English—that is, that the world court not only can see and project the laser beam, but also have the capability to contact by audio signals.

Saturday, the twenty-second, Anton couldn't come as he was busy with police work in Jerusalem.

However, Max Klausner and Sepp were scanning around the city of Nuevo Laredo, the stronghold of Zetas leader Miguel Morales. Also it was possible that the other leader, Heriberto Lazcano, joined him after fleeing his hideout in Monterrey.

It was six o'clock in the early evening that they scanned, which would be ten in the morning in Mexico. They followed the highway leading north to the border and came to a wagon; alongside stood a motorcycle cop talking to someone in the van. The policeman then walked back to his cycle and talked into a radio.

Max listened in on the conversation. The van was stopped for speeding, and the motorcycle cop checked in with the registration. When he said "All is OK then," Max quickly said (of course in Spanish), "Attention, officer. Do not turn your radio off!" The officer straightened up and looked around. Max continued, "Officer, you can't see me but I can see you. What is your name?"

Officer: Alejandro Gonzales. But who are you?

Max: Later I tell you. Just give the driver his speeding ticket and come back. And please, keep the radio on.

The officer wrote his ticket and gave it to the diver, then came back.

Max: All right, well done. I am with the world tribunal. Have you heard of us?

The officer nodded. "Yes, I heard something about such a tribunal. You did that job in Monterrey, killed the Zetas bandit Moreno and a couple others. What do you want from me?"

Max: The reason we found Moreno's place, which was also the hideout of Lazcano, is that we were able to talk to a policeman who worked for the Zetas. After I showed him what we can do and do to him if he doesn't cooperate, he told us he gave information to the Zetas because they threatened him and his family; he took us to the hideout. Now, we want you to show us the stronghold of Miguel Morales.

The officer bent even lower over the radio. "Look, gentlemen, I wished I knew. But believe me, there are honest police officers who do not work with these bandits. I am one of those officers." He stood up again and threw out his hands and shook his head. "Not me! Not every officer works for them. I hate those bandits, not so much for trafficking but their torturing, killing, and kidnapping."

Max: I believe you, Alejandro. And because you are an honest police officer, I want you to help us. Do you know of a crooked officer?

Alejandro: No, but I have my suspicion.

Max: All right then. Try to confirm your suspicion. Bring this officer here—no, better, there is something like a rest stop about five kilometers south of here; at least it looks like there is a small hut there, maybe a toilet?"

Alejandro: Yes, it is a stop and a toilet.

Max: Bring him there at ten o'clock in the morning. Let's make it the fourth Saturday in October, which would be the twenty-seventh. Just wait there with him and keep your radio on. If either you or we can't make it, let's try the fourth Saturday in November or of every month. All right?

Alejandro: OK. I work Saturdays. I'll be there even if I can't find such a bastard.

Max: Don't be too harsh with officers who work for the bandits. They threaten their families. Adios, Alejandro Gonzales.

The policeman waved his goodbye, started his cycle, and sped off.

Max: At least we made contact with a police officer and an honest one this time. Great. Let's go out and eat, Sepp.

Anton came the following Friday, 28 September. He would have to return on Saturday as Sunday is work day in Israel; rarely on a Sundays he could take off.

The fight against the pirates had dwindled to nothing. Pirates returned to fishing.

The war against the drug cartels was never ending and couldn't be won. They understood that finding and eliminating the leaders would curtail the power of each cartel, but how to find them? Max was scanning the highways leading to the border or even the scrub brush or desert regions for migrants, also for small groups of traffickers carrying drugs in packs across the border. He was scanning the waters off the Mexican and American coast in both the Atlantic and Pacific for boats carrying drugs.

Sepp wished to work on his manifesto pertaining to the Holocaust and present-day Nazis or neo-Nazis.

For that they drove to Anton's house in Planegg, but first they had lunch at the Heide's inn. Anton gave Sepp a writing pad.

Sepp: I am afraid I am not eloquent enough to write the manifesto.

Anton: Just write what you wish to say. I know it is about the Nazis and their helpers, what they did during the war to the Jews, gypsies, Slavs, to Soviet POWs.

Sepp: I was born after the war, in 1950, so I know only about the war what I read. You let me read Otto's diary so I know what happened to the thousand Jews they deported from Munich. Resettlement, they called it, resettling them in a mass grave.

I did some more research at the Munich Archives; a Dr. Heusler helped me. I read his book *Verzogen, unbekannt, wohin* (*Moved Away, Unknown, Where to*). These 994 men, women, and children did not know what would happen to them until they were brutally driven to the long ditch and had to line up to be shot with machineguns. Among them 169 children and their parents. Dr. Heusler let me read the autobiography of a Jewish boy in Nazi Munich. His name was Hugo Holzmann. Of course he wrote it much later. In the year 2000, he was then seventy-one. But he not only wrote about the murder of his classmates, whom he considered family, but about each kid. Also there was a class picture in his book of all the kids and he had named those sixteen murdered. And suddenly, these kids were no longer statistics but real-life children to me; and I could feel, or tried to feel, what they experienced as Jewish kids in this Nazi city called Hauptstadt der Bewegung (Capital of the Movement). Harassed, spit upon, called dirty names, growing up with fear in their *Heimatstadt* (hometown). Every person and kid they met became an enemy unless they knew him as a friend. The Crystal Night, Jewish businesses smashed and looted, their fathers arrested and taken to Dachau for no other reason than that they were born Jewish.

The years between November 1938 and November 1941, were years of persecutions by the SA, who handled the robbery of the Jews businesses and apartments. The house and apartment searches of the Gestapo who got a kick out of slapping old people and scare the youngster with their violent rudeness. Forced to live in barracks. The ultimate humiliations of having to wear the yellow star, the Nazi star as Mr. Holzmann called it.

Then the weekend of the 8 and 9 November '41 when they received their deportation notices. Prevented from working at their livelihoods since '38; and last robbed of all their possessions, they were herded into old trains, ten to a compartment meant for six, with all their luggage so that only half could sit at one time. Five days and nights toward the ultimate hell. The arrival in Kovno, Lithuania, and the many hours' march to Fort IX. There to be registered and then taken to the ghetto— so they were told. None of them could imagine that there awaited them a long ditch, a mass grave.

Once the sinister sound of the iron gates of the fort clanked shut the terror began.

Supervised by German SS men, their Lithuanian police collaborators drove the horrified multitude in groups of eighty along the ditch already filled with the corpses of a thousand Jews from Frankfurt and Berlin who had been shot earlier. They had to run a cordon of Lithuanian thugs who beat them with whips, clubs, and rifle butts as they ran by.

Then these victims of satanic rites of the SS had to line up facing the ditch to be shot by more Lithuanian savages who operated the machine guns on earthen emplacements.

As a last act of love, when a child tried to hide from the machine guns in front of his father, Daddy placed the child next to him so it would receive the full fuselage in the back, be killed instantly, and not suffer more horror lay wounded and being smothered by those killed later or drown in their blood. Anton, this is what happened. And those who are responsible for the murder of the innocents and those who committed the outrage deserve to be eliminated. But I cannot write all that is true into the manifesto.

Anton: No, you can't. I help you write a briefer account of what is called the Holocaust.

CHAPTER IX

The Third Manifesto

1939, the Nazi hordes conquered Poland; in 1940, France and the neutral countries of Belgium, Holland, Denmark, and Norway. In 1941, the Nazis in a surprise attack made war on the Soviet Union. And with that attack the Nazis conquered the Baltic nations and a huge swath of Russia. In these areas the Nazis established their killing centers as they also had declared war on the Jews and used their military might to fulfill Hitler's wish to murder all Jews in Europe, from babes to the oldest.

In all of mankind's shameful history of crimes against humanity, the Nazi atrocities stand foremost in numbers murdered brutalities committed to their victims in their reign of terror. Tens of thousand infants and babies murdered: shot, clubbed to death, gassed, burned alive. Infants out of their mothers' wombs dumped head first into a bucket of water, the mother shot or beaten to death because she dared to bring a Jew into the world. Hundreds of thousand toddlers brutally murdered; is it not brutal when one of these black-booted monsters took a little kid by its legs and flung it on the pyre of burning bodies, thrilled by the screams and squirms of the toddler burning alive? As it was committed in Auschwitz.

There is no specific crime against humanity we can accuse the Nazi beast of; there are too many. Let the numbers speak of the genocide committed by the Herrenvolk (master race). Six million humans slaughtered, among them over one million children.

Who were these killer we accuse? Hitler and his dictatorial government, the party, who planned the genocide. The killers who slaughtered: the SS, SA, police, Gestapo, and their brutal henchmen, Poles, Ukrainians, Lithuanians, Latvians, Estonians, and their Western collaborators.

And the shame of the German military who made it all possible and did not protest.

JUDGMENT: All those who murdered the victims—those who collaborated with the roundup, transporting, guarding the innocents and are still alive today—sentenced for elimination.

Those who harbor the same or similar believes—neo-Nazis, fascists, right-wing extremists, bigots who preach hatred toward others and incite with lies—the world tribunal warns: BEWARE. Disassociate from such groups, or you may be eliminated by death rays.

Groups forbidden are Neo-Nazis; U.S., the Aryan Nation; the Estonian and Latvian Waffen, SS veteran groups; Greeks' Golden Dawn Party; the True Finns Party; Austrian's extreme-right parliamentarians.

Anti-Semitic acts occur in many countries by individuals or groups. Lately we have read of those press releases of anti-Semitic incitements and lies in Norway, Hungary, Turkey.

BEWARE: The Force of Three will punish racial, religious, ethnic bigots anywhere!

Signed: The Force of Three.

Sepp Kainz and Anton Hofer wrote this manifesto and judgment on Friday, the twenty-eighth of September. On Saturday Anton returned to Jerusalem. He prepared the letter addressed to the *Berner Nachrichten*, also a note with FIRENCE, and a hundred-dollar bill. He placed it into the larger envelope addressed to the Rome forwarding agency and the same day gave it to Nevot.

Nevot flew on Sunday to New York and mailed the envelope on Monday. It took five days to get to Rome. Rome sent it on Friday to Bern where it arrived on Monday, the eighth of October.

Chief editor Konrad called at once Superintendent Biergli who came in the afternoon, and both discussed the manifesto and judgment.

Konrad: At last we got a political statement.

Biergli: Besides punishing any war criminals still alive—and there must be a few around, probably now in their nineties—what political statement to you read into the manifesto?

Konrad: Well, right-wing extremists, anti-Semites, generally bigots, hate mongers.

Biergli: I guess you are right. Let me take the letter and envelope along.

Konrad: I wait publishing it until I hear from you.

By Wednesday Biergli had the answers. From the Carabiniere in Rome he found out that the letter was posted in New York. His laboratory reported that both envelopes and letter were made in America.

The *Berner Nachrichten* published the manifesto in their Sunday edition, 14 October, for local and international circulation.

Super Biergli had sent a copy of the manifesto and the result of the laboratory to the chairman at EUROPOL. The chairman for October was the French legation head Pierre Dibault. Monsieur Dibault called for a Monday meeting of the legation chiefs.

Monday, Fifteenth of October at EUROPOL

The legation heads of the member and associated nations met in the small conference hall. All had a folder with the third manifesto.

Chief Dibault took the lectern. "Besides the third manifesto, we have also received new information in regard to the world tribunal." He read a fax he had received from the FBI about the rescue of forty-two migrants about to be shot by bandits of the Zetas cartel. "Two bandits were killed by laser, or as it is called death ray. One more interesting information from the FBI is that two border policemen were called over their car radio by someone who spoke flawless English, however, with a British accent. I spoke to our technical experts in regard to this, and they told me that what the tribunal uses cannot be a laser beam as they apparently can see and use audio signals to talk and listen. Therefore, a ray system that uses heat and visual and audio signal is something new and not known to exist with present-day technology. I have also received information from the Suisse

Federal Police that the letter was posted in New York. This, ladies and gentlemen, is confidential, so requested by the Carabiniere who receive inside information from the Rome agency.

Now, while the first two manifestos were directed against specific criminal enterprises, piracy and drug trafficking, this third manifesto is of a semi-political nature. To punish war criminals, I think we all agree that this is still part of combating criminal elements, though even with their apparently wide-ranging intelligence gathering, they will have a difficult time finding these old war criminals. However, the manifesto also wishes to fight against right-wing extremists and those who are anti-Semites—and there are many of those—and hate mongers, bigots. There are several organizations they list as criminal, like the neo-Nazis, fascists, the Aryan Nation in America, Baltic SS-veteran groups.

In a manner of speaking, the world tribunal has become politicized.

Now our discussion, any comments, questions, statements?

Legation head Juergens from Germany: The tribunal, by singling out right-wing extremists like the neo-Nazis, is not doing anything different than we do in Germany.

Of course we don't kill them; but we forbid the show of Nazi memorabilia, books, literature, the wearing of Nazi uniform, etc. We keep close tab on their doings.

In fact, we think of them as criminal elements.

Chairman Dibault: We know you do, and it is right. I am just surprised that the tribunal is not combating terrorists. Not a word about them.

Britain: Just wait for the next manifesto.

Hungary: I don't know why they singled our country of Hungary out for special mention. We are not anti-Semitic and treat our Jews like all other minorities.

Chairman: I had some of my French colleagues do a little research. Here is a note: "Hungarian media such as Echo TV, Magyar Hirlap, and Magyar Demokrata are now freely publishing anti-Semitic statements that would not be possible in Western Europe. Present-day anti-Jewish propaganda is very closely linked to anti-Israeli propaganda. They do not differentiate between anti-Semitism and anti-Zionism. For example, they say Israel wants to buy up Hungary, that Israeli capitalists already own the country and Hungary is ruled by Israel."

Hungary: We do not sensor our publications.

Germany: We do if the context of a publication is obvious anti-Semitic and full of lies.

Hungary: We believe in the freedom of speech.

Chairman: The freedom speech stops when someone yells "FIRE" in a crowded hall, like a cinema, and there is no fire.

Hungary: Nevertheless, we don't control the media.

Germany: You should. Or do you believe that Hungary is controlled by Israel?

Hungry: That is nonsense.

Germany: A lie?

Hungary: Well, if you put it that way, yes, that is a lie.

Britain: In a democratic country a publication is not permitted to write outright lies.

Norway: And why are we singled out? I wonder. You have any notes on us?

Chairman: You permitted the politician Anders Mathisen to publically deny the Holocaust. He wrote, "There is no evidence the gas chamber or mass graves existed.

The Holocaust never happened." You permitted him to preach his lies. Mathisen has spent the past months advocating changing history books and has accused Holocaust survivors of exaggerating their testimonies.

Norway: We cannot control what any Norwegian citizen says.

Chairman: Mathisen is not a plain Norwegian citizen. He is a politician. People listen to him. Remember the trial they had in Great Britain? The famous historian David Irving spouted the same lies publically. He was tried, found guilty that he slandered with his lies. He too tried to change history and lost. Also, liberal Norway is lately discriminating against gypsies.

Norway: We don't have any problems with gypsies and Jews.

Chairman: *Of course not with Jews; under Quisling Norway shipped its Jews to Auschwitz, like I am sorry to say we did under the Vichy government. Also I read that the few Jews who are living in Norway are leaving.*

Norway: I heard no such thing. Norwegians are by and large not anti-Semitic.

Chairman: It is not the Norwegians who make the Jews leave but the Muslims.

Norway: Look, if the Jews and Muslims don't get long, don't blame us.

Chairman: It is your liberal policies that permit Jews to be molested and harassed by Muslims. Called names, spit upon, jostled—even Jewish children are not safe anymore.

What follows harassment are beatings and killings.

Norway: Well, we had this right-wing extremist madman commit mass murder, but we did not have any Jew killings in Norway like you did in France.

Chairman: I am sorry to say that you are right. Mohamed Merah of Algerian descent committed mass murder in Toulouse. Killed three soldiers, a rabbi, and three little children. He was also a petty criminal, a purse snatcher of elderly women, an evil person.

Every country can have these madmen. But it is the liberalism of your country that breeds these malcontents. We in France, under former president Sarkozy, kept Muslim extremists at bay; they behave, or else, they go back where they came from.

The Norwegian delegate smiled. "You have a new president, Francois Hallande; things will change even in France."

Turkey: My country sent me as an observer, so I have no status at EUROPOL. But my country was also mentioned, please. We have only the best relationship with our Jewish citizens.

Chairman: My note reads: For more than five hundred years, this predominantly Muslim country was a safe haven for Jews and was one of Israel's closest allies. Now Turkey's anti-Semitic movies are finding a huge audience across Europe. This year's *Valley of the Wolves: Palestine* is a sequel to *Valley of the Wolves: Iraq*, which focused on a fictitious Jewish doctor harvesting organs of Iraqi soldiers for use in Israeli hospitals.

Both movies are spin-offs of a popular anti-Semitic TV series that enjoys a cult following in Turkey and among Turkish expats abroad.

Also your Kurdish issue. A year ago thirty-five Kurds, among them seventeen children, killed by a military jet strike in Uludere, Sirnak.

Turkey: Things change; we have a new prime minister.

Chairman: You mean Erdogan?

Turkey: Prime Minister Recep Erdogan is a true Muslim.

Chairman: Yes, that I believe.

And there is, of course, Russia where anti-Semitism is endemic. Recently, the chief prosecutor in Moscow refused to prohibit the sale of the *Protocols of the Elders of Zion*, one of the world's most infamous

outside was his. Yes, it was. The man then told him that he had violated Norwegian laws by driving through a flashing signal. Not only that, he made it his business to stop at the inn, go inside, and accuse my friend of this violation; but he wanted him to follow his car to a police station and report himself. Liberalism is fine. I am a liberal but within bounds. It is the fanaticism of some liberals that causes problems. Like a woman raped, the victim obviously, but she is guilty as she wore a short skirt and enticed the rapist. The hoodlum who robs a liquor store and shoots the clerk without provocation; he is not guilty, but society is who did not provide for him a life of leisure, so he had to rob and kill. We have had great men and women who were true liberals—Gandhi, Mother Teresa, Mandela, to name a few—but extreme liberalism is as much poison as fanatical conservatism."

NSA: Like our modern Tea Party people?

Defense Secretary smiled. "Let's not get into politics."

Director: Nevertheless, how would we classify the world tribunal?

Secretary: Conservative liberals.

They laughed.

CIA: With the latest revelations, the letter posted in New York, U.S. material used, are we thinking it is an American operation?

NSA: The most important clue is the languages used: British English, European Spanish.

Director: Jewish scientific participation? The third manifesto is all about punishment of war criminals and those who express the same philosophies.

NSA: If I had this power—and I have no Jewish connection yet knowing what the Nazis and their followers did—I might have singled them out for punishment and preventive action. While the Europeans give the third manifesto a quasi-political edge, it really is not. If we have to apply a label to them, yes, what the secretary said I agree with, conservative liberalism.

Director: Thinking along these lines, why are they not targeting terrorists?

NSA: Give them time. As a matter of speaking, pirates, Mexican traffickers, war criminals, and their followers are all terrorists.

CIA: I fully agree.

Director: The last letter posted in New York. A subterfuge for a European operation?

NSA: It seems so.

Director: I think we should have a liaison man in Hague with EUROPOL. They invited such in their fax to me. Nothing else new? We shall then meet again with any new development or a fourth manifesto.

The director chose agent Burt Johnson for this temporary assignment. Agent Johnson was the liaison to foreign police departments; he spoke French and Spanish and had connection to the Munich police department through his workings with Inspector Anton Nagil. He flew on Saturday, the twentieth, to Munich to visit Inspector Nagil; however, when he stopped by, he was told that Inspector Nagil was no longer with the police in Munich but worked as a chemist at the Max Planck Institute. When he called there, he was connected to Director Glaser who told him that, yes, former inspector Nagil was a consultant at the institute but had changed his name to Hofer. The operator at the institute then connected him to Herr Hofer.

Anton was highly surprised when his FBI acquaintance Burt Johnson was on the phone and even more so when he told him that he was in Munich, presently at the Police Praesidium, to visit him. Anton told Burt to stay there and he will pick him up.

(Anton, as police inspector Nagil, met Agent Johnson back in September 2005 when Commissioner Kolb sent him to the FBI in Quantico to get information how best to track a mass murderer who was killing couples in Munich. Agent Johnson gave him hints; foremost he recommended for him to read two certain books, including *The Great Hoax*. It was because of these books that Anton was able to find the murderer; in fact, it was that the books were missing from the library that led to the killer. Since, Anton and agent Johnson had several other cases they worked on, and Johnson knew very well that it was Inspector Nagil who had helped the FBI to intercept the terrorists on the Potomac.)

That Saturday, Anton, Max Klausner, and Sepp had been tracking groups of Hamas militants in Gaza who shot rockets into Israel. While some batteries were fired remotely, others were shot manually, and some of those terrorists were eliminated by death rays.

To Anton it was important to meet Burt Johnson since he was the FBI liaison to foreign police authorities. What was Johnson up to?

It was a hearty welcome when the two old friends met. Burt explained that he was sent to EUROPOL as the FBI's liaison in regard to the world tribunal.

Burt: I am certain you heard all about the world tribunal, Anton.

Anton smiled; it was ironic that he, Burt Johnson, the FBI foreign police liaison expert, should ask him! "Yes, whatever I read in the papers."

Burt: Why are you no longer with the police, Anton? You did marvelous work, had great successes.

Anton: As you know, I am a chemical engineer. That was my real profession. With the police, I was their explosive expert, spinning wheels; rarely that my expertise was needed. At the Max Planck Institute I can do research, my life's work.

While they drove to Planegg, Anton told about his beautiful dacha in Russia, which General Orlov gave him in gratitude for giving information that permitted Russia to intercept and destroy the terrorist. He added, "And by the way, the nuclear device exploded in a village, but they had evacuated. It was kept hush-hush."

Burt: Yes, we knew the bomb exploded, but we denied that there was a nuclear explosion that the seismograph recorded the explosion of a convoy of ammunition.

In Planegg, Anton took his friend to the inn for a good Bavarian meal, and then they sat in his house with Cuban cigars and wine. Anton told about his family in Jerusalem whom he visited weekly. That he changed his name to Hofer after his mother passed away at the dacha. He explained, "Nothing should ever let me remember Standartenfuehrer Otto Nagil."

"I understand," remarked Burt.

Then Burt told, after being assured by Anton that he will keep it all confidential, what he knew about the world tribunal. He added, "Or, as they sign their manifestos, the Force of Three. In fact, the Brits believe that this means the world tribunal is composed of three people. But we believe that is impossible. There must be a good number of scientists involved.

"Then people of the law who hold trial and the people who pull the trigger. While we believe it is all done with computers, we don't understand how they manipulate the intricate rays they must be using."

He also explained that his people believe it is an European operation, and he told why because of the British English; he looked and smiled at Anton, "Like you speak English and the Spanish as spoken in Spain."

Till late at night they talked about the case.

Burt, of course, spent the night at the house. The next morning, Sepp came by with his taxi and took both to the airport.

Burt Johnson took a plane to Amsterdam and from there the train.

In Hague, Johnson checked into one of the smaller hotels on the outskirts. On Monday morning, the twenty-second, he rented a car and drove to EUROPOL. At the gate he stated his business and showed his passport.

After a call to the office of chairman Dibault, a guide came who took him to friendly Dibault who received him. A permit was made for him that permitted Johnson to come and go as he pleased, and he also received a small office with a computer that permitted him to get at once in touch with the director's office in Quantico. He also received a manuscript of the history and functions of EUROPOL, which made for interesting reading. In a private conversation with chairman Dibault, agent Johnson assured him that the United States government was not party to the world tribunal and was very much interested in finding the source of this extraordinary agency. While at this time doing good work in combating the pirates, traffickers, and war criminals and their like-minded followers, it was the unknown future that worried the U.S. authorities.

Chairman Dibault also showed him a list of daily scheduled meetings pertaining to international crimes he was free to attend and that the purpose of his presence at EUROPOL was to attend conferences about the world tribunal, as the United States representative, and give input from FBI sources.

Johnson was also given a thick folder with all the reports and information known at EUROPOL about the world tribunal. In turn, Johnson gave the chairman a folder with all FBI meetings and documents.

After dropping off agent Johnson at the airport, Sepp and Anton drove to the institute where the three had an interesting conversation with Anton filling them in on what the Americans knew and thought and what EUROPOL knew and believed.

Of great interest was the British comment about the Force of Three being composed of three persons and their belief that the fourth manifesto will be about terrorism similar to what the American NSA delegate thought. Otherwise, neither party was close to the truth.

The three felt reassured.

CHAPTER X

Jedwabne, Poland

Jedwabne is a village in eastern Poland, about one hundred kilometers northwest of Bialystock and eighteen kilometers northeast of Lomza, the nearest town.

In September 1939, Germany attacked Poland and in the first blitzkrieg conquered western Poland in a few weeks while the Soviet Union occupied the eastern part. Jedwabne became Soviet. It didn't matter much to the village; they were poor peasants before and were just as poor under the Soviets.

Typically for Polish peasantry they didn't like outsiders. They hated the Lithuanians who lived in the village; they certainly didn't like the Russians who had occupied them, though there were no Soviet troops in the village, and as was custom in Catholic Poland, they were anti-Semitic. Yet the one thousand villagers seemed to get along fine with the Jews, most of whom were even poorer, but their latent anti-Semitism was kept alive and fostered by the village priest who kept reminding them that the Jews crucified Jesus and told them of the "blood libel"—that it is known that Jews kill babies and use their blood for making matzo on Passover. Really not any different than what Holy Fathers preached in many other villages in Poland.

In 1940, the Soviets occupied the Baltic nations, and northeastern Poland became part of Lithuania. More reason for the peasants to hate the Lithuanians and Jews.

On the twenty-second of June 1941, Nazi Germany attacked the Soviet Union and within days overran eastern Poland.

In wake of the German troops came the SS and their killer commandos to murder the Jews.

We know what happened in Jedwabne, but why it happened *there* is not known. On the tenth of July 1941, this village became infamous. The SS did not kill the Jews. But with their guidance and approval, the villagers rounded up the Jews; locked the men, women, and children in a barn; and burned them alive.

On Friday, the twenty-sixth of October, Anton came at noon to the institute and found Max and Sepp at the computer viewing Poland, in fact, the town of Lomza.

Sepp explained, "Anton, we are after Nazi war criminals. Let me read this article and get your judgment. This happened in July of this year." He read: "Recently, vandals painted swastikas and racial slurs on a memorial to the more than 340 Jews killed during the 1941 pogrom in Jedwabne, Poland. The Jedwabne memorial sits on the site of a barn in which over 340 Jews were rounded up and burned alive by their Polish neighbors. The vandals also painted messages such as 'I'm not sorry for Jedwabne' and 'They were highly flammable' on walls around the memorial. 'This is a perfect example of vandalism and stupidity, but we don't know the exact motives yet,' said police spokesman Andrzej Baranowski, the constable of the village.

"Can you imagine that, Anton? Such horrific cruelty to burn these innocent people, even their children, alive. It only happened in this one village, though Poles were known to kill Jews, beating them to death or shooting them—but burning them?"

Anton: And the stupidity of this policeman Baranowski, no motive. Only pure hatred, bigotry, and debasing cruelty can make people commit such a crime and then seventy years later write these slurs. The people haven't changed; they were miserable peasants then and still are.

Sepp: Your judgment then?

Anton: If we find someone who helped burn these Jews from those times, eliminate. Otherwise, let's burn down the village of Jedwabne.

Sepp: Exactly what Max and I said.

Max: From Goggle Earth I got to the town of Lomza. Google doesn't show the village of Jedwabne, but I found it on the map, about eighteen kilometers northeast, the only road going in that direction and no village before. Let's follow the road.

He raised the view, and they saw the road and followed it. Fields of wheat, grassland with cows, horses and sheep, isolated farmhouses. Then they saw the village from high above, four gravel roads radiating from it, several hundred houses, in the middle an open square.

Max zeroed in on the square, a church, several larger buildings, two—and three-story houses. Cars but also horse-drawn wagons or pulled by an oxen. Next to the church was a larger house with tables and chairs in front, people sitting there and eating.

Max: This must be an inn. It is one hour ahead in Poland, so it is noon there. There I see two men in police uniform, eating, drinking beer. A cellphone on the table, we have to wait until one picks it up, and it is life.

They waited. Sepp brought cups of coffee.

Then one of the men picked up the phone. At once Anton spoke in Russian "Vui panemyeti paruski [Do you understand Russian]?" The constable gave the phone to the other who said, "Ya panemyu paruski."

Anton: Are you Baranovski?

Voice: Yes, I am Baranovski. Who are you?

"Listen, Baranovski, whatever you do, don't turn off the phone. If you do, you will get hurt. Who I am? Have you heard about the world tribunal?"

"Yes, some organization that fights crime."

"Tell me, officer Baranovski, is burning innocent people alive a crime?"

"Yes. I think I know what you are talking about. A long time ago the Nazis burnt the Jews from Jedwabne."

"No, Baranovski, it wasn't the Nazis that committed that horror. The SS watched as the villagers from Jedwabne rounded up the Jews, forced them into a barn, nailed the door shut and fired the barn, burnt the men, women, and children alive."

"Maybe so, but that was a long time ago, seventy-one years ago, in fact. You can't blame today's people from here for what happened."

"Maybe yes, maybe no. How about the slurs on the wall, like 'We are not sorry' and 'They were inflammable.' Do you know who did it?"

"Just a stupid prank by kids."

"What are you teaching your kids that they would be so insensitive to say we are not sorry and make fun of the Jews being inflammable? There were kids in the barn, even toddlers and babies, who burnt to death. What little monsters are the people of Jedwabne raising?"

"Oh, you know, kids say stupid things; they don't mean it."

"Kids and drunks speak the truth. Are there any Jews living here today?"

"No. They were all killed. Those who weren't burnt were then shot by the Germans. We would welcome Jews if they wanted to live here in Jedwabne."

"So you could abuse them, harass their kids, paint swastikas on their houses. Have your priest tell the people lies about the Jews. You people haven't changed. You are the same bigots and anti-Semites your grandparents were. Given the opportunity and with Jews here, you would kill them all. Let's be honest. If the villagers were horrified by what their parents and grandparents did, they would place flowers at the memorial. And when they saw these mean slurs, they should have erased them or overpainted them. That they didn't shows they approved of the heartless writings.

Here is what the world tribunal decreed. For burning the Jews of Jedwabne by their neighbors and today their descendants possessed by the same foul philosophy, the village of Jedwabne will be destroyed by fire. Do you have a fire department here?"

"A volunteer fire brigade. I am the fire chief."

"Then let me warn you, fire chief Baranovski. Anyone who tries to extinguish the fires will be killed by death ray." Anton disconnected.

With Max zeroing in from one house to the next and Anton giving each one a five-thousand-degree jolt, soon the central part of the village was in flames as was the church, then, spreading to surrounding dwellings, many poorly built with thatched roofs.

There was little attempt to fight the many fires.

By late afternoon and with dusk setting in the village was a smoldering heap.

"Justice has been done" was the only comment Sepp made.

Deep in thought and mentally exhausted, the three went home. Saturday Anton returned to Jerusalem.

They would meet again the following Friday to continue their crusade against evildoers.

In Monday's newspaper of the nearby town of Lomza was a brief report of a fire in the village of Jedwabne, which destroyed most of the village. According to fire chief Andrzej Baranovski, the fire started in the kitchen of the village inn. The fire spread to other houses and destroyed the village. Due to low water pressure, the village could not be saved. However, a full report of the fire and reason for it was sent by constable Baranovski to the government in Warsaw.

Also, on the twenty-seventh of October, the fourth Saturday, Klausner had met police officer Gonzales at the rest stop. However, Gonzales was unable to bring a collaborator.

CHAPTER XI

Justice in Kovno

It was during forenoon of Friday, the second of November, that Anton arrived at the institute. Max and Sepp were already in the energy house viewing the Lithuanian city of Kovno.

Sepp had done research of the fate of the thousand Munich Jews who were deported on the twentieth of November 1941 to Kovno taken to Fort IX on the twenty-fifth and machine-gunned.

He explained briefly. When the nine forts were built in 1882 by Tsar Alexander II, it was meant as a defensive strategy in case of a war with Germany. In August of 1915, the Germans took the city, and not a shot was fired by the Russians. The commander, General Grigoriev, abandoned with his forces and fled. The same happened when the German attacked the Soviet Union on twenty-second of June 1941, the Soviets fled. Between the twenty-second of June and the arrival of German troops on the second of July, the inhabitants of Kovno held pogroms and killed thousands of Jews. Beat them to death or shot them with the arrival of German troops came the Gestapo and SS. Their mission to exterminate the Jews of Kovno. While other forts were used for the killings, Fort IX became the main execution site. The man in charge of the genocide in Lithuania was Standartenfuehrer Karl Jaeger

In charge of Fort IX was Obersturmbannfuehrer Otto Nagil.

Max looked at Anton. "Yes," said Anton, "I am sorry to say that Otto was my father. However, I disowned this child murderer as my father."

Sepp: They were all child killers. Alone on the twenty-ninth of October, they brought eight thousand Jews from the small ghetto and murdered them. Among them, over four thousand kids. While their elders were away on forced labor, the SS and their Lithuanian collaborators, partisans as they called themselves, rounded up the kids and took them in trucks to Fort IX. Witnesses said that they threw little ones, toddlers, like sacks of garbage on the trucks; then dumped them in ditches; and shot them. Can you imagine the horror each child had to suffer before being murdered?

Then on the twenty-fifth of November they shot almost three thousand Jews from Berlin, Frankfurt, and Munich. 994 Jews from Munich, my people from Munich, among them 169 children.

In the war diary of Otto, he details the shooting. How the Munich people came into the fort, the iron doors clunked shot, and all hell broke loose. The partisans beat them with whips, clubs, and rifle butts and drove them to the long ditch already half filled with the victims from Berlin and Frankfurt and machine-gunned them. The shooters? Again Lithuanian partisans or as I would call them merciless thugs.

Under Otto's command, over sixty thousand men, women, and children were murdered in fort IX.

Max: What we are trying to do is to find at least one of those thugs who is still around to serve justice.

Sepp: The difficulty is the language; even you, Anton, don't speak Lithuanian.

Anton: But I speak Russian. Lithuania was a Soviet Republic until '91; that is twenty-one years ago. We have to find someone who is in his late forties or fifties and was an authoritative person. An official or somebody who needed to speak Russian to the Soviets like a policeman.

Max: And where do we find such an official?'

Anton: A the police department.

They laughed.

Anton continued, "Look for a large building in downtown, one that has a flag and policemen go in an out."

Max did so, and they found a park with big buildings surrounding it, a large edifice with a flag, police cars in front. They could see people in the park, on benches. Max zeroed in on benches, and soon they found what they were looking for: a policeman eating his lunch, a sandwich and a bottle of beer or wine next to him on the bench. They also found a small radio, and when they listened, they heard music. The man was elderly, with a white mustache, in uniform; and he wore epaulets, indicating he was of high rank.

Anton took the microphone. "You speak Russian, of course. What is your name?"

The man did not move, just sat up straight, and stopped eating.

Anton: Turn off that station with the music but keep the radio on. DO IT NOW!

The man did so.

Anton: You understood me. You speak Russian. What is your name?

The man stood up and looked around.

Anton: SIT BACK DOWN. Now tell me your name. And by the way, I can see you but you cannot see me. Do as I tell you! Else, you will get hurt.

The man sat back down; speaking to the radio, he said, "My name is Inspector Juozas Mikulis."

"What do you do, Inspector Mikulis?"

"I am chief inspector of the criminal police in Kovno. And I know who you are."

"Tell me."

"I don't know you as a person but you are with the world court. We were told that such an organization exists to punish war criminals and that you speak through a radio or telephone. That you can kill with a death ray. I am a father of three and a grandfather of many. You don't need to hurt or kill me. I will cooperate with you to find war criminals.

I have connection with the Russian Police. We were occupied by the Soviets from 1944 to 1991. We had the KGB kill some and send many to Siberia. I know the name of the head-commissar of the KGB who ordered the killings. This building is our police headquarters; it was before the KGB headquarters and prison. We even have a plaque at the door that the KGB occupied the building."

"Is there also a plaque that it was Gestapo headquarters from 1941 to '44?"

"No."

"And why not? Didn't the Gestapo kill many Lithuanians?"

"There was a war then, and some Lithuanians were real partisans and fought against the Germans in the forests of Lithuania. If they captured a partisan, they sent him to Fort IX and shot them there."

"Inspector Mikulis, did you notice that you spoke about a captured partisan who was sent to Fort IX and then you added 'and shot THEM there.' Were many Lithuanians shot in Fort IX?"

"Yes. Hundreds."

"Or maybe sixty thousand. Most of them Jews?"

"Yes."

"I am interested in Russian prisoners of war. Were many shot?"

"Yes. Several thousand in Ninth Fort. However, hundred thousands died in prisoner camps in Lithuania."

"Tell me, Inspector Mikulis, why are you so reluctant to mention the war crimes committed by the Nazis?"

"You are with the world court, obviously an intelligent person. You know very well that many Lithuanians collaborated with the SS. This is a painful episode in the history of Lithuania. We wish to forget it. That is the reason why there is no Gestapo plaque."

"It was the First and Second Police Battalions under the command of Major Impulevicius who operated with the SS commandos committing these atrocities. In fact, in Fort IX, they did the shooting of the Soviet prisoners and Jews."

"Yes, that is correct. Major Impulevicius was a beast, a monster. After the war, we tried him in 1962 in absentia and passed sentence of death on him. He had escaped to America, and the U.S. government refused to extradite him. He died in America in 1971. I understand now. You are not interested in what the Soviets did to us; you are interested in what the Germans and Lithuanian collaborators did to Soviet prisoners and Jews."

"The real war criminals! We wish to find and try at least one of the Lithuanian machine gunners who shot the Jews and Soviets in Fort IX. Can you help us? You are a father and grandfather; you love your kids. Think of the many children who were exterminated in Fort IX, innocents all of them—the horror of it."

"Yes, I know and understand, and sympathize. I have always felt ashamed of what my former colleagues in the police did, collaborating with the Gestapo and SS. I know of one of those men who did the shooting and is still alive. After the war, some of them were tried by us and got prison. If the Soviets tried them for shooting Russian prisoners of war, they hanged them. But most escaped by falsifying their membership in the police. This man who is still alive is Antanas Barzda. He was twenty then, so he would be ninety-two now. He lives in Sargenai, near the Zhemaitchio road, eight kilometers from the center of town, right across from the fort."

"He speaks Russian?"

"Yes. He was with the police in 1940 when the Soviets came. All policemen had to learn Russian."

"Can you take us there, Inspector Mikulis?"

"How?"

"Just drive there in your car. Stop at his house. You smoke, yes? Drop a cigarette from the car window and drive on. That is all we want from you. And yes, tell your director of the police to either add a plaque that this building was Gestapo headquarters during the war or remove the one that is there now."

"By request of the world court?"

"By order of the world tribunal!"

They watched as Inspector Mikulis packed his things into a briefcase, then walked over to the building, got into a police car, and raising the view followed him. Through the old city, across the Slobodka Bridge, uphill along Paneriu Road—the road of sufferance for the Jews, led from the former ghetto to the fort. The car branched into the small village, which must be Sargenai. He stopped the car and got out, looked at and nodded at a small log house surrounded by a garden, and threw his cigarette down. Then he waved with his hand and drove off. At least one sympathetic Lithuanian.

Klausner zeroed in on the house. Trees in the back, a garden in front. In the garden under the shade of a tree sat an old man in a basket chair by a small table on which stood a plate with sausage, bread, a bottle and glass, and a radio from which blared music.

He could only see the man from above, the top of the head covered with sparse gray hair.

He took a bite of sausage and bread, then washed it down with a drink from the glass.

Anton took the microphone, which led to Sepp's computer. "Turn that music down!" he spoke in Russian.

Anton: Increase the volume, Sepp.

Sepp did.

Anton shouted, "Turn off the music, Barzda, but keep the radio on!"

The man did so then looked around. "Who is talking to me?"

Anton: You can't see me, but I am right with you. You understand me?

"What?" He cupped his ear.

Sepp: The man is hard of hearing. I increase the volume some more. He did.

Anton: Antanas Barzda, can you hear me now?

Barzda: Da.

"The world tribunal wants to question you. You understand?"

"Yes. The court? What have I done?"

"Have you heard of the world tribunal, Barzda?"

"No. A tribunal, like a court?"

"Yes, like a court."

"Your voice comes from the radio. So how can you see me? I don't believe you."

"You are sitting in a basket chair, a plate of sausage and bread on the table and a bottle. You just sipped from the glass. What is it, water?"

"Vodka. But how can you see me if you are not around?"

"Don't worry that you can't see me, but I can see you. Now answer my questions. You were with the police. When did you join the police?"

"Do I have to answer all your questions, to a stranger?"

"Yes, you do. We are researching the history of Lithuania during the war, so please answer. When did you join the Kovno police?"

"At the begin of 1940. Police academy, then as patrolman."

"Then the war began against the Soviet Union, and the Germans came to Kovno. You operated with the First or Second Police Battalion?"

"I was with the First, which worked in Kovno. The Second was out in the country."

"Who was your commanding officer?"

"A major Impulevicius."

"You have good memory; that was seventy-one years ago. So what did you do in the First Battalion?"

"First we worked out of Seventh Fort, then later in October out of Ninth Fort."

"Doing what?"

"I was a sharpshooter, so I was assigned as a machine gunner."

"Shooting who?"

"Jews."

"By whose order? Major Impulevicius?"

"No. He supervised us. By order of the commandant of Ninth Fort. A German SS officer."

"His name?"

"I forgot."

"Was it Obersturmbannfuehrer Otto Nagil?"

"Yes."

"On the twenty-ninth of October there was a *grossaktion*. You remember?"

"Yes. We shot over eight thousand of them."

"Over 4,200 were children. You shot the children?"

"I helped shooting them."

"Describe the shooting of the children."

"First, the real little ones were shot. I didn't do that."

"How were they shot? Babies and toddlers couldn't line up."

"Policemen would lift them up by the legs and shoot them into the head, then throw them into the ditch. Some just stomped on their heads or beat them with the rifle butt."

"And the older children, the ones you shot?"

"They were at the ditch, some bunched up, and others running around, crying and screaming all of them. We just fired our machine guns into them. Then the adult Jews had to dump them into the ditch. Then we shot them. An all-day job."

"Do you remember the big action on the twenty-fifth of November?"

"Ah, the German Jews. I remember them as they were all dressed nice. The first German Jews we had to get rid of. They were from Berlin, Frankfurt, and Munich."

"Do you remember the ones from Munich you shot?"

"I don't remember the ones from Berlin and Frankfurt, but yes, the ones from Munich I remember."

"Why do you remember them?"

"It was getting dark; the lights had come on. There were lots of children. So we wouldn't need to deflect our machine guns; the German officers Jaeger and our commandant Nagil would go along the line and shoot the little ones. Then I go *rat-tat-tat* and shoot my bunch. Each machine gunner had ten to kill."

"You aimed at each person or child?"

"I did so with the first groups. But the Munich Jews—I just moved the machine gun from left to right and went *rat-tat-tat*. Also I was drunk by then. The SS gave us shooters lots of vodka to drink."

"Were they all killed?"

"I don't know. It didn't matter. They fell in, and with lots of them on top they suffocated or were drowned in their blood. Then we buried the ditch."

"Tell me, Antanas Barzda, did you feel sorry for the Jews?"

"No, I never did. I never liked the Jews."

"How about shooting the children?"

"Children or adults—what difference does it make? They were all Jews."

"Antanas Barzda, the world tribunal accuses you of mass murder of innocent people and children. You confessed to it. You show no regret. You are sentenced to death by death ray. Prepare to die."

Barzda stood up and threw out his arms like questioning the verdict. "What do you want from me? I only obeyed orders. I have nothing against the Jews."

Klausner had zeroed in on his head. Anton gave him a three-thousand-degree jolt. At once fire, and smoke enveloped his head; he fell dead.

Max turned off the computer. "A well-deserved elimination. We all agreed on his death?"

Anton: Yes. A human monster eradicated, better late than never.

Sepp: As you said, Max, well deserved. He shot my people from Munich.

When Inspector Mikulis received the report of the strange death of Antanas Barzda, he sent a full report to the interior ministry in Vilna, the capital of Lithuania.

EUROPOL called a meeting for Wednesday, the seventh of November.

Chairman for the month of November was Signora Anna Olivetti from Italy. All legation heads from member and associated nations were present. Also Johnson from the FBI.

Chairperson Anna Olivetti took the lectern.

"Our Lithuanian representative Henri Truskas requested this meting as there is interesting news from Lithuania in regard to the world tribunal. Please, Mr. Truskas."

Mr. Truskas took the lectern. "I have a report from the Kovno police department sent to our interior ministry in Vilna. An Inspector Juozas Mikulis had an encounter with the world tribunal. Not really a physical meeting but the voice in Russian spoke to him through a radio he had. There was a lengthy conversation between the voice and Inspector Mikulis, and it would be interesting if we had a transcription, but all I have here is the verbatim report of the inspector. Here then his report: 'I was sitting on a bench in the park, eating my lunch, when the music was interrupted by the voice. It, the voice, asked me not to turn the radio off but get rid of the music. This I did. The voice spoke in good Russian, if I may add, without any foreign accent. It asked my name, told me that it is from the world tribunal and can see me. It asked me about the Second World War, what went on in Kovno. Specifically the voice was interested what happened in the Ninth Fort. I told that captured partisans were shot there. "By the Germans?" It asked. I said yes but also by Lithuanian collaborators. I also mentioned that during the Soviet occupation Lithuanians were killed and many deported to Siberia. That we have a plaque at the building, which is now our police headquarters, with the inscription that it was then occupied by the KGB. The speaker knew about the Jews being shot in Ninth Fort. It quoted sixty thousand Jews and thousands of Soviet prisoners.

Of course I had to agree. My feeling during the interview was that the voice was specifically interested in the killing of the prisoners. It asked me why we did not put also a plaque at the building that it was Gestapo headquarters when the Germans occupied Lithuania. The voice then told me that we should either add a plaque designating the building as Gestapo headquarters during 1941 to '44 or remove the plaque about the KGB. I asked, "Is this a request?" The voice answered, "This is an order by the world tribunal." Signed, criminal inspector Juozas Mikulis.'

"I cannot answer any questions about Inspector Mikulis as I had no chance to speak to him. Therefore, this is all I have pertaining to the voice. However, I received a fax from the interior ministry that on the same day—that is the second of November—a Mr. Antanas Barzda, from the village of Sargenai, which lies opposite Ninth Fort, was killed by death ray, his head burned.

"On Monday I spoke by phone to the ministry and was informed that this Antanas Barzda belonged to the police in 1941 and was a machine gunner at Ninth Fort where he participated in the killings of Jews and Soviet prisoners.

Chairperson Olivetti: Any questions for Mr. Troskas?

Britain: I doubt that Mr. Troskas can tell us anything besides the reports we received, though I have a few questions for police inspector Mikulis. Perhaps we can request his presence here in Den Haag.

Chairperson: I shall request for his visit. Now discussions?

Poland: I received a report from my government that the village of Jedwabne in Eastern Poland was destroyed by fire. That happened on Friday, the twenty-sixth of October. Officially it was reported that a fire started at an inn in the village, and due to low water pressure, the fire department could not extinguish the fires. However, a confidential report to the government by constable Andrzey Baranovski, who was also the fire chief, stated that he was spoken to by the world tribunal and the village of Jedwabne accused of a pogrom in 1941 when the inhabitants of the village rounded up the Jews, put them in a barn, and burned them alive. He reported also that he personally felt that it was not only the burning of the Jews, which happened seventy-one years ago, but that vandals smeared slogans on the walls of the monument, saying things like "We are not sorry for what happened in Jedwabne" and "They were highly inflammable"—that this infuriated the world tribunal. When constable Baranovski objected and said these were just stupid kids who did that, the voice said, "What kind of little monsters do you raise in Jedwabne?" and shouted, "You, people, haven't changed; you are the same bigots and racists, and listen to the lies your priests tell you." Further, "For punishment the village of Jedwabne will be burned down and tell your firemen that they will be killed by death rays if they try to extinguish the flames." Therefore, fire chief Baranovski prevented his people from fighting the fires too diligently.

France: May I ask the Polish delegate, did this really happen? I mean the burning of the Jews in Jedwabne?

Poland: Yes, I am sorry to say it happened. On the tenth of July 1941, after German troops entered the village, the inhabitants took the Jews they could find—men, women and children, even babies—put them in a barn, nailed the door shut, and burned them.

France: And those they couldn't find?

Poland: When the SS came, they rounded up the rest of the Jews and shot them.

Denmark: Why didn't the villagers clean up the smears on the monument? Put flowers there instead? Show their revulsion of what these vandals did and express empathy with the victims?

Poland: I guess the slogans were put there not by kids but by anti-Semitic hooligans. People were afraid of them.

France: So they rather saw their village burned down. Justice served.

Britain: Did the voice speak in Polish to Baranovski?

Poland: No. He spoke in classical Russian.

FBI agent Johnson: We have a spokesman of the world tribunal who speaks fluently Spanish, English, both as spoken in Europe, and now Russian. And you, ladies and gentlemen, still believe it is an American operation?

France: It could be Russian. The first envelope used was Russian. The emphasis of caring mainly about Soviet prisoners of war.

Holland: Russia wouldn't care about Jews killed in a Polish village. Or, for that matter, Mexican drug traffickers.

France: Camouflage?

Holland: Perhaps, but I doubt it.

Denmark: Everything we learn about the world tribunal makes it more confusing.

Holland: We have to await the fourth manifesto, if there is one.

Britain: I still believe it will be about terrorism. Iraq, the Sunnis, and Shiites at each other's throats, Afghanistan, the comeback of the Taliban. The civil war in Syria.

Iran and North Korea, the rogue countries. At least there won't be any drastic changes in the United States with Obama reelected. Any further news from Mexico, agent Johnson?

Agent Johnson: Nothing major. General Garcia would inform us. A few reports of military patrols near the border finding burned bodies of traffickers.

Britain: I wonder how the tribunal can differentiate between drug traffickers and migrants.

Johnson: They must stop individuals near the border and question them. They all had radios, so they communicated with them. Also, the reports said that their backpacks were lying there open, drugs displayed.

Of course, all these individuals are small fry and not major traffickers. Unless the tribunal can get to the top people of the drug cartels, the trafficking will continue. However, they accomplished one phase of the trafficking, the human cargo, the sluicing of illegal migrants into America, robbing and killing them.

Denmark: So far, the world tribunal is a blessing in disguise.

Herr Juergens from Germany raised his hand and was recognized by the chairperson.

"Our intelligence at the Bka has come up with an interesting time frame when the encounters of the world tribunal in regard to killings took place. Dating back to the pirate encounters, then with the drug traffickers in Mexico, it always happened on weekends, including Fridays. The radio interview with Inspector Mikulis and the subsequent killing of Antanas Barzda happened on the second of November, a Friday.

"The burning down of the village Jedwabne in Poland happened on the twenty-sixth of October, a Friday. These two reports are not even known to the Bka but only substantiates their information. The Bka believes that the apparatus for sending the rays is part of large laboratory or other technical facility and can be used only on weekends when most of the personnel is not present."

Britain: That is interesting. It shows that it is not a private enterprise but a clandestine operation at a public or industrial institution.

Chairperson: However, it does not bring the source any closer to us. How about the time frame by hours? I mean, Mexico is six to seven hours behind Greenwich time. Any intelligence from that?

Herr Juergens: Not really. The encounter of the tribunal with the forty-two migrants was as early as five in the morning, Greenwich time, early afternoon. The killing in Monterrey was at noon, six to seven o'clock in the early evening in Europe. We have to get the exact time for the killing of Barzda and the burning down of the village in Poland.

Now, only if an encounter ever took place in Mexico in the early evening hours, midnight here, could we decide if the operation is from Europe or America. I doubt that any institution is operative at midnight.

Chairperson: Any other comments, reports, questions pertaining to the world tribunal? No? Then we can get to other business.

Agent Johnson sent a full report to FBI headquarters.

CHAPTER XII

Sinmiae, Estonia

When Anton came to the institute on Friday, 9 November, he found Max and Sepp looking at Goggle Earth, imaging the very northeast corner of Estonia. After establishing the coordinates, Max used his computer and brought a small village in focus. "This is the village of Sinmiae, a small place." He showed an estate a few kilometers away, and there was activity of interest. They saw many cars, some with trailers, mobile homes, and people putting up tents. "But let Sepp tell you why we are looking at the place."

Sepp explained, "Remember Fred Schultheis, Anton? He is still with the police, got promoted and works for Inspector Wagner, but you knew all that. He is also still a member of the Nazi Bund. Anyhow I met him for coffee the other day, and he told me an interesting story I wanted to pass on to Max and you. At the last meeting of the Bund, Leader Horst Bachleiter said he received a message from their Bund headquarters that any member who wishes is invited to a meeting at Sinmiae in Estonia to attend a get-together of the Estonian SS. During the war, the Twentieth Estonian SS Division worked with the German SS. There was also a Latvian SS Division, and in Lithuania they had smaller units of police who collaborated with the Germans. In 1944, these and German divisions fought a hard battle at Sinmiae against the Soviets. The owner of this estate near the village fought in the Estonian SS. To commemorate this battle, veterans of these two divisions and new members, mostly new members as few of the old ones are left, meet on the date the battle was fought. They also meet on former Nazi holidays, like the ninth of

November, which was the day of the putsch by Hitler. However, they always have the meeting on the following Saturday when members get off work. So they have their celebration on Saturday, the tenth. They call these Saturdays Black Sabbaths, and they invited this time members of our Bund in Germany. Bachleiter explained that they even wear their SS uniforms but without the swastikas so the authorities don't complain."

Max: I thought we take a look at them tomorrow. People who want to commemorate the SS, what the SS did, belongs in the garbage pail of humanity.

Anton: When do we meet tomorrow morning?

Max: I thought at eight o'clock. They are one hour ahead. Nine means that they had their breakfast and get ready for their festivities. Also, I don't want us to come in earlier or, for that matter, late in the evening so that the guard doesn't get suspicious. You know, he makes us sign in on weekends or late at night and early hours. I know we were already a few times in the evening. Sepp and I will remain here for a while.

Anton: I guess I look up my colleagues at the Police Praesidium. Especially my friend Stefan Wagner. I haven't been there for many months. See you tomorrow morning.

Anton met Stefan Wagner in his office. Anton told Stefan about the bugging of he dacha and the result. He added, "General Orlov had not known that the dacha was still bugged. The overeager FSB agent found himself transferred to an outpost in Siberia."

Stefan laughed. "The Russian way of doing things. By the way, Anton, how was your visit to London in August?"

Anton didn't show that he was highly surprised but exhaled deeply; looking straight in his friend's eyes, he asked, "How do you know?"

Stefan explained, "The Bka sent a flyer to all major police departments in Germany with a list of names of people who flew into London on the twenty-fourth of August, asking if anyone recognizes any of the names. Commissioner Kolb gave it to me to research. I saw the name of Achmed Nabil on the list, an Egyptian."

"And?" asked Anton.

Stefan: I wrote a short notice that none of the names were familiar to me, signed it.

Anton nodded. "Yes, I remember an Achmed Nabil."

They laughed.

Stefan: What are friends for? Anything you wish to tell me, Anton?

Anton smiled. "Not this time. Yes, one question. How would you feel if Horst Bachleiter and his son Gustav were eliminated?"

Stefan shrugged his shoulders. "Bachleiter is the leader of the Nazi Bund. During Hitler's time he would have been an SS Officer in an *Einsatzkommando*. I never met the man, but Fred Schultheis tells me he is one brutal character. His son Gustav not any better. I know they kidnapped your mother and threatened to kill her. Gustav followed you in the woods and wanted to kill you. If possible, try to make it look like an accident."

Then they talked about their families.

Anton was at the institute before eight and signed in. He had coffee in the lunchroom and met Max and Sepp; they went into the energy house. Max, knowing the coordinates, brought the village of Sinmiae on the screen, moved to the estate. Many people under or near a large tent, probably the kitchen tent. Tables and chairs nearby where people sat, most men but there were a few women. All men they saw wore uniforms, the German army gray. Klausner zeroed in on a group of men. Yes, these were the gray uniforms the Waffen SS wore. But instead of the SS runes, these men wore patches on their collars showing an *E* with a sword through it.

Max: I guess they are not permitted to show the SS runes and instead the *E* for Estonia, and the sword.

Sepp: I am surprised the Estonian government even permits them to have these gatherings, commemorating their membership in the SS.

Anton: The Estonian might do it to flout their independence from the Russians. The Russians surely don't like it.

Max: I read an article in the paper not long ago that Russia complained to the EU (European Union) about the glorification of Nazism in the Baltic countries. The EU just shrugged it off by saying, "This is the liberalism of the new order in Europe."

Of course the Western European countries don't permit this type of pro-Nazi behavior.

Anton: Like I said, the Baltic countries turned extreme right to counter the left of Russia.

Max: The Russians are no longer left oriented, with Putin furthering the nationalism of Russia; they are right-wing themselves. But you are right, Anton if you say that the Baltic countries want to flout what Russia stands for. At least in Russia there is little if any love for Nazism. Teasing the big Bear. More recently I read that though on the outside government support for the Sinmiae SS rallies has decreased, but unofficial support for the former SS veterans is growing stronger.

Anton: Well, let's see if we can change that a little. Cut off the head of the viper.

Sepp: I hate those bastards. Anton, you once told me that we should not, dislike yes. But I can't help it; I just hate anything that glorifies what the Nazis did.

Anton: I was wrong in saying we should not hate. To "dislike' is not strong enough for our feelings of disgust and revulsion. Like with killing and murder. We kill or as we say we eliminate those who have committed crimes against mankind and are beyond anyone's jurisdiction. *To kill without reason, kill innocents is murder.* The same with "hate." The hatred by bigots for religious, ethnic, or racial reasons is wrong. For us to hate those who do is proper.

Max: I think they are finished with breakfast; they are assembling.

They watched as the multitude assembled in front of a podium. On each side was a large flag with the colors of Estonia: blue, white, and black. Around the podium standards, which showed the big *E* underneath an arm holding a sword.

On the podium was a lectern and chairs behind it, on each side a large loudspeaker.

The men had formed in groups in a half circle, in front a woman who held the national flag for each contingent. The men stood in rows of seven. From left to right were the Lithuanian contingent, then the Latvian, the Estonian in the middle, a small group of Germans, and just as small Ukrainians. All men in the first row were elderly, probably the veterans. One row of five old Lithuanians, a full seven of Latvians, two full rows of Estonians, three Germans, and three Ukrainian veterans. Behind each row were the younger ones, and here again the Estonian group was the largest. The Germans had only two rows of young men, the Ukrainians just four people. All in all, there were maybe a hundred uniformed men. And when Max zeroed in on the Germans, they all wore the uniform with the SS runes. At least their black-white-red flag didn't have a swastika but it had the Iron Cross of the military.

Now a group of men and one woman stepped up to the podium. The first one, an old man, wore the black uniform of the SS. Then came the woman, obviously his wife, followed by three middle-aged civilians. The SS man went to the lectern. He spoke into the microphone, and Sepp had his audio computer ready.

The black-clad man raised his hand in Nazi salute and shouted in German *Sieg Heil* three times, each heil was followed by the multitude screaming their Sieg Heil. Then he spoke in Estonian; that was followed by the playing of the national hymn. He greeted the Latvian group, after the Lithuanians, then the Estonians.

While he spoke and the anthems were played, Max zeroed in on the man. From above they could not see his face; also he wore the black SS hat. On his collar he showed patches with the SS runes. His epaulets had oak leaves. Anton explained, "The oak leaves denote the rank of a Standartenfuehrer."

He then turned to the German contingent and spoke in fluent German, "Ein herzliches Willkommen zu meinen deutschen Kameraden [A warm welcome to my German comrades. My name is Baron Feodor von Reva. My parents were of German descent]."

He introduced his wife, Greta.

He then went on to describe his membership in the SS since 1941 when Germany liberated Estonia from the Soviets and how he fought in the Twentieth Estonian SS Division and had many battles against the Red Army. He also spoke about how his division also helped the cleanse Estonia of the Jews.

Sepp: We have to get him. Like you said, cut off the head of the snake.

Max: Let him first finish the introduction. The question is, who after him?

Anton: They will scatter once we burn Reva.

Sepp: If we can, get those German SS veterans, then the Ukrainians; they were the most vicious.

Now the German anthem was played over the loudspeakers.

Reva next turned to the Ukrainians and spoke in Russian, which Anton had to translate, "My dear comrades from the Ukraine, I bid you welcome. I have to address you in Russian as I don't speak Ukrainian. Most of us speak Russian as we were for many years under the joke of the hammer and sickle. You SS veterans were the Trawnikis, the lords of the camps where we got rid of the Jews and commissars." He went on to extol their bravery in fighting Communism and the scourge of the Jews.

The Ukrainian anthem was played.

Next he introduced the civilians who had come with him and introduced them in every language, and each contingent yelled their approval and clapped their hands.

"My Latvian colleague Uldis Freimanis, who spoke truly on the television program *Without Censorship*, said, 'The Jews of Latvia need to be hanged from a pole and should be all killed.' My friend Anders Mathisen from Norway, a politician, who also spoke the truth when he said that the Holocaust did not happen, that there were no gas chambers and no mass graves existed. And let me introduce another politician, Fritz Bolkestein from Holland, who warned the Jews, 'To you, sensible Jews, I say you must accept the fact that you have no future in our land and you would be better off immigrating to Israel or the United States.'"

Sepp: Anton, are you going to talk to them before you kill that bastard?

Max: At least you must tell them that the world tribunal sentences them to death for their atrocities, that we will be there for every meeting.

Anton: There are no words to describe their evil, but I try. Maybe we can prevent any future gathering of the devils. Sepp, increase the volume; I want my voice to boom into the crowd.

Anton took the microphone. It was attached to a synchronizer to distort his voice, which made it sound metallic; since he spoke German, he needed to disguise his voice.

"THIS IS THE WORLD TRIBUNAL ADDRESSING THE MOST BARBAROUS ASSEMBLY OF MEN ON OUR PLANET. YOU ARE HERE TO COMMEMORATE THE BATTLE OF SINMIAE IN 1944 WHEN THE RED ARMY DEEATED YOU.

TODAY YOU WILL BE DEFEATED BY THE RIGHTEOUS FORCES OF THE WORLD TRIBUNAL. YOU STAND ACCUSED OF MURDER OF THE INNOCENT, SLAYING BRUTALLY EVEN BABIES AND LITTLE CHILDREN, TEN THOUSAND

OF THEM. MURDERING BRUTALLY MILLIONS OF MEN AND WOMEN. YOU HAVE BEEN FOUND GUILTY NOT ONLY OF MASS MURDER BUT ALSO OF INHUMAN BEHAVIOR, TORTURE, AND DISGUSTING BRUTALITIES TOWARD YOUR VICTIMS. YOU ARE THE CESSPOOL OF HUMANITY. DEATH TO YOU, BARBAS. AND DEATH TO YOU IF YOU EVER HOLD ANOTHER OF THESE DISGUSTING MEETINGS!"

Max had already zeroed in on the baron. Anton gave him the maximum jolt of five thousand degrees. His head exploded in fire and smoke; he fell, his black uniform aflame.

Sepp: Next the German SS veterans.

All groups still stood still in consternation and shock. Anton had reduced the strength of the infrared ray to three thousand and with quick jolts eliminated two of them; then the third one on a cane hobbled away. Klausner was able to focus on his figure, though not his head.

Anton jolted his shoulder, and his uniform burst inflame; he stood still. Another jolt to his head and he fell dead. Next he eliminated the Ukrainians. By then the groups had dissolved into men running in every direction. Some into the nearby forest, others to their cars and sped off. Some into the big house behind the podium.

"Can we fire the house?" asked Sepp.

Max zeroed in on the roof, which was with wooden shingles. In three places Anton gave it maximum half-second jolts, and the roof was on fire. Men came soon running from the house and disappeared into the forest. Soon the beautiful white house burned from top to bottom.

Justice was done.

The following week, on Saturday, 17 November, Anton was with Max. Sepp was in Stanberg, the big lake near Munich. Sepp had found out from Fred Schultheis that the leader of the neo-Nazis in Munich, Horst Bachleiter, had a beach house on the Stanberg Lake and spent weekends fishing with his son and sometimes guests. While it was already middle of November, it was a sunny, cool day. Sepp had rented a motorboat at eight in the morning as soon as the rental agency opened and driven out to the southern part of the lake, *Seeshaupt*, where near the town Bachleiter had his beach house. He was idling his motor, remaining about a kilometer from the beach house, fishing. He wore a white hat for easier recognition. Though not an avid fisherman, he managed to catch a few. In between fishing he scanned with his binoculars all around and just for a brief moment the beach house.

Max had him in view.

Max and Anton talked about Christmas, which was only five weeks away. This year, Anton had invited Max, his wife, Ingrid, and daughter Erica to spend Christmas with him at his dacha in Russia. Also Sepp and his wife, Inge, would come.

Since Anton's mother, Rosemarie, had passed away at the dacha on Christmas 2010, Anton and Hanna would make it a practice to have friends visit during that season to lessen the memory of the pain by the sudden death of his beloved mother. Last Christmas, his colleague and friend Stefan Wagner with his family had visited.

It was about ten o'clock that they saw that Sepp took his white hat off. That was the signal that Bachleiter was on the lake in his boat. Since there were many motor—and sailboats around, they followed the one from Sepp. Raising the view, they soon saw the boat Sepp was following. It was a larger motorboat with two men. That pleased Anton and Max as they did not wish to eliminate persons they did not know, though they had no doubt that any visitors were neo-Nazis.

Both boats stopped in the middle of the southern part of the large lake where it must be deepest and the fish probably more abundant and bigger. Sepp's boat pointed at the one from Bachleiter, his hat on again. Both signals that this was Bachleiter.

Max zeroed in on Bachleiter's boat. It was a good size boat with an outboat motor, next to it a large canister with gas. It would be easy.

Anton: Horst Bachleiter, you had my mother kidnapped and threatened to murder her.

Gustav Bachleiter, you pursued me with a pistol to kill me, as you confessed.

Horst Bachleiter, you are the leader of the neo-Nazi Bund in the city of Munich. The neo-Nazis the followers of Hitler and glorifiers of his maniacal genocide. Gustav raised as a Nazi, living as a Nazi with the same foul ideology as your father. You are unworthy to live among mankind. Death to both of you.

Max: Elimination is justice served.

When Max zeroed in on the gas tank, Anton gave it a maximum jolt of a half second. The fireball of the explosion destroyed both men and the boat.

Boats that raced to the area found only blackened planks of the boat. Also three life preservers with the name of *Lohengrin*, the name of the boat.

The next day, the *Seehaupt Zeitung* wrote about the accident of the boat *Lohengrin* and that the owner of the boat Horst Bachleiter and his son Gustav were killed in the apparent explosion of the gas tank. However, their bodies were not recovered.

The Munich *Sueddeutsche Zeitung* also had a short paragraph about the accident.

(Only Inspector Stefan Wagner of the Munich police understood about the accident.)

The weekend of 23 November, Anton was on duty at police headquarters in Jerusalem. In between his duties he worked on the fourth manifesto.

When it was finished Saturday afternoon, he called his friend Nevot to come by.

He let Nevot read the manifesto.

After reading it Nevot looked up. "Anything you wish to tell me, Anton?"

Anton shook his head. "No, not yet, I will soon. Can you take it Sunday or Monday to New York and mail it like you did with the last one?"

Nevot: I fly tomorrow, mail it on Monday.

Anton gave him the addressed manila envelope and the letter he had prepared, always wearing gloves. They shook hands, and Nevot left.

Nevot mailed it on Monday, 26 November. It was received in Rome on Thursday and the same day forwarded to Bern. Chief editor Konrad received it on Saturday and had it published in the Sunday edition of the second of December 2012.

CHAPTER XIII

Manifesto IV of the World Tribunal
Death to the Terrorists

9/11/2001! Three planes with innocent passengers and crews smashed into buildings incinerating men, women, and children. One plane flown on purpose into the ground killing all. The World Trade Center Towers burning, people above hurling themselves down to escape burning alive. Over two thousand innocents killed when the towers collapsed. The Pentagon crashed, over a hundred men and women killed.

Who committed these foul deeds? Moslem fanatics. Their last words were *alluha akhbar* (God is great). Did Allah permit them? Tell them to commit this atrocity?

No, Allah did not. These terrorists were not followers of Allah but of Satan.

Who ordered these wanton murders? Osama bin Laden, may he burn in hell, and this evil-spirited Mullah al-Zawahiri.

Jubilation in the Arab world. The terrorists their heroes. Palestinians do their macabre dancing in the streets and give candy to children - so many Americans killed, *alluha akhbar.*

These terrorists, monsters in human form, are not followers of Allah and the Koran. Theirs is a reign of hate and sadism, driven by the many clerics who spout lies, deceptions, and hate mongering. Throughout the world we have these outcasts of humanity do their terrible misdeeds, especially al-Qaeda and its many branches.

The world tribunal has found the terrorists guilty of crimes against mankind.

The world tribunal has sentenced all terrorists to oblivion by death ray.

The world tribunal warns certain country's leaders to desist from their mongering and hateful incitements. These include Prime Minister Recep Erdogan from Turkey, who called Israel a "terrorist nation" when they defended themselves against the rocket attacks by Hamas. The Egyptian president Mohammed Morsi, who branded Israel the "aggressor," an outright lie, when attacked by Hamas.

President Ahmadinejad from Iran, the head of the clergy council supreme leader Al-Khamenei of Iran, and the military puppet from North Korea, Kim Jong-Un. We warn Kim Jong-Un not to give any help to Iran in developing a nuclear bomb.

DESIST OR YOU WILL BE ELIMINATED!

The Force of Three.

EUROPOL met on Wednesday, the fifth of December.

Chairmanship for December was Ireland's, Mr. Charles McCallister.

Chairman McCallister: Before we get to the fourth manifesto, we have a report from our German delegate.

Michael Juergens stood up. "As it is known in Western Europe, the Baltic nations permit veterans of the Estonian and Latvian SS divisions to hold rallies to commemorate their fight against the Soviets and to brag about working closely with the German SS in killing the Jews, Soviet prisoners, and partisans fighting with the Red Army. They hold their meetings near the village of Sinmae, in northeastern Estonia, where in 1944 a big battle was fought and lost by the German army; the Estonian and Latvian SS divisions fought alongside the German army.

"Perhaps the reason for these meetings—which, by the way, are openly held and permitted by the Estonian government—is that one of the veterans from this battle has a large estate near the place where the battle took place and sponsors these meetings. His name is, or I should say was, Baron Feodor von Reva. There was a contingent of Estonians, Latvians, Lithuanians, and a small group of neo-Nazis from Germany and a few Ukrainians, Trawnikis, or as the Germans called them Hiwis. Very few were actual veterans; they are now in their nineties. After the baron greeted each contingent and they played their anthems, he gave a speech and then introduced some civilians.

"It was then that the loudspeakers on the podium boomed; and the voice, which spoke in flawless German, introduced itself as belonging to the world tribunal, castigated the assembly for the murders they committed during the war, and threatened them with annihilation if they ever met again.

"Then the baron von Reva was immolated as were the three German veterans and three Ukrainians. By then, according to the report we received, all those present were running away, some into the woods. Some sped off in cars; others ran into the estate house. The big house was then set afire and burned down; all inside the house escaped."

Britain: When did that happen?

Juergens: On the tenth of November. The meeting was to commemorate Hitler's putsch. These fascists or neo-Nazis always hold meetings on former Third Reich holidays. Of course the putsch was on ninth of November, but to make it possible for people to attend who work, they always hold the meeting the following Saturday, what they call Black Sabbath.

Britain: I saw nothing in the newspapers.

Juergens: I guess the Estonian government restricted the news. People might ask questions why they even permit these meetings.

Holland: Where from did this report emanate?

Juergens: I received it from the Bka. The Bka has a double agent with the German neo-Nazis. Please treat this information confidential.

Chairman McCallister: Thank you, Mr. Juergens.

Holland: I believe that the world press should publish this report. Another worthwhile deed performed by the tribunal. Of course without quoting the source.

France: Let's send the report to the *Berner Nachrichten*; they are like the world press.

Chairman: All agree? Good, perhaps Herr Juergens can compose this letter and send it in the name of EUROPOL. We are the center for crime reports or, in this case, for a report of important information about the world tribunal.

Juergens: I shall do so.

Bulgaria: Interesting that the voice addressed the meeting in German.

124

France: The source spoke in High German or a dialect?

Juergens: I was told it sounded artificial, disguised surely, and booming.

Chairman: Anything else about the incident in Sinmae? No? Now to the fourth manifesto.

Britain: I suggested that it would be about worldwide terrorism.

Denmark: Again a blessing for mankind.

Turkey: My government does not appreciate that Prime Minister Erdogan was threatened and included in the naming of radical world leaders. PM Erdogan is not a radical. Though a close friend of Syria, he has regretted that President Bashar al-Assad is repressing his own people.

France: What Assad is doing is not only repressing his own people but killing them wholesale.

Turkey: It is not only the military that does the killing, but the terrorists are just as brutal, if not worse.

Chairman: Gentlemen, let us return to the meaning of the fourth manifesto.

France: How can we combat worldwide Muslim fanaticism?

Turkey: We must not blame the Islamic religion for it.

Spain: We are not blaming the religion but certain factions of Islam. The fanatics like al-Qaeda worldwide, other jihadist groups, the Taliban.

Norway: We believe that if the Americans and NATO would leave Afghanistan, the Taliban and President Karzai's regime would make peace. The Afghanis were quite happy with the Taliban in charge. It was the bin Laden affair that caused all the problems there.

Britain: The male Afghans might be happy to live by Sharia but not the women.

Turkey: The women accepted Sharia because it is the religion of the Koran. As true believers, they cannot do otherwise.

Britain: Sharia, if Koran inspired or not, takes us back to the Dark Ages.

Chairman: We cannot discuss here the good and bad of religious beliefs but this force that sets itself up as judge and executor of our civilized world.

Spain: As a counterforce to religious and criminal extremism.

Norway: Who gives the tribunal the right to lord it over our civilization?

Holland: Some civilization we are; the world is afraid of these extremists. What a civilization when passengers are frisked at airports, even have to take their shoes off.

Denmark: What a religion that brings forth these extremists. Not that many of us Christians are any better. These mass killers in drug trafficking are all good Catholics.

Spain: I don't believe that religious extremists are religious. Theirs is a religion of hate and not Judaic-Christian principles or Islamic inspired. Have we ever profiled these extremists, the suicide bomber?

Chairman McCallister turned to one of his aides, "Have we done so?"

Aid: Yes, we have. Medical people, experts on terrorism; others have tried and come up with various profiles. Most bombers fit into certain categories, and not all are based on religion, though religion is the main driving force of these terrorists. However, the best profiles are by the Israelis who have the most experience with suicide bombers.

France: Perhaps we can request these profiles from the Israelis.

Chairman: I am certain the FBI has done extensive research. Since 9/11, you have prevented most attacks by terrorists, with the exception of that Major Hasan. Agent Johnson, please?

Agent Johnson: Major Hasan was a special case. Who was to expect a major in the American army to shoot fellow soldiers? Yet there were signs of his radicalism that were missed, and we in the FBI were not informed. Besides profiling, the most effective way to prevent terrorist attacks is to infiltrate reported groups of possible terrorists and also individuals. Even businesspeople have become aware of the problem and often report to us or the police the purchase of unusual amounts of fertilizers, gas cylinders, chemicals, etc. We have sent flyers to these businesses to be aware. I mean, if a known farmer buys large amounts of fertilizer as he has always done, it is different than when a stranger does so.

Norway: You don't do that with firearms bought. Anyone can buy a pistol, a rifle, even assault rifles. Like that nut did in Denver and shot these people in a cinema.

Agent Johnson: We are not perfect. There are failures, like with Holmes. He was on a danger list at the university. A psychiatrist profiled him as a person to watch and called for a meeting by an advisory group. Then when he left the university, that meeting was cancelled. The failure was not to report him to the police as a danger. Well, they did but only to the campus police. Even if they had reported to the regular police, what could the police have done? The police investigates crimes committed, not the prevention of crime. We really need a crime research lab like a small EUROPOL agency that researches and investigates people reported as dangerous. Home-grown terrorists. We in the FBI are mainly interested in persons who have connection or possible connection to international terrorism and the "nut" as my colleague from Norway described Holmes, slips by us. Just as that lunatic Anders Breivik slipped by the Norwegian police.

Italy: Wherefrom did the letter come this time?

Chairman: Again from New York. The information was sent to us by the Suisse Federal Police.

Italy: Twice now from New York. Indicating that their operation is in New York?

Chairman: Perhaps but not necessarily.

Denmark: First against the pirates, then the drug cartels, followed by ex-Nazis and neo-Nazis and other right-wing extremist groups, and now Islamic fanatics or jihadists. Why disturb their operation? Perhaps we are fortunate to have this world tribunal?

Norway: Without due jurisdictional court action?

Britain: They claim that before each action they hold a proper trial. Sounds very similar to our ICC (International Criminal Court).

France: I agree with my colleague from Great Britain. What have they done so far? Almost eliminated piracy, combating the murderous drug cartels, punishing ex-Nazis and those who still believe in Hitler's maniacal genocidal philosophy, now fighting the scourge of Islamic extremists. And while they will never stop the trafficking, we have no new reports of migrants and other innocents murdered. Also, they will never be able to stop the extremists as long as their leaders preach hatred against non-Muslims, but they may be able to reduce their effect. I am looking forward to the times when I can board a plane without being searched and having to take my shoes off. Have armed guards aboard.

Chairman: We all do. If there is nothing else? Then let me conclude this meeting.

CHAPTER XIV

Meetings of the Enemy

The work of the world tribunal did not go unnoticed by the enemy.

Several weeks after the Karin incident, the commander of the al-Shabab militia in Somalia, the leader of the pirates in Karin, and a government official who worked with the pirates met at a secret place in Mogadishu.

The pirate leader gave details of the happening in Karin. He told that when five of his men boarded the freighter *Houston*, four were killed by the death rays. One saved himself by jumping overboard and was picked up by a boat. Two of the boats returned to the cutter. Then the cutter was burned; and while the crew put out the fire, the machinery was damaged, and the cutter had to be towed by the two boats. It took several weeks to return. The same day, six men guarding the prisoners of the tanker *Star Shell* were killed by the death rays. The prisoners then took their weapons and shot several more men; the rest jumped overboard. The leader continued, "When my men on the other captured ships heard what happened, they left the ships, and all ships departed. My men in Karin are afraid the same will happen to them. They refuse to board any other ship and bring it to Karin. Then guards at the checkpoint saw the wooden barrier burn suddenly, and they ran away. Karin is finished as an anchorage for captured ships. My men rather fish than capture any more ships."

Official: I am sure that it was the Americans who used the death ray. Your men should have never shot these Americans on the yacht.

Leader: You might be right. I wasn't there; it was Amin who ordered the killing. He is now in prison in America, and they will kill him.

Commander: You have to continue. You have other hideouts for ships; the Americans don't know their anchorages. We need the money to pay my militia and buy weapons. I didn't know about the checkpoint. These were my men guarding, and now they have disappeared.

Leader: If the men in the other places hear about the death ray, they will run away too.

Commander: I give you men from the militia. You pay them well; they will capture ships.

Leader: They need to be trained.

Official: Let's do it then. It is too lucrative a business to give up so easy.

Leader: I try. I know if it happens again, all my men will run away and rather fish.

THE DRUG CARTELS MEET

In La Paz, Baja California, lived Therese Vargas, one of the mistresses of Joaquin Guzman Loera; she lived in a beautiful villa Guzman had bought for her.

As a cover for her presence, he had also bought a fishing boat rental, good business for the many tourists who came to fish in the Gulf de California. A few of the fishing boats were rather large speedboats and could transverse the Gulf from Mazatlan to La Paz, about three hundred kilometers, in five hours. This was the method of transportation Guzman used when visiting his mistress. While there were three bodyguards always present in the villa and several of Guzman's men were tending to the rental agency, most help were regular people from La Paz. Nobody knew that Senor Vargas, who supposedly was a businessman from Mexico City, was the infamous Sinaloa drug cartel leader.

Guzman had called for a meeting of major rival druglords, and boats were waiting at the Mazatlan marina to ferry them to La Paz. They left at midnight and arrived in La Paz before it got light. Nobody should recognize them—that is, if anyone even knew the leaders by sight. Cars were awaiting them at the dock to take them to Therese Vargas's villa. Of course there were more than the three leaders as each one brought his own bodyguards.

When the sun rose over the gulf, it was the third of October; there were besides Sinaloa Federation's Guzman also known as El Chapo the two leaders of the Zetas cartel Heriberto Lazcano and Miguel Trevino Morales; from the Beltran Leyva Organization Hector Beltran Leyva; Juarez cartel's Vicente Carrillo Fuentes; and from the Arellano Organization Fernando "El Ingeniero" Sanchez Arellano. Jorge "El Coss" Costilla Sanchez from the gulf cartel had been captured by the marines. While competitors and often enemies, they followed Guzman's invitation as they all were under the threat of the world court. They sat in the large dining room, minus their bodyguards as requested by their host. First, to become reacquainted and to initiate a friendly atmosphere, a sumptuous breakfast was served.

Then cigars or cigarettes were passed; tequila and cognac were on the table.

Guzman began the meeting by rapping on his glass, "Hear ye, all. Let us put aside any enmity and competitive problems. Each organization controls a certain territory and means to ship our goods. If our people have to pass through territory controlled by another organization, let us make arrangement and pay. There need not be any war between us."

Vicente Fuentes interrupted, "You tell that to the Zetas."

Guzman turned to them. "Heriberto and Miguel, can't we stop fight among ourselves?"

Miguel: It isn't just the competiveness but personal rivalries.

Guzman: Meet together, shake hands, have a glass of tequila in friendship instead of war. We all are now under the threat of this outfit that calls itself the world court. We are sure that it is an American operation. Who else has the technique to build such a death ray? I mean, with this ray they apparently can see and kill. What turned this operation against us—at least I believe that is the reason—was the killing and dismemberment of the forty-nine migrants near Monterrey. Your action, Miguel and Heriberto?

Heriberto: It was my subleader Nazario Moreno who did that with his men.

Guzman: But why? The whole world learned about it and turned against us.

Heriberto shrugged. "He had planned to rob them. Somebody told him that the migrants had plenty of dollars on them. Then when they wouldn't give it willingly, he killed them.

All they had was pesos and not many of those."

Guzman: All right, this I can understand. But why not bury them so they couldn't be found? I mean, that is not only stupid but criminal! You have to get rid of that Moreno.

Heriberto: He was killed by death ray at my villa. He and two of my guards were burned.

Guzman: That takes care of that problem. Listen, amigos, we have to stop going after migrants. It is not such a big business to bring migrants across the border.

Fernando Arellano raised his hand. "It was when we had the brothers working at the San Ysidro crossing in Tijuana. 5,000 dollars for each migrant, easy sluicing them in.

Now after they caught Hector, we have to bring them in across the desert again."

Guzman: Just don't kill them. Bringing migrants into America is not such a great business anyhow. Let's concentrate on drugs, kidnapping, extortion, and prostitution.

Now to business. I began a big operation in Chicago. I can handle all the cocaine and heroin you can get. And I need help to get them across the border.

Miguel: My Zetas people have good connection with Farc. Our routes from Nuevo Laredo to Laredo are secure. We use tunnels to get them across.

Guzman. You and I sit together and work it out. Anyone else who has plenty of the stuff, let me know. I can always be reached at this address. Just send it in care of Senora Therese Vargas and by courier only. And by the way, I am known here as Senor Vargas, Therese's husband, a businessman form Mexico City—never Guzman. Tonight, when it is dark, the boats will take you back to Mazatlan. In the meantime, relax; there are sleeping quarters downstairs. Lunch will be served here at one o'clock. Or you can go fishing as tourists. You all have cover names and corresponding driver licenses? Be sure to be back by seven. That is all, my friends.

Javier Cervantes was the mechanic who kept all boats of the Vargas running. He was a captain in the federal army and an undercover agent for General Garcia. The general had many undercover agents throughout Mexico, mostly in major cities, cities near the American border. Some were policemen, but most were associated with transportation or, as Cervantes was, the expert mechanic. Each one was first of all single so that his family could not be compromised, and each one had fake papers with a plausible history of schooling and previous employment.

At first, Cervantes had worked for another boat rental agency, but soon his expertise became known, and many times he was doing jobs for the Vargas agency when their mechanic could not fix things. He was finally hired by Senora Vargas at three times the salary. Before he was hired, he filled out employment papers, and his past was researched, but nothing suspicious was found.

In his apartment he had a computer and kept in touch with the general's office. All messages sent and received he immediately erased. What he left on his computer were only pornography pictures, but this was expected for a single man. And when he was at work and his apartment searched, as was his computer, nothing incriminating was found. The people who searched his place had an interesting time viewing his porno stuff.

Cervantes had met Senor Vargas a few times, the businessman from Mexico City. Vargas always wore sunglasses—he stated that he had weak eyes—and a bushy mustache. A clandestine picture he was able to take of the man and sent to military headquarters did not identify Vargas as Guzman. However, he was a person of interest to the army as his business address in Mexico City was only a box number.

Cervantes knew that the fast boats had been to Mazatlan during the night, ferrying who?

He had sent a short e-mail to the general: "3 Oct—cartel meeting in La Paz via Mazatlan."

When he came to work in the morning, he saw nobody but the boats were back. The boss of the rental agency came to him and told him that one of the boats had troubles on the way and to see to it. He soon found the problem: a leaking fuel line. He told his boss what the problem was and that he had no replacement but he could temporarily fix the fuel line. He suggested that whoever takes the boat to Mazatlan to buy a new line, "it takes a special one for these fast boats. I wrote down what we need. The repair shop at the marina in Mazatlan has them."

Later the boss came to him and told him that he would be the helmsman for that boat. He was to spend the night in Mazatlan and buy the new fuel line, put it in, and return in the morning.

He gave him money and told him to be at the marina at six. When he comes back, he could take the rest of the day off. He also gave him money to stay at a hotel for him and Pedro who would be his assistant. Pedro was not a mechanic but could steer the boat.

Taking Pedro along, who was one of Vargas's man, meant he would not be free.

Cervantes was at the marina at six; he and Pedro made the boat ready. Pedro also brought a basket with food and tequila, glasses. It was after seven and dark already when the cars came. The man who entered his boat he recognized at once. Part of his training had been to study the pictures of the cartel leaders. The man was Fernando Sanchez Arellano from the Arellano cartel. He was followed by three men, bodyguards. One of the guards frisked him and Pedro. Cervantes was a careful man, but he had neither his pistol on him nor his cell phone. When the cars arrived, the lights in the marina were turned off. He could not see any of the other men who boarded the boats. But if Arellano had been visiting, then this was most likely a meeting of the cartel leaders, and Senor Vargas was also a VIP, perhaps even Guzman? With the sunglasses and bushy mustache, he had never recognized him.

The five-hour night trip was uneventful. The weather was clear and the sea calm. He had instructions to follow the two boats ahead of him, though he knew the compass setting to Mazatlan and could have arrived there on his own.

It was after midnight when they arrived in Mazatlan. Arellano came to him and thanked Cervantes for bringing him safely to Mazatlan; he asked suddenly, "Tell me, Javier Cervantes, do you know who I am?" Cervantes shrugged his shoulder. "No, senor."

"Good," said Arellano and gave him 10,000 pesos. He also gave money to Pedro.

At the marina Cervantes saw several policemen, and his first inclination was to have them arrest Arellano. But then, they might be in pay of the cartels and kill him instead. If they had been marines, he would have tried. Better to get the news to General Garcia.

After his return to La Paz—he got there at noon—he had the rest of the day off. He sent a full report by e-mail to the general's office.

General Garcia in turn sent the report to the deputy of the FBI, James Adams.

The deputy informed the *New York Times* about the cartel meeting in a La Paz at the villa of Senora Therese Vargas, even giving the address.

This article was picked up by the *Berner Nachrichten* who reprinted the article on Saturday, the fifteenth of December.

There was one agency in Israel that subscribed to all major newspapers: the Mossad. Articles pertaining to Israel were copied out and sent to pertinent departments. This article, a reprint from the *New York Times*, was not of interest, but it was to Mordechai Nevot. He was an avid reader of the Suisse newspaper, and when he came in on Sunday, he found the article in Saturday's paper:

"Meeting of the Mexican drug cartels in La Paz."

Nevot made a copy and drove to police headquarters where he found Anton in his office.

He smiled when he gave the article to him. "An item of interest to you, Anton?"

Anton read the article, "I guess we have to visit Senora Vargas."

(Of interest: When Cervantes sent his first brief e-mail, the general notified his agent in Mazatlan who saw the boats arrive. He recognized the Zetas leader Lazcano and followed him to his hideout in Progreso in Coahuila state. Marines killed Lazcano in a firefight.)

And there was a meeting of the neo-Nazis a few weeks after the boat accident, which killed the leader Horst Bachleiter and his son Gustav. The new leader was Joachim Gersten, who had been the secretary before. He was chosen by acclamation of members.

Gersten stated that he and others had researched the accident and came to the conclusion that it was a bomb secreted on the boat that had caused the deadly explosion. There was one man who was a bitter enemy of Bachleiter: police inspector Anton Nagil. Nagil was also an explosive expert, and there was no doubt that he was the one who placed the bomb.

Inquires showed that Nagil had married a Jewish woman and was living in Israel.

This information came from the police department. Further, that Nagil had a cabin in Russia near Moscow and visited there sometimes, definitely for Christmas and with his family. Gersten said that he had made contact with the Russian mafia here and asked if it was possible to kill Nagil while visiting his cabin. His contact inquired with the mafia in Moscow, and it was possible to assassinate Nagil—for a price.

All this back-and-forth information took time, and it was the middle of December before a concrete offer came from the mafia. The price to assassinate Anton Nagil was 300,000 euros, 100,000 for the Munich mafia for arranging the killing, 100,000 to the Moscow mafia for finding a suitable person. It would be a one-man operation as the cabin of Hofer was in a restricted government area. The assassin would be in uniform as the area was patrolled by uniformed guards. 100,000 euros to the assassin.

Gersten knew of a rich neo-Nazi benefactor (Herr Schoenauer from Berchtesgaden), received the money, and paid it to the Munich mafia contact.

The man chosen for the killing was Ivan the Assassin; his real name was not even known in Moscow mafia circles. Ivan went at once to Alexandrov, stole from a car government plates, and purchased a uniform like the guards wear. For good money he got a map of the area and was told that the dacha odin was occupied by a German police officer; his name was Anton Hofer nee Nagil. For armament Ivan had a fast-firing 9mm Markov pistol and a long-bladed knife. Ivan was a marksman and even more skillful in using the knife—the silent assassination. He decided to do his job on Christmas Eve, when he knew the family was there. When dark, he would knock on the door of the dacha, identify himself as a security guard, tell that he wishes to report thieves in the area, and when admitted storm into the house with his pistol drawn shoot anyone who got in his way until he finds Hofer and kill him. If not admitted, he would prowl around and rattle on windows until Hofer comes out to investigate. Then he would use his knife.

Ivan had come a week before Christmas and using the map drove around during daytime to acquaint him with the layout as it would be dark when he came for the killing.

Hanukkah had begun on the eighth of December, and this was the last day of the celebration. This evening all eight candles would be lit. David would do it; he was now thirteen and would be fourteen on the twenty-fourth. Esther was ten, and their youngest, Daniel, was eight. They had received their presents on the first night of Hanukkah

The last week of December Anton was off, and they planned to spend Christmas at their dacha near Moscow, as they did each year. It was due to the close friendship he had with the commander of the Jerusalem police, Avi Barlev, that he was always able to take a week's vacation during that time when so many tourists came to celebrate Christmas in Bethlehem and of course flocked to Jerusalem.

The kids looked with joy to their visit in Russia, the winter there with snow and ice, and the many toys that awaited them, given to them for Christmas two years ago by the general.

This year Max Klausner, his wife, Ingrid, and their daughter Erika, who was twelve, would visit as was Sepp Kainz and his wife, Inge.

Therefore, the Vargas business had to be postponed until the beginning of next year.

CHAPTER XV

Christmas at the Russian Dacha

The three families met at the Domodedoro Airport in Moscow. The two families from Munich had come together shortly after lunch; they had time to change euros into rubbles and do some shopping. Anton with his family had come later from Israel, but by four o'clock they were together, and the three limousines were waiting outside. It was a cold and snowy day in Moscow, which made the Hofers' children happy as they treasured the slow sled ride through the countryside and forest with snow falling.

It took them a good half hour to reach Alexandrov, where at the government house the three sleds awaited them. The sled for the Hofer family was larger, a troika pulled by three horses, but all horses had bells. They let Erika sit with the other children; there was enough room. One sled was for their luggage. Each sled driver lit the two lanterns and made their passengers warm and comfortable with fur blankets. They walked their horses through the small town, but once on the country road, they made the horses trot; and to the joy of the children, and adults, the bells jingled. Dusk had set in, and it began to snow heavily, again to the delight of all.

When they reached the guardhouse, the entry to the restricted government area, while there was a government car, the shack was empty. This was not unusual as at night the guards were withdrawn. In fact, what was unusual was that a car was even there and no soldier in sight. However, this did not disturb the drivers as they thought that the guard was nearby or perhaps in the shack—drunk.

(The guard was nearby, hiding behind trees. However, it was Ivan the Assassin who had been around for the past couple of days when it got dark, awaiting the arrival of his victim. He was surprised to see the many visitors and children. He decided that the storming of the house was a bad idea, and he would lure Hofer out by making noises, like knocking on the window. It was Friday the twenty-first; in three days he would come back.)

Another half hour along a creek, over a stone bridge, and there was the large dacha, a warm shine from the windows.

The driver of the troika cracked the whip and yelled his "hoi-hoi," and Sasha, the caretaker, came running. He took one of the lanterns and guided his guests into the dacha.

In the large kitchen they met Isabella, Sasha's wife and gourmet cook. She already had set the table with various cold cuts, cheeses, caviar, fish dishes, and crusty farmer's bread and butter; there was also Crimean wine, vodka, and Anton's favorite bourbon whiskey.

While the drivers brought in their luggage, Sasha brushed off the snow off the children and adults and took their coats. Then the families sat around the long rectangular table, and first Isabella served her famous borscht, hot beet soup with veggies and beef cooked in.

With the cold dinner they were served the obligatory hot tea, the adults also enjoyed the Crimean wine. The conversation was mostly by the kids as David and Esther had to tell Erika of all the toys that awaited them and the many outdoor activities they would do.

With supper over, the children went into the playroom where there was a large table, covered with a green mat and blue plastic ribbon indicating a river with bridges crossing. There was the track of a miniature railroad curving around, a station in the village, and roads for Daniel to drive his little cars around. David and Daniel played there while Esther showed Erika her grocery store and all the goods it contained. The store, with shelves behind, was large, and there was a desk with a scale and cash register that contained play money—in Russian currency. The goods were of plastic, but Isabella had added real dry goods in the drawers, and there were little paper bags to put the stuff in.

While the children were busy playing, Anton and Hanna showed their guests the house, the three bedrooms, the elegant furnished living room with a bar, bibliotheca, a piano, and the television. They also showed the bathrooms with a built-in tub and took them out to the nearby sauna.

Last, they showed them the upstairs tower room from which they had a view in every direction. Of course Sepp had been here before with his wife.

Later, they all sat together in the living room. Hanna played the piano and Sasha his balalaika. Hanna also played pieces for them to sing-along, like "Dark Eyes," "Brahms' Lullaby," "Havah Nagila."

When it was late and time for bed, Hanna and Anton had their bedroom, the children with Erika in their room; an extra cot was added for Erika, Max and Ingrid had the guestroom, while Sepp and Inge went with Sasha and Isabella to their nearby cottage where there was also a guestroom.

The next couple days it snowed heavily, but on Christmas Eve the day was clear and cold. It was also David's birthday, and they would celebrate it along with Christmas in the evening. The children helped Hanna and Isabella set up and decorate the tree; presents for the children were laid around it.

In the afternoon they went skiing on the nearby hill; wisely Sasha had procured an extra pair for Erika, and the kids had fun while the adults watched.

Anton had heard from the general. He was already in his dacha and would come with his quasi-wife (his mistress) Natasha on Christmas Day, and Sasha had brought a goose for their festive dinner.

It was just getting dark, and they had supper and were getting ready for Christmas Eve and David's birthday when a car drove up. It was General Orlov who rushed into the house, a submachine gun in his hand, and motioned to Anton for a private audience. Anton took him up to the tower room.

Here is what the general told Anton, "A short while ago, one of my people from the FSB came to my dacha and told me that there would be an assassination attempt on you, Anton, tonight. He just found out himself in Moscow from an informer we have with the mafia. Well, he did right in coming at once to me, but he should have brought a troop of my men with him. It is Christmas night, and few were around, so he just got in the car to warn me. I sent him back to Moscow with Natasha. I got my gun and came to you at once."

Anton: I don't understand. Who wants to kill me? That I helped to round up the Munich mafia? That was seven years ago. Why now?

The general explained, "It has nothing to do with that. Apparently someone in the neo-Nazi organization in Munich went to the mafia there to hire them to kill you. This person also knew that you live in Israel now but that you have a dacha here. He asked the Munich mafia to get in touch with the Moscow group and do the job. As I understand, he paid 300,000 euros to have it done. The Moscow mafia has a ruthless assassin who only goes by the name of Ivan, a Georgian, a real professional killer. I called at once our security office in Alexandrov if they knew anything. All they knew was that a week ago someone removed a government license plate from one of their cars. So it looks like this Ivan has been driving around the area to find your place. The assassination is planned for Christmas Eve. He might be here already, or more likely he will come a little later when you all celebrate and it is pitch dark outside. Are you armed?"

Anton: I have my Beretta pistol.

General: Sasha has a Kalashnikov and a shotgun. Send him at once to get it. Then I guard the front door and he the back door. You take the shotgun and guard your people.

"What is his modus operandi?"

"Ivan uses a Markov pistol, supposed to be a good shot. He is an expert with a knife, uses a wicked serrated one. Likes to cut the throat for the silent kill or slit the belly open for his enjoyment."

"What if he uses explosives?"

"Ivan is never known to use them."

"How does he enter?"

"Often wears a mailman's outfit, delivery of special mail. Here he might be dressed as a security guard, I mean; he stole security plates, so he might act as a guard. Now, tell Sasha to get the rifles. What are you going to tell your people, Anton?"

"I hate to frighten them by telling them the truth, especially the children. I might just tell them that you told me there is a prowler around or a Peeping Tom."

"Not a Peeping Tom. For that you don't need an armory."

"Right. First I need to close the shutters."

"I go with you, Anton, your guard while you close up."

Anton told Sasha to get his Kalashnikov and shotgun.

When Sasha asked surprised, "What for?"

Anton replied, "The general believes there is a killer on the loose."

His families he told to remain in the living room as General Orlov warned him that a bad person is prowling round.

Anton got his Beretta and a strong flashlight. Then he and the general went outside, the general close to Anton and facing the trees while Anton closed the shutters of each window. They went back into the house, and Anton fastened the shutter latches.

Anton placed a chair by the front and back door. As he did, Hanna came out; she looked at Anton. "Now, Anton Hofer, tell me the truth!"

He knew; he could not hide anything from his wife. "The general told me that a killer is gunning for me. Now, Hanna, be a strong woman and take care of the families. Don't be frightened; they would notice it. The general, Sasha, and I will watch; both doors are guarded." When he smiled at her, she understood that he would take care of the matter.

She went to her husband and embraced him. "Be careful, Toni, please?" He nodded.

They went back outside waiting for Sasha; he came trotting back with the two rifles.

They went inside the house, the general sitting by the front door, his machine gun on his lap. Sasha took the back door. Anton wrapped a blanket around the shotgun, went into the living room, sat it by the door, and motioned to Hanna. She understood and would be a better last resort than Max and Sepp, neither a warrior. To Hanna he said, "Play something the families can sing along with. Isabella, take some wine to the general and Sasha; they are in the hallway." Sepp looked at Anton who only smiled and shook his head. He didn't need or want his help.

Hanna had the families sit on and around the large sofa; she turned the television on. "Let's watch *Swan Lake*."

Anton went upstairs into the tower room. From one window he had a good view of the road; below, in front of the house stood the general's car. It was now seven o'clock and dark, no moon yet; only the stars were giving feeble light over the snowy landscape.

It was less than an hour later that he saw from far away the headlights of a car; then they were extinguished. He knew that the assassin had arrived and would walk the last kilometer. Time to get going. He went downstairs and put on a warm jacket with a long bowie knife in his belt, in one hand his Beretta, in the other his flashlight.

"Our friend has arrived. I think I welcome him."

"Be careful, Anton; he is an expert," the general warned him.

Anton slipped out the front door. "Please lock behind me, Alex."

The snow in front of the house, as in the back, was trodden by many steps. He had to hide behind a tree to the side. He didn't have much time; it would only take at most a half hour for Ivan to walk to the dacha. He walked backward to the trees on the side of the dacha toward Sasha's cabin. There was a regular footpath nearby, but it would look like someone had walked through the snow to the house, not away from it. He stood behind a tree. How would he approach the dacha with evil intentions? Through the trees from the side. He walked farther back. Now, his eyes were adjusted to the darkness.

The first sign he had of Ivan was a soft crunching of snow. Then he saw the dark silhouette slowly approach through the trees. It stopped where he had walked backward.

The thin beam of a flashlight shined down. Ivan walked on, apparently satisfied that the track only led to the dacha. He followed the track to the door. There he stood still, just a dark shadow, not good enough to risk a shot. Then the beam of light shone against the door and just as briefly to either side where there were windows, shuttered.

There was only one way to get into the house through the door. He needed for someone to open. Anton heard him to knock against the door. A voice from the inside answered, probably the general, though Anton couldn't hear what was said. Then Ivan said loudly, "I am Dimitry, the security guard. I need to talk to the master of the house, Anton Hofer, please." Again a voice answered.

Ivan: I have an important message from the FSB office in Alexandrov for Hofer.

It was time to act. Anton sprinted toward the door; the crunching in the snow must have warned Ivan. A shot was fired in his direction; in the flash he saw the figure duck.

Anton fired low. He heard a groan; then the shadow darted away. He rushed to the door and shone his light for a moment down, a puddle of blood, a pistol, and pen light lying next to it. The door opened a fraction. "Anton?"

"I am all right, Alex. I hurt him. Lock the door again."

Using brief flashes of light, he followed the blood trail into the forest. He did not have to walk far; there was a small clearing, and he saw the shadow. He shone his light at it: a tall man in uniform, in his hand the long knife. The way he stood, legs apart, yet he stood more on his left leg, the right one to the side. He couldn't see any wound. Lower, and Anton saw that he had shot in his right ankle. The bullet must have hit the outside, and the boot was torn open on the inside, blood running out, his foot smashed. A wonder that he ran that far. He raised the beam to his face. A handsome man, his elongated face, high forehead, lush lips looked feminine. His light-blond hair almost white, smoothed down on both sides looked like a wig.

"Hello, Ivan. Is it Ivan the Terrible or Ivan the jerk?"

"Shoot me, you bastard!"

Anton put his pistol in his belt and drew his knife. "How do you want it Ivanova [addressing a female], cut your throat or slit your belly open the way you like to kill?"

With an unearthly scream, Ivan hurled himself at Anton, knocked the knife off his hand, and they both fell down. And already the strong hands of Ivan were around Anton's throat. Like a flash of memory Anton remembered when he killed the mass-murderer Huber, how he had stood too close and was surprised by Huber hurling himself at him and chocking him. And like then, Anton brought up his knees forcefully and hit into Ivan's crotch. Ivan was thrown back on his butt and then curled up in agony, squirming. Anton stood over him and then held him by his hair; it was not a wig. He lifted him partially up, then put his hands around his head, and with a powerful twist broke Ivan's neck.

He gathered up his Beretta, knife, and Ivan's knife to add to his collection of knives of assailants.

Only five minutes were gone since he left the dacha. He knocked and called "It is me, Anton." When the door opened, it was Hanna who rushed into his arms, her tears wetting his face.

"How is Ivan? Or I needn't ask," said the general.

"Ivan the Assassin is with Ivan the Terrible." They shook hands. Sasha came running and embraced Anton. They went into the living room and Max, as Sepp breathed sighs of relief. Inge, Ingrid, and Isabella were also happy though they had no idea what had happened; neither did the kids, though they all heard the shots.

It was time to celebrate David's birthday, and as a present he received a Kindle. David was an avid reader, knew English, and there was a world of literature open to him.

They lit the tree; Hanna played "Stille Nacht, Heilige Nacht." The children opened their presents. Isabella served tea, cake, and cookies; for the big people Anton made *Gluehwein* (hot-spiced wine).

The general had called the FSB office in Alexandrov. A crew came around midnight, and all men, but not the women and children, followed the bloody tracks to Ivan. When the lights of the crew shone on Ivan, they were surprised at his beauty—dead beauty.

The general remarked, "You deserve another medal, Anton."

Anton replied, "How about some of your fine Cuban cigars instead?"

The crew and the general returned with Ivan the Dead to Moscow and handed him over to the criminal police, who were mighty glad to add the infamous Ivan to the "has-been criminals."

On Christmas Day, the general came with Natasha for the goose dinner. He had brought a box of Habanas, and after dinner the men sat together in the living room with wine, vodka, and bourbon; with windows and open-smoked cigars, Anton told his story.

It had been a nice Christmas after all.

CHAPTER XVI

Traffickers, Extremists, Terrorists

The weekend at the end of the year and New Year Anton was on duty. New Year in Israel was a holiday as was the Jewish New Year of Rosh Hashanah, which had been in September. New Year of 2013 was on a Tuesday, and after a night of celebration things were fairly quiet in Jerusalem. Senior inspector Anton was the CO of the Jerusalem police for the day and sat in the duty room for the commanding officer, which was next to Avi Barlev's office. Here, with windows open, he could smoke his pipe. Barlev was a nonsmoker but permitted his officers to smoke—with window open.

He had spent the night here; there was a cot in a vestibule next to his office, and there had been nothing serious that required his presence. Now it was ten in the morning; and he was on his second cup of coffee, smoked his pipe, and read the reports of the night's activities. A call came from the guard. Mordechai Nevot came visiting. They had been close friends since 1982, when Anton came for the first time to Israel and was debriefed by Nevot, then the deputy officer of the Mossad.

Anton poured him a cup of coffee, and Nevot smoked his cigarette.

Nevot: So, Anton, what is new? Did you have a good time in your dacha in Russia?

Anton exhaled deeply. "So-so, I had an unfriendly visitor on Christmas Eve," and he related the business with Ivan then added the why he was a target for the assassin.

Nevot: Did you place a bomb on Bachleiter's boat?

"No. I exploded their auxiliary gas tank; it blew up like a bomb."

"Tell me, Anton, are there limitations to the use of the death ray?"

Anton smiled. "I guess. It is time to let you know. But you must promise not to tell anyone. Not even the Mossad, at least not for now." Nevot nodded, which was like a promise.

"Yes, there are severe limitations. The person to be eliminated must be out in the open and standing still. Walking slowly might work, but it is difficult to keep him in focus."

"Restrictions on localities, Anton?"

"No. Well, there is. Because of the locations of satellites, Australia and New Zealand are out."

"That makes the death ray almost limitless. What is it really? Our people believe it is a concentrated light beam, like a laser, but they do not understand how it is directed."

"It is not light but in the frequency of infrared, heat."

"And who invented that? You are not a scientist."

"I am, Nevot. I am a chemical engineer with a minor in nuclear science. Most of the invention was done by my friend Max Klausner. I suggested to him; it was during our discussion on astrophysics that electricity is not by electrons but a surge of photons stimulated by electrons. This led us into the idea that electricity could be transmitted wireless. Klausner is doing work on this and has the support of the Max Planck institute where he is a professor on energy. But then we realized that if electricity is a surge of photons, photons of different frequencies can be transmitted, and I suggested infrared. Klausner at once understood the implications of a death ray. Do away with baddies.

"He worked on it and succeeded. Then with Klausner's permission, I brought in my good friend the taxi driver Sepp Kainz, and we became the Force of Three. Kainz is not an academic but a good man, with lots of experience and wisdom. Also, I thought we need him as a counterforce to any extremism we might develop in going after the miscreants.

"The three of us formed a sort of tribunal where these evil people have their day in court, with one of us prosecuting, one defending, one the judge and we together are the jury.

"Each one of us has special interests to accuse those who deserve to be eliminated.

Klausner is after the Somali pirates and Mexican drug traffickers; Kainz considers war criminals, neo-Nazis, and other right-wing extremists as his targets; and I terrorists."

"And are you succeeding, Anton?"

"Yes and no. We just about stopped piracy. We can never stop the drug trafficking but *minder* the mass murder they commit. In one action we saved the lives of forty-two migrants just about to be shot by traffickers. War criminals? We eliminated a Lithuanian machine gunner who helped in shooting thousands of Jews, children, men, and women.

"We raised hell with the Estonian SS division veterans who meet regularly in Sinmae. Work like that."

"Yes, I read the manifestos. The last one was against terrorists. What terrorists, Anton?"

"Al-Qaeda and any of the other groups of Islamic fundamentalists, jihadists."

"Need the help of the Mossad?"

"If the Mossad has a special target in mind and can justify his elimination."

"As I understand it, you cannot eliminate a person in a house?"

"No. We cannot see into a house. We have to be able to see the person and hopefully a still-standing person. But we can burn a house down unless it has a stone roof."

"Limitations, I understand. How about Ahmadinejad who vowed to destroy Israel and al-Khamenei who bosses him and called Israel an insult to mankind?"

"They will be on our list of special targets but almost impossible for us to find in the open. Also the Revolutionary Guard whom I call the SS of Iran. There will be others on the list, like al-Maliki, the president of Iraq; a hate-mongering anti-Zionist; or Recep Erdogan, whom we warned in our manifesto."

"Anton, I hope you can do something with Iran before they have the bomb and use it against us."

"Nevot, this I don't understand. Remember the years of the sixties, seventies, and eighties, the enmity between the United States and the Soviet Union? At each other's throats; and yet, because of the threat of mutual annihilation, nothing happened, not even when Kennedy put a blockade on Soviet ships to Cuba. Why doesn't Israel declare in the world forum that if one bomb explodes in Israel, Tehran—in fact, all of Iran— will be destroyed?

"Besides, the Iranians would have to test a nuclear device first. When that happens, I am certain that the United States with Israel will attack the nuclear facilities in Iran. No planes needed. America can just use missiles from ships and subs. If Iran then sends missiles to Israel, like Iraq did, then it is time to warn them with nuclear retaliation."

"I pass your suggestion on. I don't know what agreements Netanyahu has with the American president. To come back to your mutual annihilation stand-off, do you know the proverb about the turtle and scorpion, Anton?"

"Yes, Nevot, I know it. And while the Iranians are not Arabs, it holds true for all fanatical Muslims. You mean to say that Iran would deliver a bomb to Israel regardless of their hundredfold retaliation? It would be suicide."

"You know that fanatics commit suicide to reach their goal."

"Ah, Nevot, but there is a big difference. The unknown fanatic commits suicide as he will become famous. In death he will be a hero, prayers will be said for him in all mosques, his family will be proud of him and receive money. But the leaders are already famous; they don't need suicide to become heroes. Have you ever heard of a bin Laden, al-Zawahiri, or Omar to commit suicide? Of course not. They treasure life. Ahmadinejad and al-Khamenei don't want to die, so the mutual stand-off is a reality."

"You are right, Anton. Well, I carefully pass on the possibility of eliminating certain evil personage, perhaps in Gaza with Hamas or with the Hezbollah in Lebanon. I just hint that I can be in touch with the world tribunal. God bless you and your colleagues."

"God has nothing to do with it, Nevot."

"You don't believe in God? You a good Christian?"

"I believe in God, perhaps not your God. I am a traditional Christian. I practice my Catholic faith because my mother was a good Christian. I don't believe in the omnipotence of God. If God could have stopped the monstrous Holocaust but did not, he becomes an accessory to mass murder. I don't want to believe that God is a mass murderer of over a million children alone. Therefore, I believe that God has only spiritual influence. He gave mankind the spirit of love, and man can be good. He chose Abraham and his descendants to receive his spiritual guidance. The Jews, his chosen people, and see what it has brought them. But I hope that Israel is not counting on God's help against the Iranians."

"The Old and New Testament, Jesus, the sayings of the Apostles, not God given?"

"Legends. I don't believe that Jesus is the Son of God. A prophet, influenced by God, yes, but not resurrection. Look, Nevot, let's not get into our religious believes. You are a Jew, a good Jew. Consider me a good Christian, that is all."

"Goodbye, Anton. You will hear from me."

"Goodbye, friend."

At a late Sunday morning meeting of the neo-Nazi Bund (many were practicing church members and attended morning mass), the leader Gersten told of the failure of the assassination attempt. Police sergeant Fred Schultheis was at the meeting, and in due time Anton was informed. He now knew why there had been an attempt on his life and who arranged the assassination. He asked Sepp to check on Gersten and find his daily habits of going to work, etc. Sepp soon found out that Gersten, who owned a fast-food store in the city but lived with his family in an apartment house in Schwabing, drove every morning at six o'clock in his white Mercedes to his place of business alone. Sepp even supplied the license number. At one of his weekend visits, Anton was very early at the apartment house. It was easy for him to get into the garage and attach a bomb under the seat of Gersten's Mercedes. He timed the bomb to go off five minutes after the car was started to give time for him to warm up and leave the building. The bomb exploded a few blocks from the building; since it was early in the morning, no other cars were involved. The same Friday, antiterror inspector Stefan Wagner and bomb squad sergeant Franz Oettinger investigated the bombing. It had been a professional job; the bomb under the seat was not powerful but enough to kill the driver. Sergeant Oettinger remarked to the inspector that it was a shame that bomb expert inspector Nagil was no longer with them, which made Inspector Wagner smile knowingly. "You are right, Franz; it is regretful."

The incident was reported in the next day's newspapers headlined new neo-nazi bund leader killed by bomb.

The knowledge that their previous leader Horst Bachleiter and his son Gustav and now their new leader Gersten had been killed caused many members of the Bund to look out for their own safety, and the membership declined.

THE YEAR 2013

They met again on Friday, the fourth of January. Max and Sepp were in the energy house when Anton came late in the afternoon. Max had the city of La Paz in view, and as he explained he was looking for a policeman to guide them to Therese Vargas's house. It was easy enough to find a policeman, but to establish voice contact, he must either find a police car that had the radio on or one walking who carried a radio or was talking on his cell phone. At last they found one talking on his phone. It was now six o'clock, 9:00 a.m. in La Paz. Max listened in. He laughed. "This man is talking to his wife, and she gives him a list of things to buy." He listened for a couple minutes. "Just chatter. Wives can talk endlessly. I better interrupt." He took the microphone and of course spoke in Spanish, "Hello, my friend, please get your wife off the line. Tell her you have important police business but leave the phone activated. All right, my friend, what is your name?"

Voice: Arturo Lopez. How can you get on my line?

Max: Don't worry about it, Arturo. You heard about the world tribunal?

"Yes, I read something about it, combating the drug cartels."

"Right, Arturo. Do you know the house of the Vargas? I can give you the address."

"I know the place. What do you want me to do?"

"You don't have a car. Take a taxi to the house and get out. Then just walk away. I am sorry if I cause you to pay for the taxi. Just tell your supervisor what you did and why. Let him give you the money back."

"No problem. Taxis don't charge us for police business. May I ask what you want from the Vargas?"

"We suspect that Senor Vargas is really the leader of the Sinaloa cartel, Guzman Lorea. His house is a meeting place of all cartel leaders."

"If I take a taxi there, can you follow me?"

"No problem, Arturo."

"Tell me, man from the world tribunal, can I tell my story to the newspaper? They would pay me well."

"I advice you not to do that. The cartel people would be after you. Just tell your supervisors—that is, if you can trust them."

"I guess I better not tell anyone. But glad to be of service to you."

"You are a good policeman, Arturo Lopez. Out."

They watched as Lopez hailed a taxi and then followed it. It took them through the city to the northern outskirts. In a street with many elegant houses, the taxi stopped by a mansion with a large garden, a pool. Lopez got out and pointed at the big white house, then got back into the taxi, and drove off.

It was early in the morning and no sign of life. Max zeroed in on the house; and to their dismay, it had a stone roof, with a balustrade around it, in the middle a stone staircase.

This would lead to a door, but from above they could not see it.

"Let's try the chimneys," suggested Anton. There were two. "Chimney fires can be dangerous." Max brought the view close to the larger chimney. Anton used five thousand degrees and a one-second pulse. Nothing. A second pulse and nothing could be seen. A third pulse and thick black smoke came from the chimney that quickly increased in intensity.

Then smoke streamed out from an open window on the first floor. Windows were opened on the third floor. People looked out. Then men and women exited from the main entrance. Most were still in their night cloth, one, a beautiful woman in a fancy robe, maybe Mrs. Vargas? The fire had started on the first floor and quickly burned up to the second and third floors. By the time the fire department came, the house was aflame, black smoke billowing up. They could not save the house; it was a total loss.

Max wondered if Guzman realized that it was the world tribunal who fired his house.

Anton said, "He should. I am certain he will be told that on a nice, sunny, and warm day in La Paz, they didn't use the fireplace. Anther chip in the war against the cartels."

Sepp wondered how to find members of the American neo-Nazi Aryan Nation group.

"Aren't they somewhere in Texas?"

Anton thought that they held their meetings in Idaho. "Probably east of Boise in the forest or around the Coeur d'Alene area or farther east in the mountains. I read that they hold their war games there, though we have to be careful to differentiate them from regular gun clubs."

Sepp: How can we?

Anton: Knowing how the neo-Nazis operate, they will have something Nazi-like around. Maybe even the swastika flag or a flag showing the Iron Cross. Wear uniforms and the *Stahlhelm*.

Max: Isn't it winter there? All full of snow?

Anton: You are right, Max. We have to wait for spring.

Sepp: How about in Texas?

Anton: I know nothing about their war games in Texas. But I try to find out.

Max: In the meantime I get acquainted with the area there; that is in Idaho.

Max showed Anton a newspaper article advertising a seminar at the University of Munich in regard to the world tribunal. "One of the speakers is your friend and former colleague Stefan Wagner." The seminar was sponsored by the university and scheduled for Saturday at three o'clock in the library hall.

"I think I'll attend," replied Anton.

All three decided to attend, and Sepp brought them in his taxi. Shortly before three, they entered the hall, which was really a theater where movies were shown. On the stage were the chairs of the participants in a half circle facing the audience. The theater was full with students, the first row reserved for the press, teachers, and guests. The three compatriots sat in the back near the center, and when the participants entered along the aisle, Anton and Inspector Wagner made eye contact and smiled. It was ironical that the subject matter presented, the world tribunal, had the Force of Three present and one of its founders' friend, police inspector Wagner, was supposed to discuss this subject. Inspector Wagner strongly suspected that his friend Anton was with the tribunal, though he was not 100 percent certain.

Professor Baumgaertel from the law department of the university was the MC and introduced the members of the panel, including chief inspector Wagner from the antiterror unit of the Munich police. In fact, at the beginning of the panel's discussion, Prof. Baumgartel turned to the inspector and asked, "The newspapers this morning reported the bombing of a car in Munich and the killing of a Herr Joachim Gersten. Since Herr Gersten is also reported as a member of the right-wing neo-Nazi's Bund, might there be any connection to the world tribunal? The tribunal in its third manifesto accused neo-Nazis of belonging to an organization, which the tribunal considers as targets to eliminate."

Inspector Wagner: I, as responsible police officer of the antiterror unit, investigated the bombing this morning. While it is true that Herr Gersten is, or was, a member of this right-wing group, we in the police see no connection to the tribunal. The tribunal exclusively uses the death ray to eliminate those it designates as criminals against mankind.

Someone in the audience shouted, "How about the bombing of Herr Bachleiter and his son when they fished peacefully in Lake Stanberg?"

Professor Baumgaertel: At this point, please do not interrupt the proceedings of the panel. Later, there will be time to take questions from the audience. However, since the question was asked, please, Inspector Wagner?

Wagner: The matter was extensively investigated by the Seeshaupt police. Also, our police laboratory investigated by examining debris. They reported that no traces of explosives were found. We accepted the conclusion of the police that apparently there was a leak in the auxiliary gas tank. Herr Bachleiter who is known to be a heavy smoker most likely brought a burning cigarette near the fumes and caused a fire, which exploded the gas tank.

Therefore, the explosion of the boat and the subsequent death of Herr Bachleiter and his son Gustav was ruled an accident. As to the bombing of Herr Gersten's car and his death, the police department is investigating. We are also searching for a motive; was it by an anti-Nazi person or group? Or perhaps a feud within the Bund? All we know at this point is that Herr Gersten was the new leader. The use of a bomb or explosive is a rare occurrence in Munich and Bavaria. We don't know of any criminals who use such methods or, for that mater, any political group. Our forensic people stated that the bomb used had a small output; the explosive was plastic and the mechanism by an expert.

The next speaker was chief inspector Vogel from the Bka (Bundeskriminalamt) who spoke about the manifestos received by the Suisse newspaper. The various reports by foreign departments detailing actions of the world tribunal in their countries, including the saving of forty-two migrants in Mexico about to be murdered by drug traffickers.

He concluded, "So far, the achievements of the tribunal have been remarkable. Piracy in the Gulf of Aden and the Indian Ocean has practically stopped. Combating the Mexican drug cartels has resulted in diminished killings of both innocents and warfare between the various cartels. The third manifesto was directed against former war criminals. Though there are few around and probably difficult to find as they would be in their nineties, we had a report from Lithuania that a former machine gunner who killed thousands was eliminated by this death ray. From Poland we have a report that a village, which at the beginning of the World War killed 340 Jews by locking them in a barn and burning them alive, was torched. This third manifesto also stated that the tribunal will punish, if this is the right expression to use, neo-Nazis, fascists, and those with like political philosophies; and here we had a report of action in Estonia where at a meeting of SS veterans of the Baltic countries, several veterans were killed by death ray. The sponsor of this meeting, a baron Feodor von Reva, a former veteran of the Estonian SS division, was killed and his mansion torched.

"The last and fourth manifesto was directed against terrorists, specifically Islamic extremists. Also in it certain world leaders were warned to desist from mongering and inciting against other nations or persons of other than Islamic religion. So far, there are no reports that such actions have occurred."

Professor Baumgaertel: Chief inspector Vogel, would you please describe the confusion that exists to pinpoint the origin of the tribunal?

Inspector Vogel: The power of the tribunal seems limitless. They apparently can reach any place of earth. He then spoke about the many localities from where the paper and envelopes came, the places of mailing, the different languages used in communications.

Nothing pointing to a definite country and place of origin.

Professor Baumgaertel: Chief engineer Huber from the technical school can give us an idea what techniques are used by the tribunal.

Engineer Huber: The technique used the world tribunal is far advanced to anything known to exist on our planet. The so-called death ray must be a laser beam as its effect is heat. Simultaneously they have the capability to see, to speak, and to hear. How can a laser beam be directed, as it is light and surges in a straight line? We can do it both in tiny distances and long but again only in a straight line, like a visual beam. At first, when the pirates were killed and their ship set on fire, we thought it was projected from another ship. The Mexican actions made us believe that the beams came from above, from perhaps a plane or a drone.

However, the American government assured us that they are not involved, and we at the engineering department believe them. Then the killings in Lithuania, a pinpoint heat radiation at the head of the machine gunner, similar to the killings in Estonia. A careful analysis showed us that the beam comes from above. If not from a plane or drone, then perhaps from a satellite? But again the pinpoint accuracy is puzzling to us. Besides, few nations have satellites, and those who do assure us that they have nothing to do with the laser beams. We just don't know!

Professor Baumgaertel: Thank you, engineer Huber. Our last panel participant is Professor Moll from the political science department.

Professor Moll: In my department I established a panel similar to this one, with eminent doctors and professors of psychology, history, social sciences, jurisprudence, and related fields to get at the root of our problem: who are these people of the world tribunal? From a political point of view, they are not right-wing. Of course not as they wish to eliminate right-wing extremists, radicals. Left-wing extreme liberals? They are not known to kill people, rather persuade within the political process. We finally decided not to give them a right—or left-leaning designation. Now, what do they want? They give us their desires in their manifestos. Basically to combat those who harm mankind and are beyond anyone's judicial jurisdiction. Therefore, they do not have a political agenda and seem to be free of any national association. What have they done so far? Brought a mass murderer to justice in Lithuania who should have been brought to trial eons ago. All their killings for punishment or to prevent killings were conducted in third-world countries where these miscreants are either tolerated or protected, or as in Mexico where the government is willing to combat them but unable to control them. While there is an obvious danger to have such a private group or organization with such power in existence, we concluded that so far the world tribunal is not a danger but rather a benefit to the nations of earth. Let me add. Let the rogue nations such as Iran and North Korea beware.

Professor Baumgaertel: Thank you, Professor Moll. Now, questions from our students?

There were many intelligent questions, most pertaining to the origin of the tribunal. Many thought that America was involved despite their denial, basing their opinion on the fact that the American government was concerned about the drug trafficking from Mexico. Also that the last two manifestos were mailed from New York and American paper and envelopes were used. One student thought that it was a Russian operation since the first letter was sent in a Russian envelope. He stated, "The tribunal was careless the first time, wrote the letter on German paper to disguise the source but then only had a local envelope available. They did not think that it could be examined and found to be local. Also, as Inspector Vogel reported, the voice in Poland and Lithuania spoke Russian without a foreign accent. And the tribunal spokesman who had this conversation with police officer Mikulis in Kovno stated that the spokesman was mainly interested in the shooting of Soviet prisoners."

This was countered by a student who stood up (all students who were asking a question or making a statement stood up and said their names) and said, "My name is Karl

Ludwig. I believe the operation is Jewish. I read the *Protocol of the Elders*, and this book tells about the Jews wishing to dominate the world. The Zionist country has many Jews who are smart and must have developed the death ray. Also, I read that the Jews wish to fight the Mexican drug cartels as they are in competition with their own drug trafficking. By poisoning the world with drugs, the Jews want to dominate the world." The student sat down. He was the same one who asked about the Bachleiter accident. Now Anton could see him, a young blond man.

Professor Baumgaertel: I believe I speak for the panel and most students when I declare your statement utter nonsense. In fact, it is pure anti-Semitic slander. I cannot believe that in our new liberal Germany such slander is still in vogue as it would have been during the Nazi period. Young man, grow up and fit into our modern society.

It was past five o'clock when the meeting was over. Sepp had left a few minutes earlier to start the car and heater as an icy wind blew; also, it was getting dark outside. When Anton and Max walked to the taxi, they saw a commotion there. Several students were arguing with Sepp; apparently they had wanted to use the taxi, and Sepp had refused them.

Anton saw at once that one of the loudmouthed students arguing was this Karl Ludwig.

He smiled at the student. "Can I help you, Ludwig?"

Karl Ludwig: We wanted to use the taxi, and he said it is reserved. There is no such thing as a reserved taxi; the driver has to take first come, first serve.

Anton: As it happens, I reserved the taxi. You are the student who made this asinine statement about Israel making the death ray to dominate the world?

Ludwig yelled, "You call me stupid?"

Anton still smiled. "Stupid is complimenting you, Ludwig. I should call you a lot worse things!"

Ludwig sneered, "You must be a dirty Jew!"

Anton was now angry. "I am neither a Jew nor dirty. Now scatter or I teach you a lesson in civility if this is possible."

Ludwig screamed, "LET'S GET HIM!" He jumped at Anton and swung his fist at his face.

Anton parried the arm, held on to it, and forcefully swung it around his back, dislocating his shoulder. The three companions of Ludwig also came at Anton with their fists swinging; the first Anton hit at his chin, breaking it; he fell down stunned. The second Anton kicked in the right knee; he crashed to the ground squirming in pain. The third he grabbed by the arms, hurled him around like a sack of potatoes, and slammed him against a street lamp post. He too was just a formless heap on the sidewalk.

Students stood around and clapped their hands.

Then Inspector Wagner appeared. "I saw what happened. You were attacked by these hoodlums. I guess I better call the police wagon."

Anton smiled at his friend. "I think they better need an ambulance."

While Inspector Wagner made his call, he waved Anton off to leave.

They left in Sepp's taxi. After taking Max home, they went to Anton's house and enjoyed good cigars, a couple bottles of beer, and fine bourbon.

As Inspector Wagner told Anton at a later meeting, when he wrote his report, he referred to Anton as an unknown person who was attacked by four belligerent students, defended himself, and in the process injured the students.

Also, Fred Schultheiss told him that Karl Ludwig wore his arm in a sling for a long time as his shoulder was wrenched; one of the others had a broken chin, one had broken ribs, the third had his leg in a cast for many months. All four students were members of the Bund. The Nazi-Bund was just a small group as many had left for safety concerns.

Gratifying to Anton was when Stefan Wagner told him that the university expelled Karl Ludwig and his three companions for hooliganism.

A few days after this incident, Professor Moll from the political science department visited Inspector Wagner at police headquarters.

Inspector Wagner, after welcoming the professor in his office, asked, "What can I do for you, Professor Moll?"

Moll: One of my students who witnessed this debacle about the taxi saw that you spoke to this man who roughed up these four hoodlums and then waved him off. Yet the newspaper account spoke about an unknown person. May I venture the thought that you wished to not cause this man any troubles or perhaps retaliation? Who is this man? We would like to have him speak to our students, and by the way, Karl Ludwig and his rowdy companions were expelled from the university.

Wagner smiled. "Yes, dear professor Moll, your student saw it right. I did not wish to involve this man as he is a friend of mine and a former police colleague."

Moll: This man—and I do not need to know his identity at this point—seems quite extraordinary and skillful in hand combat. Anything special about him? And if I may ask, with his abilities, why is he no longer with the police?

Wagner: He is really a chemical engineer, an expert in explosives. He was our bomb disposal officer. But how often did we encounter this problem? I believe his first love was science; therefore, he left the police department and now works for the Max Plank Institute as a chemist.

"He studied at our university?"

"No, though he was born in Munich. He has a most interesting background. His father was during the war a SS officer, in charge of a killing commando in Lithuania. Declared a war criminal. However, after the war he took flight to Cairo. That is where this man grew up. Attended the university in Cairo and took his master's in the United States.

"He was in the Egyptian army where he became an explosive expert, of course speaks fluently Arabic. Interestingly, he went to Afghanistan in 1998 with a Muslim friend of his as his protector since Afghanistan was at that time under the reign of the Taliban.

"His friend was killed by a fanatic; and this man had to flee from the Taliban, crossed through Afghanistan, and escaped into Uzbekistan."

"May I ask, with his father having been in the SS, surely a prominent Nazi, is his son, this man we are speaking of, also a neo-Nazi? This Karl Ludwig and his cohorts did not seem to know him?"

"Oh no, this man is not a Nazi. In fact, as he told me, when he was a boy, his father died and his mother let him read his father's war diary. How he was the commandant of Fort

IX in Kovno and participated in the killings of Jews. The boy was so shocked by these revelations that he disowned this SS officer as his father. After his mother died a few years ago, he even changed his family name to his mother's maternal name. His mother returned to Munich in the midnineties to her ancestral home here in Munich, and that is the home of this man."

"That is most interesting. In my class we are just studying the war against the Taliban by the NATO forces and in general the popular uprisings in Muslim countries. Would it be possible for your friend and ex-colleague to talk to my students about these subjects, specifically about the Taliban, their goal in Afghanistan?"

Inspector Wagner smiled. "I can ask him. Perhaps if you do not advertise it as a seminar and keep it small, just your class."

Inspector Wagner queried his friend Anton about giving this class in regard to the Taliban and Anton; as a favor to Stefan, Anton agreed.

Anton had come Friday, the eleventh of January. Sepp had picked him up at the airport; they had lunch and then went to the university. The class was scheduled for 2:00 p.m., and it was not in the classroom of Professor Moll but in the theater as several classes wished to attend.

He was invited to sit with Sepp in the first row with teachers.

Professor Moll was on the podium and used a microphone to be heard by the several hundred students. "Before I introduce the speaker, let me briefly tell about him. As you all know, he had an altercation after the seminar, was attacked by four students, and rendered them incapable. The four students were members of the neo-Nazi Bund, and to avoid retaliation by the Bund, our speaker will remain anonymous. Since he has a master in chemical engineering, you may address our speaker as doctor.

"Briefly, the doctor was born in our city but lived with his family in Cairo, Egypt. He attended the Cairo University and took his master's in the United States. When his mother returned in the midnineties to her home in Munich, he joined her with his family. He was for three years active in the Egyptian army where he became an explosive expert. In 1998, he visited Afghanistan—that is, Taliban Afghanistan. Since my class is studying this country and the Taliban, you may ask the doctor questions pertaining to this subject.

Please, doctor."

Anton came on the stage and took the microphone.

(Each student who wanted to ask a question raised his hand and when recognized by Professor Moll, who remained by Anton, stated his name. While different students asked, some had follow-up questions.)

Student: Do you speak Arabic, doctor?

"Yes."

"Are you a Muslim?"

"No, I am like my family was, a Catholic."

"Where you discriminated in Egypt since you were a Christian?"

"No. Under President Mubarak there was little discrimination against Christians or Jews. Most Christians in Egypt are of the Coptic faith; however, they are a minority."

Different student, "Why did you visit Taliban Afghanistan?"

Anton smiled. "It is a long story. Briefly, I grew up with a Muslim boy; his name was Ali Nasr. He went to the famous religious school and mosque Al-Azhar and became an imam. Ali and I were the best of friends; in 1998 Ali wanted to visit Afghanistan to bring his message of peace given by the Koran to Egyptian freedom fighters. Ali wanted me to accompany him as his protector, not physical protection but spiritual influence so he would not fall under the spell of jihadists. We were assigned to the el-Badr camp for freedom fighters, near Khost in southeast Afghanistan. However, Ali was shot by a jihadist, and I had to flee."

"How could you go to a Taliban camp as a Christian?"

"Having black hair, suntanned as I was, growing a beard, I looked like an Arab. My Arabic was fluent Egyptian. Only the camp commander knew who I was. Besides, there were a number of Europeans in the camp, albeit all the Muslim faith. It was one of those who knew me as a Christian who told the others."

"Why was your friend Ali shot? And by whom?"

"Now you make me branch out and tell you more. I went with the blessing of the Egyptian Islamic jihad. I was supposed to teach the jihadists bomb making, I, the explosive expert. Let me assure you. I taught them nothing. I showed them, that is all. The reason that they— that is, the Taliban—permitted me to come as a Christian was that their explosive experts were in Africa and they were in desperate need to have a teacher. Those in Africa detonated big bombs in cars or trucks at the American embassies in Nairobi and Dar es Salaam and killed hundreds, though few were Americans. The American retaliated by sending missiles against Taliban camps, including ours. This infuriated the jihadists, and knowing I was a Christian by then, they came after me. This Yemeni raised his rifle to shoot me, but Ali stepped in front of me and was shot. I hit the Yemeni with a shovel, smashed his face, and blinded him. My stay became impossible, and the camp commander gave me a van to flee. With me, the friend of Ali a young man by the name of Sidqi. We managed to escape and fought our way into the Panjshir Valley, which was under the command of Shah Massoud. Masssoud was in opposition to the Taliban and helped us escape to Uzbekistan. From there we went to Russia and back to Cairo."

"Why was this Massoud in opposition? I thought when the Taliban ruled they controlled all of Afghanistan?"

"No, there was the Northern Alliance under Shah Massoud in opposition. You must understand that Taliban rule is by the law of Sharia. There are many who do not wish to be ruled by these extreme religious really medieval laws. Rural people and most members of the various tribes favor Sharia but not the men of education and culture, in fact, city people."

"Why should we care what religion people follow? Why are we even in Afghanistan?"

"That is a good question. It is, of course, mainly the Americans who are fighting there.

The Americans went there to get Osama bin Laden after 9/11. They wanted the Taliban to either extradite bin Laden or kick him out of the country. The Taliban didn't want to do that, so the Americans with NATO went there to get him. Once he escaped to Bora-Bora and hid in

Northern Waziristan or Pakistan, they should have left. They are fighting a religious war as most Afghan men wish to live under Sharia."

Other student: To liberate womanhood?

"Well, yes and no. Most women who live in tribal areas are content to live under Sharia. But those who are educated and have tasted freedom from oppression do not."

Female student: What is so bad for women to live under Shariah?

Anton took a slip from his pocket. "Just in case someone asked me, I brought this note along. I copied this note from a Taliban hospital where our friend Sidqi was recovering from a severe concussion. Let me read it; it was nailed to the wall by a Taliban clergy."

1. Under the law of Sharia, this being a hospital for men, women are forbidden to enter.
2. Ban on women being treated by male doctors.
3. Women doctors and nurses only are permitted to treat female patients.
4. Sick women may travel by bus to Kabul only in buses designated for women.
5. Ban on women working outside the home.
6. Ban on women dealing with male shopkeepers.
7. Ban on females studying in schools and universities.
8. Requirement for women to wear the burqa.
9. Women will be publicly whipped for having uncovered ankles.
10. Public stoning of women accused of extramarital affairs.
11. Ban on women using cosmetics. Punishment is cutting off fingers.
12. Ban on women shaking hands with non-mahram males.
13. Ban on women laughing loudly.
14. Ban on women riding in a taxi without a mahram.
15. Ban on women playing sports.
16. Ban on women wearing brightly colored clothes.
17. Changing all names of places including the word "woman."
18. Ban on women appearing on the balconies of apartments or houses.
19. All windows of apartments and houses where women live must be painted black.

"Not to your liking, miss?"

"Terrible. Yes, I can see the war in Afghanistan to liberate womanhood. Even those women who don't know any better, once they taste freedom from oppression by the men, they would chuck Sharia. What is a mahram?"

"A male relative."

"Public stoning? They kill her?"

"Yes. She has to kneel. Then men hurl stones and rocks at her until she lies severely injured on the ground; then a relative, often the father or a brother, kills her by smashing a rock on her head."

Other female student: Doctor, you call the Taliban a religious movement and not a terrorist organization. And even the fourth manifesto of the world tribunal—while condemning terrorists, al-Qaeda, and its many branches—does not mention the Taliban as being terroristic. Yet I read in the newspaper—it was back in October of last year—that a young girl by the name of Malala Yousufzai was shot by a Taliban. Malala was a fourteen-year-old schoolgirl. Since she was eleven, she became interested in the suppression of the women by the Taliban, that they don't want the girls to go to school.

School meant so much to Malala as she wanted to become a doctor and help people. On that day in October, she was in the bus with other girls going home from school. This was in the Swat Valley, wherever that is in Pakistan. A car came and stopped the bus. Then a Taliban walked into the bus, asked which one Malala Yousufzai is. He then shot Malala into the head and neck. She was taken to a hospital in Peshawar, in critical condition. I never read a follow-up story if she survived and if she did if she is a living girl again or just comatose. I sincerely hope she is all right. But the deed! A Taliban goes into a school bus to assassinate a kid. And the Taliban was quick to claim responsibility for shooting Malala. A Taliban spokesman even said, "This was a new chapter of obscenity, and we have to finish this chapter." Threatened to shoot her again if she survives. I mean, what kind of people are the Taliban if they murder even children? You say it is a religious movement who prefer the extremism of Sharia. I believe that either this religion is monstrous or that the Taliban are really murderous terrorists and not religious at all.

"DEATH TO THE TALIBAN!" someone yelled and like a chorus, the students repeated in unison "DEATH TO THE TALIBAN!" until Professor Moll raised his hand for silence.

The female student continued, "While the fourth manifesto of the world tribunal does not mention the Taliban as terrorists, yet they are obviously just as bad as al-Qaeda."

Anton pointed at her. "Perhaps you should write to the world tribunal to include the Taliban as terrorists."

Student: How can I do that? How does one get in touch with the tribunal?

Anton: Write a letter to the editor of the *Berner Nachrichten*. I believe his name is Sebastian Konrad. The world tribunal communicates exclusively with this Suisse newspaper, the *Berner Nachrichten*. I am certain that they read the paper.

Student: I think I shall do that.

Another female student: Write in the name of all the female students of our university.

Male student: Why not in the name of all students? We men are just as abhorred by this assassination attempt of a young schoolgirl.

Professor Moll: Anyone here who objects? No? Then please, in the name of all students.

Student: Doctor, do you approve of the Arab Spring?

"I never called it the Arab Spring. From the beginning of the Tunisian uprising, I called it the Arab Winter. The freedom we enjoy, the democracy we seek or have, cannot exist in an Islamic nation. It goes against their very culture, the ancient culture of desert people, unchanged since the times of the Prophet."

A student: But the educated Muslims, the city people, young people who want freedom, they demonstrated against the rulers, didn't they want a democratic form of government?

"Yes, that is true. But they are also a minority and without power. All these uprisings against their leaders, who were dictators, were in the end dominated by those who seek government by religion according to the Koran, by Sharia. A good example is Egypt where the Brotherhood won the election and presidency. Under President Mubarak, the Brotherhood was banned, yet tolerated as long as they didn't make mischief. Egypt was then a free country: Christians could worship freely; so did Jews. Egypt had diplomatic relations with Israel. Tourist enjoyed visiting the country. Today, after free elections, the Brotherhood rules. Tourists are afraid to visit. Egypt is in economic distress, unemployment is sky high, and if it weren't for American help, the people would starve."

A student: Why is America helping them? I mean, Egypt is again a totalitarian country, even worse than under Mubarak.

"This is a good question. If it were up to the Brotherhood and their president Morsi,

Egypt would at once abrogate the peace treaty with Israel and start troubles in the Sinai against Israel, probably leading to another war. However, there is the military that doesn't want this war; neither does the business and educated class. While they are the minority, they have the power of arms. America supports the military financially and with weapons to keep them in power and keep the peace. America also provides economic aid to the government of the Brotherhood. I am certain that Washington threatens the Brotherhood with loss of economic aid if they don't behave, like they did in September of last year after the demonstrations against the anti-Islamic film. These demonstrations were sponsored by President Morsi until President Obama called Morsi and told him to stop the upheavals or America would stop their economic aid, and it worked. President Morsi called off the million-man march to demonstrate against America."

A student: What is it with the Muslims? Why are they so sensitive when someone says something nasty about Mohamed or the Koran? I mean, you can say something bad about Jesus or even deny god, and while it may lead to an argument, it won't lead to demonstrations or bloody warfare. Another question, is their Allah the same God as ours?

"First of all the correct name for the prophet is Prophet Mohammad. Yes, Allah is also our God, the God of the Jews and Christians. Why are Muslims so sensitive about their religion? Well, again you have to split the Muslims into two factions. The educated, the business oriented—in fact, the city people versus the uneducated, the tribal people who are the majority. To the various tribes—and here it doesn't matter if they are Shiites or Sunnis—religion is to them a way of life; they are very devoted, pray five times a day.

Tribal life is simple life; and it is directed by religious laws, either Shariah, which is the extreme interpretation of the Koran, or a more moderate version."

A student: What is the difference between the Shiites and Sunnis? Why do they hate and fight each other?

"Ah, remember the medieval times when the Catholics and Protestants were fighting each other? Today we can only wonder about the why. During the past five centuries, we have become civilized. Let me put a question mark to that statement. But in our modern times we would not think of holding the religious beliefs of someone against him. Catholics, Protestants, and there are many split-offs—Mormons, Jehovah's Witnesses—they are all Christians. We accept anyone's religion, right? Muslims are mainly split into these two factions, though again there are smaller groups who practice Islam differently, mainly due to tribal customs. But the difference between Shiites and Sunnis has to do with the heir of the Prophet. He did not leave or designate an heir. Islam's schism goes back more that 1,300 years. It began in 632, after Prophet Mohammad died without naming a successor. Many Islamists believed that the role of Caliph, meaning Viceroy of Allah, should be given to the bloodline of the Prophet, his cousin or son-in-law. However, the majority chose the Prophet's friend Abu Bakr, who then became Caliph.

The son-in-law Ali ibn Abi Talib became the fourth Caliph. Ali was killed, and the succession was again disputed and led to a formal split. Ali's followers became the Shiites. So there you have the origin of the schism. Usually the two groups get along fine, but anything can set them off like the holiday of the Ashura, when Shiites commemorate the killing and decapitating of Ali's son Hussein or a clergy mongers against either sect or a ruler exploits the schism for power, like Hussein did in Iraq. Hussein was a Sunni, and Iraq discriminated against Shiites. Today we have al-Maliki in power; he is a Shiite, and they rule over the Sunnis and fight each other. Iran and Syria are Shiites; so is the Iran-supported Hezbollah in Lebanon. We have to understand the mind-set of the Arab. Most Arabs are rural and subscribe to tribal customs dating back a thousand years, as are their religious laws of Sharia. Are then these tribal people rather primitive? In our eyes they are. They are very emotional, especially if you criticize their religion or the Prophet. Then they easily hate and can be very brutal and sadistic. On the other hand, they are very friendly, and hospitality is like a religious command to them.

"The main problem is that we live in the twenty-first century; and tribal Arabs live like they always did and see no reason and willingness to change, become modern, and tolerate nonbelievers. Fanatical Arabs wish for the rest of the world to convert to Islamism and live under one Caliph."

Female student: I once believed that our problems with the Muslims are because of Israel. But when Iran and Iraq fought a war and Iraq invaded Kuwait, I realized that Israel is only one problem. Who is right there in the Middle East, the Zionists or the Arabs?

"First of all, you call the Jews or Israelis there Zionists. But many who refer to the Israelis as Zionists, or Israel as the Zionist entity like Ahmadinejad does, mean it derogatory. A Zionist is a person who believes that the Jews should have a homeland, especially after the Holocaust, to let the genocide never happen again or give a safe haven to Jews. Winston Churchill was a confirmed Zionist. So are most leaders of our modern world. Are you familiar with the Old Testament, miss?"

She smiled. "I read about Adam and Eve, that they were naked in the Garden of Eden, about the snake and apple."

There was snickering and laughing in the audience.

"Well, I am glad that you remember something about the beginning of God's relationship with mankind. Let me ask you, dear miss. Are you a believer in God or an atheist?"

"Of course I believe in God and I guess in the Jew's Bible as it precedes the New Testament."

"Then let me go back in the Old Testament and refresh your memory, the times after the flood and Noah. There was a man by the name of Abram who was an Aramean and lived in Ur of Chaldee. God chose him to go to the land of Canaan. Canaan was a descendant of Noah, a man whom God favored over all other men. Then it was Abram whom God favored and spoke to him, named him Abraham and his wife Sarai Sarah.

God made a covenant with Abraham and told him he will be the father of many nations.

His descendants would receive the land of Canaan for perpetuity and God said, 'And I will be their God.' Now here comes the split as Abraham, or Ibrahim as the Muslims call him, is the father of both people, the Jews and Muslims.

"Abraham, when eighty-six, had gone unto Hagar, Sarah's handmaiden and servant; she bore him a child, which was named Ishmael. Ishmael was revered by the Muslims as their true ancestor; and accordingly, as he was the firstborn, inherited all lands of Canaan, which at that time was a huge swath of land that included Israel, Jordan, and more. However, an angel of God predicted that Ishmael would grow up to be a 'wild man: his hand will be against every man and every man's hand against him.' How prophetic? It was only after Ishmael was born that Sarah conceived; Sara then was ninety years old. Muslims don't believe that Sarah could have conceived at that age and that the Jews only tell the story to legitimize Israel as their land. Yet they believe that God could do wonders. Sarah's son was named Isaac. Isaac's wife, Rebecca, was barren, but God spoke to Rebecca, 'Two nations are in your womb . . . the one people shall be stronger than the other people; and the elder shall serve the younger.' The firstborn was called Esau, his brother Jacob. According to the narrator of the Bible, the two already fought in Rebecca's womb. Esau sold his birthright to his younger brother, and Jacob appeared before his dying blind father and was blessed by him as his rightful heir. Esau, incensed by this treachery, vowed to kill Jacob who fled.

"When Jacob returned with his two wives, during the voyage, at night, Jacob wrestled with an angel, was lamed, but was told by the angel, 'Your name from this day forth will be Israel, for as a prince hast though power with God and with men.' The Bible continues and tells that when Jacob arrived in the land of the Canaanites, God appeared to him and told Jacob, 'Your name is Israel. The land I gave to Abraham and Isaac I now give to you.'

"The descendents of Abraham, Isaac, and Jacob are the Jews. From the religious point of view, this land in the Middle East belongs to the Jews for eternity. The Islamists have no claim whatsoever to the land. But they have a case of possession by rights of inhabitants.

The land of Canaan was inhabited by Hebrews (Habiru), meaning wanderers, and Arabs, the desert people. Secular history tells of both people living there and the land conquered by stronger neighboring tribes and nations like the Romans. Whoever was in power owed the land. From medieval times the Ottoman Empire ruled. When Turkey sided with Germany in the First World War, they lost the land to the British. England received a mandate from the League of Nations to administer the land, then called Palestine. With British perfidy they promised a national home to both the Arabs and Jews. They split off part of Palestine and created Trans-Jordan. They never fulfilled their promise to the Jews.

By then, and under British administration, the land of Palestine was in turmoil. The Mufti of Jerusalem incited the Arabs to either expel or kill the Jews. And when the Mufti visited Hitler in Berlin in 1942, Hitler promised him to include Palestine in his "final solution." When the Mufti returned to Palestine, he told the Arabs that all Jews will be killed and their possessions given to the Muslim Palestinians. Murder and robbery his clarion call. In 1947, the United Nation decided to split Palestine into a Jewish Homeland and a Palestinian Country. It was a bad split but according to where the majority of Jews and Arabs lived. The Jews accepted and in May of 1948 proclaimed the nation of Israel.

The Palestinians did not accept the UN resolution but instead made war on the Jews, together with Egypt, Iraq, Syria, and Lebanon. The Jews defeated them and did so again in 1956, 1967, and 1973. Only Egypt and Jordan made peace with Israel.

"Today, here in Europe, we condemn Israel for still occupying what is called the Palestinian territory. The reason for that is that Israel would love to live in peace with the Palestinians; but periodically the Palestinians instituted a reign of terror with suicide bombers and murder of men, women, and children. The Palestinians are still seeking to destroy Israel. So finally the Israelis built a wall to keep the terrorists out, and it works.

That is the up-to-the-present history of the Middle East."

Same female student: But President Abbas wants to make peace. Why don't the Israelis accept if they so much love to live in peace?

"The peace Abbas offers is by his terms. You don't make a war four times and institute periodically terror and then present your terms. You take what is offered. Like Germany made war on the world and then accepted the terms of the victors and not vice versa."

Same student: All the Palestinians want is the West Bank without the Jewish settlements. I understand there are three hundred thousand Jews living in the West Bank.

"And there are over 1.6 million former Palestinians living in Israel."

Student: Wouldn't an exchange of population make sense, both countries being homogenized?

"You might be right there. But try to sell that proposition to Abbas, the Palestinians living in Israel, and the settlers. Besides, Abbas wants more. He wants Old Jerusalem.

Jerusalem was designated by the UN under an international administration. Instead the Jordanians and Palestinian occupied it and did not let the Jews visit their holy places.

169

Abbas recently even declared that the *Klagemauer*, the Western Wall, is not part of the Second Temple, even though the world's archaeology accepts it as such. Another term of Abbas is for Israel to accept all former Palestinian refugees back, who lived in what is now Israel. While there were a half-million refugees, now there are two and a half million. Israel, during the years after its establishment as a nation, accepted about a half-million Jews from Arab countries into Israel and gave them homes and jobs. The Arabs kept most of their refugees in camps for political reasons. President Abbas and the Palestinians are not a good partner to make peace with. Look what happened in Gaza. The Israelis left Gaza and in return got bombarded by thousands of rockets, Gaza now in the hands of the terrorist group Hamas. The Palestinian Territory may be next under Hamas."

Student: Doctor, you were raised in Egypt, went to school there, you were in the army. Are you familiar with the Koran? Was the Koran God inspired? Was Mohammad a prophet? What is the Koran all about?

Anton smiled. "So many questions in one. We Christians do not believe that Prophet Mohammad was a prophet. The Koran God inspired? Prophet Mohammad was a very intelligent and eloquent man. You see, I call him Prophet Mohammad so as not to offend any Muslim. What is the Koran all about? I studied the Koran in its classical Egyptian edition. The Koran, according to Muslims, is universal, being the continuation of all previous revealed scriptures in Judaism of the Abrahamic tradition as delivered among other by the Prophets Moses, David, and, last, before Prophet Muhammad, by Jesus and the Apostles. Jesus is accepted as a prophet but not as the Son of God by Muslims.

The Koran is in flowery prose and in continuous praise for Allah, the All-Merciful.

I quote here what Muslims believe, and the Koran bears it out: for a scholar it is knowledge; for a politician in Koran-restricted politics; for a ruler in its justice system of Sharia. The Koran is all-inclusive. Was the Koran God given, a revelation to Prophet Mohammad? As I said before, we Christians don't believe so. There are substantial differences to our Christian scriptures. Ours are for all mankind; the Koran is rather for Arabs, people of the desert. Differences foremost between God, man, and woman.

"Perhaps of more interest are the commentaries; these commentaries are written by scholars. Through times they bear different interpretations and are supplemented by *fatwas*, decrees pronounced by clerics. It is with the fatwas that the trouble begins. Let me just quote from the beginning of the Koran. It is the opening sura 1:7. The Prophet admonishes his followers: 'The way of those on whom thou has bestowed thy grace, those whose is not wrath.' We know very well that for fundamentalist it is all wrath. They misinterpret the Koran as it suits them or disregard the Koran altogether.

The Koran doesn't make war on civilians. Mohammedans can pick up the sword to defend. There are sure in the Koran of drawing the sword against the infidels.

The Koran permits Muslims to own slaves by purchase or as bounty in war. Can you imagine Jesus owning slaves? Slavery is still practiced by some.

"As Prophet Muhammad progressed from visionary and teacher to warlord and ruler, his style and messages became more violent and intolerant. It is these later revelations that are considered definite by Islamic authorities when they conflict with earlier ones cited for Western consumption. Let me quote the perhaps most important late revelation as it is part of the reason that war can be declared against all infidels. It comes from sura 9:5, from verses called sword verses: 'Fight and slay the pagans wherever ye find them and seize them, beleaguer them and lie in wait for them.' All non-Muslims are pagans.

In Islam, the definition what is right or just is not empirical but changeable by divine decree, the fatwas, enabling the most heinous sins and crimes to be declared 'the will of Allah' but not admitted to by moderate Islamists who like for us to think of Islam as religion of peace that promotes charity, tolerance, and freedom.

"Remember the paradise promised the martyrs? The joys and glories of the Islamic paradise are tangible and sensual and include the many young virgins. Let us look at that paradise through the eyes of a Christian. The God of the Jews and our same God and his son Jesus the Savior regarded man and woman as his creation and not woman as a mere pleasure object to man. It is just ungodly in its basic tenet. Yet this promised paradise seems such a powerful motive for suicide bombers. To sit in the presence of Allah and have these virgins cater to his pleasure."

A teacher: Is this part of the Koran?

Anton shook his head. "Not directly. Perhaps from a fatwa or more likely a legend."

Teacher: Propaganda then?

"More than propaganda. It can't be quoted as a verse from the Koran, but when drilled into the believers by a religious leader as a revelation, it becomes truth."

Teacher: What motivates the suicide bomber? Do they actually believe they go to Allah in paradise and that nonsense of a bunch of virgins waiting for them?

"A mixture of many motives. Religiously, it may be based upon a verse in the Koran, sura 3:169: 'Think not of those who are slain in God's way as dead. Nay, they live.

Finding their sustenance in the Presence of their Lord.' Let's look at this sura more closely and its interpretation by fanatical clerics. Suicide is forbidden by the Koran; it is murder. Mullahs interpret 'slain in God's way' as a Muslim who was killed serving Allah. If he was killed by the enemy or by his own hand, it becomes the same thing; therefore, the injunction against suicide is overruled by the deed of having committed it in the service of Allah. The suicide bomber becomes a martyr. 'Nay, they live.' The bomber believes his mutilated body becomes whole again. 'Finding their sustenance,' a man's pleasure fulfilling his lust with virgins. 'In the Presence of their Lord,' sitting next to Allah. Certainly a gross misinterpretation of the sura. Let's look at the suicide bombers and who they are. First of all, most are young men, uneducated, and a failure in everything they did, a shame to their families; they are terribly frustrated. They see the world around them, an affluent society. They envy those who have; they begin to hate them and the society that makes it possible but excludes them. Religion at that point has little influence in their lives. Then they meet someone who is part of a secret organization, or they attend a mosque were the imam is a fanatic and teaches hatred for the infidels and gives the young men an outlet for their frustrations. They become easy recruits for fundamentalism; they become recognized as important members. Now they find a direction for their hatred. The leader or mentor of their clandestine group sends them to a madras, a religious school, usually in Pakistan where they learn the Koran, fatwas of hatred towards the nonbelievers; they turn into terrorists."

Teacher: They are brainwashed.

"Yes, indeed. Once they have become religious fanatics, they have to be trained as warriors and are sent to secret camps in Pakistan, Afghanistan, and Yemen. They are taught to use weapons, explosives, how to travel, live within the society they hate without arousing suspicion. The trigger of becoming a suicide bomber lies in each individual's personality, fostered by the leader's ability to recognize these traits.

"The thought of becoming such a self-destructive bomber is not one of an instant decision but rather a spark that ignites all sorts of emotions, even a thrill TO DO IT. The living martyr has become a special person, a hero. Besides, the act will not happen tomorrow or soon. These primitive minds live by the hour, by the day. They never consider themselves as terrorists but freedom fighters for Allah. There are exceptions, of course, like that American major Hasan or Mohamed Atta who flew the first plane into the World Trade Tower. Atta belonged to a terrorist cell in Hamburg, and one of his co-conspirators wrote this: 'The victors will come. We swear to beat you. I came to you with men who love the death just as you love life. Oh, the smell of paradise is rising.'

"But you don't see a fanatic like al-Zawahiri or Ahdmadinejad put on an explosive vest.

When Osama bin Laden was killed, he was not the warrior he claimed to be and didn't even try to defend himself."

Anton glanced down at his watch, and Professor Moll at once stepped to the lectern. "I believe this was an inspiring lecture about the evil of fanaticism. We wish to thank you, doctor." He shook hands with Anton, and the students stood up and gave him an enthusiastic ovation.

Anton left with Sepp. "That was a fine lecture, Anton. Looks like we have to do something about these fanatics." They drove home.

Later, Anton had a call from Max who asked him to be at the institute at nine in the morning. "I have to show you something interesting, Anton," Max promised him. "Be sure to bring Sepp."

Saturday, the twelfth of January, Anton picked up Sepp early in the morning. Sepp never came in his taxi to the institute or rarely; nobody there knew that he was taxi driver. Sepp was the computer expert and working for Professor Klausner.

They signed in at the desk and joined Max in the energy house.

Max: I have been snooping around for you, Anton, to find terrorists. I think I have found one of the training camps of al-Qaeda in Yemen. It is about sixty kilometers southwest of their capital Sana'a, in the hills. Let me show you.

Anton: What is the time difference?

Max: Yemen is three hours ahead of us. It is a little past eleven here; it would be after two in the afternoon there.

Sepp: Would they have training now? Isn't it broiling hot in the desert?

Max: Remember, it is winter there too, should be a comfortable afternoon for them. I read that al-Qaeda in Yemen is now the major operation of al-Qaeda, right, Anton?

Anton: It has been for some years, even before bin Laden was killed. The other active al-Qaeda operations are in Iraq, Afghanistan, North Africa, what they call al-Qaeda in the Moslem Maghreb. Besides, they might have training camps in Somalia, Indonesia, even in Chechnya, and in the tribal areas of northwestern Pakistan. The terrorists who rammed that American destroyer in Aden with a speedboat loaded with explosives were trained in Yemen, and so was that terrorist who concealed a bomb in his underwear. It is really the major training camp for al-Qaeda now.

Max showed the desert and hills of southern Yemen, moved in closer, and they could see the camp at the foot of a large hill. A tent city with people moving around, camels, bunched together, a few pickups. Moving closer to the hill, they saw men firing weapons at targets. To the side and at a greater distance, men were using rifle grenades at car wrecks.

To the other side of the men firing Kalashnikovs was an obstacle course and men were running through it.

Anton: You found a real training camp, Max.

Sepp: Can we be sure it is al-Qaeda? Maybe it is of the Yemenite army?

Anton: Max, return the view to the tent city. Find a large tent with a flag or banner by it.

Max did so, found the largest tent, and there was a flag. He zeroed in on the flag while the view was from above; the wind waved the flag, and they saw it was black.

Anton: It is of al-Qaeda. Their flag is black with Arabic writing, something like Aluha Akbar, Allah is great or something praising Allah; also they are not in uniform.

Max: Let me show you something else that is interesting.

He moved the view along the hill, away from the target practice, and showed a barbed wire enclosure with a several mud huts. An open truck stood by one hut, and men were carrying wooden boxes out and placing them on the truck.

Max: An ammunition dump?

Anton: Looks like it. Zero in on the hut. The metal door is open, and a box propped against it, probably so the wind doesn't close it. Let's hope the box contains dynamite or grenades; rifle ammunition wouldn't explode it forceful enough to destroy the hut.

Max zeroed in on the box while Anton was at the infrared computer and gave it a five-thousand-degree jolt for one second. Not only did the box burst into fire but at once it exploded; the hut blew up, and then the ammunition dump erupted into a huge ball of fire and smoke. The truck and the men working there were engulfed; then there were just fires and smoke, the truck a skeleton of metal, many charred bodies.

Anton: Max, return the view to the big tent. I want to see who is in it.

Max did so; in front of the tent stood several men looking at the conflagration, one with a white beard, frock, and turban.

Anton: He must be their leader, religious leader like an imam or mullah; they are the ones who incite the terrorists to murder. Let's get him.

Max zeroed in on the turban, and Anton gave him a brief five-thousand-degree jolt. His turbaned head exploded in fire, and he fell dead. The other men first looked stunned then ran off in different directions, some to cars; others ran into the hills, some on camels. So did the men in training. In a short time the camp was emptied.

Anton: Let's burn their tents.

With Max moving the view from tent to tent, Anton gave each one a brief one-thousand-degree jolt; from some men came running out, and soon the whole camp burnt down.

Raising the view they saw only smoke come from where the camp and ammunition dump had been.

Anton: A fine piece of work we did.

Max: A beginning against the terrorist scourge.

Sepp: Amen.

On Thursday, the seventeenth of January, the advisory board met at FBI HQ in Quantico. The defense secretary had called for the urgent meeting.

Defense secretary: I was just informed by the state department that an apparent action against terrorists was committed on the twelfth. The White House was also informed. The news comes from the Saudi embassy; they have an informer with al-Qaeda in Yemen.

According to this informer, during the afternoon of the twelfth, the ammunition dump of the al-Qaeda training camp, which is located to the south of Sana'a, exploded mysteriously. Many were killed, among them foreign fighters. While the main camp is about a mile from the dump, the explosion was felt by all. The shockwave was hot, and some of the tents were blown over. The informer states that he was near the tent of Imam Ayman al-Azzawi, who is the spiritual leader, and happened to look at him when suddenly his turbaned head exploded in fire and smoke and he fell dead. Everybody ran away; some hid in tents. A short time later he saw from a distance as one tent after another burst into flames. The whole camp was destroyed. The men who hid in the tents all escaped; there was no one else killed. So much for the report by the Saudis.

FBI deputy: Looks like a first action by the tribunal against terrorists.

NSA: A good action too. I wonder, with the Saudis having an informer at that al-Qaeda training camp, why have they never told us? We could have sent a drone or missiles.

CIA: The Saudis are playing a two-headed game. They fight their own terrorists but either support those in foreign lands or hush it up.

Secretary: Yet they told us.

CIA: After the fact. But they never revealed to us the existence of the camp.

FBI: The question is, shall we let the media know? What does the White House propose?

Secretary: They leave it up to the state department. The information came to them by way of the Saudi embassy here in Washington. The secretary of state wishes for us to decide since we are the advisory board for news and actions of the world tribunal.

FBI: But we, the advisory board, are a secret panel. Neither the media nor the public knows of its existence.

NSA: The media and public know that the FBI is concerned in the matter. Sooner or later the media will find out, and then they will ask the FBI about transparence.

Secretary: The state department wishes for the news to come out, but we must not quote the Saudis as the source.

FBI: Let me suggest this course of action. I inform EUROPOL. They will tell the media, at least the Suisse newspaper. Let them quote the FBI as source. Then when we are questioned, we can say that our information was from a dubious source and had to be first confirmed.

This was the course of action accepted by the board.

The deputy sent a fax to EUROPOL, who in turn informed the media and all European newspapers to print the story in their Sunday editions. When the FBI was queried why they did not tell the media, they stated because of the dubious source they did not report it, which by now has been confirmed as true. However, the FBI informed EUROPOL.

In fact, the media lauded the FBI as being the first to report the world tribunal's action against terrorists.

Friday, 18 January.

When Anton arrived at noon at the energy house, he found Max and Sepp viewing Hamburg.

Sepp explained, "Anton, I made contact with a student of history who researched the killing operation of Reserve Police Battalion 101. This battalion was activated in 1941 and comprised mostly those who had not yet been drafted into the army. They consisted mainly of dock workers, workers in the industry, truckers, farmers or farm workers. Many were members of the Nazi Party; some were members in the SS but not gung-ho Germans who volunteered in 1938, '39, and '40 for the army or Waffen SS when Germany was victorious. By enlisting into the *ordnungspolizei* [order police], they were freed from conscription into the army, *and it being a regional police unit they were safe from the dangers of fighting, also being stationed near their homes.* Really ordinary men. And that is what made this student. His name is Gerhard Schneider, interested in doing his research how ordinary men can become killers. I read an article by him and found his name in the phonebook. I called him and told him that I too do similar research. We had a long conversation, and I asked him if anyone from that 101 Battalion was still around. Schneider said yes and that he was interviewing a member periodically. I told him that I was interested in this interview, and he invited me to join him for one of the sessions. He asked me who I was, and I said that my name was Johann Bauer and that I was gathering information for the world tribunal and therefore could not tell him more about myself or where I am from. If that was acceptable to him, I would continue to talk to him; otherwise, I would have to break off.

"He then told me that he was in full agreement with the work of the world tribunal. But how would I join him in the interview? I told him that when interviewing this member, he should have a cell phone with him or a radio that was activated and I could hear then, even speak to him or ask questions, and I would be able to see him and this man.

"He then asked me if I would harm that man. I told him that I would not send the death ray, but if he was found guilty of murder, someone of the world tribunal would be listening in and would send the death ray but not in his presence. I told him that if he objects to that procedure, we just discontinue our conversation. No, he did not object. He had already talked to this man who had confessed to killing many Jews, and that was at the first action of the battalion in Jozefow, Poland, on 13 July 1942. He told me that two books were written about this battalion, one by Christopher Browning, *Ordinary Men*, and the other by Daniel Goldhagen, *Hitler's Willing Executioners*. Both published in English, but German translations are available. I found both books at the Munich archives and read them—unbelievable."

Anton asked, "Who is this former policeman Gerhard Schneider is interviewing?"

Sepp: His name is Friedrich Kammer; he was in charge of a platoon of first company.

His platoon was detailed to do the shooting. He was then twenty-two, now ninety-two.

I told Schneider that for the world tribunal to be a witness, he must be out in the open where he can see both. Schneider arranged the interview to be at his mother's home and he would sit in the garden. Instead of the address, I asked him to meet me. She lives near the town of Wedel, to the west of Hamburg. There is a big church in the center of town, and he would be there with Kammer at ten in the morning. He would drive a yellow Volkswagen, the old Beetle type, can't miss it. He would wait until a quarter after ten and then drive to his mother's house, a sort of bungalow along the Elbe River. There is only one major road coming out of town going to the southwest. I told him I'll be watching for him at the church, and if he leaves the car radio on, I would tell him I am there by giving the time. Also, it would help if he has a portable radio and to put it on the table, turn it on but not on a station. Increase the volume and adjust it when I talk to him or Kammer.

So it is all arranged, Anton. We meet tomorrow at nine.

Then Max explained that he was supposed to give a demonstration today to Director Glaser and transmit wireless energy to a receiver in Erding, about twenty kilometers away.

For his experiment he had them build a hundred-meter-high transmission tower. Max explained, "I have to give some satisfaction for my work on wireless energy transmission. And I told Glaser that the energy can only be transmitted in line of sight.

The tower has an apparatus I built, which does nothing; we transmit to satellite and back to earth. Glaser will be with his engineers in Erding."

The experiment was a huge success. Though the current sent was of low voltage and not yet suitable for household use, it promised a revolution in energy transmission. Instead of many towers to be built and strung with high-voltage wires, it needed far fewer towers and no wires. Professor Max Klausner assured Director Glaser than within a few years he would be able to send high-voltage current.

Saturday, 19 January.

They met at nine o'clock, and Max brewed a pot of coffee.

Shortly before ten, Max switched to the town of Wedel, which he had monitored before. By the big church they saw the yellow Beetle. Sepp increased the volume on his audio receiver, and they heard music. How proper—it was a church chorale. A minute before ten, Sepp spoke into the microphone, "The time is ten o'clock."

They watched the Beetle drive off and followed it from high up. It took the highway to the southwest, out of town, and in the distance they could see the River Elbe. Along the river was a village, mostly with small homes; and in front of a bungalow, surrounded by a home garden, the Volkswagen stopped. Two men came out, one using a cane, and wore an overcoat as it was a sunny but cool day, surely the ex-sergeant Kammer. They went into the bungalow.

A short while later, they came back out and went to a table near the path to the house; it was already set with a tablecloth, cups, a radio. The two were followed by a woman, Schneider's mother, who brought a tray with a coffeepot and condiments. Schneider poured the coffee.

Kammer: I am glad you brought us out here, Herr Schneider. I wouldn't wish to talk in front of Frau Schneider.

Schneider: You are right. She knows nothing and doesn't need to know.

"Your father, Herr Schneider?"

"My mother is divorced. My father is a rich businessman, took up with a woman many years younger, really just a girl. Divorce followed. He pays, gave us his bungalow, pays for my education. I rarely see him."

"He was in the army, SS perhaps?"

Schneider laughed. "You must be talking about my grandfather; he was in the war. Before the end, taken prisoner by the Soviets and didn't come back until 1950. A slave laborer somewhere in Russia."

"Yea, yea, the Russkies. Big mistake to start the war against the Soviets, a war we could never win. Well, we could have taken Moscow, Leningrad, and Stalingrad at the end if the Americans wouldn't have come in then build an *Ostwall* along the Wolga.

It would have worked but to declare war on America that the Fuehrer should have never done. America didn't want to come into the war even though the Jews wanted it. It was the stupid Japanese who started it all. We should have told the Japs, 'Now you started it, you finish it by yourself.' We could have had all of Europe and Russia up to the Urals.

I don't think the Fuehrer wanted this world war, but Himmler and Goebbels did, and they talked the Fuehrer into declaing war on America."

"Yes, there are different versions of who started it all. I am glad to listen to your comments, Herr Kammer, your personal experiences."

"Well, it was, of course, the Jews, world-Jewry who started it all. And our Fuehrer told the Jews, 'You start a world war and we destroy you.' I just want you to have all the facts that when you become a history teacher, you know the truth."

"And that is why you participated in the destruction of the Jews?"

"Yes, though when I joined the Reserve Police Battalion 101 in 1941, I did not know that this would be our mission, to help eradicate our archenemies, the Jews."

"At the last interview, you told about the deportation of Jews in Poland to the ghetto in Lublin, to the KZ Majdanek, and that your first action against the Jews was in Jozefow.

"Yes, that was on the thirteenth of July 1942. We got there early in the morning, before sunrise. Second company surrounded the village. Then when it got light, third company and my company, the first, went into the village to round up the Jews and take them to the marketplace—that is, those who could walk."

"And the ones who could not walk? Who were they?"

"Very old people, the infirm, little children, and infants. Also the patients in the hospital, and of an old age home."

"What happened to those?"

"We were instructed to shoot all those who could not walk."

"Even the infants?"

"Of course, infants don't walk. Often we had to find them they hid them in blankets, under the bed, in the attic. Most cried and screamed, so they were easy to find."

"Did you shoot any infants?"

"Yeah, several."

"How does it feel to shoot an infant Herr Kammer?"

"No feeling. They were enemies of state. I had some bad feelings later when we shot children at the execution site."

"And the sick patients, the old in the home—they were all shot?"

"Orders."

"Now the Jews are at the marketplace. How many were there?"

"I believe about 1,600."

"What next?"

"My platoon was detailed as shooters. I called my men together—there were about thirty—and I didn't have any shirkers. Before the action, the battalion chief, Major Trapp, explained the action and asked if anyone cannot participate. There was a captain Buchmann who volunteered out and a few more men, not from my platoon. My platoon made a half circle and our battalion medic, Dr. Schoenfelder, explained how to execute.

Point the tip of the bayonet against the nape of the neck and shoot. Then we marched to the forest, a couple kilometers away, and soon the trucks arrived with the Jews. Then I saw that the men from the third platoon did not do a good job in the village; there were women with infants and little children. Now I understood why Captain Hoffmann was angry with them and told them they had not proceeded energetically enough, meaning to shoot the little ones.

"I, as the platoon leader then assigned one of my men with a Jew. They walked together about a hundred meters to the forest; the Jew lay down and was shot like the doc showed us. After each one did his job, he came back, and I gave him another Jew to finish off."

"Did you participate in the shooting?"

"Yes, of course, I did not want my men to think I am a coward."

"Who did you shoot? Can you remember?"

"First an old man. He happened to be from Hamburg. Begged me not to shoot him but let him run away. Orders are orders, I told him. Then I executed a twelve-year-old girl. I felt almost sorry for her; she was a pretty blond, could have been a German girl. She cried bitterly, but she was a Jewess. Then a woman—she had trouble laying her little girl on the ground; the girl clung to her. So I shot the women, then the kid.

"The next action 101 participated in was on the seventeenth of August, in a village called Lomazy. 1,700 Jews were to be shot. In Jozefow a few men were selected as laborer and sent to Lublin, but in Lomazy all Jews were to be killed. Early in the morning the Jews were driven out of their homes. The procedure to execute them was different this time.

"First, Jew men had to dig a ditch, about three meters deep and fifty meters long. They couldn't dig deeper as groundwater came up. Also, the men were separated from the women and children. My platoon was to guard the men. The shooting would be done by the Hiwis, Ukrainian militia. Oh, did they hate the Jews. Lieutenant Gnade was in charge of the executions. Isn't that a strange coincidence that a man with than name GNADE [meaning 'mercy'] would be in charge? Lieutenant Gnade was a real sadist. He believed in the order from above that the Jews should be killed in an aura of terror. Before the Jew men were shot, he selected about thirty of them, all old ones with beards, made them strip naked, then crawl on all fours to the ditch, which at one end was sloped down. He then made them stop and turned to me and ordered me and my men to take clubs and beat the Jews while they crawled to their grave."

"Did you do that?"

"Yeah, we beat them. Orders are orders; some beat them brutally. Then lying in the ditch, Hiwis shot them. They went right down in the ditch and shot them from close. But after about three hundred Jews were shot, the thing became messy. The Hiwis stood by now in knee-deep water, and corpses were floating around; besides, they were constantly supplied with bottles of vodka and were drunk. Couldn't aim properly and mostly wounded the Jews.

"That is when Lieutenant Gnade ordered my men to do the shooting. I had my men stand on either side of the ditch and shoot down at the Jews. About six hundred men Jews were executed there."

"A real massacre!"

"I don't want to call it a massacre, just an action as ordered. Except for Lieutenant Gnade's sadistic game, the way he played with the old Jews, it was done very decently."

"Herr Kammer, you still approve of these actions?"

"Well, it was wartime, and we only followed orders. Remember, '*Die Juden sind unser Unglueck* [The Jews are our misfortune].' It was drilled into our minds. Our deadly enemies."

"They did you no harm."

"Well, that is your opinion now, Herr Schneider. If you had lived then, all the propaganda that the Jews are our enemies and want to dominate the world. Remember, we were just ordinary men."

"Tribunal, are you listening in? Any questions for Herr Kammer?"

Sepp: No, no questions. Send Kammer home. We pronounce him a war criminal.

Kammer: Who was that? The radio speaks to me?

"That was the world tribunal. Have you heard of them? No? You will in due time. The coffee got cold by now; you want a fresh brew, Herr Kammer?"

"No, just take me home. I don't think that you understand what we went through in the war and that we had no choice but only obeyed orders."

Max followed the yellow Beetle back to Hamburg. In front of an elegant apartment house, the car stopped and let Herr Kammer out. He walked slowly on his cane to the entrance.

Schneider who watched him saw his head suddenly explode in fire and smoke; he fell dead.

Schneider drove off. He understood—justice was done.

Sunday, twentieth of January 2013.

The *Berner Nachrichten* printed a letter to the editor received the day before:

> Sehr gehrter Herr Redakteur Konrad:
>
> We, the students of the University of Muenchen, wish to propose to the world tribunal that the Taliban is classified as a terrorist organization. Several of our classes met and listened to a lecture on the Taliban in Afghanistan and Pakistan. The lecturer stated that the Taliban were mainly an organization who fight for their religion, the Sharia. However, he also read us a poster put up in a hospital in Khost that specified laws pertaining to females. These religious laws were ridiculous, in fact, totally oppressive toward womanhood. Let me state a few: "Women cannot go out without a male relative. Women and girls cannot go to school. Women cannot participate in sports. Women who show their ankles will be whipped. Women who use cosmetics have their fingers cut off. Women who have an affair without being married will be stoned to death. Women cannot laugh loudly. All windows in a house or apartment where a woman lives must be painted black—and more of those stupid laws. We also heard of a Taliban assassin who stopped a school bus, asked the students which one was Malala Yousufzai, and then shot the fourteen-year-old girl in the head and neck. All the girl wanted to do was to go to school and become a doctor to help people.
>
> Malala was critically injured. The Taliban claimed responsibility and stated that if the girl survives she will be killed the next time. At this point, all students shouted together repeatedly, "DEATH TO THE TALIBAN!"
>
> We students hope sincerely that the world tribunal classifies the Taliban as a terrorist organization and eliminates this scourge of mankind from our planet.
>
> Signed: THE STUDENTS OF THE UNIVERSITY OF MUENCHEN

Sunday, the twentieth of January 2013.

The plane from Bern arrived at noon in Israel. With it came a stack of the *Berner Nachrichten* newspaper for distribution to addressees. Three copies are picked up by a courier and taken to the Mossad office. Moderchai Nevot made it a practice to come to the Mossad Sunday afternoons to read various newspapers that arrived from Europe, including, since the world tribunal published its first manifesto, the *Berner Nachrichten*.

When he read the letter to the editor by the Munich university students, he made a copy and drove to Jerusalem, to police headquarters, to see his friend Anton.

Anton read then shook his head. "It was on purpose that we never included the Taliban in our manifestos, especially the fourth one pertaining to terrorists. I did not wish to give our warnings or judgments against religion, not even Sharia. I mean, I was in Afghanistan in 1998, when the Taliban were in power. What I saw and heard was that the majority of the Afghans supported the Taliban because they believed in Sharia. But the students are right. The practice of Sharia deprives all females of their rights for freedom and happiness. The laws of Sharia are cruel and belong to the Dark Age. I saw the practice of it at a soccer stadium when thieves had their hands chopped off and a robber lost both a leg and arm. And I saw a woman stoned to death, not a pretty sight to see, and she suffered cruelly until a relative killed her with a rock. But I also saw the jubilation of the thousands of spectators who believed in these judgments. Is it right to practice these mutilations on minor criminals? Of course it is not. To oppress women under Sharia? No, it is not right, even if most of these women don't know any better. The Taliban are evil and use the umbrella of religion to justify their murderous campaigns. The problem we of the world tribunal have is that we did not want to infringe on religion. But the assassination attempt, trying to murder a young girl, puts the

Taliban into the category of terrorists. The students are right. 250 students spontaneously stood up and yelled, 'DEATH TO THE TALIBAN!' I think a fifth manifesto is in order. Looks like you have to take another trip to New York, my friend."

Nevot: I am ready to go.

"Let me write it up. I call you when the letter is ready."

"You are doing the right thing, Anton. 250 students can't be all wrong. Tell me, Anton, what kind of person can target a child, a religious fanatic?"

"We don't know who the shooter was. The order to assassinate the girl was given by a mullah, a fanatical Muslim clergy. Was Mullah Fazlullah motivated by religion? What kind of religion orders the killing of a child? I don't believe that even those Muslims who believe in Sharia condone this horrible act. There is more to it. Fazlullah is a psychopath who uses religion as a mantel for his inhumanity. Like this deranged young man in Newtown, Connecticut, who methodically shot these twenty children and six teachers.

Adam Lanza was a psychopath, a man with serious personality defects who was amoral, impulsive, and cruel. He would have been a worthy member of the SS.

"On the same day, the fourteenth of December, a man entered the Chenpeng Primary School in a village in China and injured twenty-three children with a meat cleaver before he was chased away by people with broomsticks. Authorities believe that if China had such loose gun controls as in America, it would have been a slaughter of children. Another psychopath who, thanks God, did not have a gun."

"What is it with America that they permit everybody to have a gun?"

"It is their Second Amendment that permits citizens to bear arms. I am certain that the originators of this Second Amendment had plain single-shot rifles in mind and not modern assault rifles that can fire thirty and more bullets in a short time or pistols with High-capacity magazines as are permitted now. At one time they outlawed these assault weapons, but then in 2004, under the republican administration the law expired."

"A good reason now to reinstate this law."

"It is not that simple. There is this powerful gun lobby, the National Rifle Association that opposes any restriction on arms. Their executive vice president Wayne LaPierre says, 'The NRA is not going to let people lose the Second Amendment in this country, which is supported by the overwhelming majority of the American people.' This is, of course, a lie. President Obama and the administration do not wish to change or do away with the Second Amendment but only outlaw assault rifles and high-capacity magazines, which is supported by the majority of Americans. You don't go hunting with an assault rifle; if you did, you wouldn't be a hunter but a nut; and if you fire at targets, you want to check your shots and not demolish it with rapid fire. Only an idiot would do that. The NRA says you need a machinegun-like weapon to protect your house and family, but I never heard of an American army attacking a local's house. LaPierre is one of those fanatics who twist everything around, lies and deceives to have his way. There is also big businesses involved who manufacture these weapons, the darlings of the NRA and their financial supporters. Look, not everything in America is golden; they have their share of fanatics. In politics they have the Tea Party, extremist Republicans who act more like fascists. Anything President Obama wants to do for America they are against."

"But why? Why do they hate Obama?"

"Mainly because he is a black democrat, very smart and eloquent; they are all a bunch of bigots. They believe a black man should shine shoes, wash dishes, sweep streets, but not become president of a White America. They would have been fanatical Nazis if they had lived in Germany during Hitler's regime."

"I think you are right, Anton."

The next day on Monday, Nevot flew to New York. The manifesto was received by Saturday in Bern and published in the Sunday edition of 27 January 2013.

CHAPTER XVII

Manifesto V of the World Tribunal

The World Tribunal Designates the Taliban as a Terrorist Organization

The world tribunal has purposefully refrained from declaring religious beliefs and practices as terroristic and evil. Therefore, the world tribunal has not judged the Taliban and the practice of Sharia. However, the tribunal is dismayed to read about terroristic acts committed by the Taliban, most of these not against the NATO troops in Afghanistan but brutally murdering their own people, often with suicide bombers.

The tribunal realizes that one aim of the Taliban is to force foreign troops to leave their country; Afghanistan has always fought and expelled invaders.

While the tribunal looks akin at the practice of Sharia, the mutilations of criminals, the oppression of women, it realizes that a multitude of Afghans wish to live by Sharia.

The tribunal hopes that under the moderate government of President Karzai, a less brutal form of Islam can be instituted and accepted if not by all by a majority of Afghans and practiced even after NATO troops leave next year.

However, certain violent acts in the name of Taliban have occurred that makes the tribunal realize that Taliban does not mean Sharia but political domination by terrorism.

There cannot be a more horrendous act than when on 9 October 2012, a Taliban stopped a school bus, entered the bus full of children, and asked which girl was Malala Jousufzai. When Malala answered the call, the Taliban shot the girl at point-blank into the head to assassinate the child. Thank Allah that Malala lives. The Taliban then claimed responsibility and threatened to kill the child if she should survive.

This dastardly and cowardly act is symptomatic with the rule of Taliban.

The assassination of Malala was ordered by Mullah Fazlullah, the Taliban commander in Swat Valley of Pakistan. A CLERGY!

250 students at the University of Munich who heard of this foul crime stood and shouted in unison, "DEATH TO TALIBAN!"

The world tribunal declares the Taliban in Afghanistan and Pakistan to be an outlaw terrorist gang, foremost Mullah Fazlullah who ordered the killing of Malalah, and the judgment is ELIMINATION BY DEATH RAY.

Further, the Pakistani Taliban have emerged as the most ruthless. In January 2013, a group calling itself Lashkar-e-Jhangvi, allied with the Taliban and al-Qaeda, exploded bombs that killed 120 people, mostly Shiites, 81 persons in a billiard hall in the city of Quetta.

In December, in the Khyber Pakhtunkhwa Province, the Taliban murdered nine health workers who immunized children against polio. Seven more were killed in January. The Taliban claim that the immunizations make Muslim children sterile.

Such vicious lies are spread by the Muslim clergy to justify the killings.

Also, the world tribunal declares Hamas a terrorist organization after the unprovoked rocket attacks against Israel.

Signed: The Force of Three

Friday, the twenty-fifth of January, Anton and the family—that is all but Amal—flew to Munich to spend the weekend in Anton's ancestral home in Planegg. Anton had promised the children to take them to Circus Krone and on Saturday to take them to the world-famous zoo. Taxi driver Sepp picked them up and brought them home. It was snowing in Munich to the joy of the children and Hanna. They had lunch at the Heide Inn, then went shopping for food. Dressed warm they went out in the garden and with Daddy's help built a snowman. For eyes Anton used small oval charcoal, for a nose a carrot. "And what can we use for a mouth?" Anton asked. David suggested a pickle, but Esther wanted something red; so Hanna went into the house and carved a mouth from a red pepper.

Anton stuck one of his pipes into the mouth, then a broom alongside, and they had a genuine snowman. By then they were covered with snow and frozen, and since Sepp had turned on the water heater before he went to the airport, they went into the Jacuzzi. With all dressed in swimming suits, they warmed up in the churning water into which Hanna had thrown pine tables that turned the water green and smelling of forest.

Anton told them of the circus he had visited many times as a boy and told the story of little David who when five years old had visited the circus with Daddy and Mommy and became so upset when the clown came into the arena on a bicycle, had a flat, and when someone brought him a pump had affixed it to the wrong wheel. The family had sat in the first row, and Danny yelled in Hebrew at him that he pumped the wrong tire. The clown, who didn't understand a word, finally motioned to Danny to show him, and little Danny went into the arena and showed him to the joy and laughter of the audience.

Danny then told of the big lollipop the clown brought him—he remembered that part.

After super, which Hanna had prepared, Sepp came in his taxi and took them to the circus where they met Max Klausner, his wife, Ingrid, and Erika. Max had procured the tickets, and they sat again in the first row. The children were especially fascinated with the antics of the clowns, though none came in on a bicycle and had a flat.

Saturday, they, along with Sepp and Inge, were invited to the Klausners for lunch. Ingrid and a maid cooked while Inge, Hanna, and the children went out into the garden to build a snow castle; it was snowing again, and the men sat together with hot-spiced wine and Habanas Anton had brought.

Sitting comfortable in the warm office, they could talk freely about their accomplishments as world judges.

Max: We did well in regard to the pirates, but with the drug cartels in Mexico, it is a battle we cannot win.

From an article he read:

> Two months after President Enrique Pena Nieto took office promising to reduce violent crime, the killings linked to Mexico's drug cartels continue unabated. Eighteen members of a music band and its retinue were kidnapped and apparently slain in the northern border state of Nuevo Leon. Fourteen prisoners and nine guards died in an attempted prison escape in Durango State. Nine men were slain Christmas Eve in Sinaloa. Near the capital more than a dozen bodies were found last week, some dismembered. The difference under this administration is that there have been no major news conferences announcing more troops or federal police for drug-plagued hotspots. Pena Nieto has been mum, instead touting education, fiscal, and energy reforms. On Monday, he told a summit of Latin American and Caribbean leaders in Chile that he wants Mexico to focus on being a player in solving world and regional problems. Critics suggest the country's new leaders believe that the best way to solve a security crisis is to create distraction. What Pena Pieto is doing is sweeping violence under the rug in hopes that no one notices, said security expert Jorge Chabat. An area known as the Laguna, where Coahuila and Durango States meet, has been the scene of numerous battles between faction of the Sinaloa and the Zetas cartels.
>
> The newspaper *Reforma*, one of several media outlets that count murders linked to organized crime, said in December, the first month of the new government, there were 755 drug-related killings compared to 699 in November.

Sepp: Give him time.

Anton: What President Nieto is doing will not solve Mexico's drug problems and the violence of the cartels. Former president Calderon was right in combating the cartels openly and vigorously. Drug traffickers are like terrorists, and you must not go soft with them; you just cannot find an accommodation with either group. What Nieto should do is to let the federalis—that is, the army—combat them. Not the police as they are corrupt and so are the judges and prison officials and guards. Best to put the marines in charge. Let the army and marines try traffickers and put in prison camps located in their compounds.

We can help Mexico by not only going after their leaders who are just about impossible to be found by us but after their lieutenants—that is, their subleaders like this Moreno we eliminated. Those we might find through the police like Carlos Villarreal, who works for the cartels. Max, continue your war against the cartels, and we'll help you.

You, Sepp, in your search for war criminals, there are few left, but we can judge those who have the same unsavory philosophy, like the neo-Nazis and other extreme right-wing groups. Most of the information about these groups comes from newspaper and magazine articles, like the *Berner Nachrichten*, the *Spiegel* magazine from Germany, the *New York Times*. And we may be able to get information from the American Eli Wiesenthal Center and Anti-Defamation League.

Max: They sit in their offices, so how can we question them?

Anton: I can get Nevot to visit them in America. He is not part of us but a trustworthy person who can get us this information.

Sepp: I can have the Spiegel sent to me. Also, I can ask Fred Schultheis to bring me any newsletter from the Munich neo-Nazi party. They had an article about the Estonian SS meeting that is about their coming meeting. Nothing after we raided them.

Max: Anton, how about your fighting the terrorists? Don't you think we should go after the Taliban, especially the Pakistani Taliban who seem more brutal than those from Afghanistan?

Sepp: And these terrorists from Algeria and Mali? I read about their terror.

Anton: You mean the jihadist group that calls itself the al-Qaeda from Muslim Maghreb, meaning North Africa? But, Max, you are right about the Pakistani Taliban being more brutal and active.

Max: Why is that? What makes the Pakistanis crueler? Are they by nature more vicious?

Anton: Nobody is by nature cruel; well, the capacity for it is inborn. That is not correct either. I believe some children seem to have a mental defect so that certain human traits like kindness, mercy, compassion do not develop properly. Take children who, when young, perhaps already in kindergarten, turn into bullies regardless of proper upbringing by their parents or guardians.

Max: A mental aberration that turns them into psychopaths?

Anton: I think it is rather the lack of ability to develop these more gentle and loving traits that most children develop. The child that finds pleasure in hurting animals will develop into this bully and hurt other children. As an adult, he will turn into a person with serious personality defects; he will become amoral, irresponsible, and impulsive.

Sepp: So these psychopaths become such because of mental defects, regardless of having good parents?

Anton: The black sheep. In some cases, yes, though I think it is rare. I also believe that the violent behavior of children comes from adults; it is mostly nurtured. A son sees and experiences the brutal nature of his father and becomes like him.

Sepp: The mother has no influence?

Anton: Yes, she does; in fact, she develops good traits in her child. Babies already learn, though it is a selfish learning. The newborn is only living, surviving; its brain knows neither good nor bad. It is really devoid of anything. It needs food, to be changed when dirty, sleep. A baby is like a sponge, soaking it all up. The hugging by Mommy, the gentle words, songs—it all feels good. The babe is happy. In return the baby learns to smile to show its satisfaction; it is also the beginning of return loving. It already learned to cry to show it is unhappy. If she is a cold mother who provides only essentials but not love, the child doesn't have a chance to become a normal person. Add a mean and unjust father and you develop a bad child and youngster. Under Hitler, the brutality was also nurtured by the Hitler Youth. The family then played a secondary role. There was also peer pressure to be like the others. A well-indoctrinated youth then became a brutal SS man who could shoot men, women, and children and do it merciless. We cannot even call these killers psychopath. Today's children and youths in Germany are from the same stock as those were born and raised in Nazi Germany, yet they are decent and normal. This is why I say that evilness is mostly nurtured and not inborn.

Sepp: Women by nature not as brutal as men?

Anton: That is right. I am not a psychologist to tell you why that is so. Perhaps because they are physically not as strong therefore less aggressive and brutal. In fact, in Egypt where I went to school and higher education, we didn't even have, well, let's call it sociology 101. It would have had to treat females like males a no-no. Nor Christian ethics like love thy enemy or the famous "do unto others." If anything it was "hate thy enemy and kill him." To come back to females, women can be very evil; but when it comes to physical cruelties and killings, it is done by men. There are and were exceptions; take the female guards in concentration camps. But all these mass murders in America and in the rest of the world are by men, never by women.

Max: Then it is by nurturing that the Pakistani Taliban are more cruel than those from Afghanistan?

Anton: Yes. What I have seen and learned, the most vicious men come from Pakistan, Iraq, and the Palestinians. The Palestinians have been nurtured with incitement and hatred for three generations to kill the Jews. It is in their blood; of course, this is a matter of speech. It is not their genes, only learned and taught to hate and kill, to torture.

I read the book *Because They Hate* by Brigitte Gabriel. Gabriel is a Maronite Lebanese, and she writes about her youth in Lebanon during the civil war. The cruelties of the Hezbollah who are mostly Palestinians living in Lebanon.

Max: How about the jihadists from North Africa? Killing these hostages in Algeria. Also in Mali and Nigeria they are active.

Anton: You have a big problem in the northern parts of Africa. To the south of the Arab countries of Morocco, Algeria, Libya, and Egypt are the nations of Mauritania, Mali, Niger, Chad, Sudan, Ethiopia, also Nigeria, and Somali. These countries are multiethnic; you have Arabs, Muslims to the north and blacks, Christians, or heathens to the south. Until America abolished slavery, the Arabs would send expeditions to the south and other African countries to capture blacks and bring them to ports, either on the west coast or east coast, and slave ships brought them to the Americas. As I said, the Koran permits slavery. This, of course, was inhuman business to tear families apart and to treat the slaves cruelly. If a warship came in sight, they often just drowned the slaves. The Arabs today do not enslave the blacks but want them to convert to Islamism and the religion of Sharia. One way or another, the Arabs have always dominated the blacks.

The blacks in the south of those countries—most of them are Christians—do not want to be dominated and live under Sharia therefore these clashes. In Algeria the Islamists were mainly bandits, like their leader Moktar Belmoktar. He uses religion to mask his banditry. In Mali and Nigeria it is religious; the Muslims came south and wanted the introduction of Sharia with the usual excesses of amputations, whippings, enslaving women.

Max: I have to check around northern Mali and Nigeria for these Islamists. I read that the French forces liberated Timbuktu.

Anton: It will be difficult to differentiate between Islamists and local inhabitants. The Tuaregs who live there are always armed.

Sepp: Aren't Tuaregs bandits?

Anton: They are both desert warriors and bandits—given the opportunity. Now to something else, Sepp, I know you are still looking for war criminals; and while they are old, few left, some are still around. Why don't you query Fred Schultheis about old-timers in the Bund?

Sepp: Good idea. I ask him if there are and who they were in the war years.

Just then the door opened, and Ingrid stuck her head it; she waved her hand around. "Oooh, all that smoke. Max, open the window. And all you, men, the kids need you to build the snow castle. They want a door and windows and a roof."

The men got dressed and went out. The women with the children had built four walls but forgot an entrance. It was easy enough to cut a door and then hang a bath towel for a door, the same with windows. A large bedspread became the roof, fastened at the corners with snow. The kids disappeared into the castle, the adults into the house.

Hanna, who watched through the kitchen window, suddenly burst into laughter. "Come!"

Hanna screamed; when they looked out the window, they all laughed. It was still snowing and good, and the roof heavy with snow had caved in on the kids.

It was time for lunch anyhow.

Then in their three cars they drove out to Hellabrun, the zoo. Many of the animals were inside their enclosures, but they enjoyed watching the polar bears have fun in the snow.

Early Sunday morning Sepp came in his taxi and took the Hofer family to the airport for their flight back to Israel. It had been an enjoyable visit to snowy Munich.

Monday morning Sepp drove to the Tuerken police station and had a cup of coffee with Fred Schultheis. They sat in the coffee room and were alone; the coffee came from a machine, and Sepp made a face. "I wonder, is this coffee or soup?" They laughed.

Sepp: How are things in the Bund behaving?

"You know, they hold their meetings, give vent to anti-Semitism, condemn Mayor Ude for helping the Jews build their center and synagogue, blame the Jews for everything that is wrong in Germany and the world. Want the foreigners out of Germany, and when they make a *krawall* [rumpus], they carry placards with 'FOREIGNERS OUT OF GERMANY' and find sympathy with the citizens."

"Tell me, Fred, are there any old-timers left, I mean SS, SA, real Nazis from Hitler's times?"

"Out of the 240 members—and we were over three hundred but many left due to the warning of the world tribunal—there are about six of them. Of course, all former party members. I don't know if any were SS or SA, but I know two who were with the Gestapo."

"Who are they? Tell me about them."

"One's name is Horst Pfeuffer. I know he is ninety-five, still in pretty good shape, though hard of hearing but he remembers, tells sometimes about his work. The other is Xaver Lorenz. He worked then for the chief investigator of the Gestapo, a Robert Mohr. The good Catholic he is, he goes to church every Sunday. He seems like a decent person."

"He has family?"

"I don't know."

"And Pfeuffer—can you find out where he lives?"

"You want to meet them Herr Kainz?"

"Maybe. I like to find out more about the Gestapo. I am doing some private research about the Nazi time."

"Pfeuffer lives in the Stift, the old people's home in Schwabing."

"By the way, who is their new leader?"

"A Waldemar Wegner. We voted him in, a pretty good speaker. Radical Nazi, anti-Semite, and, of course, anti-foreigner."

"You vote with them?"

"Of course. I am an honored member, their police informer. Inspector Wagner still tells me when they conduct a *razzia* [search of their premises]. So I am trusted. And because I am police and can't be known as a member, I don't have to participate in their marches or any outdoor activities. I'll get you the information about these ex-Gestapo officials."

Fred Schultheis supplied the address of both to Sepp Kainz, who in turn asked Anton to investigate these Gestapo officials. Anton came to Munich on Saturday, ninth of February; and after checking in with Max and Sepp at the energy house, both were scanning in northern Mexico for cartel members. He drove to the address of Lorenz in the Schellingstrasse. It was afternoon by then. When he rang the bell at the second-floor apartment of Xaver Lorenz, the speaker by the entrance door asked, "Who is it?"

"I am Alfons Maier. Your leader Herr Wegner sent me with a message for you."

"So what is the message, Herr Maier?"

"I have to give it in person to you."

When the buzzer sounded, Anton opened the door. He walked upstairs and found the door to apartment 8. He knocked. "Come in, Herr Maier, the door is open." He went in and closed the door. Light came from the living room; he stepped in and found two old men sitting in basket chairs by the table.

"I am Xaver Lorenz; my friend here is Horst Pfeuffer." A cane leaned against the table where Pfeuffer sat. A bottle of wine and a half-filled glasses on the table.

"Heil Hitler," he was greeted by Pfeuffer. "Heil," he replied briefly.

"If you care to join us in a glass of wine, there are glasses on the sideboard."

Anton shook his head. "This Beaujolais is not my favorite." He sat down.

"I am surprised that our leader sent a messenger. Why didn't he just call me?"

"He told me that you don't hear very well and dislike to be called."

"That is Pfeuffer. But, Herr Maier, you are not a member of our Bund?"

"I belong to the group from Berchtesgaden. Bund member Schoenauer is our leader, and he cleared my visit to you with Waldemar Wegner. Do you know Leader Schoenauer?"

"Yes, I do. Fine man, good *Nationalsozialist*. So what can I do for you?"

"I am writing the history of members of the Bund who during the Fuehrer's time held important positions in the government, like you, Herr Lorenz; you were a Gestapo official as were you Herr Pfeuffer."

Anton saw old man Pfeuffer sit up straight as if at attention; his eyes, which seemed tired, were now wide awake. "You wish to learn about the good old times, Herr Maier? Yes, I was with the Gestapo in Munich. I am glad that somebody finally recognizes that we in the Gestapo did important work for the Reich, ferreting out opponents to the regime, taking care of the Jews, arresting Jehovah's Witnesses, and sending them to the KZ."

"When did you join the Gestapo?"

"In 1940, I was then twenty-two, just finished at the university. I had majored in political science. I was already a member of the SS. I had an uncle, Hans Pfeuffer, who was a high-ranking inspector in the Gestapo here in Munich.

He arranged for me to join. I worked out of the Wittelsbacher Palais, Gestapo Headquarters."

"And you worked there as an agent?"

"At the beginning I worked with another official, checking people in the street, at the railroad station. I learned fast that when we stopped someone and showed them our badge and said, 'Geheime Staatspolizei'; the reaction told us if they were suspicious characters.

They would turn white in the face; some had trembled hands when they showed their identification. We were like the bogeyman to them." He laughed. "Of course we had a profile whom to stop, learned that in training sessions. The usual riff-raff, Jews, foreigners, homosexuals, *Bibelforscher* [men who should have been in the army]. It became easier for us when in September 1941, the Jews had to wear the Star of David.

Checked that it was sewn on and not just fastened with snaps. Off to Dachau if we caught one like that or hiding it. Checking in movies or other places they were prohibited to go to."

"What were your most memorable moments during your work as a Gestapo agent?"

"I liked the house searches of Jews. I worked then with the SA Scharfuehrer Mugler who knew where the Jews lived. The SA was in charge of everything that pertained to the Jews, especially the aryanization of Jewish property. They conducted the house searches but needed an authoritative person with them, usually a Gestapo agent. By then I am talking about late 1941 when the Jews had to wear the star.

We conducted the raids to find weapons. Of course we knew that the Jews didn't have any weapons but other illegal items they were forbidden to have. Jewelry—anything of silver and gold—money, furs, pets. I was mainly interested in finding food stuff they were not supposed to have as their ration cards had those stamped void. Butter, cold cuts, any meat or fish, fruits, white bread or bakeries, wine or anything alcoholic. Mugler let me confiscate those items while he took things of value and money. Mugler could be rough. I remember in one dingy apartment the old woman had a cat. He grabbed it by its hind legs and smashed its head on the table that blood spattered all over. When the old woman cried out, I slapped her then hit the old man with my fist in the face when he interfered. I didn't go for killing pets, but that was Mugler. We also checked their clothing to see if their star was sewn on correctly. Just before the deportation in November 41, we got calls from neighbors that they smelled gas, Jews using gas to commit suicide, or they took poison, sleeping tablets. Then came the first deportation, the big one of a thousand Jews. Several of us Gestapo agents worked with the SA. All the Jews to be deported were already in the Jew camp in Milbertshofen. SA Mugler, Schrott, and Gestapo Wegner were in charge. We Gestapo just assisted, and so did Jews from the camp, opening suitcases and backpacks. The Jews had much too much baggage; they had a list of what to take, but we allowed them only forty pounds of baggage. So anything of value, new or pretty things, we took away from them. The same all their mementos, pictures, documents, money, bankbooks, etc. Lots of crying, screaming and yelling by us. Then we conducted strip searches even on children. They didn't need any of that stuff they were told to take, not where they were going."

"Where were they going?"

"We were told to work camps in the East, supposedly to the ghetto in Riga. Later Mugler told me that they are destined to Kovno to be shot."

"Did you agree with that Herr Pfeuffer?"

"Of course. That was the 'final solution' the Fuehrer decreed."

"How about you, Herr Lorenz?"

"Well, it is kind of brutal to shoot people, especially families with children. There must have been a better way to get rid of the Jews."

Pfeuffer: Like later gassing them. Or just work them to death.

Lorenz: It is kind of un-German to shoot children. I thought then and I think now. Of course, as I found out later, the shooting was done by Lithuanians.

"Herr Lorenz, your work as a Gestapo agent was then mainly concerned with Jews?"

"Oh no. In 1942, I was assigned as an aid to chief inspector Mohr of the Gestapo. He handled real criminals, opposition enemies of the Reich. With him I learned real detective work and investigations. There were still former Communists around, Jehovah's Witnesses, people who listened to foreign broadcasts, making anti-Nazi remarks. Mohr was great in investigations and always had good results. He used psychology instead of beatings and tortures. Our big coup came at the begin of 1943 when we eliminated the Weisse Rose group led by the brother-and-sister team Hans and Sophie Scholl. That group of students printed and distributed anti-Hitler and anti-Nazi leaflets, also painted slogans on walls in the city. Nobody knew who they were; we in the Gestapo and the police were on high alert to find them. With the city in blackout we couldn't see a person smearing on walls if they were just a few houses away. Then luckily the caretaker at the university, a Jakob Schmidt, saw a young woman throw a stack of leaflets from a staircase. He then saw her joined by a student and had the two arrested, Hans and Sophie Scholl. Searching their apartment we found the names of others and were able to arrest the group. I, as the aid to Inspector Mohr, brought them to his office for interrogation. I took notes, and while at first they denied everything, he soon had them confess using psychology; he was a master at that. Then came the trial before the *Volksgerichthof* [people's tribunal]. Roland Freisler came down from Berlin and sentenced them and six others to death. The next day their parents came to visit them in the prison of Stadelheim. Later the same day they were guillotined. Stupid students—I really felt sorry for Sophie. She was such a nice girl. Shortly after, I joined the Viking Waffen SS division and went to Russia."

"And you, Herr Pfeuffer, you had anything to do with the White Rose Group?"

"Of course. While the Scholls were only interrogated by Mohr, I was in arresting and questioning the others of the group. Christoph Probst, Alexander Schmorell, Willi Graf, and Professor Kurt Huber. Graf was a tough nut to crack. I slapped him numerous times, but we were told not to hurt them so it showed. Good blows against the kidneys not only hurt but led enviably to a slow death. Some of us had a course on 'rigorous questioning.' Of course Roland Freisler sentenced them to death, and their heads were chopped off."

"What do you mean by rigorous questioning, Herr Pfeuffer?"

"Application of force. Beatings—my specialty—actual torturing like thumb screws; only we had an apparatus that squeezed all fingers breaking fingers, electric shock. Ice water immersion, but that was done in the KZ Dachau. I know in the east in KZs, they used acetylene torches. But all in all, we were not as harsh as the inquisition with their auto-de-café; we didn't use boiling water, and we didn't rape the females. Sophie Scholl was never molested, right, Xaver?" Herr Lorenz nodded his head.

"Let me ask you, Herr Lorenz, now, seventy years after it all ended, you are still a confirmed Nazi?"

"Herr Maier, you are writing the history of the Gestapo, and as you said, you belong to the Bund from Berchtesgaden. Can we keep this conversation just between us? Yes? All right, I was a Nazi, and what else could I do as a former Gestapo agent and SS man but join our group here in Munich to find understanding, if you know what I mean? But while I liked the comradeship of first the Hitler Youth, then the Gestapo and especially the Waffen SS, I was never an admirer of Hitler or Himmler. With their crimes against the Jews, gypsies, and Jehovah's Witnesses, they shamed Germany before the world. Instead of starting this war against the Soviets Hitler, should have stopped the war. Let England shrivel away. No war with America. We were the masters in Europe. Ship the Jews to Palestine and solve the problem this way instead of shooting and gassing them in camps, and to hell with the Arabs if they didn't like it. Look at them here in Munich, the Muslims trying to take over, into crime, taking our women away. We in the Bund want all the foreigners out. That is the main reason I am still in the Bund and not because of their anti-Semitic program. To uphold what the Nazis stood for. Some were good; some were bad. Hitler was Germany's downfall. Just between us, Herr Maier?"

Anton smiled. "Just between us. And you, Herr Pfeuffer, any last words?"

"My friend and colleague from the Gestapo Xaver never was a steadfast Nazi. I was and still am. The Fuehrer at least succeeded in wiping out the Jews who started the war, though he made the mistake of declaring war on America. He did it mainly to wipe out the Jews worldwide. We present Nazis still have as our main aim the *Endloesung* of the Jews."

Anton concluded the interview and thanked Herr Lorenz for his openness and promised him not to reveal his low opinion of Hitler. He turned to Pfeuffer. "Can I give you a lift to the Stift? I have my car downstairs."

Pfeuffer drained his glass, said goodbye to Lorenz, took his cane, and hobbled out of the apartment. At the stairwell Anton said in a whisper, "Pfeuffer you are an abomination to mankind, to decent Germans in particular. Go to hell!" He tripped him; with a push, Pfeuffer fell head over heels down the staircase. There was the commotion of his fall. Lorenz came to the stairs and called down, "What happened? Did Horst fall?"

Anton examined the old man. The way his head was deformed he knew he had broken his neck—saved him from doing it.

Anton called up, "Herr Pfeuffer stumbled and fell; you better call the medics."

(When the ambulance came, they recorded Pfeuffer's death and called the police. The police concluded that the man was drunk, stumbled, and fell. It was an accident. In a byline the police added that a stranger by the name of Alfons Maier was with Horst Pfeuffer, said he was sent by Herr Wegner. Wegner stated that he did not know Maier.)

Anton returned to the institute and told Sepp and Max of his discussion with Pfeuffer and Lorenz.

"When I first met them, I had in mind to eliminate both Gestapo agents, terrorizing people, beating, and torturing them But Lorenz was not a bad person; he was not anti-Semitic. In fact, he thought that Hitler should have solved the Jewish question by shipping them to Palestine."

Sepp: The Arabs and British wouldn't have liked that.

Anton: He didn't say anything about the British, probably didn't even know about their white paper prohibiting the emigration of Jews to Palestine. As for the Arabs, he said, "To hell with the Arabs"; he doesn't like the Muslims being in Germany.

Sepp: You did right in not eliminating Lorenz.

Max: I agree. We want to be very selective whom we eliminate. Anton, we have an interesting project. I thought we take a look at the illegal entry into America by boats, bringing people and drugs. I found a fishing cutter which looks mighty suspicious. Here let me show you.

Max projected the coast of Southern California; a good distance west of San Diego he showed the cutter. "They are just standing there doing nothing. A few times a fighter, probably from the air base in Coronado, flew over; and then they are fishing. Just a fishing cutter in international waters. Now watch when I bring the cutter up close."

Max zeroed in close, and they saw nothing happening but a hose extended from the cutter down into the sea. "This could be first of all a connection for air, also for electricity and communication. Now watch the water by the cutter. You see the shadow?"

What they saw was the outline of a long narrow boat, almost as long as the cutter.

Anton: A submarine?

Max: I think so. Not for illegals but to bring drugs into America, probably when it gets dark. For now we just let them do their fishing and come back at sunset. Let's see. It is now after five, eight in the morning in California; in February it should get dark by their time at five. Let's go home and come back at midnight; then we still have a couple hours.

This they did and met again at midnight. Max said that if asked why they signed in so late for work and on a Sunday, he would explain that they needed radiation-free access to the atmosphere to project electricity. Max brewed good coffee.

By two o'clock in the morning Max had the cutter back in view; the sun was just setting. He explained that the cutter had moved about twenty miles to the north and as many miles from shore. A close-up of the cutter showed its radar antenna turning.

Max: They want to be certain that there is nothing around for a distance of ten or more miles. Max raised the view until they could see the coastline of southern California; they didn't see anything either except the bright lights of nearby towns.

Twilight, then it was dark. The view was again close to the cutter, which now shone a spotlight down at the water at the leeward, away from the coast. And slowly the submarine rose, cables fastened it to the cutter. From the small conning tower, three men emerged and seemed to be talking to men on the cutter.

Max: If there were illegals on the cutter, they would get into small boats here, right?

Anton: Right! To use a sub to bring immigrants would be expensive; it must be drugs.

Max: But why the cutter? Why not bring the sub up from Mexico by itself?

Anton: A small sub like that has a limited range. It was attached to the cutter, so it wouldn't need to use its batteries. It couldn't go on top using the diesels; else, it would be spotted by the American Coast Guard, other ships, or planes. We can be sure that it is a drug sub. It will go underwater close to shore, then surface, and unload on boats waiting or launch rubber rafts. It has to be at a protective cove. But how can we sink it?

Max: We can eliminate the three. They are probably the only ones who know how to maneuver the sub.

Anton: Let's wait and see what they do.

Sepp: You mean if they transfer drugs from the cutter to the sub?

Anton: No. The cutter couldn't afford to carry any drugs. They might be stopped by the Coast Guard and searched. A Mexican fishing boat off the California coast is always suspicious. The drugs are on the sub.

They watched and saw men from the cutter bring Jerry cans to the railing.

Anton: Here is our chance. They need to refuel their diesel. Let me get my infrared rays going. There are six cans, Max; after they lowered three into the sub, zero in of the fourth one. When it is lowered into the tower, I give it a good jolt. Most likely they will drop it and ignite the other cans for a good fire or even an explosion.

A man climbed back into the sub, and then one on the cutter tied a rope into the handle on a can and lowered it into the sub. When the fourth can was lowered, Max showed a close-up when the can was in the tower. Anton gave it a five-thousand-degree, one-second jolt, and the can burst into flames. The man on the sub holding the rope let go, and it fell down. The man in the sub scrambled up, his clothing on fire; the others used a blanket to smother it. There was a swoosh of fire emerging; then dark smoke came boiling up. The three on the sub went up the rope ladder to the cutter as fire engulfed the submarine. The cutter cut all cables to the sub and moved away.

They watched the sub sink.

Max then zeroed in on the coast by tracking the lights of the coastal town of Solana Beach. They saw high cliffs and then an open cove. A ramp led from the beach to the street, it all of was sparsely lit. There stood a van in the parking lot. Several men were standing by the van; one was talking on his cell phone. Then the men got into the van and drove off.

Max: Let that be a lesson not to use subs bringing in drugs. Mission accomplished. Let's go home. It was six o'clock in the morning when they left.

With Max's and Sepp's approval, Anton wrote a letter on the computer and addressed it to chief editor Sebastian Konrad of the *Berner Nachrichten*. On Monday, the eleventh of February, Sepp went by train to Vienna and bought a packet of envelopes. He used plastic gloves to insert the letter, then mailed it.

The letter was received by the secretary Matilde Gruber on Wednesday who at once gave it to Herr Konrad (the letter was in English).

To: Herr Sebastian Konrad, chief editor Berner Nachrichten
From: The World Tribunal

Adjunct with fighting the Mexican drug cartels, agents of the world tribunal are surveying the American coast. Beginning of February a Mexican fishing cutter was observed fifty miles off the coast of San Diego. Upon closer observation, a small submarine was seen attached to the cutter. At dusk, the cutter was seen twenty miles north and about as many miles due west off Solana Beach. It was dark when the sub surfaced.

When the sub was fueled, eliminator agents were able to cause a fire on the sub, and it sank. One man from the sub was injured by fire; no one was killed. The cutter then departed. Searching the cove the agents saw a large van, which soon left.

Please inform the American Coast Guard of the matter.

The Force of Three

Meeting of the Advisory Board, Monday 25 February 2013.
The meeting was as usual at FBI headquarters in Quantico. It was called by the director of the FBI. Invited was the commander of the sub base in Point Loma, San Diego, Rear Admiral Wilson. Present, the new secretary of state Kerry.

Director: I have interesting news from our agent John Adams, who is with EUROPOL. Apparently, the world tribunal sent a letter to the *Berner Nachrichten* newspaper who in turn informed EUROPOL. Accordingly, a Mexican cartel submarine penetrated our coastal waters off San Diego to deliver a load of drugs. The sub was attached to a fishing cutter. With nighttime the sub surfaced, it was then about twenty miles due west of a town called Solana Beach. Apparently, the world tribunal caused a fire on the sub, and it sank.

We informed the naval authorities in San Diego who had Admiral Wilson dispatch a rescue ship to the indicated area. Admiral Wilson, please.

Admiral Wilson: It was easy to find the sub in the fairly shallow water. Our rescue ship raised the small sub. The fire destroyed most of the sub's control area. It seemed that someone was in the control area, directly under the conning tower, and hit the flooding controls, probably to put out the fire, but then left. This caused the boat to sink.

The submarine was built by North Korea and of the Nahang costal submarine class.

This small sub is of one hundred tons displacement and used for insertion of agents; it can carry five personnel and about three tons of supplies. We found that much of cocaine. We did not find any personnel; they must have abandoned the sub when the fire started. In the control room right under the tower, we found four burst canisters of diesel fuel.

Director: This must have been the cause of the fire. The tribunal with their heat ray bursting one can, which then caused the others to burn or explode.

CIA: Interesting that North Korea deals with the drug cartels.

NSA: Giving it to them or selling them the sub?

CIA: The North Koreans don't give anything away for free.

Director: They might, anything to hurt the United States, even dealing with the criminal cartels.

Secretary: Clandestine of course. They would never admit to have dealings with drug cartels. Lately the North Koreans have become quite belligerent towards South Korea and us.

CIA: What is Kim Jong-Un trying to prove?

Secretary: Mostly for internal consumption, showing his people how tough he can be. Also, impressing the military, solidifying his leadership over his officer's corps. As a dictator, he always must be aware that he rules only because the military permits him.

NSA: I don't understand that the military plays his game. Don't they want to be free and enjoy international relationships? Travel to foreign countries? Rub elbows, so to speak, with fellow officers from abroad? Work toward a unification with South Korea?

Secretary: Unification on North Korea's terms. Every dictator cuddles his military by giving them high salaries, villas, cars. Officers are the princes of the realm. Even enlisted men are better off than the common worker or farmer. So the military desires the status quo, even if their leader looks and acts like a bully.

Director: The question is, should we publicize the capture of a Mexican cartel's submarine in United States water? A sub given or sold to the cartel by North Korea?

Secretary: The North Koreans would only deny it.

Director: A coastal sub of the Nahang class. We can show North Korean writing.

Secretary: The same writing South Korea uses.

Director: A North Korean production. The South Koreans do not build submarines.

Secretary: They will say it was built by the U.S., given to the South Koreans, all done to embarrass the United States. Dictators do not need to speak the truth. Let us just display the sub in a navy yard. Yes, for public viewing and a plaque describing the capture of the North Korean sub, used by the drug cartel to sluice cocaine into the United States. Let the media pick it up and print the story.

Admiral Wilson: It is now at our sub bas in Point Loma, San Diego. We shall do so as you suggested, Secretary Kerry.

With that the FBI director concluded the meeting.

Anton did not come to Munich for several weeks. Professor Klausner was still tracking the drug cartels in northern Mexico. And while news media wrote of renewed warfare between the cartels, there were no new reports of innocents murdered. At least that much had been achieved by the world tribunal. Nor were there any reports of Somali pirates capturing ships. To find former war criminals was also a difficult task as few were still alive. The campaign against terrorists was at a standstill. Klausner could not find any new camps in Yemen, Pakistan, or Afghanistan.

Nevot, who visited Anton frequently, brought an interesting article his friend Resnik had sent him. Dated 6 February, it was now several weeks old. It was headlined survivalists seeking families for walled "citadel" in Idaho.

It was a report from St. Maries, Idaho, and stated that a group of survivalists want to build a giant walled fortress in the woods of the Idaho Panhandle. Christina Kerodin, the promoter of the project, provided little details but points to a website that shows drawings of a stone fortress with room for up to seven thousand families. The compound would include houses, schools, a hotel, a museum, and a firearms factory to manufacture semi-automatic pistols and AR-15 assault rifles. Applicants must pay a $208 fee, and the website claims several hundred people already have applied to live in the citadel.

Such communities are hardly new, especially in northern Idaho, which has long been a magnet for those looking to shun mainstream society because of its isolation, wide-open spaces, and lack of racial diversity. For three decades, the Aryan Nations operated a compound about an hour north of here before the group went bankrupt and the land was sold.

The number of so-called patriot groups has grown since President Obama was first elected, and the renewed debate over gun control is further deepening resentment of the federal government among such faction.

Anton looked at Nevot after he read the article. "Probably the former members of the Aryan Nation wish to live in this fortress, also other bigots who don't wish to live with the diverse makeup of America, meaning with blacks, Latinos, Asians, Jews. I hope they build this place and live there; then, we can control this rabble easier, and so can the local police and FBI."

"I heard from Resnik that the people in St. Maries already complain about such a fortress being built near their town."

"I doubt that it will ever be built. But thanks for the information. Now we don't have to look for the camps of the Aryan Nation."

"You were looking for such camps Anton?"

"In our fight against neo-Nazis."

Other news of a terrorist nature in February came from Egypt where two ultraconservative clerics issued a fatwa urging the killing of opposition figures as Sharia demands it. Cleric Ahmed Mohammed Abdullah, also known as Abu Islam, justified a string of mob sexual assaults on women protesters in Cairo's Tahrir Square by saying, "They are going there to get raped. Nine out of ten of them are Crusaders [Christians]."

And in Nigeria, gunmen of the radical sect known as Boko Haram killed nine nurses

These women were giving oral polio vaccines to children. This dastardly crime happened in Kano, the largest city in Nigeria's predominantly Muslim north.

Anton saved this article to give to Max and research the city of Kano.

March, 2013.

They met again Friday, the fifteenth of March. Sepp had picked up Anton at the airport at noon. At the institute they went to the cafeteria for lunch.

Max: Have you seen the papers about North Korea threatening South Korea and America?

Anton: Yes, the papers in Israel are full of such reports.

Sepp: What is that crazy Kim Jong-Un up to?

Max: Kim Jong-Un doesn't like the new sanctions the UNO has targeted North Korea with. In retaliation he threatens South Korea and America. The apocalyptic rhetoric included a threat to launch a preemptive nuclear strike against foreign aggressors, which again means South Korea and America. Here, I cut the warning from the paper as I feel we have to do something to counter these threats: "A foreign ministry statement published by Pyongyang's news agency decried the new sanctions as part of a U.S. led 'war of aggression, vowing that the North would respond with a display of might and put an end to the evil cycle of tension.'" The statement further warned that Pyongyang would exercise its right for a preemptive nuclear attack to destroy the stronghold of the aggressors. North Korea is also preparing a new long-range missile test on its east coast and directed into the Pacific, toward Hawaii.

Sepp: Is Kim trying to start a war, a war with atom bombs?

Anton: Like Max said, apocalyptic but empty threats. North Korea doesn't have long-range missiles to hit anything and, besides, not the capability to put a nuclear device into a missile. There is an outside chance that he might start a war against South Korea. He has a powerful army with many good Russian tanks, a strong air force and navy. I read where on the twelfth North Korea carried out a threat to cancel the 1953 armistice, which means that both countries are again in a state of war.

Sepp: This Kim is a war criminal. Didn't his navy sink a South Korean destroyer a few years ago? And bombard an island, killing people? He deserves to be eliminated.

Max: Even if we eliminate him, what comes after? With the aggressive military in charge, it may easily come to war. Can't we warn him, threaten him with the heat ray?

Anton: I doubt that he is even aware of the world tribunal and its power. He is also a bully and threatening him would turn him into a raging bull. We have to work on the Chinese. They are his best friends and give him the economic aid to permit him to exist.

Max: Who is the president of China or chairman?

Anton: His name is Xi. We don't need to talk to him. I don't even know if he speaks English. We can talk to the Chinese ambassador in Washington. Washington is six hours behind us. Let's try at six in the afternoon, which would be noon there. Let's see if we can catch him perhaps in the garden.

Max: I get a map of the city in the meantime and through Google find the place.

Anton: Gives me a chance to go home. Sepp, want to drive me there? You used my car to pick me up.

Sepp: Yes, to keep it in running order. I rarely come here in my taxi.

They met again at six in the energy house. Max had already the Chinese embassy in view and showed the garden. It was a nice sunny day in Washington and apparently pleasant enough to have lunch in the garden. On the veranda behind the house a small table was prepared, and two men sat there eating; a servant stood nearby. On a sideboard stood a radio, and when Sepp turned his audio ray on, they could hear the news. The two men spoke in Chinese. Anton told Sepp to increase the volume.

Anton (in English): We interrupt the news with an important message for the Chinese ambassador.

One of the men looked startled then said, "I wonder that the news bureau wants to speak to me." (He spoke in English.)

Anton: Please, ambassador. This is the world tribunal who wishes to address you. Please turn the news off but keep the radio active.

They watched as the ambassador stood up, went to the sideboard, and adjusted the radio.

He said something to the servant who left. He then sat down again.

Ambassador: Yes, please. I heard about the world tribunal.

Anton: It is a most important message I have for you, perhaps even a discussion. I am glad you sent the servant away. May I ask who the man is sitting with you? You wish for him to remain?"

Ambassador: This is Li Baodong, the Chinese UN envoy. If it is world politics you wish to discuss with me, I believe that Mr. Baodong should remain.

Anton: Yes, a splendid idea. In fact, I welcome Mr. Baodong's presence as it concerns the present tension in Asia, specifically the aggressiveness of Kim Jong-Un.

Baodong: I understand. But why not take it up with Kim Jong-Un directly?

Anton: First of all, I doubt that Kim speaks English or Russian or any other European language. Secondly, one cannot reason with a person like Kim Jong-Un. Could one have reasoned with a Hitler or Stalin? North Korea at this stage is just a hermetic Stalinist state. And while not a puppet state of China, it has no other friend and depends upon China for its existence, its aggressive army for your weapons.

Ambassador: And your organization believes that he will listen to us?

Anton: Of course he will. We are certain that China—who has become a world power, an economic giant—does not wish for a war on its doorsteps. Stop your daily delivery of food and fuel, just for a few days, a week, and he will notice that you are serious and determined to keep the peace in Asia. It is not what you say to Kim, but certain actions you can take to stop him from his rhetoric. Threats plus provocation can lead to war.

A war Kim can never win but it would devastate his country.

Baodong: The threatening theoretic is due to the vote in the UN pursued by your United States government.

Anton: My dear ambassador Li Baodong, the world tribunal is not an agent or agency of the United States. We are an international group of eminent scientists and jurists who have this power to punish and warn.

We have no allegiance to any nation. We punish with elimination mass murderers past and present, terrorists; we warn hate and war mongers. We could warn Kim Jong-Un in a public manifesto, but that takes time. We believe that the matter is urgent and that China can persuade North Korea to stop the threats of war and stop the testing of missiles.

Baodong: I shall fly immediately to China and speak to our chairman and government officials. While I don't believe that Kim Jong-Un would accept an invitation to come to Beijing, I believe that he would send his foreign minister at once. I personally believe that one of the reasons of Kim's belligerency is to impress on the United States to hold talks and rescind the UN sanctions.

Anton: While I cannot speak for the U.S. government, I am certain that they will agree to talks of denuclearization of the Korean Peninsula and if that happens with the rescinding of UN sanctions.

Ambassador: May I ask one question of the world tribunal? Are you in association with any European nation or perhaps Israel?

Anton: No. As I said before and as our manifesto proclaimed, we are international.

Goodbye then, gentlemen, and good luck, Ambassador Li Baodong.

Anton gave Sepp a sign to interrupt the broadcasting.

Max: I hope we succeed.

Sepp: Good job, Anton.

Apparently Ambassador Li Baodong succeeded in his mission to China. China summoned the North Korean foreign minister. By the end of March the long-range missile was withdrawn from the east coast of North Korea, and Pyongyang asked for talks with the United States.

It was early in the morning of Friday, the tenth of May, that Nevot came to visit his friend Anton at police headquarters. Anton was surprised at the early visit, had tea brought in, and the two friends sat together with windows open smoking.

Anton: So early? What happened, Nevot?

Nevot: Yesterday, the Hezbollah leader Hassan Nasrallah made a speech marking the twenty-fifth anniversary of the founding of Al-Nour, Hezbollah's radio station. It was televised in Beirut. In his speech he made boasts that Syria will supply Hezbollah with "game changing" weapons. It was only last week that we targeted trucks in Damascus, which carried advanced Iranian guided missiles destined for Hezbollah. They have tens of thousand rockets, though most are unguided. These trucks carried precision-guided missiles that could reach even Elath, in fact, any place in Israel. The strike was successful, the shipment destroyed. Nasrallah knows that our planes can pinpoint any target; therefore, he asked Iran for antiaircraft weapons to hold our planes at bay. Iran has such weapons, of course, made in Russia and provided by them to Iran. Syria doesn't even have this advanced weapon system. Iran at once shipped these weapons to Syria, and they are stored in a warehouse in an industrial park near Damascus. We have, of course, people in Damascus who supply us with information. The question for us is which warehouse; there are hundreds of them in that park, large and small, office buildings in between. We cannot afford to hit the wrong building, kill people not involved. Assad and the Syrians would scream to high heaven if we did. Probably drag us before the United Nations.

We have an exact description of the warehouse, but with so many, our planes would have a hard time identifying the right one. I thought if the world tribunal could help us, somehow mark this building before our planes arrive—understand what I mean, Anton?

"I do, Nevot. I guess it is very important for Israel to destroy this weapons system."

"Once they have the capability to ward off our planes, they are free to ship these guided missiles to Hezbollah or anything else they wish to send them."

"Would it help your planes if we set the roof of the warehouse on fire?"

"It would make a fine target."

"How much time to we have?"

"It has to be done as soon as possible. We have information that they are dismantling the systems into small parts so they can be carried by cars and vans then leave individually so as not to attract attention. The first shipments are to leave on Sunday."

"Which means the warehouse has to be destroyed tomorrow."

"Yes, Anton."

"I wasn't planning on going to Munich this weekend. I have to send at once an e-mail that I am coming. Number two, you need to get the description of the warehouse today and come to Munich later today, take a taxi, and come to my house. Coordinate the action to take place on

Saturday with exact timing. At a certain time we set the roof on fire, and within minutes the plane or planes have to appear. Once we start the fire, we have to expect that a nearby fire department comes and extinguishes the fire. That is, at the time the fire starts within ten minutes the action has to take place."

"It can be done; the Mossad will coordinate it with the air force."

"There is the possibility that the roof is not inflammable—a tin roof, for example, or even tin sheets placed on concrete—which means we cannot burn holes into it. Does the air force have the means to guide their bombs with infrared?"

"I don't know, Anton. I need to call the Mossad, and they might have to call the air force."

"Do it now. In the meantime I notify Munich that I am coming. Call my wife that it is urgent that I fly to Munich today."

While Nevot called, Anton sent his e-mail to Max.

Nevot: I talked to the chief. Of course he was highly surprised. He expects me shortly so he can have the right people show me how to recognize the pertinent building. He also calls the air force in regards to the infrared bombing system. I expect his return call any minute. He asked if this phone connection is secure.

"It is, Nevot."

A few minutes later the phone rang. The caller asked to speak to Mordechai Nevot.

Anton gave him the phone.

Nevot: The chief says that the bombs cannot be guided by infrared but the planes can home in on a hot target.

Anton: Then the pilots might see smoke of a burning roof or hot spots on a roof.

"All right, Anton. Visually they will look for smoke, with instruments a hot roof. I have a time element to coordinate. Fifteen minutes after noon, that is, 12:15 p.m."

"Israel is an hour ahead of our time in Germany. We will fire the roof at 11:05 a.m."

"Done, Anton. I leave now for the Mossad. See you this evening."

"One more thing, Nevot. We have to sign you in as it is the weekend. Get a passport for a German, if possible with a title of a scientist."

"No problem, Anton."

Nevot left. Anton reported to the commissioner of police Avi Barlev that he had to leave urgently and went home.

Saturday, May 11, Anton and Nevot went to the Max Planck Institute. In the foyer they signed in—that is, Nevot did after showing his passport, a Dr. Hans Schmitt, professor of energy at the institute in Dresden.

In the energy house Max awaited them. Anton introduced Nevot. Max was already appraised of him and the action.

Through Google, Max had already greater Damascus on the screen. Nevot pointed to the northeast, zeroing closer they soon saw the industrial complex. Nevot had a large picture, an aerial photograph of the area. One mid-sized warehouse was circled. Max found it and closed in on the building. Yes, it had a tin roof.

Anton: The tin sheet must lie upon a roof structure; if it is wood, we can burn through and start a fire. If it is concrete, we can only heat it and do so at several places.

It was now eleven o'clock.

Anton adjusted the infrared ray to five thousand degrees and gave it a one-tenth-second pulse. They could see a small hole and smoke was pouring out.

Anton: It is wooden underneath. We can start nice fires. I hope nobody sees the smoke."

Nevot: In the harsh sunlight it is hardly noticeable.

Max: Ready to go, Anton?

Anton: Let's wait five more minutes. Can't have premature smoke attracting people.

Eleven seven. Anton used five thousand degrees and one-fifth-second pulses; and at different places he used the ray to burn holes through the tin sheeting and started fires underneath. He did so for ten pulses and by eleven twelve, the roof was enveloped in smoke.

Max raised the view, and they saw people standing by the building and staring up. No fire engines in sight so far.

Eleven sixteen. Suddenly the building was torn by a fireball, a moment later a second, and then a third ball of fire—smoke, dust, debris flew apart; and then only black smoke came from the area where the building had stood.

Max: Mission accomplished successfully.

Nevot shook his hand. "We thank you and are grateful for what you have done," then thanked Anton likewise.

Max put his fingers to his lips.

Nevot: I have seen nothing; in fact, I was not even in Munich.

Anton wanted Nevot to stay in Munich for the day, but Nevot needed to fly back to Israel and report to the Mossad. Anton flew back with him.

The director of the Mossad wished to see him; it was Sunday, the twelfth of May. Nevot went to his office.

Director: Have a seat Mordechai. Tea or coffee?

Glasses of tea were brought in.

Mordechai: The raid was a success?

"Each directed bomb hit the warehouse, and it and its contents were destroyed. The roof of the warehouse was marked with smoke. How was it done?"

"A number of five-thousand-degree heat radiations burned through the tin-roof and set the wooden layer on fire."

"Now, Mordechai, tell me all about it and the people involved."

"Director, I can't. I gave my word of honor, and any future cooperation between them and Israel depends on my silence."

"So far, we only know that it is not a laser beam; are you permitted to tell me about the technique?"

"I can only divulge that it is infrared radiation."

"Directed by a plane, a drone perhaps?"

"No, it is satellite directed."

"You are telling me secrets now?"

"Not really. Common sense explains it better than technical guessing."

The director laughed. "Nobody seems to have this common sense.

We thought for certain that it is an American operation. And now we find out that it is German, directed from or near Munich."

"You traced me?"

"Of course! We did not promise you that we do not check on the destination of your mission. Let me ask you this, the people involved . . . Jewish?"

"No. But let me tell you this much: the group involved is Israeli friendly. I was told that if the Mossad has a special target to be eliminated, if possible they will help."

"May I ask, what are the technical capabilities?"

"By switching to different wavelength they can see, hear, and speak. By using infrared they can kill or, as they prefer to call it, eliminate a person. The individual has to be outdoors and stand still. I cannot tell you any more, director."

"One last question, Mordechai, are they careful in communicating with you? We know, of course, that America, as is Russia and China and many other technically advanced nations, listen in to wireless communication."

"They don't use any such communication; they are aware of the pitfalls. Is that it, director?"

The director smiled. "I have many more, but I understand your promise to be discreet.

Let me ask you this then: they cannot see at night?"

"Like you, darkness prevents seeing."

"Your visits to America then have nothing to do with the world tribunal?"

Mordechai smiled. "Then you also know about my visits to New York. I visit a good friend of mine Jack. Resnik is a philanthropist who benefits Israel. I advise and give seminars sometimes to Israel-involved groups."

"Goodbye then, Mordechai. Keep up the good relation with them. Any news of interest, you know where to find me as I know how to find you."

"Director, my advice to you is to keep your knowledge guarded. No one else in the world knows as much about the world tribunal as you do now."

"Only my deputy will learn these facts in case something happens to me, and the PM must know."

"Not the cabinet I hope."

"Of course not." Mordechai Nevot was satisfied and left.

In June there was no action in the energy house. The Hofers—together with the Klausner family, Sepp Kainz, and his wife, Inge—spent two weeks together at Anton's dacha in Russia. Since it was too early for the berries to be ripe, the lake was free of bears and the families enjoyed swimming and fishing, picnics with barbecues.

Once, Anton went on a boar hunt with General Alex Orlov. Alex got a wild boar, and the next day they have a festive dinner at the general's dacha with the boar roasting on a spit.

After, with the men enjoying good cigars and the adults good wine, they had a sing-along with Alex playing the accordion, mostly Russian songs. And when he played "Havah Nagila," the children formed a circle and danced the hora.

They returned home at the end of June; it had been a pleasant vacation for all.

On Saturday, 29 June, Max Klausner was alone in the energy house. As was his practice, every last Saturday of the month, he zeroed in on the rest stop near Nuevo Laredo to meet with the Mexican police officer Alejandro Gonzales.

He tried it at four in the afternoon, which would be eight in the morning there. The rest stop was empty. He tried it again an hour later, and this time the motorcycle cop was there, his cell phone in his hand.

"Buenos dias, Alejandro Gonzales." Max hoped the phone was activated.

He saw the police officer put the phone to his ear.

"Hello, man from the court. Today I have important news for you. Through a friend and colleague of mine who works for the Zetas cartel, I was accepted as an informer. The news I have for you is that the Zetas leader Miguel Angel Trevino Morales will be in Nuevo Laredo in July. I am not certain on what dates or perhaps for the whole month. He has a mistress there. Do you know what he looks like, man?"

"No, I never saw a picture of him."

"It wouldn't help you much as I understand he wears a disguise, a mustache or even beard, tinted glasses, and dresses like a common laborer."

"Do you know his address, Alejandro?"

"Yes. It is on Calle Nardo, number 16, a small white-painted villa."

"I pass the information on to trustworthy authorities."

"Not the police I hope or even army, best the marines."

"I let the FBI know; they will get in touch with the marines. You are a good police officer, Alejandro. Don't get in trouble with the Zetas."

"I try not to. All they want of me is to let my colleague know when a roadblock is set up on my route."

"Goodbye, Alejandro, see you next month."

"Goodbye, man from the court."

When Anton came on Friday, the fifth of July, with Sepp, who had picked him up at the airport to the energy house, Max at once told him of the news about the Zetas leader.

Anton: I need to let the FBI know at once.

Max: How? If he is just visiting his mistress, after a few days he may be tired of her and leave.

Anton: I have to notify the FBI at once; they can get in touch with the Mexican marines.

Max: How? You call the FBI from here and they might trace the call.

Sepp: From a public telephone.

Anton: I don't even want the FBI be able to trace the call to Munich. I'll call my friend Nevot; he can fly to New York and call from there by public phone. I use my cell phone from here.

He dialed Nevot's number in Israel. When it was answered by Nevot, Anton at once said

"Amcho here [codename for Anton Hofer; Amcho is Hebrew and means 'one of the tribe']. I want you at once to fly to New York and call my Tall Friend [codename for FBI] and tell them that Miguel Trevino Morales is visiting with his girlfriend in Nuevo Laredo. Her address is 16 Calle Nardo. Let me spell that. N-A-R-D-O. You got that?"

"Yes, 16 Calle Nardo in Nuevo Laredo. Urgent?"

"Very. Shalom, Nevot."

"Shalom, Amcho."

(Nevot managed to take a United Airlines flight at four in the afternoon to New York. Without reservation he had to fly first class. He arrived at La Guardia at three in the morning and called at once the FBI office in New York. His message was brief and not repeated, "Please tell Director Mueller at once that Miguel Trevino Morales is with his girlfriend at 16 Calle Nardo in Nuevo Laredo." He hung up. This call was traced by the FBI, however, except that the trace came from a public telephone at La Guardia Airport, nothing else was known about the anonymous caller. Director Mueller was at once informed.)

Friday, 12 July

Sepp picked up Anton at the airport, and by noon they were at the energy house where Max awaited them impatiently.

Max: Anton, did you read last Sunday's newspaper?

Anton: Yes, it was full of the news that President Morsi was overthrown by the military.

"Yes, I know. No, I don't mean that event. There was an article in our paper islamic militants kill 30 nigerian students."

"No, I didn't see that. Tell me about it."

Max took a report. "And that happened on Saturday, the sixth of July."

He read:

> Islamic militants attacked a boarding school before dawn Saturday, dousing a dormitory in fuel and lighting it ablaze as students slept. At least 30 students were killed in the deadliest attack yet on schools in Nigeria's embattled northeast. Authorities blamed the violence on Boko Haram, a radical group whose name means "Western education is sacrilege." The militants have been behind a series of recent attacks on schools in the region, including one in which gunmen opened fire on children taking exams in a classroom. "We were sleeping when we heard a commotion," Musa Hassan, 15, said of the assault on the government school in Mamudo village in Yobe State. "They burned the children alive," he said, the horror showing in his wide eyes.
>
> On Saturday, at the morgue of Potiskum General Hospital, a few miles from the scene of the attack, parents screamed in anguish as they attempted to identify the victims, many charred beyond recognition. Farmer Malam Abdullahi found the bodies of two of his sons, a ten-year-old shot in the back as he apparently tried to run away and a twelve-year-old shot in the chest.

By Saturday afternoon, thousands of students had fled several
boarding schools around Potiskum, leaving deserted campuses in
fear of more attacks.

He continued, "Isn't this an outrage? Burning children because they
want an education?"

Sepp: This is just as horrible as what the SS did to the Jews. Often
burning them alive, even children, locking them into a house or shed,
and burning them to save ammunition.

Anton: And the good citizens of Jedwabne in Poland who rounded
up the Jews in the village and locked them into a barn and burned them,
children and all.

Max: This I didn't understand at all. The Nazis did it because their
propaganda claimed the Jews were *Untermenschen* (inferior humans) and
were told to kill the Jews brutally.

The Islamists claim that Allah wants them to kill because they go
against their strictest religious obligation, the Sharia, though I doubt if
even in Sharia there is a dictum to burn children alive. But the Polish
villagers, why did they commit this atrocity?

Anton: The savagery of ordinary man. The dark side in man it is
still with us, not that we have become truly civilized. Too many plain
and educated people are half human half beasts. I wished I could
venture a guess of what percentage of man is truly civilized, but I am
not a psychologist, and I doubt anyone knows. But whenever you have
a fanatic, be it religious, racist, or political, you have a man who can be
turned into a savage. To come back to the Boko Haram, brutal killers
they are, we have to punish them.

Max: I have found the town of Potiskum in northeastern Nigeria
and scanned the villages around it. I found one place that showed several
buildings burned down; that must be the Mamudo Village. The people
there are all blacks. Some wear the white frocks of devout Muslims but
most just slacks and T-shirts, some women burqas but most shoddy
dresses. I am pretty sure that most if not all are Muslims. The north of
Nigeria is Muslim, the south more Christian. Looking farther around,
about thirty miles north from the village I found a tent encampment
with many vehicles, all armed and in white frocks with bandoliers of
ammunition around them and Kalashnikov rifles, machine guns on their
pickups. They are not government troops; else, they would be in uniform.

Anton: Did you see any soldiers in the village of Mamudo?

"No, I saw policemen, Red Cross vehicles, ambulances."

"In the encampment, did you see any flags?"

"Besides all the tents, there were a couple mud huts. Yes, there was a flag there, black with Arabic writing."

"Those are the militants, the Boko Haram. Let's pay them a visit."

Max brought the encampment in view.

The area was barren with few trees, though not really desert. Around a dirt road were some two dozen tents, many vehicles along the road, most of them pickups. A little ways from the road were three mud huts, an open square in front. People in white were milling around. Most were blacks, all of them armed. Many were also carrying eating utensils. It was lunchtime. From one mud hut came smoke; it must be the kitchen. There, as here, was in the same timezone—it was noon.

A man in a black turban, unarmed, came out of the middle hut and apparently called to the multitude. Many ran to the tents to dispose of their plates; all assembled in the square in rows, placed a prayer rug before them, and knelt down.

Max: Are you ready, Anton? I zero in on the mullah.

"Ready. I give the mullah a five-thousand-degree jolt. I really want to torch him then reduce to three thousand. After, I zero in on those in the first row; they are the mullah's favorites and probably the most fanatical and brutal."

When Anton saw a close-up of the turbaned head; he pushed the key, and the head burst into a fiery explosion. He fell down, and his frock was aflame, all eyes of the kneeling militants on him. They must have never heard of the world court's punishment rituals as they remained kneeling and one after the other was eliminated. Only after the twelve in the first row were dead did the others get up and ran in many different directions, some tumbling over each other in their haste to get away. A few more Anton eliminated when they ran to their pickups and sat in the seat starting the car. Some hid in the tents.

The six pickups with dead drivers, Anton managed to set them on fire by exploding their ammunition boxes. Then methodically he burned down each tent, from which some militants came running.

When Max raised the view, they could see running figures in every direction.

Sepp: They will probably run until they fall exhausted.

Max: I hope they got the message not to burn children anymore or kill them or anyone else. Burning alive is the most horrible death.

Anton: These people are more superstitious than devout; they probably believe that Allah punished them for their deeds.

Max: Ours was a good deed. Let's finish and go home to our families.

Anton: I think I shall return to my family in Israel.

Sepp: I take you to the airport.

16 July 2013.

All Media reports in the Western world and the Americas carried the news that the leader of Zetas drug cartel was captured:

Miguel Angel Trevino Morales, the notoriously brutal leader of the feared Zetas drug cartel, has been captured in the first major blow against an organized crime leader by a Mexican administration struggling to drive down persistently high levels of violence.

Trevino Morales, known as Z-40, was captured by Mexican Marines in Nuevo Laredo.

Morales's capture removes the leader of a corps of special forces who splintered off into their own cartel and spread across Mexico, expanding from drug dealing into extortion and human trafficking. The Zetas authored some of the worst atrocities of Mexico's drug war, slaughtering dozens, leaving their bodies on display, many Mexican and Central American migrants and gaining a reputation as the most terrifying of the country's numerous ruthless drug cartels.

CHAPTER XVIII

Special Investigator Andreas Vogel of the Bka

A ndreas Vogel's title was special investigator; however, he was on loan from the Munich Police Department and had been at the Bka (Bundeskriminalamt) for many years, in fact, since 2004, the year Anton Nagil began his career with the Munich police in December of that year. Since Inspector Vogel had left for the Bka in the summer, the two had not met. Inspector Vogel had been the chief of the antiterror unit, and Inspector Stefan Wagner, who had been his deputy, replaced him.

Andreas Vogel was fifty-five years old, single, though he had a lady friend in Wiesbaden and hoped to marry her in the near future.

Vogel was of average height; a little heavy (potbelly as he enjoyed good food); brown hair, which he kept short; a round and pleasant face, brown eyes, which could be piercing or friendly. His easy smile showed a pleasant disposition.

Despite his charismatic appearance, he had the habit of tilting his head down and then looking up at the person he questioned with piercing eyes that said, "Don't fool me. Don't lie," adding a knowing smile. He had been an astute investigator.

Munich police commissioner Kolb hated to lose him, but it was always prestigious for a police department to have one of its members working at the Bka, and repeated requests to return him to Munich were politely refused by the head of the Bka.

Once he married, he would cancel his employment with the Munich police as he liked it in the spa city of Wiesbaden where he had bought a small villa.

At the Bka he had continued his expertise in unraveling terrorist plots, and the chief had assigned him to research the authorship of the world tribunal, the Force of Three.

On the fifth of September 2012, Inspector Vogel had a visitor. Superintendent Willi Biergli of the Suisse Federal Police had requested an appointment with the Bka in regard to the world tribunal. For this meeting Inspector Vogel had invited Professor Kohl from the Free University of Berlin to give a psychological and political profile of the tribunal.

Of great interest to Inspector Vogel was a possible German connection in that the papers of the letters sent to the *Berner Nachrichten* newspaper were made in Germany.

All information pertaining to the WT (world tribunal) from EUROPOL, INTERPOL, the FBI, and concerned departments of the EU (European Union) and national police departments came to his office.

Inspector Vogel had started a log of known facts and rumors/ suppositions on the world tribunal (which he shortened to WT).

Hugo Wolfgang Holzmann

CONTACTS & FACTS	ACTIONS	SUPPOSITIONS
23 July 2012, 1st letter & 1st Manif received at the *Berner* newspaper. WT established July 2012—hostis humani generis—crimes against mankind. Signed STE Judgment against Somali pirates.	First action reported: 4 Aug. 2012, 10 pirates killed from 2 American ships. Ships freed. near Karin, Somalia.	Prank or real? Somali time 3 & 7 p.m. By laser? From ship/plane?
Sat. 30 Aug. 2nd Manifesto/Judg. against Mexican drug cartels Posted in London.	Sat. 25 Aug. In Monterrey/Mexico subleader & guard killed, Villa and drug shed burned	Action 6 days before Manif. received. Time: at noon
5 Sept. *Meeting with Suisse Super Biergli* and Prof. Kohl at Bka. Biergli: 1st Manif. from Vienna, envelope/ Russia, paper/Germany. Facts: Paper used in both Manif. came from Germany.	*Requested log of passengers to/from* London on 24 Aug. of Scotland Yard. Sent list to major police departments in Germany for possible identification. Requested laser research work from major science centers & universities in Germany.	
	Answers to queries rec. from departments. All negative! I shall get in touch with our foreign office to send a query to our embassies of foreigners who arrived/ departed on 24 August at both London airports.	

Report from EU.

Saving lives of 42 illegals!
Sat. 15 Sept. In the desert near Ciudad Laredo/Mexico, 42 illegal's wishing to cross to El Paso/USA, were robbed & about to be shot when the WT killed 2 bandits with laser. Other bandits fled. Interesting, WT spoke to illegals in Castilian Spanish. Later to American border uards in British English. WT not only can kill with rays but also see, listen and speak. Scientists state that our present scientific knowledge does not permit such technology. Ray beams used are not of the laser type.

Time element:
Bandits killed at sunrise—
5-6 a.m.?
Border guards contact at 8 a.m.
Local times.

14 Oct. 3rd Manifesto.
Directed against war criminals,
Also fascists, neo-Nazis, right wing radicals.
Gives specificwarning against hate mongers.
Posted from New York withAmerican paper, envelopes.

Inquiry to foreign office. They state that query requests were sent to pertinent embassies in foreign countries
No answers as yet.

Is WT American?
Some believe that it is European—
Castilian Spanish British English!

Friday, 26 October
Reported by EUROPOL.

Village of Jedwabne/Poland burned for defacing memorial to alive burned Jews from village by neighbors.

Time element:
noon. Police spoken to in Russian.

Friday, 2 November.
Reported by EUROPOL.

Lithuanian collaborator/mass murderer killed by death ray.

Time: noon.
Russian spoken.

Saturday, 10 November.
EUROPOL report

Sinmae/Estonia meeting of Baltic former SS. Lithuanian, German, Ukrainian SS men killed Estate burned down.

Time: 9:00 a.m.
German spoken, distorted.

Reports from embassies—all negative. Outstanding from Egypt. Morsi authorities there are un-cooperative with German embassy. No replies from Saudi Arabia and Russia. Sent a 2nd request.

Sunday, 2 December.
4th Manifesto published
by B.N.
Death to terrorists.

Also warned were North Korea and Iran,
Pres. Morsi.

This was expecte
by many, by me.
All non-political.

Friday, 4 January 2013
Seminar at Munich
university with insp.
Wagner, prof. Moll and
Dr. Hofer. Spoke about
WT problems.

Dr. Hofer well
versed in Afghan
history also
Muslim history
and Muslim terror.

Saturday, 12 January.
Report from FBI.

Al-Qaeda camp in Yemen attacked by
death ray.
Ammo dump exploded, many killed.

Time: 3:00 p.m. in
Yemen.

Saturday, 19 January.
Report from Hamburg
police.

Friedrich Kammer from Wedel killed by
death ray.
Kammer was with Hamburg Reserve
police in 1941 nd participated in mass
shootings of Jews.

Killed in Wedel.
Time: noon.

27 January.
5th Manifesto
published in
B.N. Posted again N.Y.
American material.

Taliban are designated a terrorist org.
because they tried to kill the girl Malala
Yousufza; other killings.
Hamas declared terror org.

Friday, 8 February.
Report from Munich
police (at a later date).

Horst Pfeuffer killed—fell downstairs.
Pfeuffer was a former Gestapo agent and
known, for his brutality.

Accident or ?
His friend Lorenz
Spoke of visitor
with bogus name.

13 February.
Letter received by B.N.
from WT. Letter in
English, Posted on 11th
February from Vienna.
American m.

WT reports of the sinking of a drug
cartel sub off the coast of San Diego,
California, on 9 Feb.

FBI reports sinking
of sub at dusk.
Local time:
6-8 p.m.

Saturday, 11 May.
Possible action of WT in
Damascus/Syria. Report
to German embassy in
Damascus by anonymous
source.

Israeli planes bomb Damascus warehouse
storing advanced missiles—to be shipped
to Hezbollah in Lebanon. Warehouse
with tin roof was possibly set on fire by
WT minutes before planes arrived?

Time
element; noon.
WT working with
Israel? Or just a
one-time operation?

Inspector Vogel had a secretary, Elizabeth Stiegler; actually she was a student at the university where she majored in criminology and worked only part-time for him—that is, the afternoons. Since Fräulein Stiegler was highly intelligent, he used her for occasional research projects.

It was in June of 2013 that he gave her the project to research the time elements when the WT took actions against evildoers.

He asked her to project the action times in certain locations as detailed in his log, specifically the time in Central Europe (Germany), time at the USA East Coast, and time at the USA West Coast versus the days and times the actions happened.

They had discussed the fact that all actions happened on weekends, Fridays included. His log documented that most acts happened on a Friday and Saturday.

Inspector Vogel voiced his opinion that perhaps the agency from which the death rays were sent was an industrial or educational complex and only available on weekends. To that Fräulein Stiegler objected that this would not include Fridays. She believed that it was rather the unavailability of a member of the Force of Three who could only attend on Fridays and Saturdays, came on Friday, and returned on Sunday, a working day for him.

Here then is her report:

TIME AND PLACE ACTION OCCURRED: (day/month/year)	ECT (European Central Time)	U.S. EAST COAST	U.S. WEST COAT
4/8/12 Off Somalia Saturday, 3 & 7 p.m.	11 a.m. 3 p.m. Saturday	5 and 9 a.m Saturday	2 & 6 a.m. Saturday
25/8/12 Monterrey Saturday noon	8 p.m. Saturday	2 p.m. Saturday	11 a.m. Saturday
13/9/12 Ciudad Laredo Saturday 5-6 a.m.	1-2 p.m. Saturday	7-8 a.m Saturday	4-5 a.m. Saturday
26/10/12 Jedwabne/Poland Saturday noon	11 a.m. Saturday	5 a.m Saturday	2 a.m. Saturday

2/11/12 Kovno/Lithuania	11 a.m.	5 a.m	2 a.m.
Friday noon	Friday	Friday	Friday
10/11/12 Sinmae/Estonia	8 a.m.	2 a.m.	11 p.m.
Saturday, 9 a.m.	Saturday	Saturday	Friday
12/1/13 Yemen	noon	6 a.m	3 a.m.
Saturday 3 p.m	Saturday	Saturday	Saturday
19/1/13 Hamburg/Wedel	noon	6 a.m.	3 a.m.
Saturday noon	Saturday	Saturday	Saturday
9/2/13 San Diego	3-5 a.m	9-11 p.m	6-8 p.m
Saturday 6-8 p.m.	Sunday	Saturday	Saturday
11/5/13 Damascus	11 a.m	5 a.m	2 a.m.
Saturday noon	Saturday	Saturday	Saturday

When they scanned the list together, they realized that if the operations were conducted from Europe, while always on Fridays and Saturdays with one exception, they were active during daytime or early evening. If in the United States, these were night operations.

"What good for is this list? There is consistency in days, namely, on weekends, Fridays included," thought Fräulein Stiegler.

"There is one clue: the submarine operation off San Diego. Europe shows that it was conducted early Sunday morning. All other operations were Fridays and Saturdays during the day or evening. If you are right in that one or more of the operators were from out of town and could only attend on weekends, returned on Sundays, then we need to find the place of operation; and if there is a log of personnel in attendance, this exception would become an important clue."

"This sounds farfetched, Inspector Vogel."

"I know. It is like we have a fingerprint of a suspect. We catch the suspect we can confirm his culpability. If there is a log that shows this exception of a European operation on a Sunday early in the morning, we can confirm. How was it to get the proper timing from the different places?"

"What sounded like an easy arithmetic became totally confusing. Do I add time or subtract time elements? My head was swimming after a while, and I had to stop. Start again the next day and day after."

"Well, I thank you Fräulein Stiegler. You did a fine job, and it may be very useful information."

It was on Monday, the twenty-second of July 2013, that Inspector Vogel received a call from the *Auslandsamt* (foreign office) in Berlin.

The caller was a Bernd Lederer.

Lederer: Inspector Vogel, I just had a call from the German embassy in Cairo. Your queries to them in August and November of last year were finally answered. Though the requests are now almost a year old, I sensed some urgency in your writing; therefore, I thought I call you. A letter with the complete information will be sent to you later today.

"I remember the queries. I was seeking information about the Egyptian Achmed Nabil, who flew to London on the twenty-fourth of August and returned the same day."

"Right. A. Nabil flew into Heathrow on the twenty-fourth of August from Munich and returned to Germany on the same day. According to the information supplied to the embassy, this gentleman Achmed Nabil is a German Egyptian citizen. He was born in Munich on 27 March 1965. His mother was Rosemarie Nagil, his father Otto Nagil. The Nagils lived in Cairo, and shortly after the birth of her son, whose name was Anton Nagil, she returned with her baby to Cairo. Anton Nagil attended the university there and became a chemical engineer. Herr Nagil was also in the Egyptian army; he then used his Egyptian name. I understand he had both a German passport and an Egyptian. In November of 2004, Herr Nagil sold his house in Cairo and moved to his mother in Munich, as we were told by Brigadier Amer. In December of 2004, Nagil found employment with the Munich police department. You should find him there."

"One question, Herr Justizrat, why did it take so long for the Egyptian authorities to answer my queries? Not that it is important, just curious."

"Apparently your queries ended up with military intelligence. Why there? Who knows? The military intelligence apparently was not very cooperative with the German embassy under President Morsi. Now, Brigadier Amer, whom the Morsi government had dismissed, was reinstated. He found the queries unanswered in the in-basket. Since Egypt under their new government seeks to establish normal relation with the European governments, he at once called the German embassy. The information is still useful, Inspector Vogel?"

"Oh yes, and I thank you very much. Auf Wiedersehn."

"Auf Wiedersehen, inspector Vogel, always glad to oblige the Bka."

Inspector Vogel knew he had to visit the Munich police department.

On Wednesday, the twenty-fourth of July, inspector Vogel flew to Munich and went to the police headquarters for a visit with his boss, police commissioner Max Kolb.

He was heartily welcomed by Commissioner Kolb. "My errant inspector Vogel, how nice of you to visit your old hounds, though I expect you have a good reason for your sudden visit?"

"I do, Commissioner."

"Let's go to lunch, and you can tell me all about your business."

Kolb took Inspector Vogel to the Hofbrauehaus for a good Munich lunch. Then they sat in a vestibule for smokers and enjoyed good cigars.

Kolb: Now tell me all about your mission to Munich.

"It is rather a personnel problem I am researching." And he told Kolb about his research project in finding a connection to the world tribunal.

"And how can I help you, inspector? You mentioned a personnel problem, someone I know who might be connected to the tribunal?"

"It is perhaps a thread, the thinnest of a connection I am following." And he told the commissioner about his research into the people who flew into London on the twenty-fourth of August of last year, the day the second manifesto was posted in London.

Kolb: Yes, a query came to us. I glanced at the list. There were several thousand names. I gave the list to one of our inspectors to research. I believe the inspector did not find any familiar name, and the list was returned to you, yes?

"Yes, Inspector Wagner signed the query negatively; so did all other major police departments in Germany. However, since there were also foreigners on the visit to

London that day, I sent queries to our embassies in those countries to check with pertinent authorities and received replies except for Egypt, Saudi Arabia, and Russia.

Well, it was just a slim chance that one of the names would be recognized by the authorities, but I persisted and sent a second query. No answers. Two days ago—that is, Monday—I received a call from our foreign office. The German embassy in Cairo was notified by Egyptian military intelligence that one of the names was familiar to Brigadier Amer, the head of military intelligence. The name was Achmed Nabil. Herr Nabil is a German Egyptian citizen and apparently uses both names for convenience. His German name is Anton Nagil. Supposedly employed by the Munich police department?"

Commissioner Kolb showed surprise. "Inspector Nagil? Our inspector? Connected to the world tribunal? I can't believe it."

"Of course, even if it was he who flew into London that day that doesn't mean that he is connected. As an investigator, I have to examine any and all clues. What can you tell me about Inspector Nagil? And let me add here, Commissioner, that my investigation must remain confidential.

"I understand. Inspector Nagil came to our department in December of 2004. You had left for the Bka in the summer, so you never met him. Nagil had never before worked for the police, but his credentials were so impressive that I had him hired as inspector. He worked for the antiterror unit under Inspector Wagner and became most valuable for his friendly connection to the Muslim community and mosque here in Munich. However, not to spook the Muslims, he was assigned to the criminal division under Inspector Keller.

Inspector Nagil became my most accomplished investigator. Already in the first year with us, he foiled a bomb plot against the president of the Jewish community center and infiltrated the Russian mafia, which led to their demise here in our city. Then we had a serial killer on our hands. I remember the day when Inspector Keller came rushing in my office and handed me a card Nagil had given him with the name of the killer. Then Nagil was with the arresting team and handled a hostage situation so brilliantly that the murderer just handed him the knife with which he threatened to cut the throat of a woman. For that and the mafia arrests, I promoted him after a year of service.

"Oh yes, he was deeply involved in the foiling of the terrorists' attempt to atom bomb Moscow, Tel Aviv, and Washington. For that, PM Putin gave him a dacha near Moscow, which we from the Munich police can visit; my family and I have been there.

"However, Inspector Nagil is no longer with us. He resigned in March 2011 and joined the Jerusalem Police Department who accepted him as a senior inspector. His wife is Jewish, and his family and wife's mother live in Jerusalem. He comes to Munich occasionally and then visits with Inspector Wagner; the two are the best of friends. More details about Nagil and his present life, you have to visit Wagner. Oh, one more thing, he changed his name from Nagil to Hofer. I understand that he wanted nothing to do with the name Nagil as this was his father's name, that of SS-Standartenfuehrer Otto Nagil, an infamous war criminal. When in Munich he also visits Professor Klausner."

"Is that by any chance the famous Professor Klausner from the Max Planck Institute?"

"I believe so. I understand that he is a friend of his and is a sort of consultant to him. Nagil—I should say Hofer—is by profession a chemical engineer. But again, for more details, you have to speak to Inspector Wagner."

"Again, Commissioner Kolb, please consider this a confidential matter."

"Of course, Inspector Vogel. You wish to visit with Inspector Wagner?"

When Vogel nodded, Kolb called Wagner and told him he had a visitor. "I send him to your office. In an hour or so? All right."

Inspector Vogel understood that if Nagil/Hofer and Wagner were the best of friends, and Wagner even had falsified the query by signing that none of the names were familiar; he could not expect to get any useful information. He went to his office.

The two greeted each other like friends. Of course they knew each well. Inspector Wagner had been his deputy of the antiterror unit and met again at the seminar they gave back in January at the university with Vogel as the Bka representative speaking about the world tribunal.

As is custom at the department, both of the same rank, they called each other by their last name, leaving off the title.

"My dear Vogel, how nice to see you. How are things at the Bka, keeping busy?"

"My antiterror occupation is busier than yours Wagner, we have all of Germany to safeguard. Yours is just this city."

"But you, Vogel, you have nothing to do with the neo-Nazis and other fringe groups, like I do."

"You are right there."

"So what brings you to the Munich department? You visited with the commissioner I understand?"

"Just a courtesy visit. I came to see you."

"And?"

"Remember the seminar back in January where a Dr. Hofer spoke about Afghanistan and generally about Muslim terror? I received a transcript of the seminar from Professor Moll. Dr. Hofer also explained the present status of Israel and the Palestinians. He spoke so well and explained matters so eloquently that I like for him to give a similar seminar at the Bka. By the way, from the commissioner, I found out that Hofer was our Inspector Nagil before he changed his name and joined the Jerusalem Police Department."

"That is correct. And what do you want from me, Vogel?"

"Arrange Hofer's visit to us. All expenses paid by the Bka of course. Perhaps when he is in Munich? The commissioner said that he comes frequently to the city and works as a consultant for the Max Planck Institute. Maybe he can add a day and visit us?"

"He comes on weekends. Sundays he has to be back in Jerusalem, a working day in Israel. But it isn't that often that he comes by here, three to four times a year."

"I could write to him. Do you have his address, Wagner?"

"Hofer keeps his personal address confidential. You could write to him in care of the Jerusalem Police Department; he is senior inspector there."

"You have his address there?"

"Jerusalem PD. One Clermont Ganneau, 93580 Jerusalem. Or you can e-mail him ^antonhofer@jpd.il."

Wagner had coffee brought in, and they talked about each other's work and problems until five, time to go home.

Of course it was too late to visit the Max Planck Institute. Inspector Vogel would do that the next morning. He spent the night at the Bayerische Hotel.

Thursday, 25 August.

What time would the director of a science institute come to work? Inspector Vogel called the Max Planck Institute at nine o'clock. He called the number listed in the phonebook and asked the operator to speak to the director.

"Who may I say is calling, please?"

"Chief Inspector Andreas Vogel from the Bka."

"And what organization is the Bka, please?"

"Bundeskriminalamt in Wiesbaden."

He was connected.

"Director Glaser."

Vogel identified himself, and the director knew what Bka stood for. He received an appointment for ten o'clock. He took a taxi from the hotel.

He was on time, and the receptionist guided him to the director's office.

The man he met was elderly, with a goatee, and he was greeted by Director Glaser.

Director Glaser smiled. "A visit from the Bka. I hope we are not in trouble of any sort."

"Oh no, Director Glaser, I am just interested in one of your people. And let me first establish that my inquiries are formal but also must remain confidential. Also, that the person in question is not in any sort of trouble, just an investigation I was asked to conduct; its purpose is strictly one of national security."

"I understand. And who is this person?"

"A Herr Anton Hofer, a chemical engineer."

"Dr. Hofer the chemist? Yes, he works part-time as a consultant to Professor Klausner.

"Hofer is a doctor of what?"

"As I saw in his credentials, he took a minor in nuclear physics in America and earned the doctor title as diploma engineer."

"A consultant to Professor Klausner? May I ask what his specialty is?"

"Professor Klausner is our energy expert."

"Specifically, what type of energy?"

"Inspector Vogel, why are you interested in Professor Klausner and what he does? I thought you wish to learn about his consultant."

"It is a matter of national security. The subject of his research and that of Dr. Hofer is secret, yes?" The director nodded. "Therefore, we are concerned. Dr. Hofer worked before for the police department. Before that, he lived in Egypt, was in the Egyptian army. He now resides in

Israel, is a senior inspector at the Jerusalem Police Department. He is a citizen of the three countries. We at the Bka are concerned about his interest and loyalty to which country. therefore this investigation, which, of course, must remain confidential.

May I ask what the research of Professor Klausner pertains to?"

"It is our secret, that of the Max Planck Institute. We will be the beneficiary if they succeed. Let me just hint that is has to do with wireless transmission of energy. More details you have to bring me a warrant from the Bka."

"Yes, I heard something of this nature, therefore our concern. It would be a tremendous undertaking and greatly benefit your institution as it would Germany. Or Israel, Egypt?"

"Professor Klausner is a loyal German citizen, so is his assistant Herr Kainz, and I am almost hundred percent certain of Dr. Hofer's loyalty."

"And these three work on this secret project. Dr. Hofer apparently only comes on Fridays and Saturdays? Busy with police work in Jerusalem on all other days."

"Yes. He has never visited on a Sunday or other days during the week."

"Are you certain of that? We projected Dr. Hofer having been attending here on Sunday, the tenth of February of this year?"

"I don't believe so, Inspector Vogel."

"Could you check on that, Director Glaser, please? This confirmation or denial would be my last question I have for you."

"All right, inspector. I don't understand why this particular date is so important."

Director Glaser picked up the phone. "Frau Maierhof, please bring me the logbook for weekend sign-ins."

Director Glaser opened the log register. "What date was it you are interested in?"

"Saturday, the ninth of February, and the next day Sunday. That would be the tenth."

The director thumbed in the logbook.

"Here it is, Saturday, the ninth of February. You wish to take notes? There are a number of entries."

Inspector Vogel took his notebook.

"Klausner and Kainz signed in at ten in the morning. Hofer came at noon. Hofer signed out at 1:00 p.m. then came back at 4:00 p.m. All three signed out at 5:00 p.m. The three then signed it at midnight on Saturday. You are right. They left at six o'clock in the morning of Sunday, the tenth. There is a note to justify their early Sunday morning work.

Reason for early Sunday morning research: needed free atmospheric radiation. Does that satisfy your investigation, Inspector Vogel?"

"Completely, Director Glaser. I thank you for your full cooperation. And again, please keep my visit and inquiry confidential. Not a word or even hint to Dr. Hofer and the others."

Inspector Vogel shook the director's hand and left.

From the hotel he phoned Commissioner Kolb.

"Commissioner Kolb, Inspector Vogel here. I talked with Inspector Wagner. Everything is fine. One question, is the name Kainz familiar to you in connection with Herr Hofer?"

"Josef Kainz—or Sepp as we call him—yes, he is a good friend of Hofer. He is a taxi driver, and when Hofer was with us as Inspector Nagil, he helped him in many phases of police work. In fact, we dubbed Kainz as Nagil's private detective."

"Thank you, Commissioner, and goodbye."

Commissioner Kolb heard a distinct chuckle. Before he could ask "What is so funny?" he was disconnected.

Inspector Vogel took the afternoon flight back to Wiesbaden.

26 July, Friday morning, he was back in his office at the Bka.

He skipped lunch, too agitated to have an appetite.

Shortly after one o'clock his secretary Fräulein Stiegler came. "Well, Inspector Vogel, how was your trip to Munich? Success or failure?"

"Fräulein Stiegler, you have top-secret clearance working for the Bka for me?"

"Of course, but you know that."

"Sit down here. I need your personal promise that what I confide in you will remain our secret. Ours for now."

She put her hand to her heart. "I swear my lips are sealed!"

"I solved the puzzle of the world tribunal, specifically of the Force of Three."

Her eyes widened in surprise; she stared in silence at Inspector Vogel.

"A professor of energy, a chemical engineer with a minor in nuclear energy, and a taxi driver." Fräulein Stiegler broke out in a nervous giggle. "Really?"

"Yes! The clue of your research, the Sunday morning action of sinking the drug submarine, confirmed my suspicion. The three entered the facility at midnight of Saturday, the ninth of February, and were there on Sunday morning, signed out at 6:00 a.m. According to your log, the submarine surfaced and was sunk at dusk or when it got dark, at 6:00 to 8:00 p.m. on Saturday, the ninth of February, off California. The log showed that it was between 3:00 and 5:00 a.m. Sunday morning, local. That is our time."

"Maybe a coincident, inspector?"

"Look at the facility, the famous Max Planck Institute. The professor, an expert on energy, one a chemical engineer versed in nuclear science. The director of the institute told me that the three are working on wireless energy transmission. Just the type of people who may invent the death ray, which is wireless energy transmission."

"And with help of the taxi driver?" The two broke out in laughter, which helped release them from their excitement.

"I don't know what he helped with. The question is now what do we do with our secret information?"

"NOTHING!" exclaimed Fräulein Stiegler.

Inspector Vogel looked in silence at his secretary. At last he said, "This was a most eloquent statement, Fräulein Stiegler."

She lowered her eyes in light embarrassment, though her smile showed her pleasure.

"Can you justify your statement, Fräulein Stiegler?"

She looked at him. "You, like I, read the book by Michael Juergs *BKA, EUROPOL, Scotland Yard Die Jaeger des Boesen—the Hunters of Evil*. Juergs writes about the evils committed in the various chapters, evil deeds against the laws of society and civilization, and therefore punishable by courts. That is all the world tribunal has done or, as you specify them, the Force of Three. And while Juergs writes that immoral thoughts are not punishable only the deeds committed, the Force of Three goes one step further and warns hate mongers, often the messengers and cause of evil, to desist or they will be eliminated. Immoral thoughts and mongering are punishable.

"Apparently the three hold court; there is the prosecution, the defense, the judgment by jury. Perhaps the taxi driver is a wise man and the judge?" She giggled though she meant it not as a joke. "Look whom they have killed or as they call it eliminated pirates who kidnapped for ransom and killed innocent seafarers. Ruthless drug traffickers who commit grizzly crimes, trade in poison, extortion—they, like the pirates, did it for money. Ex-Nazis and their collaborators who committed the most horrible crimes we classify as genocide, they were the racists. Terrorists who claim religion but are possessed by hate.

I never heard of an innocent they eliminated, not even by mistake. And all those they eliminated, the most wicked evildoers, were criminals we couldn't touch or find."

"Well spoken, Fräulein Stiegler, like an advocate. Maybe you should go into law, criminal law. NOTHING, you said, do nothing! The world tribunal a blessing for mankind, even in disguise?

There is, of course, the other side of the coin in that I am committed to find the source of the Ttibunal. I swore an oath to be a loyal employee of the Bka."

"My suggestion is to take it up with the chief. He is a decent, thoughtful man, not a radical *boese Jaeger*."

"Perhaps you are right. Let it be a Judgment of Three."

"Right, the chief, you, and little me."

The inspector smiled. "You are not so little, Fräulein Stiegler, rather a VIP to me."

The former president of the Bka Horst Herold build the institution into the formidable crime research agency it has become. "Crime-research" might be the wrong term to quantify the Bka. Crime (*das Boese*) is well documented. The work of the Bka is to find the criminal and not the criminal activity. In this respect it is similar to the American FBI. However, while the FBI actively pursues the criminal and has arresting powers, the five-hundred-plus personnel of the Bka do only research to identify the criminal who has committed acts forbidden by national and international laws.

As such it cooperates with EUROPOL, INTERPOL, Scotland Yard, the Surete, FBI, and national police agencies of the EU, also with the police of nonmember countries.

President Joerg Ziercke is generally referred to at the Bka as the *Chef* (the Chief).

Friday afternoon Inspector Vogel made an appointment to see the Chief at three o'clock.

When he went into the Chief's office, he brought Fräulein Stiegler along.

"Ah, Inspector Vogel, and your secretary I assume? What brings you to me for a personal visit? Don't tell me you found the identity of the world tribunal? Please have a seat. Maybe you can bring a chair over for the lady, miss or misses?"

"Fräulein Stiegler is my secretary and student at the university, majors in criminology in the morning and works for me in the afternoon."

The Chief stood up and walked around his desk to greet her. "Don't let Inspector Vogel poison you with his extravagant lunches unless you don't pay attention to your figure, Fräulein Stiegler."

They sat down.

Inspector Vogel: I have a request, Chief. May we discuss first the possibility that we discover the Force of Three and then what?

The Chief stared at Inspector Vogel for a minute; then he took a deep breath. "Two thoughts flashed in my mind, first that you discovered their identity and, now, what do we do with that knowledge?"

The inspector nodded.

Another deep breath and then the Chief stood up, walked to the large picture window, and looked out. A few minutes passed in silence. He came back, sat down, and looked at the inspector.

"And what have you two decided?"

"When I asked Fräulein Stiegler, who is not only a brilliant researcher but also a fine and decent—" He was interrupted by the Chief who raised his arm. "No need to qualify Fräulein Stiegler's credentials. I am certain she is highly intelligent and a decent person. So?"

"Fräulein Stiegler emphatically answered NOTHING and then justified her statement."

"I gather she worked with you on this project? Yes? Good. And you, Inspector Vogel, agreed with her?"

"Yes, qualified. I would also like to mention that we discussed the doings of the world tribunal, its pros and cons. Eliminating the worst, never an innocent, only those who were beyond justice. And apparently they hold a trial before eliminating."

Again the Chief raised his hand. "I know very well what they have done. The reports, before they come to you, are seen by me. I admit I have never given it any thought that if we should find them, what next?" And softly he added, as if talking to himself, "Doing nothing—what a brilliant and tempting suggestion." And to Inspector Vogel he said, "You mentioned 'qualified'; you meant by that?"

"It seems realistic that we can't just sit back and do nothing. I have to mention a similar situation though on a minor scale. An American film shown here at the Bka called *Death Wish* with Charles Bronson. He was a successful architect in New York, had a wife and daughter. Hoodlums came into his place, killed his wife, and brutally raped his daughter, who had to be confined to an asylum. Bronson became a vigilante, and whenever he saw a violent crime committed, he shot the perpetrators. The laws couldn't punish them—he did. He never killed an innocent person. The papers were full of the vigilante killer. Especially violent crime was reduced substantially in New York. The public generally supported his vigilantism; so did the chief of police and the mayor. However, elected officials put pressure on the mayor and police chief to find and stop the vigilante.

"A brilliant police inspector discovered who the vigilante was. At a meeting of the mayor, police chief, and the detective, they decided to stop the vigilante by making him leave the city. This the detective did; he had a talk with Bronson and told him to leave the city within twenty-four hours. He did."

"If I understand you correctly, Inspector Vogel, you suggest that you tell them, or whoever their leader is, to stop?"

"Briefly, yes."

"I see. Now tell me who they are and how you discovered their identity."

"The first clue I had—in fact, it was more a thought only—was when I read a police report of the Munich police that a former Gestapo official had an accident, fell down a flight of stairs, and broke his neck. It was ruled an accident, but there was a byline to the report. It stated that this man, a Herr Pfeuffer, had ben visiting a friend, a Herr Lorenz. Lorenz stated that they were together having a glass of wine when a stranger came to visit, gave his name as Alfons Maier, said that he was sent by Wegner, the leader of the neo-Nazi Bund. That he belonged to the Bund in Berchtesgaden under the leadership of a Herr Schoenauer. His purpose of the visit was to write the history of former Gestapo officials and their work. According to Lorenz, this friend of his, Pfeuffer, confessed to brutalities he committed as a Gestapo agent. Pfeuffer and this stranger left together. Lorenz heard a commotion in the staircase and was told by the stranger or Maier that Pfeuffer stumbled and fell down the flight of stairs and broke his neck. While this may have been so, subsequent inquiries by the police with both Wegner and Schoenauer showed that they did not know an Alfons Maier. An accident? Or was Pfeuffer pushed or tripped? By whom, a man with a bogus name and credentials? It just fitted in with the third manifesto of punishing former war criminals. Munich became just a little clue in my mind; as we know, detective work is based upon building a house brick by brick."

Inspector Vogel then told of the log he made of tribunal actions reported with day and time sequences. The only clue available was the London visit for the second manifesto.

He received the requested list from Scotland Yard of persons who flew in and out of London that day.

All reports negative except those from Egypt, Russia, and Saudi Arabia. In June he received an answer to the query sent to Egypt. Yes, they recognized the name of Achmed Nabil, who was a German Egyptian citizen and presently employed by the Munich police department. His German name was Anton Nagil. Inspector Vogel told of his trip to Munich and conversations with the commissioner of the Munich police; *Inspector Wagner who was a personal friend of Herr Nagil. And last with the director of the Max Planck Institute in Munich who told him that Herr Nagil, who had changed his name to Hofer, was a consultant to a Professor Klausner and his computer expert Herr Kainz.* The three worked together on weekends. Professor Klausner was working on wireless energy transmission. "The first clue in Munich came to my mind, now a second clue from Munich, plus computer paper from Germany for the first two manifestos."

Then Inspector Vogel related how Fräulein Stiegler made a list of days and times when the actions of the tribunal occurred. Comparing the time of the submarine sinking, which was at dusk or early night off California, with a visit of the three to the institute during the early morning hours of the next day, a Sunday when Herr Hofer normally returned to Israel, he was able to confirm that the three were present at the institute when the sinking of the sub occurred.

He concluded, "I don't know what function Herr Kainz has or plays in this trio or the Force of Three as he is only a taxi driver, but—" He was interrupted by the Chief, "He represents the public, the common man. Tell me about this Hofer and his connection to Israel."

Inspector Vogel told of what he knew about the man, also what the commissioner told him about the brilliance of Hofer as a police inspector in Munich and his personal courage and martial arts expertise when he subdued four hooligan students after a seminar at the university. And while he did not witness the altercation, he heard about it. "Four students who were members of the neo-Nazi Bund Blut und Erde."

"Fits right in" smiled the Chief. "Brilliant work, Inspector Vogel. You too, Fräulein Stiegler, fine work. So far, as I understand, only we three know about the results of your task? Yes? Good, not a word to anyone else."

Fräulein Stiegler: Inspector Vogel dubbed us the Judgment of Three.

The Chief smiled. "Let it remain the Judgment of Three. Let me think about it for a few days. We here at the Bka have a certain commitment to EUROPOL."

Fräulein Stiegler: Oh god, so they can fight over the matter like hyenas over a carcass.

The Chief waved his finger at her as if admonishing her, but his smile showed he meant it in jest. "Dear, Fräulein, you should have a better opinion of EUROPOL; they are not like the EU meetings. Then we meet Monday morning in my office for coffee." He smiled.

When Inspector Vogel and Fräulein Stiegler left, they saw the Chief leaning back in his chair, his eyes closed, deep in thought.

29 July.

They met on Monday morning at nine o'clock in the Chief's office. A small table had been placed near the window. They were four; Michael Juergens from EUROPOL was the fourth person. The Chief introduced him to Inspector Vogel and Fräulein Stiegler. "Inspector Juergens is from the Berlin PD but has been with EUROPOL for many years and is our delegation head there. This is Chief Inspector Vogel from the Munich PD, long-time member of Bka, and his competent secretary Fräulein Stiegler. Let's sit down, have good coffee, and discuss our problem." The Chief poured the coffee; there were sweet and plain rolls, butter, and marmalade. Nobody ate anything.

Chief: First, Inspector Juergens, I need your personal assurance that what we discuss here remains strictly confidential. Juergens gave this assurance.

The Chief continued, "Inspector Vogel is our expert on terrorist groups and individual terrorist. I gave him the task, if possible, to discover the persons behind the world tribunal. With brilliant detective work and help by Fräulein Stiegler, he discovered the identity of the world tribunal, or I should say the Force of Three."

Inspector Juergens sat stunned; after a moment of silence, he asked, "Who are they?"

Chief: That is not important at the moment. Let me just say that it is an operation out of Germany. The question before us is what we do with this information.

Juergens looked at the Chief. "And what have you decided?"

"We have discussed but made no decision. This information is only a few days old. I had the weekend to think about its ramification. The first question we need to answer is, should we involve EUROPOL? I get their reports from your office and understand that the membership has voted in the majority to spare no efforts to find out who they are. Then what?"

"Of course stop them, arrest their people."

"Has that been decided?"

"No. It just seems the logical conclusion. Well, perhaps not. We had voices raised that what the tribunal is doing benefits mankind. But there are concerns that so powerful an organization is or may be a detriment to the national interest of membership countries. There is fear that the tribunal might extend its power politically. Some Scandinavian nations call it vigilantism; Muslim nations think it is anti-Muslim."

"We don't have any member nations who are Muslim."

"No, but Turkey as an associated member nation raised concerns. Turkey is the spokesman for the other Muslin countries."

"Your personal opinion, Inspector Juergens?"

"I, as delegation head from Germany, voted with the majority that we should find and stop the tribunal. Berlin concurred, and I sent a letter to the Bka accordingly."

"Yes, I received your letter and also concurred. It was then that I gave Inspector Vogel this task. But I wish to know your personal opinion what to do if we find them—and we did."

"You mean I, as Michael Juergens, and not Inspector Juergens and head of the delegation?" The Chief nodded. "I understand. What we have seen so far—let me personify this—what I have seen so far, the tribunal has only benefited humanity. Their five manifestos are directed against individuals and groups who have or are harming mankind and who are beyond normal national jurisdictions. The tribunal is an extranational power and supposedly holds quasi-trials before they eliminate. As long as they confine their power to their stated principles, I condone.

"There is, of course, this problem that we, as a member nation of EUROPOL, have concurred in the majority's request to find and stop the tribunal."

"This is the reason I asked for your presence today. I had time over the weekend to think about this problem and came to this conclusion. Let us test the waters, so to speak.

I like for you, Inspector Juergens, to call a meeting for EUROPOL. Explain that the Bka has through time elements discovered that the tribunal is a European operation and that the Bka is perhaps close to discover their identity. The question is what then? What should EUROPOL or the EU do? I would like for you to submit four proposals: [a] to look upon the tribunal's doing—that is, combating evil-doers beyond anyone's jurisdiction—as benefit to mankind and support them; [b] to do nothing, neither help nor stop them; [c] to demand of them to stop their activities; [d] to arrest them and bring them to trial probably before the International Criminal Court in Hague." He turned to the others. "You agree?"

Inspector Vogel: I concur.

Fräulein Stiegler just nodded.

The Chief smiled. "Fräulein Stiegler gave us an emphatic Do NOTHING."

Chief: Please continue with your coffee. Have something to eat. I must write a report to the ministry of interior in Berlin. Inspector Juergens, I shall look forward to your report after your meeting.

Wednesday, the thirty-first of July, at 10:00 a.m., EUROPOL met.

Alexander Talef from Bulgaria who was the chairman for July took the lectern.

Chairman Talef: This meeting was requested by our German legation head, Inspector Juergens; please take the lectern.

Inspector Juergens did so. "Ladies and gentlemen, I had a meeting at the Bka on Monday and was informed that the Bka has learned that the work of the world tribunal is an European operation and that they may be close to identifying the members.

"The question then arose what to do if these persons of the WT are known and can be apprehended. The president of the Bka wishes to cooperate fully with the member nations of EUROPOL and the EU. He asked me to propose four scenarios if the Bka succeeds in finding these person of or associated with the world tribunal: [a] accept the WT as a bona fide crime fighting organization and support them; [b] do nothing, essentially let them operate under their five manifestos; [c] contact them and let it be known that they have to stop their operation; [d] arrest the members and bring them before the ICC [International Criminal Court] here in Hague."

He returned to his seat in front of which stood a small German flag.

Chairman Talef took the lectern. "Comments please?"

Many hands were raised. "Britain please?"

Britain: We have discussed this possibility in our highest government circle with the prime minister present. Our conclusion was that we wish for them to stop their activities but not arrest and prosecute them.

France: At a meeting of the cabinet with the PM and president present, we decided to let the tribunal continue and to support the world tribunal with information in accordance with their five manifestos.

Italy: We never went so far as to discuss this possibility. But the president of Italy has voiced his opinion that if we should make contact with the world tribunal to support them. Of course, as France has stated, within the context of their manifestos.

Holland: We also have never thought that the members of the tribunal would be found. I am certain that my government would support the statements of both France and Italy.

Belgium: We have talked about the time when the identity of the world tribunal is discovered. Our conclusion is to demand from them to stop their actions.

Denmark: As secret and confusing the reports about the world tribunal are, my government did not express any decision if the tribunal's identify was found. I am certain we would support the conclusion of the French and Italian governments.

Germany: My government is at the present time notified. The president of the Bka would support a stop-and-desist order.

Austria: My government has informed me that if the perpetrators are found to arrest them and bring the members of the tribunal before the ICC.

However, the majority delegates of member nations could not express a definite conclusion by their governments or even express an opinion. Therefore, Chairman Alexander Talef tabled the vote on any of the four proposals for one week to give the delegates a chance to query their governments.

The voting for any of the four proposals was postponed for a week. The next meeting was scheduled for 9:00 a.m. on Wednesday, the seventh of August.

Delegate Juergens phoned the results to the Chief of the Bka.

The Chief, Joerg Ziercke, decided to follow up his written report to the German government with a personal visit to Chancellor Merkel. Together with other members of the cabinet they decided to vote for a stop-and-desist order.

Wednesday, the seventh of August, 9:00 a.m., EUROPOL meets.

Chairman for the month of August was Salvador Jesus Salazar from Spain.

When all delegates were seated, Chairman Salazar took the lectern. At the rear of the hall, and sitting separately from the large roundtable were associate members (who had applied for membership in the EU or attended meetings of EUROPOL as interested observers and participants for international crime research, such as Norway, Turkey, Albania, Switzerland, USA, Mexico, among others).

Chairman Salazar: Unless any delegate present wishes to clarify his vote, let us just vote on the four proposals as presented a week ago by the German delegate inspector Juergens.

Several delegates raised their hands.

Bulgaria: We are voting here in regard to a powerful organization, which seems to have the ability to kill just about anyone on this globe. My government believes that the matter of finding this organization and brining them to justice is to bring it before the United Nations. There are major nations that are not represented here, such as Russia, China, and India, having more than half of the world's population.

Chairman Salazar: While this may be the more correct way to discuss, solve, and act upon the possibility of finding the members of the tribunal, we here at EUROPOL are only in an advisory capacity. It is then up to the EU to act upon our advice and also to decide if the matter should be brought before UNO. Since we understand of the close relationship between Bulgaria and Russia, perhaps you can give us Russia's point of view?

Bulgaria: Our foreign minister met with Russia's foreign minister, and both agreed that arrest and trial are the only proper course of action.

Chairman: Thank you. Anyone else here to voice an opinion before we vote?

Sweden: We the Scandinavian nations are together as one to demand the arrest and trial of this vigilante organization.

"Thank you. Anyone else? No? Then let us proceed with the voting.

"The first proposal was accept the world tribunal as a bona fide crime-fighting organization and support them. Please raise your hand if your government supports proposal A. I see France, Italy, Holland, and Denmark. To these four votes, my government, Spain, wishes to add its vote. Makes five votes for proposal A.

"Proposal B: do nothing, essentially let the world tribunal operate under their five manifestos. Show of hands please? Three member nations voted for proposal B.

"Proposal C: contact the world tribunal and let it be known that they have to stop their operation. Votes? I see twelve hands, twelve votes for proposal C.

"Proposal D: Arrest the members and bring them before the ICC. Seven votes.

"Therefore, in agreement with EUROPOL and the EU, we shall request the German government to try to establish contact with the world tribunal, if that is possible"—he smiled—"and request of them or order the WT to stop and desist from any further elimination actions. Perhaps if contact is established, we can request of them to cooperate with existing legitimate crime-fighting organization such as EUROPOL, INTERPOL, Scotland Yard, Surete, Bka, the FBI, or other national police agencies.

"Any other comments? Yes, our associate member Mohamed Khamal from Turkey?"

Khamal: Turkey, as the spokesman for the Muslim countries, we are abhorred that the perpetrators of these illegitimate actions are not arrested and tried before a court.

Norway: We likewise condemn the actions of this vigilante tribunal and like to see the members arrested and brought before justice. We consider the tribunal a lawless organization.

USA Burt Johnson, the FBI liaison, spoke up, "I spoke with director Mueller of the FBI. Secretary of State Kerry was present; so were the heads of CIA and NSA. It is a delicate subject. So far, as we know the world tribunal has eliminated pirates and just about stopped piracy. It has eliminated members of the violent drug cartels and as we know has rescued immigrants from certain death in the desert. It has punished war criminals who have escaped justice. It is combating terrorists, mostly those we cannot find. These actions justify their continuation according to the principles written in their five manifestos. None of the members present ever voiced the opinion that the people of the tribunal should be apprehended and punished. For what? That they eliminated evildoers whom we could neither find or stop from committing crime? The question was that if we find the members of the tribunal, should we stop or support their actions? What is ominous is their power apparently over anyone on this planet. This scared us, to be frank. We decided on two options.

"One, if we know their identity, we would let them continue their work as long as they abide by their five manifestos, which we all agree are important statements and benefit mankind. Yes, we would like their cooperation and they have done so. They notified the FBI where to find the Zetas Cartel leader Miguel Trevino Morales. We in turn told General

Garcia, the head of the cartel-fighting organization in Mexico. Their marines captured Morales. They also notified us when they sank the cocaine-carrying cartel submarine off the southern California coast. We found the sub, raised it, and it is on display in San Diego. Perhaps we can form an international advisory board to cooperate with the tribunal and work together with them. Option two is for the world tribunal to supply us with information leading to criminals and terrorists but let us do the work of apprehension and trial. Of course, having no vote in Europol we can only advise.

Chairman Salazar: America's two options would connect to our options A and B, which as we saw were defeated.

Mexico: My country is benefitting from the tribunal and hope they continue their action against the violent drug cartels.

Lithuania: I believe I speak for the Baltic nations when I demand the arrest and prosecution of the tribunal members.

Suisse: As a country that believes foremost in law and order, we hope that the members of the tribunal can be arrested and tried before the ICC.

Chairman: Anyone else? No? Then I believe we can suggest to the European Union, if possible, to find the members of the world tribunal and demand of them to stop and desist from further elimination actions. I have our legal department prepare the documents to this effect and request of the twenty-seven members of EUROPOL to sign as representatives of their respective countries. As far as bringing the matter before UNO, I doubt that we shall ever find agreement with Russia and China.

The meeting is adjourned.

On Friday, the ninth of August, Inspector Juergens visited the Bka and had a meeting with the Chief and Inspector Vogel. He gave an account of the EUROPOL meeting on the seventh and that the Chief's proposition C—that is, to advise the world tribunal to stop and desist from further elimination actions—carried by twelve nations out of the twenty-seven member countries, as Germany did. He told of France, Italy, Holland, Denmark, and Spain who voted for proposition A, to let the tribunal continue and offer the EUROPOL's and INTERPOL's cooperation. *Juergens told of the strange fellowship of the two Scandinavian countries, Sweden and Finland, they together with Norway the most liberal countries in Europe—with the conservative or right-leaning country of*

Austria, and the nationalistic Baltic nations of Lithuania, Latvia, and Estonia, and Russian friendly Bulgaria who in a block of seven voted to have the members of the tribunal arrested and tried before the ICC.

The Chief looked at Inspector Vogel. "Looks like you have to visit Jerusalem, my dear inspector, and take Fräulein Stiegler along to keep record of the interesting conversation you will have with Senior Inspector Anton Hofer of the Jerusalem police. Explain the advisory voting of EUROPOL that twelve countries out of twenty-seven members voted for the tribunal to stop and desist. Here is a personal observation you may suggest: no more overt actions that make the headlines. No added manifestos. The five posted are inclusive of the worst crimes against mankind. Mexico is very much interested that they continue combating the drug cartels but without taking credit for any action. No more communication with the Suisse *Berner Nachrichten*. On the other hand, let them, if they continue with small and isolated actions or wish to communicate with a friendly agency, establish a very private relationship with you, Inspector Vogel, AND ONLY WITH YOU. Not by wireless or telephone but let someone bring a message to you, directly to the Bka.

"The guard post at the gate will acccpt such messages and forward them to the right person. And don't use your plastic card when you fly to Israel. Use cash only. Give to me privately your expense account, and I shall have you reimbursed. Now get ready and apply for your and Fräulein Stiegler's visas to Israel. Ask our liaison office for foreign embassies to send for visas. He can expedite it as the Bka has good relations with the Israeli embassy."

Inspector Vogel did so and took his passport and that of Stiegler to the liaison office who sent them directly to the third attaché at the Israel embassy in Berlin. The attaché was a Shin Bet representative and cooperated with Bka. His computer listed Chief Inspector Vogel from the Bka as a "friendly" person, as would be his secretary Elizabeth Stiegler.

A visa was issued for both, and their passports returned within a week.

The travel office of the Bka then made reservations for a Lufthansa flight from Frankfurt to Tel Aviv for Tuesday, the twentieth of August to return on Friday, the twenty-third.

CHAPTER XIX

THE END OF THE
WORLLD TRIBUNAL

Inspector Vogel Visits Jerusalem

Tuesday, 20 August 2013.

Their Lufthansa plane left at 11:00 p.m., Monday night, from Frankfurt and arrived in Tel Aviv at 4:30 a.m. Israel is one hour ahead of Central European time.

While still on the plane, they had to fill out a form every foreigner had to do; besides stating their personal data, they had to indicate the purpose of their visit to Israel. Inspector Vogel wrote "professional visit to Senior Inspector Anton Hofer of the Jerusalem police." He had Fräulein Stiegler write the same notice.

At the control, their passports with visa were checked, and so was the form.

The comtroller, a woman, called a man over who scanned the forms, then came around the booth. "I don't speak German. Do you speak English? Yes, of course." He identified himself as a security agent. "A professional visit from an inspector of the Bka to one of our police inspectors. Can I be of any assistance? There is one of our vans leaving at seven for Jerusalem, if you care to wait. No? There are taxis outside.

I recommend you change euros into shekels first, though the taxis will take euros. But you get a better rate from our money change booth. Do you have hotel reservations?"

Vogel: No. Can you recommend a nice but inexpensive hotel?

Agent: Ask the driver to take you to the Ron Hotel. It is a small but nice hotel and near the Ben Yehuda Street where you find typical Israeli life and shops, a street like a mall. Your first time in Israel? I wish you a nice stay. Shalom.

"Shalom," Vogel answered; and to Fräulein Stiegler, he said, "My only Hebrew, shalom—it is the greeting. It means peace and is said when coming or going."

They changed money, got a taxi, and drove the one-and-a-half-hour ride to Jerusalem.

It was getting light by the time they left Ben Gurion Airport, and they saw orange groves as they went past the flatlands, small picturesque towns coming alive, then uphill toward Jerusalem. The driver, who spoke English, pointed out rusted wrecks of cars, armored busses, and trucks "from the 1948 war when Arabs were shooting up traffic."

The Ron Hotel was just a three-story building of white stone. They got two nice rooms, air-conditioned. Vogel asked, "Fräulein Stiegler, would you like to rest a little?"

"I slept on the plane," she answered. "Look, Inspector Vogel, please, just call me Elizabeth or better Liz. We have been together for so long, and this adventure in Israel makes us rather close companions."

The inspector smiled. "Just what I had in mind. But then you must call me Andreas."

"Hello, Andreas. Let's go out and have breakfast. I am starving."

First they changed from their rumpled traveling clothing into something more suitable and summery; it was already getting warm, though the nights are cool in Jerusalem.

They went into the Yehuda Street across the plaza, and while many of the shops were still closed, the restaurants were open. They had fresh orange juice, cheese omelets, rolls, and the obligatory salad. The coffee was strong and good—Arabian coffee, which came in little cups.

By nine o'clock they hailed a taxi and drove to the Jerusalem police headquarters, which was north of the city.

At the gate was a control booth. They showed their passports. Purpose of visit? To visit Senior Inspector Anton Hofer. The man called on the phone; of course, he spoke Hebrew, which neither understood. But they heard their names mentioned and a repeat spelling of bet-kof-patach (bka).

"Inspector Hofer is coming down." He smiled.

Senior Inspector Hofer meets the visitors from the Bka.

It was nine thirty when the phone rang in Inspector Hofer's office. It was the guard at the entrance who called and told him that a middle-aged man and a pretty girl wished to see him. "An Inspector Vogel and his secretary from the Bka."

For a moment, Anton felt a tingling in his spine—a danger signal? Or just discomfort that an unknown inspector from the German Bka came to see him? He wondered for a moment. Should he speak German to them? Inspector Vogel? Then he remembered; at the seminar Professor Baumgaertel gave back in January, there was an inspector Vogel from the Bka who spoke about the world tribunal or, as he referred to it, the Force of Three. He had spoken very positive about the work of the tribunal but also the confusion that exists to find their source. While he knew that a forwarding mailbox was used from Rome, the sender was from Vienna or London. Also, the materials used—envelopes, computer paper—from different countries. The languages spoken, Spanish like from Spain, English with a British accent, Russian classical, German. That many thought it was an American operation as the USA benefited most from the anticartel actions and American ships were freed from the pirates. Yes, he remembered Vogel. As he walked to the gate—and while he thought that Vogel was interested in the tribunal and therefore visited him—he was no longer worried. Nothing had changed in their procedures except that the letters were now posted from New York.

And there by the gate stood this man Inspector Vogel, a little pudgier than he remembered him. He wore a white linen jacket. With him was a pretty young woman, supposed to be his secretary. If a man shows up with his secretary, he meant no harm, Anton thought.

Inspector Hofer was in the khaki uniform of the Jerusalem police.

Anton smiled as he shook hands with Inspector Vogel and spoke German, "I remember you from the seminar in January at the university."

"I did not meet you then, Inspector Hofer. But I heard of the trouble you had later with those four hooligan students. And Professor Moll sent me a transcription of the seminar you gave shortly after pertaining to the Taliban, Islamic terrorism, and a fine explanation of Middle East problems or should I say of Israel versus the Palestinians? Such a seminar at the Bka would be most helpful."

"And that is the reason for your visit, Inspector Vogel? And by the way, you speak English, yes? Let us speak in English then, please."

"First let me introduce my able secretary, Fräulein Elizabeth Stiegler; she speaks English well." They continued in English—all three speaking with a British accent.

Anton shook hands with the young lady. "Your first visit to Israel, Fräulein Stiegler? Yes? You must stay at least a week."

Vogel: We must leave Friday night; the Chief expects me back on Saturday.

Anton: Well, let's go up to my office, and you can give me then the particulars for your visit.

At the front office sat his secretary whom he shared with other inspectors.

Anton turned to his visitors. "Tea, coffee, or perhaps orange juice?"

"Something cold would be fine, maybe ice tea," suggested Fräulein Stiegler.

Anton ordered a pot of tea with ice cubes.

In the corner of his office was a small round table with four comfortable chairs. They sat down.

Anton: Now, Inspector Vogel, what is the reason for your visit? A seminar at the Bka?

Vogel: First, if you are recording our conversation, please turn it off; it must remain private and confidential.

Anton went to his desk and turned the switch off. "As you requested." He smiled.

Vogel took a deep breath. *"I first thought that I would introduce this request. But after learning more about Chief Inspector Hofer, alias Nagil. Your achievements as a criminal inspector with the Munich police; before your upbringing in Cairo, your visit to Afghanistan; with the Egyptian army, friend of Brigadier Amer",* . . . *he lowered his head and looked up with piercing eyes at Hofer, yet there was a friendly smile . . .* "You are a man of integrity, I shall be honest Inspector Hofer. I know that you are one of the* *three . . . together with Professor Klausner and Josef Kainz . . . the Force of Three.*"

Anton stared at Vogel who raised his head and his eyes, now looking at him as friendly as his smile.

At last, Anton sat up straight from his comfortable relaxing posture. "Is this a suggestion? Or do you have proof?"

"All the proof I need to know that you three are the world tribunal."

"I see. And?"

"I came to talk about it."

"Of course at this point I regard your accusation only as a supposition. May I ask who else knows about what you believe?"

"This knowledge is restricted to four people, well, perhaps there are five. My secretary and I, my chief at the Bka Joerg Ziercke, and Michael Juergens our German delegate at EUROPOL."

"And the fifth?"

Inspector Vogel smiled. "Perhaps your friend Stefan Wagner."

"What makes you think so?"

"You see, after your visit to London to send the second manifesto, I requested from Scotland Yard a list of all passengers who flew in and out of the two airports in London. Sent copies to all major police departments in Germany to see, if by chance, anyone recognized the name of Achmed Nabil—any name really. Your friend returned the query negative, though he knew very well who Achmed Nabil is. I personally do not call it a falsification but rather a protecting of his close friend."

"With hundreds, if not thousands of names, he might have missed Achmed Nabil?"

"Yes, that is true, and it may have been at that time only a supposition, but there were other clues."

"But that was almost a year ago. Why now?"

"You see, Achmed Nabil was listed as an Egyptian citizen. I sent also queries to the German embassies in other countries. I received negative replies from all except Egypt, Saudi Arabia, and Russia. I sent a second query. No luck. Then suddenly in July the German embassy in Cairo called our foreign office that a Brigadier Amer replied. He had been replaced by the Morsi government, and when he returned to his job at military intelligence in July, he found the two requests in his in-basket. He told us that Achmed Nabil was the Egyptian name for Anton Nagil, whom we can find with the Munich police department. I then flew to Munich and had a talk with Commissioner Kolb. I only mentioned a possible connection to the tribunal. He doesn't know that you are one of the three.

"However, I had already a suspicion that someone in Munich was involved when I read a police report in January—or was it beginning of February? A former Gestapo agent by the name of Pfeuffer was killed. It was ruled an accident, but in a byline the police reported that it was possible that he was killed by a stranger, supposedly a Herr Alfons Maier, a member of the neo-Nazi Bund. They questioned both Herr Wegner and Schoenauer who did not know such a man. With the third manifesto, the tribunal condemned former war criminals, and Pfeuffer had bragged about the brutalities he committed while with the Gestapo. So Munich was a clue. Herr Maier had been visiting a Herr Lorenz who was also Gestapo. That you didn't kill Lorenz showed me that you are very selective whom to eliminate. I applaud that.

I had also a talk while I was in Munich with Director Glaser from the Max Planck Institute. I told him that the Bka was concerned with the secret work that was going on at the institute since one of the project members was an Egyptian citizen, served in the army there, was with the Munich police, and now senior inspector in Jerusalem. You, Inspector Hofer. A security matter. He vouched for you as he did for Professor Klausner and his computer expert Herr Kainz, the taxi driver.

"I was only interested in where you were on Sunday morning, the tenth of February. All other actions happened on Friday or Saturday. Sunday you had to be back at work in Jerusalem. Well, the sign-in book showed the three of you were present that Sunday night or morning between midnight and 6:00 a.m. when the sub was sunk off California.

"You are a multilinguist; besides your native German, you speak Arabic, Russian, English with a British accent, and, of course, Hebrew. Professor Klausner speaks Spanish as they do in Spain. Oh yes, Director Glaser told me that Professor Klausner is an energy expert and works on wireless energy. What else is the death ray but wireless energy? You are diploma engineer of chemistry with a minor in nuclear physics."

Anton smiled. "And Herr Kainz, the taxi driver?"

"My chief answered that particular person with he represents the public, the common man.'"

"Well spoken. Let us assume that you are correct. Where do we go from here?"

"Let me explain, Inspector Hofer. Bka works close with EUROPOL. This multinational agency has decided to find the members of the tribunal and bring them to justice."

"Justice?"

"No. Please, Inspector Hofer, let me continue. Some nations felt that a private group, not restricted by and responsible to a certain country, might prove harmful. While they accepted the five stated manifestos as a noble effort to fight evildoers past and present, that it is nonpolitical, they were afraid of what the future brings, therefore the vote to find and bring to justice. The president of the Bka gave me the responsibility to find the world tribunal or, as I refer to them, the Force of Three. Assuming, as you put it, that I am correct, I told the Chief what I knew, whom I suspect. The Chief mulled it over for a few days and then invited Inspector Michael Juergens from EUROPOL, and he was told under fullest confidence. Juergens is also our delegation head at EUROPOL.

"The Chief proposed the following for Juergens: to call a meeting of EUROPOL and confide in them that Bka has established that the tribunal is a European operation and may discover its members. The question is then, what to do? Juergens was to propose four solutions: [a] to let the tribunal continue their operation under the five manifestos and support them with information,[b] do nothing and let them continue without our cooperation, [c] to stop them and tell them to desist from further eliminations, and [D] to arrest and bring the members to trial before the International Criminal Court in Hague. Some countries had proposed this before.

"This meeting took place and was tabled for a week so that member nations could consult with their governments. The matter was put to a vote before the twenty-seven-nation membership. Proposition C, the stop-and-desist request, won with twelve votes. Five votes were cast for proposition A, three for B, and seven for D."

"May I ask who voted for D?"

"An interesting group: the conservative or should I say right-leaning government of Austria; the two liberal nations from Scandinavia, Sweden, and Finland; the ultranationalistic nations of the Baltic, Lithuania, Latvia and Estonia, and Bulgaria. Interesting, a month before when the legation head for Bulgaria Alexander Talef was the chairman of

EUROPOL, he spoke positive about the accomplishments of the tribunal. But after consulting his government and probably Russia, he voted for proposition D.

"And who are our five friends?"

"France, Holland, Denmark, Italy, and Spain."

"Germany?"

"Our xhief flew to Berlin and consulted with Chancellor Merkel. The chancellor in turn with the cabinet. Their vote was for proposition C, as was that of Britain."

"Cease and desist—is that beneficial to mankind?"

"Inspector Hofer, let me add a qualification we four decided upon."

"The four? You, your secretary, the president of Bka Herr Ziercke, and legation head to EUROPOL Inspector Juergens?"

"Exactly. We four in the know propose to let the Force of Three continue in their mankind-beneficial work but without publishing any added manifestos, letters to the *Berner Nachrichten*, in fact, not publicizing any elimination. In fact, to do their work as secret as their Force of Three is and shall remain."

"Inspector Vogel, one question, you don't carry any recording device on you by chance?"

"My dear Inspector Hofer, you insult me."

"I apologize, but I needed to know. Therefore, it was all assumption. Now it is fact. You are a brilliant detective. Sherlock Holmes would be proud of you. And your secretary was assisting you?"

"Fräulein Stiegler was the brilliant detective. When I questioned the times of action by the tribunal, always on weekends, and that therefore it must be at a complex that is otherwise closed then, she pointed out that Friday is not part of a weekend. And more likely that one of the three is from out of town and can only participate on Fridays and Saturday, has to be back at work on Sunday. Also she worked out the time elements when the actions happened, wherever. Compared these actions with Central European Time, like in Germany. Sunday's sinking of the cartel sub was the only exception.

"When Director Glaser showed me the sign-in sheets, I saw the three of you present Sunday morning, and I knew. Fräulein Stiegler also gave me a definite do nothing when I wondered what do we do now with out discovery of the Force of Three."

Anton smiled at Fräulein Stiegler. "Thank you." And turning to Inspector Vogel, "Our agreement is then for both of parties to remain mum."

"Silent as Sherlock and Dr. Watson."

They shook hands on their agreement, both having a tight handshake.

Inspector Vogel asked, "How is the wireless energy transmission business proceeding?"

"We cannot use satellites as we do for the rays. High-capacity current would damage them. But we project using towers in sight of line, doing away with transmission wires. Still years away from practical application. Someday."

Anton guided them downstairs where they left in a taxi. Fräulein Stiegler waved a goodbye.

Anton was quite satisfied with the meeting. Yes, their identity had been unexpectedly discovered, but they could continue their mankind-benefitting work in secret, without publicity and on a reduced scale.

As soon as his strange guests had left, Anton went to his friend Avi Barlev, the Jerusalem commissioner of police, and asked for furlough for the rest of the week, which was at once granted. He then rushed home and told Hanna that it was urgent for him to fly to Munich. And yes, it was in connection with his "secret" business he had with Max and Sepp.

David, who was now fourteen, wanted to come along. Esther and Daniel were in summer camp. David was interested in science, specifically electricity and the phenomena of lightning, and he remembered a few years back they had been in the Deutsche Museum in Munich and saw the display of lightning strikes. Since Hanna supported his wish and school didn't start until September, Anton let his son come along. They both packed their most essentials and were ready to go. Hanna had called their housekeeper Eliahu Zamir who drove them to the airport in Tel Aviv. They took the evening flight to Munich, first-class accommodation for which they didn't need reservation, and arrived after midnight. A taxi took them home to Planegg.

Anton had sent an e-mail to Max: "Amcho coming. See you and Sepp Wednesday morning."

It was seven o'clock in the morning, and Anton was preparing breakfast for David and himself when the bell rang. It was Sepp. Max had called him yesterday with the message that Anton was coming and most likely would be home. Sepp had come in his own car; he joined them for a little breakfast.

While they drank coffee, Sepp asked, "Why the urgent visit, Anton?"

Anton smiled. "I tell you later, Sepp. I hate to have to tell things twice."

Before they left, Anton gave instructions to his son not to let anyone into the house and gave him the institute's phone number. "Ask for Professor Klausner's office if you need to call me. You can go back to bed; you didn't go to sleep until two in the morning."

Then Anton and Sepp left for the long ride to the institute.

Wednesday, 21 August 2013. Shortly before nine o'clock in the morning.

Since it was normal working hours, they didn't need to sign in. They found Max in the energy house; a pot of coffee was on the hot plate.

Max looked quizzically at Anton. "So what is the emergency visit about?"

Anton: Our identity has been discovered!

Max: I can't believe it. After so carefully disguising our presence? The identity of all three of us, our work at the institute? Yes?

Sepp: Are they coming to arrest us?

Anton looked at Sepp. "First let me assure both of you that no arrests are contemplated. It is a stop-and-desist order by EUROPOL, transmitted by our Bundeskriminalamt, Bka for short."

He then told the story of this unexpected visit by Inspector Vogel from the Bka, accompanied by his secretary, a Fräulein Stiegler. "By the way, Inspector Vogel is that somewhat pudgy man who gave a discourse on what was known about the tribunal back in January. Remember? We all attended that seminar at the university. Vogel is a sharp investigator. The first minor clue he spoke about was that German computer paper we used printing the first two manifestos. A German operation? Possible, but with the many other confusing clues, just a thought. My London visit established the first real clue, though that was not known to him until July of this year. What he did was to send to Scotland Yard a request for a list of all passengers who flew in and out of London on the twenty-fourth of August of last year. However, he didn't get an answer that an Egyptian by the name of Achmed Nabil was on the list and recognized until July this year. Before, he believed it was a European operation because of the languages spoken, mainly British English and Spanish as spoken in Spain.

"Another thought of a clue came to his mind when he read a police report from Munich that the former Gestapo agent Pfeuffer was killed in a fall. Vogel still belongs to the Munich PD and is only on loan to the Bka, so he gets their monthly newsletter. While the Munich police officially declared it an accident, there was a comment that possibly he was pushed down the staircase by a visitor, a Herr Alfons Maier. Pfeuffer and Maier left together. Maier had come at the invitation of the Bundleader in Munich, Waldemar Wegner, and said that he belonged to the Bund in Berchtesgaden under the leader Schoenauer. Investigation showed that neither Wegner nor Schoenauer ever heard of an Alfons Maier.

"This happened shortly after the third manifesto was published announcing the elimination of former war criminals and Nazis who killed or committed violent acts. Pfeuffer was bragging about his brutality as a Gestapo agent to this mysterious Alfons Maier. A clue. And by the way, Vogel believed that the Force of Three was a threesome and not a group of scientist, jurists. So he thought, how did this mystery man know about Pfeuffer and Lorenz being former Gestapo agents? Knew where both lived? He made it a point to leave with the evil one, Pfeuffer, who lived in an old age home, promised to take him home. Could Maier be from Munich? One of the three from Munich?

"Then came the confirmation in July that this Achmed Nabil was a German Egyptian citizen by the name of Anton Nagil who is with the Munich PD.

"Vogel flew to Munich and visited Police Commissioner Kolb. I don't know what they discussed, but I am certain that Kolb told Vogel that Inspetor Nagil was now with the Jerusalem police and also worked as a consultant to Professor Klausner at the Max Planck Institute. He then visited Inspector Wagner who had signed the report that none of the names on the passenger list were familiar to him. A falsification as he knew that Achmed Nabil and Anton Nagil were one and the same. From Wagner he learned very little except perhaps that Anton Nagil had changed his name to Hofer and was working as a consultant on weekends for the institute. The next day he went to the Max Planck Institute, which he knew was one of Germany's most prestigious science centers, and had a talk with Director Glaser. Now, Vogel had kept a log of happenings of the world tribunal. Actions, places, time, etc. He had his secretary work out the times, when they happened, where the action took place versus the times in Germany. She had suggested to him that since all actions took place on Fridays and Saturday, one of the participants was out of town and had to be back on Sundays, working time for him. There was one exception, and that was the sinking of the cartel sub, which happened on Saturday evening off the California Coast, German time on Sunday early morning. Vogel needed to establish Hofer's presence on Sunday morning, the ninth of February, in the institute. The sign-in log of the institute of employees working on weekends and nights showed that Anton Hofer, together with Professor Klausner and his computer expert Josef Kainz, was present between midnight and 6:00 a.m. on that Sunday morning.

That information, together with Glaser revealing that the three are working on a secret project of transmitting wireless energy, confirmed to Vogel that the three were the Force of Three."

Max: Brilliant detective work.

Sepp: That pudgy man who looked so friendly and tame and was so confused about the Force of Three—hard to believe it is him who discovered us.

Max: Continue, Anton, I am fascinated.

Sepp: What happens now?

Anton then told of the visit to Jerusalem by Vogel and his secretary. The "cease and desist" order by EUROPOL. As he explained, "After consulting with their governments, twelve out of the twenty-seven member nations voted for the stop of further actions by the world tribunal. Five had voted not only to let the W.T. continue under their five published manifestos but support their efforts to rid the world of evildoers. Three had voted do nothing. Seven voted to have the members of the tribunal arrested and brought before the International Criminal Court.

Max: Who were the seven?

Anton: The government of Austria with its right-leaning Parliament; the two liberal Scandinavian members of Finland and Sweden; the three Baltic nations Estonia, Latvia, and Lithuania. I am certain they didn't like the publicity of having been collaborators to the Nazis and having some of their SS thugs eliminated. And yes, Bulgaria, certainly Russian influence.

The three sipped their coffee.

Sepp: Let me ask again. What happens now?

Anton: First of all, Vogel assured me that only four persons know who we are: he, his secretary, the chief of Bka, and the German delegation head at EUROPOL. All promised to keep their knowledge secret. Also, that we can continue in our work, in context of the five manifestos, without publicity, further manifestos, and letters to the *Berner Nachrichten*. Basically, to continue on a smaller scale and secretly.

Sepp exhaled deeply. "That was a shock. All is then, as it was, minus any publicity and publicized eliminations."

Max: We can continue our operations against the drug cartels.

Anton: And especially terrorists. Al-Qaeda and its affiliations won't complain or publicize the eliminations of its members. It was then that the telephone rang.

CHAPTER XX

A Tragedy

The new leader of the neo-Nazi Bund in Munich, after both Horst Bachleiter and Joachim Gersten had been killed, was Waldemar Wegner.

His father was Karl Wegner, a former Gestapo official who had died a long time ago.

Karl Wegner and Horst Pfcuffer worked often as a team and were known for their brutalities, and both used by the Gestapo as "strict questioners" (read torturers) in the Gestapo cellar.

Waldemar Wegner remembered fondly Uncle Horst Pfeuffer when he came visiting, always to him the "old uncle Horst." Therefore, he was shocked when he heard of Horst Pfeuffer falling down the staircase and breaking his neck back in January. An accident—the tottering old man had stumbled and fell. Maybe he was drunk?

It was a few weeks later that a detective from the police department came by Wegner and asked about a visit to Herr Lorenz by a man who called himself Alfons Maier and stated that he had been sent by him. Wegner said that he did not send a Herr Maier and did not know such a person. His suspicion was aroused, and he visited Herr Lorenz. From him he found particulars about this mystery person who had said that Wegner sent him to write the history of the Gestapo. Also that he belonged to the Bund from Berchtesgaden.

A description of this Alfons Maier didn't help much, nothing special about him, neither his language; it was of Munich dialect. It was this Maier who offered to take Pfeuffer back to the senior home. Lorenz had said goodbye to them at the door, closed it, and a minute later he, Lorenz, heard a commotion; he went out, and from downstairs this Maier had called up that Pfeuffer had stumbled, fell down, and was hurt badly or even dead. To call an ambulance. He had called the police. That was it.

It all seemed to be just an accident. However, it bothered Wegner that there was this person who claimed that he was sent by him. A member of the Berchtesgaden group? A few weeks later Wegner called Schoenauer, the leader of the group there. No, Herr Alfons Maier was not known to him.

Wegner's suspicion fell on their archenemy, former police Inspector Anton Nagil. He was now with the Jerusalem police, had changed his name to Hofer. That he came frequently to Munich as he had a house there or rather in Planegg, a suburb.

This information came from a member of the Bund who worked in the records division of police headquarters, a Frau Fleischer. (The police did not know of her sympathies, that she was a neo-Nazi.)

At their next Bund meeting, he spoke to Frau Fleischer and asked her if she could procure a picture of former inspector Anton Nagil; it would be in his application to join the police, which was back in 04. It took a few weeks; but she found the file, made a copy, and gave it to leader Wegner.

He paid a visit to Herr Lorenz who at once recognized the picture as of Alfons Maier.

Wegner was now certain that this had not been an accident but that Nagil probably had pushed old Pfeuffer down the stairs to his death.

Something had to be done with this "devil" that caused havoc with the leadership of the Bund.

The leadership of the neo-Nazi Bund Blut und Erde consisted of the leader, who was Waldemar Wegner, his deputy leader, secretary, treasurer, and three *Kaempfer* (fighters)—men well versed in hand combat, marksmen, and designated as bodyguards to the leadership. One of the "fighters" was Karl Ludwig, the former student who had his jaw broken by Nagil back in January.

Wegner called a private meeting of the leadership at his home and discussed the problem of Inspector Hofer alias Nagil. There was a long list of complaints against this devil, who was not only an anti-Nazi but also married to a Jewish woman and was now an Israeli policeman. Complaints dating back to 2005, when he gouged out Seitz's eye (to find where his kidnapped mother was). He injured Gustav Bachleiter severely, breaking his ribs. He caused the death of their leader Horst Bachleiter and his son Gustav by placing a bomb on his boat, then rigging a bomb in the car of their new leader Gersten. And as Karl Ludwig explained, he severely injured him and three other students.

Wegner also told of the assassination attempt by the Russian mafia at the dacha of Nagil, which failed and caused the death of the assassin "and cost us 300,000 euros," said the treasurer.

They were unanimous that Nagil had to be killed. But how and when?

They knew that Nagil had a house in Planegg, and from talk at police headquarters, Frau Fleischer had learned that Nagil came to visit frequently as Inspector Wagner was his friend. One suggested to bomb his house when visiting was the surest way to get rid of him. How to find a bomber? Leader Wegner said he would make discreet inquiries with other cities where the Bund functioned. Once they had such an expert, he would have to be hired, live in Planegg, and be available at a moment's notice. He also had to pay him generously for his work.

Wegner thought he could get the money from leader Schoenauer in Berchtesgaden, a rich industrialist, who had paid the 300,000 euros for the assassination attempt.

Karl Ludwig vonlunteered to keep watch on his house once the bomber was hired and present. He would do so with the other two former students whom Nagil had also injured in their fight with him; they all knew what he looked like.

Wegner also proposed that those present would leave Munich before the deed was committed as surely the police would blame the Bund for the blowing up of Nagil's house. They needed a good alibi. He then proposed that as soon as the presence of Nagil was confirmed, they would drive to Berchtesgaden where Schoenauer had a place up the Watzmann Mountain they could use. And he explained they would have to take along tents as the cottage up there was burned down twice by Nagil and never rebuilt. When the time came, they would have to have everything prepared and ready to go at a moment's notice.

They would use their mobile telephones, and the codename for Nagil's presence would be "stork"—the stork has arrived.

A bomber was found; he was from Wuppertal, with the Bund there, and worked in the coal mines, an explosive expert.

The bomber was invited to Munich and met with Wegner. He was apprised of the situation of former police inspector Anton Nagil who had caused tremendous problems to the Bund in Munich and was now an Israeli, "A Jew!" Wegner told him. He offered the bomber 50,000 euros and all expenses paid while in Munich. Wegner drove the bomber to Planegg and showed him the house of Nagil. In front stood his BMW. A few cars behind was the Mercedes of one of the students who watched over the house.

Wegner told the bomber that he would be called when Nagil arrives. The watcher would only briefly state, "The stork has arrived."

"I get that Jew bastard," the bomber assured Wegner and took the money as he insisted on prepayment.

The bomber took lodging at the Heide Inn, just a block away, and rented a white van. He had his own car with which he had driven from Wuppertal, and in it he had plastic explosives enough to blow up a small house. He also had brought two large signs, which he would affix to both sides of the van he rented.

INSTALLATEUR—*plumbing.*

All was ready by the middle of August. The watchers each took an eight-hour shift. Karl Ludiwg admonished his friends not to fall asleep, especially at night. They could use the Heide Inn for toilet facility, even have a quick bite there. Also report if Nagil's BMW had been moved. That meant that he came and his entry was missed.

It was past midnight on Wednesday, the twenty-first, that one of the watchers saw a taxi drive up and stop in front of Nagil's house. A man and boy came out and went into Nagil's house. The watcher, as he had been instructed, at once called Wegner, "The stork has arrived" and hung up. Wegner called the bomber with the same message. Added, "We seven are off to Berchtesgaden; you too get out with first daylight." Then he called his deputy and in turn his secretary and treasurer. The deputy called the three fighters. The arrangement was for all seven to meet in Ramersdorf by the church, leave their cars there, and drive together in Wegner's VW camper to Berchtesgaden. By 2:30 a.m. they had met, loaded their equipment into the camper, and were off.

The bomber got into his car and drove the one block to Nagil's house. He parked behind the BMW. The house was dark. He must be asleep coming home so late. He went into the back of his van and affixed the sign to each side; they were paper signs with sticky backs. One last checked his two batteries; to his dismay, one was dead. Where to find such a battery at night? Impossible. He had planned to put each charge by the doors in front and back. Would one charge be enough to demolish the house? He wasn't sure. Better wait, get another battery, and do the job right. By eight in the morning, he was at the nearest drugstore; it just opened. He showed the clerk the type of battery he needed and was told that this was a special battery the store didn't carry; in fact, the clerk told him that he **d**oesn't know of any place in Planegg that would have this type. He gave him the address of a place in Pasing (a surburb of Munich), which carried all types of specialty batteries. The bomber drove there, bought two, and returned. By the time he was back at Nagil's house, it was close to ten o'clock.

Nagil's BMW still stood in front of his house. He parked in front of it. He was in overalls as becomes a workman; he carried a box, a backpack, and under his arm a long pipe and a plunger. He went first to the back of the house. By the door, he placed the box containing the plastic explosive; from the backpack, he took the detonator wrapped in a cloth bag with the battery and a timer, which he set for ten fifteen.

He went back to the car, still carrying the pipe and plunger; got the second box; and set it by the front door, making the connections. The timer he set also for ten fifteen. In five minutes the house would blow. It was time to disappear.

(When he went back to his van for the second charge, he was observed by David. Looking through the living room window, David saw the man carry something to the door: a long pipe and plunger in his arm and hand. Shortly after, the man went back to the white van that had something written on the side, still carrying a pipe and plunger, and drove off.)

David thought his daddy didn't tell him that a workman would come. Having always been drilled to observe and report strange things, he called his daddy. When the phone was answered, he asked for Professor Klausner. A moment later, the voice said, "Klausner here."

David: May I speak to my daddy please, Anton Hofer.

"Hi, David. Remember me, Max Klausner? We were at the dacha together. I get your daddy," and handed the phone to Anton. "Your son David."

With the sinking feeling of foreboding, Anton took the phone. "What's up, David?"

"There was a workman here and did something by the door. He came in a white van."

"What kind of van, David? Was there a company's name on it?"

"Yes, it said 'installation' or something like that in German."

"Listen, David, are you dressed?"

"No, I am still in my pajamas, barefoot."

"Doesn't matter. Run to the back door and get out of the house. Climb over the neighbor's fence and run to the Heide Inn. I meet you there. DO IT NOW. RUN!"

At that moment Anton heard a strange almost screeching noise, and the connection was broken.

"Something happened at my house; you two stay here. I might need you," and Anton ran out and drove at breakneck speed home.

What took normally fifty minutes took him barely thirty minutes in the traffic, but from afar, he saw black smoke curling up in town. The dark smoke, intermixed with white-boiling clouds, became heavier as he neared the town. When he drove by the Heide Inn, he glanced at a white van, read INSTALLATEUR on the side. He turned the corner and saw his house destroyed, still smoking. Several fire engines were directing streams of water at it; ambulances were in the street. Just then he saw two men carry a litter to an ambulance. He jumped out of his car and rushed to them.

"Halt! I need to see who that is."

"You don't want to see that, a charred body of a boy."

"That is of my son. Show me! Please."

A medic came over. "What is it?"

"This man says it is his boy."

"Is that your house? Yes? Show him." The medic unzipped the body bag. Anton, with a wrenching pain in his heart, saw the charred form of David; only his lower legs were recognizable, and he was barefoot. The good boy had done what he was told—he ran—but the blast had cought him and the fire burned him. Anton threw up.

"I told him not to look," said one of the carriers.

"Shut up, you fool. How would you feel if your boy was killed like that?"

Anton managed to ask, "Whereto are you taking his body?"

"To the funeral home here in Planegg."

"Please tell them to take good care of David. I will be in touch." And Anton rushed off in his car around the corner to the Heide Inn and parked next to the white van. Though he was deep in pain and sorrow, when action called, Anton was with steady nerves. He got his Beretta from a hidden fold under the seat and walked into the part of the inn that was for hotel guests. The lady behind the desk knew him as he had been for years a steady customer at the inn, what Germans called a *Stammgast*.

"Ah, Herr Nagil, what was that explosion about? I heard a house blew up, near yours?"

"Frau Singer, I desperately need your help. It was my house they blew up and killed my son. The bomber—no, Frau Singer, please don't cry. Help me find the bomber. The white van outside belongs to him. Who is he? Is he here? What room?"

Frau Singer trembled; she was crying and literally shook in despair. Anton placed his hand over hers. "Please."

She stood up straight, tears still running down her face. "I am so . . . so deeply sorry. His name is Kurt Tauber; he just checked out. He is in room 12. Paterre, all the way back.

"One more thing, Frau Singer, tell no one that I came for him." She nodded.

Anton walked the long hall to room 12. He knocked. "Porter, any baggage to take to your car, Herr Tauber?" His voice steady but hard.

The door opened. Anton met Kurt Tauber, a middle-aged man, the face Slavic with pronounced cheekbones, a small but firm chin, bald. He carried a wig in his hand. "Just getting ready to make myself pretty for the ladies." He grinned.

Then he saw the pistol in Anton's hand; he looked up at Anton and saw his eyes glaring at him, and he understood. "You are An—" he stopped, the wig fell from his hand, and his grinning expression changed into one of shock and fear.

Anton, with piercing eyes and holding the pistol in his face, nodded. "Anton Nagil."

"What do you want of me, Nagil?" his voice quivering in fear.

"Your confession, Tauber. All of it. Names, who sent you, why, how much they paid you. All!"

"I am not very good in writing confessions. About what?" He tried to grin, but his face still showed cowardly anxiety.

"Tauber, you don't seem ro realize how much I despise and hate you. The things I want to do to you and maybe I will."

Tauber walked to the small desk and picked up the phone; his hand was shaking.

"I call the police. You are threatening me with a gun; it is illegal to carry a pistol, Nagil."

"The police are here already. Right by my bombed-out house. It depends now if they arrest you as Kurt Tauber or as unrecognizable piece of meat."

"You seem to accuse me of having bombed your house, Nagil. I heard a loud explosion before. Any witnesses?"

"Mhm, my son who saw you go to the house and put something at the door. Then get into the white van with the inscription INSTALLATEUR, like your van outside."

"And where is your son now?"

"With the undertaker as a charred former live boy."

"Look, Herr Nagil, I didn't know your boy was in the house. They told me nothing about a boy with you. Honest, I am not lying this time."

"Confession, Tauber, write it all down."

"Then you let me go?"

"If you were just their tool, maybe yes. Now sit down at the desk and write all or you don't realize how bad I can be, the things I will do to you."

Tauber, still with trembling hand, wrote his confession, implicating Waldemar Wegner who hired him, paid him 50,000 euros to blow up Herr Nagil's house. Though he didn't admit to try to kill Nagil, it was the murder of his son David he would be accused of.

Anton read the confession. "Tell me, Tauber, after you committed this deed, how were you to contact Wegner? Visit him to get the money?"

"The money is in my suitcase. No, I called Wegner already, told him I succeeded. I do you a favor since I am sorry that I killed your boy. Wegner and his crew went to Berchtesgaden to have an alibi."

"With whom? How many of them?"

"I don't know who went with him, I guess his top people who would be suspected, five, six, or seven of them. Can I go now?"

"First let me make certain that you never again blow up someone's house!"

Anton rushed to Tauber and gave him a powerful karate jab against his neck and let the body fall to the floor.

When Anton left, he waved to Frau Singer who was still crying.

(Frau Singer waited till noon before she entered room 12. On the floor she found the unconscious Kurt Tauber. She called the local police. The Planegg police department consisted only of seven officers, and they were busy this morning. The explosion was attributed to a leaking gas line, especially after smelling gas coming from the ruin and a broken gas pipe.)

Unfortunately a boy in the house was killed. The house belonged to the former Munich police inspector Anton Nagil. A medical attendant with the ambulance stated that a man, who identified himself as the father of the boy, saw the body and said he would be in touch with the funeral home, then rushed off.

It was noon that the police had a call from the nearby Heide Inn that a body was found in one of the rooms. One of the policemen went to the inn and was shown room 12, with the unconscious but obviously alive man on the floor. The man was identified as Kurt Tauber from Wuppertal by Frau Singer.

The police then found the confession on the desk. An ambulance was called who took Kurt Tauber to the hospital where he was placed on a police hold. In searching his belongings, 50,000 euros were found in his suitcase and in his jacket a further 3,000.

Since a crime had been committed with explosives, the Munich police was requested to investigate as they had experts. Chief inspector Wagner came at once with his explosive expert Sergeant Oettinger.

Wagner, the personal friend of Anton, was shocked by the news that his house had been destroyed and Anton's son killed. He was advised that a man who claimed that the charred body of the boy was his son David had been seen but then disappeared. Sergeant Oettinger in searching the car of Tauber found some more plastic explosives and detonaters, also a dead battery. Wagner knew of the feud between his friend Anton and the neo-Nazis in Munich. He arranged with Commissioner Kolb warrants for the arrest of the Munich Bund leadership.

Doctors who examined Kurt Tauber found that his neck had been fractured, and the man, while still alive, was a paralytic. When he awoke, he could only mumble incoherently. He was kept alive with a breathing apparatus and fluid fed.

Commissioner Kolb agreed with Inspector Wagner to record Tauber's paralyses as the result of a stroke he must have suffered in a fall after bombing the house.

More serious was the possibility that Anton might catch up with the missing leadership of the Bund. When detectives served the warrents for their arrests, they were told that the men left the day before on an excursion into the mountains. *While the police report did not implicate Anton Nagil/Hofer in the severe injury to the bomber—he had a stroke, fell and broke his neck, not so if Wegner or any of the other Bund members were found killed. Or, as the commissioner posited, that Nagil might be killed, Wegner claiming self-defense.* "In any case," Commissioner Kolb stated, "the confession of Tauber will be enough to put Wegner away for many years, if not life."

The seven neo-Nazis arrived in Berchtesgaden shortly before six and went to Wegner's favorite restaurant that just opened. They ordered a sumptuous breakfast and were in a jolly mood. In fact, they were boisterous enough that some of the early customers complained to the waitress. Wegner wanted as many witnesses to remember them in this place at that early hour. At eight, they left for the short drive to Schoenau on Lake Koenigssee. They parked by the boat ramp and paid for the two days they wanted to climb up the mountain. Then carrying their equipment and supplies in Rucksaecks, they walked up the path toward their destination. A three-hour strenuous walk, always uphill and through the forest until they came to the clearing where once stood Schoenauer's cottage, now just a ruin of stone. The only part standing was the outhouse behind the ruin. Nearby, in the meadow, they erected their tents.

Rudolf Hart, the secretary, called a Bund member who lived in Planegg; however, it was the wife who answered. Hart told her that he and his *Spezies* (comrades) were camping in Berchtesgarden and if she and her husband wish to join them they are welcome. The wife thanked him but told Hart that her husband had to work during the week. Then she added, "Guess what, Herr Hart, the house of that pesky inspector Nagil, was bombed."

Hart faked his surprise. "Really? I can't believe. Who would do such a dastardly deed? I hope that Nagil didn't get hurt." The woman then told him that a neighbor of hers saw a litter being carried away with someone dead who was in the house.

That news called for a celebration, and Wegner took a bottle of Schnapps from his rucksack; and after the seven yelled their "Sieg Heil," the bottle was passed around.

They put up three two-men tents and one large tent with a small folding table and chairs, a primus stove. First, Wegner checked their individual weapons; the four leaders had brought their hunting rifles. The fighters each had a 9mm Luger. With Nagil dead they didn't need to worry, but Wegner was a cautious man and even posted one of the fighters by the path at the forest. "One never knows." He smiled. They finished the bottle, and since they had gotten up so early, they all took their sleeping bags to the big tent and took a well-deserved nap.

By noon Anton was racing on the Autobahn to Salzburg. On his mobile phone he had called information for the undertaker in Planegg and then spoke to the director. He told him who he was and to please take good care of his boy David. The director told him that the police had come by and the body cannot be released until an autopsy was performed since the boy's death was due to a criminal act. The director added that the police was looking for him.

Next he called Max Klauser and told him the sad news and took his sincere condolences. Then likewise from Sepp Kainz. He could hear Sepp cry (something he had not had time to do yet). He told Sepp that he was on his way to the Watzmann where the Nazi leadership was hiding from him. To have Max project the area on the lower reaches of the mountain where the cottage once stood. He told Sepp that the best way was to start at the Koenigssee and work their way up along the path to the clearing. Report to him who was there, how many, and what they were doing and continue to observe them. To report to him even if no one was there; then he would have to look for them somewhere else.

"Maybe they visit Schoenauer, though I doubt it that they involve him," he thought.

Sepp wanted to join him and help him get the killers, but Anton thought it was more important for Sepp to help Max find the clearing as Sepp had been there, to report their presence, and how many there were.

The next call was to his friend Stefan Wagner who was still in Planegg at the ruin. Stefan, his long-time friend, was devastated by the killing of David. "Anton, I guess you are after those bastards. We found the confession. Commissioner Kolb says that we can assume that the bomber, this wretched Tauber, had his neck broken by you, but the police report will list him as having fallen and thereby breaking his neck.

"However, if Wegner and any of the others turn up dead, the police will have to charge you. My advice is, if you catch up with Wegner and his cohorts, wherever, make certain they disappear never to be found again, kapisch?"

"I understand, Stefan. They will disappear forever or I will. One more favor, Stefan, ask the commissioner to have the body released. I don't want an autopsy. If I find out that David was not killed by the explosion but burned to death, it will give me a never-ending grief and pain. I call the Israeli embassy to make arrangements to have David shipped to Jerusalem. If the police release their hold on David, it can be done within a few days instead of weeks."

"Tell me, Anton, have you called Jerusalem yet?"

"No, Stefan, it breaks my heart just to think about it. After—"

"I know and understand, Anton. Good luck and a safe return, buddy."

Anton drove for a while, the sorrow of losing his son.

He then called the Israeli embassy and spoke to the third secretary who knew him.

He explained briefly what had happened and that he was after the murderers. Told the secretary what he needed. The man promised him to fly to Munich and take charge of David who most likely would have to be transported in a tin coffin. He would certify for David so the coffin would have no problem being accepted in Ben Gurion Airport and transported to Jerusalem.

The thought of calling Hanna was so terrible that he decided to do it after, or as it may happen, he would not have a chance to call at all.

Speeding as he did (and there are no speed limits on the Autobahn), he arrived in Schoenau shortly after two o'clock. Just armed with his Beretta, a tire iron, flashlight, and a dozen plastic handcuffs in his pocket, he walked speedily up the path through the forest. It was a hot, muggy day; clouds were boiling up in the west promising a storm.

His phone rang; it was Sepp. He reported that they had trouble finding the clearing; following up the path didn't work as the forest hid it. They finally found the clearing by checking areas along the timberline.

"Here is what I see. Off to the side of the ruin they put their tents. I see three small and one big tent. They must be in the big tent or were when I first saw the place. Then I saw one man come out; he carried a poncho and a broadrimmed hat, walked to the forest path, came back without it. Maybe there is a guard at the path. He then went back into the tent. That was a few minutes ago. Where are you now, Anton?"

"Less than an hour away. Keep you eyes on them, Sepp, and call me if anything changes. Looks like a storm is brewing. You can see all right?"

"Yes. Max says that even if it storms and rains, we will be able to see, maybe not as good as it gets darker too. But until almost eight, seven thirty anyhow, we will be able to observe."

"Sepp, when I get close, I call you. Don't call me as the jingle might be heard."

"Anton, why don't you just have the phone on vibrator?"

"You are right. I forgot. Out for now." He turned the ringing off.

It was close to five o'clock that Anton knew he was near the clearing. He walked off the path into the forest and worked his way carefully from tree to tree.

Then he saw the man; he was standing leaning against a tree and looking down the path.

The first raindrops fell through the trees; the man was wearing a poncho and a broad hat.

Anton worked his way behind the man; on the soft needle-covered forest ground, his steps were noiseless. Then he stood directly behind the tree; one step to the side of it, he gave the man a shove. Free from the tree, he hit him with the tire iron across the neck.

The man collapsed.

Anton bent down to take his poncho off; he saw that it was Karl Ludwig, the loudmouth from the seminar. He felt his pulse—the man was dead. In his belt was a Luger; he put it in his pocket. Then he put the poncho and his hat on.

Anton stepped to the edge of the forest and looked out at the clearing at the tents about a hundred meters away. What had been heavy drops before was now a downpour, whipped in his face by the storm as he walked toward the tent. Just then a light came on inside.

Max and Sepp sat fascinated and apprehensive before the monitor as they watched the man step from the forest and walk toward the tent. He wore a poncho and broadrimmed hat.

"Is it Anton?" asked Max.

"It sure is," exclaimed Sepp. "Look at the tire iron in his hand, his favorite weapon when going after the Nazis."

Anton also was observed by one of the fighters who stood guard in the tent looking out a plastic window.

"There comes that fool Karl, afraid to get wet in that storm."

"Let him. No danger anyone coming in that storm," answered Wegner; he had to shout to be heard as the rain sounded like drums against the canvas roof. "Unzip the door for Karl."

The guard did, and in stepped Anton, a tire iron and pistol in his hands.

"Na-Nagil!" Wegner stuttered in surprise.

The first reaction was by one of the guards who reached for his Luger and sank with a scream to the floor, shot into his navel.

"A surprise party?" Anton said, but his remark wasn't heard or undertood; they all just stood there in fearful consternation. Besides, Anton thought, they weren't worth even a sarcastic remark. "HAENDE HOCH, SCHNELL [HANDS UP FAST]!"

They raised their hands.

"Anyone who doesn't obey me gets shot in his belly like he did."

At last Wegner sort of protested, "What do you want of us, Nagil? We have been camping here the past couple of days."

"I want you all just stand still. Hold your hands in front!" They did. Anton observed one man who was trembling with fright, the least dangerous one. "You!" He tabbed him on the shoulder with the iron. "What is your name?"

"Rudolf Hart." His voice quivered.

"What is your function at the Bund?"

"I am the sec . . . sec . . ."

"He is the secretary," Wegner said.

"Here. Hart, take these cuffs and fasten each man's hands together. And anyone who makes the slightest resistance gets shot in the belly, tears your insides, so remember!"

Hart did and had difficulty doing it with trembling hands.

Last, Anton cuffed Hart's hands. They were now helpless. He made them stand in a row, looked closer at them.

"My, my, if it isn't one-eyed Karl Seitz. You have come up in the hirachy of the Bund, from a messenger boy to what?"

"I am just the treasurer, Inspector Nagil. All I do is collecting the dues and . . . and . . ."

"And pay the mafia 300,000 euros to assassinate Nagil. Or more recently pay Tauber 50,000 to blow Nagil's house up."

Wegner: That you are here shows that nothing happened. If you just leave us alone, we forget this episode and don't report it to the police. This is kidnapping; you should know as a cop.

"I tell you later why I am here and what I want of you, bastards, you Nazi dogs."

Wegner: Where is Karl Ludwig? What have you done to him?

"Ludwig is dead. You want to join him in his hell? Now just shut up until I tell you to speak."

Anton found a rope and tied it to each of his prisoner's arms. He took the lead and made them follow him out into the downpour, lightning flashing overhead, thunder exploding in the clouds. It was half dark outside. Pulling them by the rope, he walked the five to the nearby outhouse. Behind the toilet was a square hole with a ladder to get down and lift the barrel out when full and dispose of the foul contents. He untied the rope from each one and made them kneel around the edge of the hole; then he cuffed their ankles together. He lifted the lid to the cesspool.

"Now dig, you Nazi pigs, dig dirt up. Make the hole larger."

"What for?" asked Wegner.

"I tell you what for. When the SS, those other Nazi pigs, killed Jews, they made them often dig their own graves. When they didn't have shovels, they made them use their hands. If they didn't dig or weren't fast enough, they beat them. Oh yes, they made them undress first. Do it naked. You want me to have you undress? No? Then dig!" And he jabbed Wegner into the side of his ribs that the man screamed in agony. They dug first grass, then dirt, and mud up; while the downpour continued, so did the lightning and thunder.

It was a macabre sight, the five man digging with their hands, making piles of dirt and mud, encouraged with blows at their ribs when they flagged, kneeling there in the storm that raged unabated. "A picture worth of a Wagnerian scene," to Anton, "the gods hurling damnation with fire of lightning, the drumbeat of thunder, the storm of their anger."

Their doings observed by Max and Sepp who felt no compassion for the killers of the boy David. In the storm and approaching evening, they could hardly see them but understood that they were digging their own graves.

"Now comes the time when the SS dogs had a deep enough hole to burry the Jews. There were no last words, no prayers permitted. True to the dictum of their satanic leader

Adolf Hitler, they shot the Jews. They were innocents, did no one any harm, only wanted to live happily with the families. Instead the SS pigs came, terrorized them, beat them, murdered their wives and children in often gruesdome fashion. You, neo-Nazis, subscribe to the same foul philosophy. I know about your devlish meetings in which you proclaim your bloodlust for killing Jews. I find you guilty of wanton mass murder in your hearts and of the murder of my son David who perished in my house you had blown up. DIE, YOU DISCIPLES OF SATAN. GO BACK TO HELL WHERE YOU CAME FROM!"

Anton drew his pistol and one after the other eliminated them with the SS's favorite Genickschuss. Then he threw them into the deep hole. "Scheisse zu Scheisse," he intoned his act of punishment like a prayer.

In the continuing downpour of the storm, he carried the guard, who had in the meantime gone into shock, and threw him into the hole. Then carried Karl Ludwig to it and had him join his kindred. Next he folded up the table and chairs and threw them into the hole, joined by the dismanted tents and all their equipment, weapons, utensils and food, also the poncho and hat of Ludwig.

Last he used his hands and feet to shovel the dirt, mostly mud by then, into the hole, which was almost level with the ground, placed the lid over it.

It was dark by the time he went into the forest and leasurely felt his way down the path into Schoenau. Washed of mud by the rain and wet to the skin he sat in his car and called Max.

"Mission accomplished, Max. David can rest in peace."

"We know, Anton. We watched until it got dark. Yes, peace to David. We love you, Anton. Goodbye."

"Please tell Sepp that I drive back to Munich and stay in his place. I should be there by midnight."

"He will be up waiting for you. He says a terrible job well done and to drive careful."

(A couple wceks later, a detective from the Berchtesgadener police came by Herr Schoenauer's Haus Tanneck and asked Herr Schoenauer if he knew where a Herr Wegner from Munich was or might be. His Volkswagen bus had been parked at the boat ramp and paid for two days but had not been picked up. Herr Wegner and some of his friends from Munich were missing. And with a wink of his eye, the detective added, "We all know that you, Wegner, and his companions belong to the Bund and they came to visit you."

Schoenauer assured the detective that, yes, he had befriended with Wegner, but no, Wegner and his friends did not visit him this time. "Maybe they went mountain climbing and had an accident?" he suggested.

This explanation was accepted by the police, especially after the parking attendant told that the group all carried heavy rucksacks and said they would attempt a climb up the Watzmann Mountain. A search party was then organized and went up the usual route but did not find a trace of the missing men.

The Munich police was then notified, and they accepted the explanation that the men, in attempting this difficult climb, must have taken a different route and since there had been a severe thunderstorm that evening met with an accident.

Only Inspector Wagner and Commissioner Kolb understood about the "accident" that overcame the climbing party of Herr Wegner.

A few days later Herr Schoenauer, who had divided sympathies in regard to Anton Nagil, a dear friend of his daughter Betty; and the Bundmembers from Munich, went up the mountain to his private holding. He took a shovel along—just in case. Nothing was any different; there was the ruin of the stone cottage he had built and was burned down by Anton. He went to the outhouse; behind it the hole to get the barrel out was filled in.

He went into the small wooden structure and at once smelled the stink of human cadaver coming from the open toilet, a round hole in the wooden bench. He knew then.

His first impulse was to rush down and call the police. But then, contemplating the trouble all around, let Wegner and his companions rest in peace.

He fired the wooden shack; then when burned down, he shoveled ashes and small half-burned wooden pieces into the hole, dirt over the foundation of the outhouse.

He raised his arm in Nazi salute, and with a firm "Heil Hitler," he said goodbye to his comrades.

CHAPTER XXI

Finis

I t was shortly after midnight that Anton arrived at Sepp's house in Planegg. The two old friends embraced. "Thank God that you returned safe!"

Anton wanted to say that God had nothing to do with it but then remembered that Sepp was a good Christian man.

Sepp served hot tea with a generous shot of rum in it. "We watched them digging around the hole, but then it got dark. Those bastards were digging their own grave?"

"All seven of them are down in the cesspool."

"Let's go to sleep, Anton; you didn't get much sleep last night."

"Four hours Sepp, enough. I couldn't sleep now. I think I walk over to the funeral home. I don't want David to be all alone."

"I understand, Anton. But at least, let me give you dry clothing and shoes."

Anton changed into a new outfit Sepp gave him and shoes. Sepp gave him a house key to get back in whenever he wanted to. Anton left.

When Sepp went into his bedroom, his wife, Inge, lay awake, crying softly.

Anton walked first by his house. A thunderstorm that had come at night had extinguished all residues of fire, and not even steam arose from the ghastly ruin. He would not rebuild but try to remember how it was and remember the good times when his mother, Rosemarie, was living there with him and Hanna.

Hanna—she did not know.

He walked over to the funeral home and set on the broad steps, keeping watch with David in his eternal sleep. At last he could let the tears flow and be at peace, though in pain.

With the sun coming up on a new day, he walked into the nearby forest. He needed to call Hanna. Just then his phone rang. It was Hanna.

"Tony, you didn't call yesterday as you promised. Something happened?"

Hanna took the terrible news more bravely than he expected; only when she said "If I only hadn't insisted on David's coming with you" he stopped her. "No recriminations, Hannerle; if I only would have taken him with me to the institute in the morning. We are not guilty of anything. Fate, Hannerle, fate was against David, against us." He heard her cry. He explained that he would stay with David and bring him home to Jerusalem.

And this he did.

There was the funeral attended to by friends of the family, by Avi Barlev, the commissioner of the police, his friends from the department, by Nevot. The chief rabbi spoke when the tin coffin, emplaced in a simple pine coffin, was lowered. Tears were in many eyes when he said, "God gave you David and Esther; now he took David back."

They recited the Kaddish, the prayer for the dead.

So many people, so many flowers. Hanna was so brave until Esther, David's sister, turned to her and said, "Mommy, if I die, will I have such a beautiful funeral?"

A mother can endure only so much pain. Anton put his arms around his wife who fainted; he carried Hanna to the car followed by Amal, Esther, and Daniel. He took the family home. Nevot then functioned in place of the Hofer family.

In the days to come, Anton promised Hanna that Munich would be to him—to them—at least for the moment an accursed city as it was after the Olympic debacle. He would sell the lot; though the house had been insured against fire, it was not against bombing. He got little for the lot.

He would still come occasionally and stay at the Pension Freizeit to visit Max and Sepp at the institute if his visit was needed or even if the Mossad requested a special job, eliminating terrorists.

Or for that matter, inspector Vogel, who had become friends with the Three and made use of the observational power of the computers in the energy house to track criminals or terrorists.

Max Klausner and Sepp Kainz were still fighting the drug cartels, but it was a war they could not win.

Nor could they win the war against terrorists. But those who became infamous because of their dastardly, violent, and sadistic acts against innocents they would seek out and destroy.

However, every Christmas the three families would gather at the Russian dacha.

Max continued his research on wireless transmission of energy or electricity, but there were unforeseen problems when using high-voltage current.

Time heals. Esther grew up into a lovely young lady no longer thinking of beautiful funerals. Daniel did well in school and would become a career officer in the IDF.

Anton Hofer was a highly respected senior inspector in the police department.

Munich was just a bad memory in their hearts if not in their minds.

END

BIBLIOGRAPHY

TERROR
By Hugo W. Holzmann
Published by Xlibris Corporation, 2008
Orders@Xlibris.com

THE GREAT HOAX
By Hugo W. Holzmann
Published by Xlibris Corporation, 2011
Orders@Xlibris.com

Various newspaper and internet articles.

EPILOGUE

The author doesn't know of any book where you, the reader, can add your own opinion.

BUT WHY NOT?

You might have just as strong feelings as the author has to eliminate evil doers, be they criminal, religious, or racist fanatics who murder innocents in often gruesome fashion.

Psychopaths like Lanza, Holmes, Tsarnaev, or the Norwegian Breivik who killed seventy-seven young people and was given a twenty-one-year prison sentence, and of course war criminals who are still around.

In the following pages you are given the opportunity to express your fantasy or wish to eliminate those who deserve to be removed from the earth or issue a warning to desist from hate mongering.

YOU ACCUSE (INDIVIDUAL OR GROUP):

_____

ACCUSATION:
hostis humani generis_____

_____

*DEFENSE:*_____

_____

JUDGMENT
*GUILTY:*____
*NOT GUILTY:*____

SENTENCE
*ELIMINATION:*____
*WARNING:*____

YOU ACCUSE (INDIVIDUAL OR GROUP):

_____

ACCUSATION:
*hostis humani generis*_____

_____

*DEFENSE:*_____

_____

JUDGMENT
GUILTY:____
NOT GUILTY:____

SENTENCE
ELIMINATION:____
WARNING:____

YOU ACCUSE (INDIVIDUAL OR GROUP):

_____

ACCUSATION:
*hostis humani generis*_____

_____

*DEFENSE:*_____

_____

JUDGMENT
GUILTY:____
NOT GUILTY:____

SENTENCE
ELIMINATION:____
WARNING:____

YOU ACCUSE (INDIVIDUAL OR GROUP):

_____

ACCUSATION:
*hostis humani generis*_____

_____

*DEFENSE:*_____

_____

JUDGMENT
GUILTY:____
NOT GUILTY:____

SENTENCE
ELIMINATION:____
WARNING:____

YOU ACCUSE (INDIVIDUAL OR GROUP):

_____

ACCUSATION:
*hostis humani generis*_____

_____

*DEFENSE:*_____

_____

JUDGMENT
*GUILTY:*____
*NOT GUILTY:*____

SENTENCE
*ELIMINATION:*____
*WARNING:*____

YOU ACCUSE (INDIVIDUAL OR GROUP):

_____

ACCUSATION:
*hostis humani generis*_____

_____

*DEFENSE:*_____

_____

JUDGMENT
GUILTY:____
NOT GUILTY:____

SENTENCE
ELIMINATION:____
WARNING:____